Karma Never Sleeps

Karma Never Sleeps

Gus Wheeler FBI Thriller

R. John Dingle

TULE
PUBLISHING

Karma Never Sleeps

Tule Publishing First Printing, April 2025

The Tule Publishing, Inc.

First Publication by Tule Publishing 2025

Cover design by Croco Designs

ISBN: 978-1-965640-68-5

Dedication

To Lis. Without you, life would be but a blank page.

It is mine to avenge; I will repay. In due time their foot will slip; their day of disaster is near and their doom rushes upon them.

—Deuteronomy 32:35

Chapter One

Everyone knew Sarah Nelson loved to run. She was a triage nurse, so her days were filled with alarms and buzzers and life-or-death decisions. Running gave her much-needed quiet time, a chance to decompress and get lost in her own head without any distractions from work or kids or social media. She loved the alone time on the trails, just her and her music and the fresh smells of nature. And the endorphins; oh, how she loved the endorphins. Sarah would rave to the girls, the Posse as they called themselves, that as good as sex was with Steve (and it was pretty amazing), when she hit the zone on a run and the world melted away, the endorphins she'd get afterward were simply orgasmic. But, of course, all this was a lie, especially the Steve-sex thing. Sarah hated running, she absolutely loathed it. But deep down she loathed her vile friend, Jules, even more. Jules was a liar and a drunk and a constant thorn in Sarah's side. Any day Sarah didn't see Jules was a good day. But worst of all, Jules was a runner and a big-time one at that. And Sarah would be damned if that bitch did anything better than she did.

The drizzle that had been ongoing throughout her run had turned intrusive, the wind thrusting it inside her collar and up her pant legs. All around her, tree trunks were stained a sinister black from the dampness. She fought her way up the steep incline and over the crest of the hill and relief washed over her. This was the three-mile mark and that hill was the hardest part of her run. She knew she'd be at the exit to her backyard just around the next bend. But, as she turned the corner, the first thing Sarah saw was someone lying in a fetal position across the trail, their back arched her way. She stopped short and, peeling wet hair from her face, thought a moment.

She pressed pause on the phone strapped to her bicep and the music in her wireless earbuds was gone. The person wore baggy exercise pants and a form-fitting cold weather running top with its hood pulled tightly over their head. Long arms and legs uncoiled and Sarah heard a low, pain-filled moaning.

Just what I need on my day off, Sarah thought. *Another patient.*

She kissed the endorphins goodbye and stepped closer. "Oh, hey. You okay?"

The runner twisted their torso and pressed their face into the dirt. "Ah, it's my knee. My leg bent the wrong way around that corner and I heard a pop. I can't seem to put any weight on it."

Sarah knelt down. "Here, let me take a look."

"Ah, ah AH."

"Sorry," she said, sliding the pant leg up. The runner's leg was a solid, condensed muscle. "The good news is I don't see any swelling, so it's probably just a mild strain." Sarah looked to the opening to her yard a few feet away. "Let's get you up and bandaged to keep it from swelling."

"I'm such an idiot," the runner moaned into the dirt.

"Ah, don't worry about it. Accidents ha..." Sarah's words were interrupted by a sharp prick to the back of her neck, and before she knew what was happening her throat and shoulders began to go numb. She swatted at it as if it were a bee sting and, as she did so, scrambled to her feet but not before her cell phone was tugged free from the strap on her arm.

"Wait...what...what the...?" Sarah muttered, confused, stumbling away. She looked at her assailant, who was holding up a scalpel and smiling wide, all traces of anguish and pain gone. Sarah tried to say something but slurred her words so severely even she couldn't understand what was said. Her mind was racing and she began to have trouble breathing as the numbness made its way to her chest. Her legs wobbled and fear gripped her insides.

She turned to run but a hand grabbed her from behind and she felt searing pain erupt across her lower neck and shoulder. She pulled free and saw a thin red line blooming through her shirt as she began to shuffle-run toward the entrance of her yard. Gusts of wind spread tears across her cheeks like scattering bugs and her legs felt heavy, sluggish, as if she were running on a beach. She tried to focus on the opening in the trees to her yard but her eyes served it up in pairs.

Sarah staggered from the woods and nausea gripped her so severely she vomited down the front of her shirt. She heard a distant voice calling her name before she dropped to one knee. The world spun violently and she collapsed onto her shoulder, then her side, coming to rest atop her flowerless rosebushes. Hot pain consumed her body, her screams of agony trapped in the bile collecting in her throat.

Someone gripped her arm and the back of her neck and it felt like her flesh was on fire. She felt herself lift off the thorny branches as a mix of words and sounds swam to her confused brain. She struggled to peel her eyes open and, when she finally did, terror gripped her once again.

Then the world snapped black.

Chapter Two

THE ELEVATOR DOORS closed behind Gus Wheeler, swallowing that God-awful music in the process. Sure, once or twice when he was alone in the box, he'd bobbed along to the occasional song—Lawrence Welk's "Calcutta" was a particularly foot-tapping tune—but not today.

The fading smell of chemical cleaner was still in the air from the building's night janitorial crew, and his eyes yearned for the old, tread-worn carpet that used to greet him at One Center Plaza. The move to the new digs had happened almost four years ago, and with it much fanfare. The politically embattled director had flown in for the ribbon cutting, marking the first time the FBI's Boston Office had its own stand-alone headquarters. The fact that the new glass-and-marble building was now located not in Boston, but Chelsea, was a fact that Gus never let the office's director and his old friend, Jeff Cattagio, forget. It wasn't that Gus had anything against Chelsea; it's just that it wasn't within walking distance of Faneuil Hall and Quincy Market and, most importantly, Pizzeria Regina.

Lost in familiar thoughts of whether he should change the strings on his concert bass, Gus swiped his key card and used a hip to open the fourth floor's large glass door. The dulcet sounds of crime fighting for the masses rose up and spanked his eardrums. Conversations mixed with occasional laughter and the buzzing of phones.

He walked past pod after pod of gray cubicles, each identical to the last, and as a thin arm shot out, Gus put the Diet Coke he had picked up into Vanessa Lambert's expectant hand. Unusually relaxed from a few days off, he leaned his six-foot-four frame against the side of her cube as she cracked open what was sure not to be her first or last Diet Coke of the morning.

"Stoked to have you back!" she greeted him. Her green eyes sparkled.

Vanessa was a dichotomy to most people she met. She had strawberry-blond hair with vibrant red streaks that was curly on top, shaved along the sides, and had a single foot-long ginger braid stemming from the back. Her fair complexion bordered on ivory and the bridge of her nose and upper cheeks were dusted with golden freckles. And while her attitude—her 'tude, as she would say—had gotten Vanessa far from her Detroit roots, it was the behavioral psychology degree she received with honors from Notre Dame that got her into the FBI.

"Miss me?" he quipped.

She leaned back in her chair, twirling her red leather-framed eyeglasses beside her cheek. She wore her favorite Pistola camo-green denim jacket with its sleeves rolled up over a clean white T-shirt, high-waisted skinny black jeans and her new black leather Ziggy biker boots. To suggest that Vanessa didn't stand out amongst her conservative colleagues, with their gray and navy suits and yellow or red ties, was to suggest the sky wasn't blue.

"How'd the gig go?"

Gus had been a musician nearly all of his life. After years of struggle, his former college roommate and close friend, Jeff Cattagio, convinced him to apply to the FBI. At first Gus had laughed at him, pointing out that he didn't think his bachelor of music in jazz studies nor his philosophy minor in classical studies was what the FBI was desperately seeking. But Jeff reminded him of all the stories he'd heard from Gus over the years of Gus tracking animals in the Colorado wilderness for hunters and that this was just another form of hunting and tracking. He then went on to sell Gus on it by pointing out he'd earn a steady income, have reliable health benefits, and still have time for his music. But it was the availability of sabbaticals when needed that snagged Gus in the end.

"It was killin'."

"Pats won big." Vanessa topic-hopped. She toasted the air between them and took a swig.

"Shocker," he deadpanned. "They cheat?"

"Dude." She took a second to burp under her breath. "How long have you been here?" She didn't wait. "They're your team now." Her head wagged side to side. "Haters gonna hate."

Gus was raised in rural Colorado to be a diehard Broncos fan, and when he stayed in New Orleans after graduating from Loyola he adopted the Saints as his surrogate team.

"Never." He dug in. "I might be able to adopt the Sox,

but the—"

"Hey, Wheeler," a voice interrupted from the corner office. "Got a minute?"

"Ah." He smiled. "Saved by the bell."

"Sure." He thumped the top of the cubicle with the palm of his hand and walked away.

"Pats rule, ya jack monkey!" followed him. He chuckled and made his way over to Jeff's office. It took about three seconds to realize Vanessa was right behind him.

They walked into the large, cluttered space with its stacks of boxes crowding the door. Jeff didn't wait for meets or greets. He slid two identical manila folders across his desk toward them.

"Remember Kendalton?"

"Of course," Vanessa replied before Gus could finish a quick nod.

"The woman murdered in the woods five or six months back," said Gus as he flipped open his folder. Vanessa plopped into one of the guest seats and opened hers. She then took the pen from her mouth and began spinning it quickly back and forth across the top of her hand.

Jeff sat and took a deep breath. "That's right, a Laurie Turner. Well, another woman was found murdered there this morning. We got the call about an hour ago. The state police have been assisting the locals with the Turner murder and, apparently, now with this second one they're all too happy to hand it off to us."

Gus eyed him suspiciously. "You know my tour starts in two weeks, right?" He waved the thin folder. "This, this does not sound like a quick hit."

Jeff raised a hand. "Just go up there and suss it out, so we know what we're dealing with. It's a small town and the local force is only a few officers; they don't have the expertise for something like this. And the stateys came up with nothing on the first murder."

Gus stepped to the window and gazed out over Route 1 toward the Chelsea High School. He tried to pull the details for the first murder to the front of his mind. Something about a frenzied bludgeoning but details were elusive. He turned back to the room. "What do we know?"

Jeff gestured to the file in Gus's hands. "What little there is, is in there. The two women were friends. But, unlike the first one, this woman wasn't beaten. Rob's got it." Jeff was referring to the pathologist, Dr. Robert Pappas.

"The stateys must've come up with something on the first one."

Jeff shook his head. "Nothing, really."

"Suspects? Leads? Theories?" Gus pressed.

"None. None. And none."

Gus glanced to Vanessa, who was already looking at him with a raised eyebrow.

Jeff continued, "You two need to get up there. The crime scene guys are on their way and the locals officially called us in so it's ours now."

"So, these women were friends," parroted Vanessa, seeming to stare through the wall behind Jeff. "Who else is in the friend group?"

Jeff looked at her, confused where she was going.

"Girls…"

Vanessa caught herself when Gus raised an eyebrow.

"Sorry, women. More often than not they run in packs."

Chapter Three

GUS MADE A few calls on the drive from Boston but kept each brief, more out of necessity than desire. His late-sixties Land Rover was perfect for all his gear once he removed a few rows of seats, but its rugged ride, thin metal doors, and sliding windows were not conducive to quiet time. But Gus couldn't get rid of the old workhorse; it simply held too many childhood memories.

His first call was to a pet-sitting service for the stray cat that had recently adopted Gus as its human; he knew they'd be spending the night in Kendalton. He then called his luthier to schedule a new bridge for his concert bass. And when he wasn't on the phone, Gus's brain bounced between walking a bassline through a blues in F and thinking of a way to solo over it that wasn't boring to a nonbassist.

Vanessa used the time to begin stalking Laurie Turner and Sarah Nelson online to get a sense for the vibe of their crowd. As far as she could tell, the two women were part of a close group of friends that seemed to do everything together as evidenced by their intertwined Facebook and Instagram feeds. There were the typical photos of family parties, group vacations, birthdays, graduations, and other lifetime milestones, but there were also a large number of older, grainy photographs of proms and marriages and newborn babies that chronicled these women throughout their lives. Not only had they all grown up together, they'd lived and shared their lives with each other every step of the way.

The main road from the highway dropped them right into Kendalton's center, a half-mile stretch of antique brick and shingle-style New England architecture featuring a variety of shops and merchants to appeal to the nonstop tourist traffic. A fine mist began to collect on the windshield as they turned onto Main Street and saw a group of people busy decorating the gazebo in The Commons, a large open space that sat at the end of the town's businesses and shops. Ladders leaned against its roof as balloons and streamers danced in the air. A gaggle of preschool kids toddled around the adults, chasing each other in wobbly circles. Gus watched as a banner got raised across its front announcing to all an upcoming 5K road race fundraiser. One end of the banner slipped loose and flapped in the breeze like a wounded bird, before being wrestled back down. Off in the distance he saw a tapestry of red, orange, and yellow mountains. It was a cold, dreary late-September day, the first bitterly cold day in weeks. Unseasonably warm weather had teased its way into the norm as of late, and balmy days had begun to feel like an entitlement.

Vanessa gestured to the mountains out the windshield. "Maybe you can get a hike in."

When Gus wasn't working or gigging, he could be found hiking in some forest somewhere around New England. He had told Vanessa so many stories of him hiking and camping in the woods growing up that she'd begun calling him Mowgli from *The Jungle Book*.

"I wish."

It was another ten minutes of closely following the GPS on Vanessa's phone before Gus eased to a stop beside the entrance of the Nelsons' driveway. The narrow country road sliced through thick woods in both directions and scattered along its sides were small, intermittent mounds of dirt—remnants from past plowing seasons. A small SUV slowly passed by followed closely by a gray sedan, then a large, lumbering farming tractor, its trailer stacked high with bales of hay. Vanessa watched it pass, eyes squinted, head tilted to the side.

"That was…unexpected."

Gus whistled a few bars of Duke Ellington's "Jack the Bear" as he hopped from the truck, feeling the stares of a group of neighbors huddled together like penguins near the end of the driveway. He and Vanessa worked their way between cars up the driveway until they came to a Kendalton police officer standing just inside crime scene tape that circled the backyard. Gus flashed the officer his badge and they exchanged greetings as he and Vanessa slid on nylon booties over their shoes and entered the scene. Gus noticed another Kendalton officer sitting off in the distance away from the crime scene, consoling a distraught woman at a picnic table. The woman eyed them as they passed while the officer left her and made his way to Gus and Vanessa.

"Agents." His shiny gold badge read *Chief Lincoln*. "Jim Lincoln. Thanks for coming so quickly."

Jim was not a tall man, but what he lacked in height he made up for in mass. He had rolling, broad shoulders, large biceps, and the forearms of a dock worker. Gus pegged him for mid to late thirties, not yet forty. His uniform was taut across his chest, with short pant legs highlighting rugged, high-top black boots. Jim Lincoln was the type who had excelled in every high school sport imaginable; Gus bet he had been a fine tailback in his day. They shook hands and, as expected, the chief's grip was deliberate and firm.

"Thanks for having us, Chief."

"Absolutely. And, please, Jim." His stare was as serious as his tone.

Gus gestured to the woman. "Witness?"

Jim's jaw tightened. "That's my wife, Maria. She and Sarah—the victim—were best friends." He glanced beyond the trees at the side of the yard. "We live next door. Maria saw Sarah stumble from the woods, but by the time she got to her she was already barely responsive."

With at least six inches on him, Gus struggled to not overtly look down at Jim so looked past him to where crime scene techs were erecting a tent in front of a large pool area.

"We've gone over the murder from this past spring. Any other suspicious deaths in town over the past year or so?"

The chief shook his head. "Suspicious? No. A young high school girl died last year of a drug overdose but other than that nothing out of the ordinary. We have had some other weird things go on here in town recently, though."

Gus met the chief's eyes. "Like what?"

Jim was about to respond when his name was called by

the pale officer manning the entrance to the crime scene. Gus turned to see a middle-aged, well-dressed man holding a large umbrella, his face red, speaking into the officer's ear.

Jim's eyes narrowed. "Sorry. That's the mayor. Excuse me a moment."

And as Jim walked away a brawny, thick-chested state trooper approached. He was easily six-foot-something tall, had a thin mustache and hair buzzed short to hide its sparseness.

"You must be agents Wheeler and Lambert." They nodded their hellos. "Mike. Mike Morrow. I caught the murder here a few months back, so when this came up guess who they called?" His words were plain and clear, with no distinguishable accent. "The boss said you folks would be taking this mess off our hands."

"That's what I hear." Gus continued to take in the scene. With the tent now set up, the CSI team—each clad in a white bunny suit—worked the area around the body. They pecked at the brown, dormant grass and barren bushes, pinching things from the flowerbed with long silver tweezers. In the center of their busywork crouched the pathologist, Rob Pappas. His heavy down jacket was zipped up tight and his sturdy black eyeglasses delineated a round, hairy face from a smooth and shiny head. He was kneeling over the body of a blond woman dressed in a tight long-sleeve shirt and white exercise pants, carefully evaluating every inch of her whitish-blue arm as he spoke into a microphone headset. Against the backdrop of the expedient CSI techs he appeared to be moving in slow motion.

"You guys get any traction with the first one?"

The trooper took a deep breath and squinted through the mist to the sky, as if he was just asked to recite the philosophies of Friedrich Nietzsche, then looked back to Gus.

"There was really nothing to go on. No witnesses, no evidence at the scene, nothing."

Gus gestured to the chief's wife, Maria. "You interview the friend yet?"

"No. One of my guys got her details, but I thought you'd want to talk with her."

Gus's eyes shifted to the chief's house, then he looked over the Nelsons' house behind him.

"Any security cameras?"

Mike shook his head. "Not at either house."

"Let's get the phone records for the vic's home phone and cell," Gus said to Vanessa. "And get her cell phone and computer to the lab."

"We were there when the techs bagged the scene," interrupted Mike. "I didn't see any cell phone with the body, so you might check inside the house."

Jim rejoined them after sending the mayor on his way. "Sorry about that."

Having watched Gus take in the scene, the trooper asked, "What're you thinking?"

"Well, the MOs are very different but the fact remains that two women who were close friends in a very small town have been murdered on the same trails in a span of months." Gus spoke slowly, confident. "And that raises a number of possibilities. Either the person who killed Laurie Turner has returned to the area to continue his killing or he's been here all along." He arched an eyebrow as he met the trooper's eyes. "And it is a male committing these murders—almost certainly Caucasian. But what's more troubling is the pace with which he's killing. Two murders in six months is fairly quick, which means either he's impulsive or he's enjoying it." Gus looked to the chief's house just beyond the tree line, and he recalled that Turner's body was found floating facedown in a pond just off a busy walking trail. "But, regardless of which it is, he's not going to stop, and it's likely the duration between this murder and his next will be shorter. He wants to be noticed or heard, wants attention for what he's doing. But he's not getting it."

"What makes you so certain it's a man and he's Caucasian?" asked the chief.

"Well, there're the numbers: There's been four-hundred-and-twenty-some-odd known serial killers in the US, and only sixty or so have been women. But, really, mostly because of the extreme violence of the Turner murder. The strength required to overtake and subdue her, to inflict the wounds she had, and then to get the body into that pond. That has male written all over it. And, as for being Caucasian, it's very rare for serial killers to cross ethnic boundaries, but we won't mark that as an absolute."

Gus looked back to the trooper. "All that said, what we should be asking is: Why have two close friends been murdered?" His eyes shifted to the chief. "What did these women do and who wants them to pay for it?"

The chief's eyes fell to the ground for answers, but before

he could reply, the pathologist caught Gus's attention. And as they joined Rob beside the body, Gus saw the creamy clouds in Sarah Nelson's partially open eyes.

"What've we got?"

"Caucasian woman, approximately forty years of age. Laceration beginning on the lower neck and extending across the shoulder. Very clean cut, likely a scalpel or something similar but not a fatal wound." The pathologist gently turned Sarah Nelson's head to the side. "Injection point here at the base of the skull." Rob angled the head away to elongate the neck. The small red dot left from the injection was surrounded by a red discoloration that had a slightly mottled appearance. And farther down the red discoloration blended into a patch of skin the size of Gus's hand that was so vibrantly blue it looked as if someone had painted it on. Rob waved his finger over the red spot.

"That reddish skin there, surrounding the injection mark? That's ischemia, the result of a local deficiency in blood supply, usually indicative of a vasoconstriction or some other local obstacle to the arterial blood flow." He moved his gloved hand down to the bluish patch of skin. "And this is cyanosis, which indicates an imperfectly oxygenated blood."

Rob rested her head gently back onto the thorny bush. "The woman who found her described her stumbling from the woods, struggling to stay upright. She also said the vic was unable to speak and seemed confused. And"—he pointed to the front of her shirt—"she was vomiting as she collapsed. There's a trail of it back toward the tree line. But this is what I wanted you to see."

The pathologist rolled Sarah's rigid body up slightly onto one side, exposing the other. He pointed to her arm just above the empty gray armband Velcroed around her bicep. Gus leaned in closer and saw the corner of what looked like a photograph sticking out from behind the strap.

"What is it?"

Rob leaned in with his tweezers. "Well, it's certainly not medical, so I've been waiting for you to get here to find out." He took hold of a corner of the object and carefully slid it out from between the strap and Sarah's arm.

Hanging from the end of the tweezers was a portrait of a young girl the size of a playing card. Its edges were rough and yellowed, its corners bent and frayed. The young girl's freckled face was clear and bright but the edges of her hair and background were blurred to give her an angelic look. Written across the card in sweeping, cursive script were the words *In Loving Memory of* and beneath that was the name *Rebecca Gillian Munroe.*

"Holy shit," muttered Jim.

Gus turned to him. "Who's Rebecca Munroe?"

Jim looked to Gus and Gus saw the flicker of fear in the chief's eyes.

"Rebecca Munroe—that's Becca—she committed suicide when we were in high school."

Chapter Four

"HOW LONG AGO was that?" asked Gus, his voice smooth, his tone thoughtful.

The pathologist had bagged the memorial funeral card of Rebecca Munroe and Gus now held it in his hand. It felt like the baseball cards he collected and traded as a kid. *Got it, need it. Need it, got it.* He stared at the picture of the young girl, her crooked smile awkwardly trying to hide chunky silver braces, her eyes clear yet hesitant. He read the quote from Matthew 5:4 again that was printed beneath her photo.

Blessed are they that mourn for they shall be comforted.

Not being raised in a religious family, the words didn't particularly resonate with Gus, but he guessed they would with some. He wondered about her family. He made a mental note to find out as much about Rebecca Munroe as he could before Jim's voice interrupted his thoughts.

"She did it the summer between sophomore and junior year. So that would've been nineteen…ninety-seven, I think."

Gus caught a raised eyebrow from Vanessa but remained quiet. He stared at the baggie with the card inside and began to think through its implications for the case. Then, turning his attention back to the chief, he held the card up between them.

"This girl died twenty-five years ago." He gestured toward the body beside the pool. "Any idea why her funeral card would be found on the vic? Were they friends?"

Jim's forehead wrinkled and his eyes narrowed as he shook his head. Gus looked to Jim's wife, Maria, who was still sitting alone at the picnic table and watching their discussion with renewed interest.

"Did your wife know this Munroe girl?"

"Of course—we all did. Agent, there were only sixty-nine kids in our class back then. Everyone knew everyone."

Gus's eyes remained on Maria, and after a few moments she looked back to her hands and tissues. He had felt her stare since he'd arrived at the scene and thought it was time to find out what she knew. So, after delivering the funeral card back to one of the CSI techs to be fingerprinted and put into evidence, he, Vanessa, and Jim started toward the picnic table. The state trooper, Mike Morrow, saw this as his chance to exit so, after making sure Gus knew how to reach him, he and his men left the scene.

Maria was a slight woman with creamy-white skin and a thin, petite nose. Her hair had small, gray flecks like metal shavings throughout and was styled into a bob cut that cupped her face. She wore plain jeans and a light blue cotton blouse that was baggy enough to obscure her disproportionately large chest. As they approached, she finished whispering something, then kissed the small gold cross that hung around her neck and rested it back onto her chest. Jim sat beside her, while Gus and Vanessa settled on the bench seat across from them. Vanessa slid her phone over the umbrella hole in the picnic table and pressed the record app.

"Mrs. Lincoln, we're very sorry for your loss," began Gus. Maria lowered her head slightly, fighting back the tears, and Gus could see her reach for Jim's hand beside her on the seat. Her movements were sluggish and deliberate, as if she'd just awoken. "We understand you were with Mrs. Nelson when she passed. I'm sorry to have to ask you this, but can you walk us through what you remember step by step?"

Maria's hand went to her cross and she began to roll it back and forth between her finger and thumb.

"Sure, like I told Jim I was rinsing a cup in our"—her voice cracked and she cleared her throat—"in our kitchen sink when I saw Sarah sort of stagger from the woods." She pointed toward the tree line at the far side of the house. "From the entrance over there. At first, I thought she was just coming to a hard stop from running. But as she kept going I noticed her legs were moving oddly. You know, like they wouldn't do what she was telling them to do.

"Then I saw her vomit violently, and as I ran down the steps of our back porch she continued to vomit, then collapsed onto the bushes. And that's when I heard this horrible sound." Maria wiped away fresh tears with her tissues and paused, reliving her friend's final moments. "It was this guttural, roaring moan but sharper, more intense, like a wild animal when it's being attacked." She met Gus's eyes and he saw the vacant look of trauma staring back. "It was awful."

"Was she conscious when you got to her?"

"Barely. Her eyelids were drooping terribly, so much so

that I could only see tiny slits of her eyes. I held her in my arms and rubbed her forehead and face but it seemed like every time I touched her she'd moan that awful sound again."

"Did she say anything?"

"No. She started to gag like she was having trouble swallowing, then her body started to lurch up off me toward the sky. Like she was convulsing." Tears breached her eyes and raced down her cheeks. "Then it was as if she choked on something 'cause she made this horrible gagging sound, then just went still."

Jim pulled her close while she furiously wiped her cheeks with the tissue.

Gus waited a moment before asking, "Can you think of anyone who would want to harm Sarah or Laurie?"

Maria was shaking her head before Gus finished the question. "No, no one. This is Kendalton, not some big city. Things like this just don't happen here."

"Mrs. Lincoln," interjected Vanessa. "Just for our notes, can you tell us where you were the morning of Ms. Turner's death?"

Maria's eyes flicked to Jim. "We were at home that morning when Jim got the call."

"I had the morning off but the guys called me when they got the 9-1-1 alert," added Jim.

Vanessa nodded and, turning her attention back to Maria, continued, "And can you tell us who the women are in your immediate friend group? Other than Laurie and Sarah?"

Maria swallowed. "There's me, Lizzy Porter, Melainey

Idlewilde, and Jules Russell."

"Was Sarah into anything odd or dangerous that you know of?" continued Gus, picking up where he left off.

She shook her head. "No, I would've known. Sarah and I were best friends; we told each other everything."

"So, no secrets? Nothing she wouldn't want to get out?"

Maria bit her lower lip for a moment and, as she did so, looked around to see who was within earshot. She leaned forward onto her forearms, closing the space between her and Gus.

"Nothing dangerous, but Sarah was having an affair with some guy at the hospital. George something. And he wasn't her first." She paused and Gus saw a nearly imperceptible shake of her head. "I told her it was a sin, and heaven knows I prayed for her, but she wouldn't stop. She maintained that, just like the others, this was only a casual fling, nothing serious, but I knew otherwise. She wasn't very happy in her marriage."

"And you don't know his last name?"

"No, but he was one of the other triage nurses."

Gus looked to Vanessa to be sure she got it. "What can you tell us about her husband?"

"Steve? He's a nice guy and all but he's no match for Sarah. Sarah's stubborn and independent and absolutely in charge." She exhaled. "She's an alpha in every way." She tilted her head to the side, dabbing at the corners of her eyes.

"And what about the women in your group? Any issues there we should know about?"

Maria pursed her lips. "Well, as headstrong as Sarah is,

Jules is equally so. Sarah and Jules butt heads often."

"Anything serious?"

"No." Maria paused, choosing her next words carefully. "It's complicated. Let's just say they tolerate each other."

"Barely," commented Jim, and Maria shot him a disapproving look.

"I have no doubt that deep down they love each other," she continued. "They're just in this constant power struggle. It's totally a control thing."

Maria got quiet, pulled elsewhere by some memory. Gus thought about the funeral memorial card wrapped neatly inside the thick protective evidence bag. How could a twenty-five-year-old suicide be connected to the recent murders? Maria cleared her throat.

"Thank you, Maria," said Gus. "We know how difficult this must be for you. Just one last question. What can you tell us about Rebecca Munroe?"

Maria's eyebrows scrunched and she looked to her side at Jim. "Becca? From high school?"

The chief nodded before looking back to Gus, and Maria followed his gaze. "Ah, I don't know. That was so long ago now. She was a girl in our class in high school who committed suicide. It was tragic."

"Were she and Sarah friends?"

"Sarah and Becca?" Maria asked with an air of disbelief. "No," she said emphatically.

"Were they enemies or did they fight? Can you think of any connection between them?"

Maria shook her head throughout Gus's questions. "No,

you don't understand. They weren't friends *or* enemies. They weren't anything; they just...were. Becca was a nice kid but we didn't have anything to do with her. Not Sarah or any of us. We ran in very different circles."

"Could she and Sarah have been on the same team at some point or in the same club?"

"I mean, we all played some sports. Maybe not very well, but it was a small school so making a team wasn't very hard. But I don't remember Becca being into sports at all, and as for clubs she and Sarah might've been in together, Sarah wasn't the club type so, no, I don't think so."

"Do you remember who Rebecca's friends were, who she hung around with?"

"She was sort of a loner. But the one person she was close with was Maury, ah, Maureen Ferguson. She runs the library over in Ashby now."

Maria looked to her side again at Jim. "What's going on?" When he didn't answer she turned back to Gus. "Why all the questions about Becca? What does she have to do with Sarah's death?"

"We have reason to believe that Rebecca's and Sarah's deaths may be connected."

Chapter Five

Melainey Idlewilde stood by the bay window of Maria Lincoln's family room and looked out over the driveway and side yard. Her eyes followed a bird from one tree to another, and she thought of the mysteries surrounding John James Audubon's masterpiece, *The Birds of America*. She wondered if some of the species included were, in fact, contrived or mistakes as some people theorized.

It was early afternoon and the large crowd that had gathered at the edge of Sarah's yard had dispersed. Maria had just finished speaking with the FBI, so when she got back to her house she texted the Posse to come over, threw her soiled clothes in the wash, and jumped in the shower.

Mel heard the water upstairs stop and the metal-framed glass door to Maria's shower clang shut. She gazed out the window, past the lawn, through the row of bushes, and into Sarah Nelson's side yard. Ever since junior high, Maria and Sarah had always planned to live next to each other. And they all guffawed the day Maria and her husband, Jim, put an offer in on the house next to Sarah's. But none of them were surprised. Maria was a planner. With lists and schedules. And rules, lots of rules.

Two kids—one boy, one girl—a golden retriever named

Charlie, a tabby cat named Patches. A big house so everyone can come over.

The yellow crime scene tape strung up around Sarah's yard earlier that morning had begun to droop, and its playful flapping in the autumn breeze pissed Mel off. Her eyes moved to the elaborate inground pool just inside its borders, then to its hot tub, and the splashing and laughter of past pool parties hijacked her thoughts. CSI people sealed tight in white bunny suits drifted in and out of her frame, faceless shapes from another world.

But inevitably her eyes kept settling back on the same spot, the one she tried her best to avoid. Not thirty yards from where Mel stood, amongst the bare rosebushes lining the outside of the pool—the same pool Sarah had dreamed of and planned and designed and saved for—was the flattened spot where Sarah had taken her last breath just hours ago. The concept of another one of her friends being dead shredded Mel's reality.

Maria's text about Sarah's death had once again opened the floodgates of emotions surrounding Laur's murder, emotions that had taken Mel months to wrestle down. Mel had convinced herself that Laur's murder was some random act of violence, a tragic event that could have been avoided. Wrong place, wrong time. But now she knew that was not the case; now she knew how terribly wrong she was.

Mel was lost in a haze, until her eyes were drawn to a group photograph—on the wall beside the window—of Maria's and Sarah's families together. They had saved up and gone on a trip to Disney World one spring vacation a few years ago before any of the kids hit high school and the rigors of college prep classes. Her eyes drifted over the photo, past the smiles and goofy faces and sun-kissed cheeks until they came to Sarah's two daughters: Jessica, her now-eleventh-grader, and Abigail, her ninth-grader. They were in the center of the group, their faces painted; Jess's like a tiger, Abby's like a character from *Frozen*. They looked straight into the camera, each caught mid-laugh, and Mel immediately saw Sarah's goofiness in both young girls.

Mel had never married, nor did she have any children. She wasn't opposed to either; she'd just raced too fast through her twenties and thirties to fall in love. After college, she'd lived in Boston, climbing the ranks of one technology firm after another and traveling the globe. And before she knew it, she was selling the company she had started eight years before and moving back to Kendalton to "downshift." And bumping up against forty.

But Mel knew deep down inside that her Facebook status was as much a result of the shit-show marriage her parents had as it was her Global Elite standing on United Airlines. So, while Mel didn't have any children of her own, she co-opted each of her friend's kids and spoiled them rotten. And as she stared at Jess and Abby in the photo, their happiness on display for all to see, her heart cracked just a little more. She knew she and Sarah's girls would now share an odd common link, whether ever spoken about or not. Although Mel's mother wasn't murdered, Mel was a young teenager when she came home one afternoon from school to find her mother gone for good and, in her place, a Department of

Social Services officer. So, Mel knew the chasm of loss that grows inside you when you lose a parent—even a shitty one—at that young age.

She heard light footsteps on the stairs and turned to see Maria step into the room. Her friend's pale complexion was a touch more ashen than usual and her wet hair was disheveled, as if she towel-dried and shook it out on the way down the stairs. Maria's eyes welled up when they met Mel's. They were all in anguish about Sarah's death but none more than Maria. She clenched her jaw and Mel could see the lines around her mouth were deeper, more pronounced, as her chin began to quiver. Mel quickly went to her and the two women hugged tight, the type of profound embrace that says *I love you* and *we'll get through this together* all at once.

As Mel and Maria rocked back and forth in silence, Mel opened her eyes to see Lizzy Porter on the far side of the room. Lizzy, who was the free spirit of the group, with her soft, tawny skin, wavy chestnut hair, and generally carefree attitude was anything but Zen today. She paced back and forth with her three-year-old son, Nicolas—Nico or the Surprise, as she jokingly referred to him—on her hip. Her white peasant blouse with the three-quarter-length sleeves brushed the top of faded jeans. Mel watched Nico play with the collection of leather and yarn bracelets around one of Lizzy's wrists while she dangled her large, retro-style wristwatch on the other in front of him.

"Niiicooo," she cooed, trying to keep the restless toddler occupied, but her eyes remained locked on Maria.

Nico lolled his head straight back between his shoulders

and with an infectious laugh looked to the ceiling. “WhaaAaat?” He swung his head side to side like a pendulum.

Distracted, she went through the motions of their private game once more before Jules, without saying a word, gently touched Lizzy’s shoulder and took Nico into her arms. Mel released her hold on Maria, and Lizzy slid right in, as if they’d practiced this particular move a hundred times. Lizzy crouched slightly to hold her shorter friend.

“I’m so sorry,” Lizzy whispered into Maria’s ear. “I’m so sorry.”

The two women cried together, causing them each to hug tighter. Jules Russell slowly rocked little Nico for another moment before setting him down on the floor beside his toys and stepping beside Mel. The thick straps of Jules’s sports bra bulged beneath her white tank top and her thin, black nylon shorts accentuated firm runner’s legs. Mel got the faintest whiff of the medicinal cream she knew her friend used for the faint, pink spots of psoriasis dotting her elbows and upper forearms. Jules tilted her head and cupped her hand along her ponytail, leaving it to rest on the front of her right shoulder. Scooping up her cup of tea, she put her hand on Maria’s shoulder.

“Hey, love, you okay?”

Maria wiped tears away with the outsides of her palms and whispered, “I don’t know…”

Collecting herself, Maria brought them through it all: from seeing Sarah stumble from the woods to her dying in her arms and to the needle mark she heard the pathologist found on Sarah's neck. And throughout it all, there were tears and tissues for all. When Maria had finished, Jules leaned against the credenza and the others naturally gathered around her as if she were holding court. The look on her face had turned to concern.

"So, what'd the FBI say?" she asked, her expression becoming stoic.

"Do they think it's connected to Laurie?" blurted Lizzy.

"Of course it is," dismissed Jules.

"You say it like it's nothing!" hissed Lizzy, trying to keep her voice low for Nico. Her chest heaved and her mouth was quivering and Mel saw the tears pooling in her soft, hazel eyes.

Frustrated, Jules glared at Lizzy. Her eyes were intense, cold. "Lizzy, stop. You think I'm not concerned? Not devastated at what's happened?" she asked, eyes wide. "Of course I am, but we have to keep it together." She turned her attention back to Maria.

"After we talked about finding Sarah, they asked about Sarah's personal life, if she had any enemies, anyone who'd want to harm her or Laurie." They all remained quiet as Maria added, "If she had any secrets she wouldn't want anyone to find out."

"What'd you say?" asked Jules, curiosity carrying her voice higher.

Maria's eyes narrowed. "I fed them her affair."

The room fell quiet as the reality of the situation settled in with each of them. Someone had murdered two of their closest friends. Would one of them be next? Jules took a deep breath, then rubbed the small, light brown beauty mark on her upper lip as she was apt to do when thinking something through. She grabbed the half-empty bottle of Ketel One vodka next to her on the top of Maria's credenza, twisted its top off, and poured a splash into her tea.

Maria caught Jules's eye and raised an eyebrow, but Jules just stared at her with a vacant look before taking a gulp. She bit down hard and wiped a drop from her lower lip using her fist.

"You better fill up," said Maria, her eyes locked with Jules's. This time it was Jules's eyebrow that was raised. "They asked me what I knew about Becca."

Jules's head twitched and her eyes narrowed. "What?" But before Maria could reply, Lizzy's hushed shriek filled their ears.

"Why'd they ask about her?"

"I don't know," said Maria in a near whisper, frustration mixing with fear. "I tried to find out but they wouldn't say. I'll ask Jim tonight."

The four of them drew quiet, the air sucked from the room. The FBI asking about Becca Munroe introduced a fear they had not experienced in decades. But, worse, it had ripped off the scab covering old questions. Could anyone else know? Had they missed something, some tiny detail a fresh pair of eyes would find? If the FBI connected Becca's death to Sarah, they'd soon connect it to the rest of them. If they hadn't already.

Mel looked around at her friends, at the new, leaner Posse. In Lizzy's and Maria's eyes she saw fear, but in Jules's only suspicion.

"Has anyone said anything to anybody?" asked Jules. "Anything at all?" She looked from one to the next; they each in turn silently shook their head. "Laurie, Sarah then?" she speculated.

"Oh my God!" moaned Lizzy at the suggestion, cupping a hand over her mouth.

"Lizzy, enough," snapped Jules, her jaw clenched.

Maria put her small hand on Lizzy's shoulder and leaned in close. "Hey, hey, c'mon. We're gonna figure this out."

Jules tipped another splash of vodka into her mug and looked around their shrinking circle. She saw the stress in the others' eyes, and her face softened. "Listen, I get it. What happened to Laur and Sarah is horrendous. And, we're all scared." She looked to Mel then Maria. "And mourning our best friends. But, we have to keep it together." Her eyes grew intense. "Everything depends on it." She eyed each of them. "*Everything.*"

"But what if we're next?" said Lizzy, her bottom lip quivering.

Maria held Lizzy close and, looking over her friend's shoulder, made a wide-eyed expression at Jules.

"Lizzy, we're going to figure this out," said Jules, softly rubbing her shoulder. "But we can't panic." She looked at each of them. "We can't raise any suspicions. Two of our friends have been murdered. So, like everyone else in town, we too want answers. We're just like them, no different. So, we go out, we see people and they see us. If people don't see us mourning it'll only raise suspicions." She looked to Maria.

"But first, we find out why they're asking about Becca."

Maria nodded and, locking eyes with Lizzy, said, "And I'll pray for us."

Nico toddled over holding up an empty sippy cup. Lizzy pushed tears away, then knelt and hoisted him up onto her hip.

"Thirsty, bud?" She held him close and headed toward the kitchen. "Let's get you some more juicy."

As Lizzy left the room, Maria looked up at Mel and Jules. Mel could feel the fear radiating off her. "We've got to get in front of this, Jules. Come up with a plan."

"The plan's the same as it's always been: keep our heads down and mouths shut," bit back Jules. "But..." She tipped her chin toward Lizzy through the doorway.

"That one's the weak link," finished Maria.

"Amen," sighed Jules. "Amen."

Chapter Six

MEL YANKED THE emergency brake on her Jeep and, sliding her foot off the clutch, noticed the large clumps of dead leaves littering the gravel parking lot around her. The Johnson Sports Complex was situated on the outskirts of town in a small area known by the locals as The Pit, a name one would not find anywhere on the brochures available at the Kendalton Tourist Center. The Johnson family—one of the oldest in town—had donated the fifty or so acres that made up the complex years ago, with a vision of creating a regional athletic mecca. But, as is the case with many dreams, it had proved elusive and, after the initial phase of three regulation-sized soccer fields and a mile-long walking path surrounding them, development was ceased due to "lack of demand." As it turned out, Kendalton was so remote a destination that only its own teams used the fields, which, in the end, suited those in town just fine.

Mel had stayed and consoled Maria long after Lizzy and Jules left and, as a result, was emotionally spent. So now, alone in the quiet sanctuary of her Jeep, lost in her own thoughts, she took a minute for herself before joining the other humans. Mel was an introvert, so if she had her way she'd be home by herself, curled up on the couch in her sweats with her rambunctious yellow Labrador retriever, Fred, by her side. But Jules's voice rang in her head.

We go out, we see people and they see us. If people don't see us mourning it'll only raise suspicions.

She looked off into the distance at a large green farm tractor, its hay rake in tow, forming clean lines of windrow as it went. While Kendalton was most known for its fall festivals and apple picking or its antique shops and close proximity to New England's most prominent ski areas, there were also several large farms in town, and for them haying season was well underway.

Through the silver chain-link fence in front of her she could see the soccer fields stretching into the distance. Just inside the gate sat a small concession hut, around which parents and kids alike gathered to eat burgers and hot dogs and a variety of candies and drinks, both hot and cold. Mel scanned the fields for the right game and as she did so caught a glimpse of herself in the rearview mirror and winced. The brown eyes—so dark they looked black—staring back at her and the painfully straight brown hair were familiar but slightly off, as if someone had traced a picture of her over the original, yet placed it slightly askew. Mel was fried and she knew she had let herself go. Losing Laur was like a cancer to Mel; an invasive, fast-spreading disease eating away her insides. Nothing smelled right, nothing tasted right, nothing made her happy, nothing made her...her. It was like death with the lights on.

She turned away and found Lizzy's daughter, Terry, standing with her teammates on the sideline. She had her warm-up clothes on and her arms were in the air cheering on the players as she watched the game, laughing with the other girls. Off to the side, away from all the other parents, stood Jules next to her husband, Shane. She had changed since leaving Maria's earlier, replacing her exercise outfit with dark, tight-fitting jeans, ankle-high leather Frye boots and a formfitting cream cashmere sweater. Her shiny hair fell perfectly to the center of her back, and she wore dark sunglasses with black lenses that hid her eyes. Jules was always a walking fashion statement and Mel wondered how she did it, what with kids and a husband and a house to take care of. Mel could barely pull on jeans some mornings or remember to feed Fred.

The crowd cheered, drawing Mel's attention to the field of play just in time to see Jules's daughter Emily—aka Milly—rifle a shot that caught the top corner of the net. And as the teammates congratulating Milly dispersed, Mel watched her jog back to the center of the field and it struck her, as it had so many times over the years, just how much daughter was like mother. And it wasn't just her eyes or chin or hair. It was the tilt of her head a certain way when she was thinking or that rare but unmistakable look in her eye that told you she got you. Really got you.

Mel's thoughts went to Sarah's two daughters: Jessica and Abby. She knew the long road they had in front of them, growing up without a mother. Could they survive adolescence—arguably the toughest years for a young girl—without a mother? Once again, Mel found herself lost in her thoughts of the past and of the futures—the ones taken from her, and the ones put in their place without her consent.

Closure was Grief's nemesis. Or its puppet.

She had that tingling in her nose again and found herself dabbing away stubborn tears with her fingertips. Her hands dropped to her lap and, in a haze, Mel looked off into the distance at the trees lining the far side of the fields while her sluggish brain served up old, fuzzy memories.

Mel and Laur squished on Laur's bed with their heads at the bottom, their elbows propping them up while their bare feet rested on the pillows. Laur's frizzy hair was tied back in a ponytail with a red scrunchie that matched her choker necklace wrapped high on her throat. Mel played with the new slap bracelet Mrs. T had given her earlier that day. At first she was confused about what it was for; she couldn't remember the last time someone thought to get her a gift for nothing. She blew her hair out of her face for a third time, then grabbed an elastic from the nightstand and tied it back like Laur's.

Sarah was on the floor leaning against the foot of the bed close to Mel, her long, athletic figure folded into a tight sitting position. She had toned athletic legs, the kind her mom always told her she'd miss one day. Her face was red from laughter, and she covered her mouth with a hand to stifle the sound. Maria sat next to her, hunched over a stack of thick construction paper she had been cutting and folding, and laughed into the crook of her arm wrapped around her mouth. The town phone book sat open on the floor between her and Sarah, and they had stretched the phone cord from the hall into Mel and Laur's bedroom and were prank-calling boys from school. Sarah took her finger off the button that hung up the phone, then took the receiver from Laur and hung it up properly. They all burst into a raucous laughter.

"Shhhh," said Laur through her hands. "My mom will hear us."

"I don't think Tommy could tell it was you," said Lizzy to Laur through laughter. She sat atop one of the desks, behind Jules, who was sitting in the chair. The two of them faced the others across the tiny room. Jules had a wide grin and her face was flushed from laughing. Her low-cut shirt was tight across her chest and abdomen and, coupled with her developing body and meticulously styled blond hair, she bore a striking resemblance to the young women pictured in the windows of the newest store in the mall: Abercrombie & Fitch.

"He totally could," proclaimed Jules in a hushed whisper. "And even if holding your nose worked, the fact that Maria yelled, 'Hang up, Laur!' at the end probably gave you away."

They all burst into a new fit of muffled giggles. Lizzy held her aching sides for a few moments before her laughter subsided and she went back to braiding Jules's hair. She had drawn a picture of a woman with braided hair that Jules really liked, which now lay on the desk beside her. She continually consulted the sketch as she carefully wove Jules's hair into its form. Lizzy's loose-fitting denim overalls were unbuttoned on one side, its top flapped open. She kept sliding the cluster of bracelets up her forearm, exposing thin white tan lines around her wrist.

"If he talks to you at school," said Laur to Maria, "say it

wasn't you who yelled and you don't know what he's talking about. And if he talks to me I'll say I wasn't even with you."

Maria nodded, all in with the collusion, before turning back to the paper she was writing on. Her penmanship was tight and crisp. Mel looked to Laur and the notebook on the bed by her hand. Laur had repeatedly circled Tommy Dumont's name and phone number, and Mel noticed below it she had signed *Mrs. Laurie Dumont* over and over down the page.

"Laur, I'll talk to him," declared Jules. "You should know if he likes you or not."

"No!" pleaded Laurie, the smile fading from her face. "Jules, don't. I mean it."

"Have you seen him at all this summer?" asked Lizzy.

"We saw him," burst out Sarah. She looked over to Maria. "At Eddie's around the Fourth of July," she said, referring to Eddie's Ice Cream shop on Main Street.

"That's right," confirmed Maria. "He was outside with Troy and Brian and they pretended not to see us. He totally likes you," said Maria to Laur. "He's just shy."

"Shy?" asked Jules in disbelief.

"I heard Stephanie Stromb likes him too," interrupted Sarah.

"Me too," added Jules. She leaned forward and with a raised eyebrow said in a hushed whisper, "I heard he and Stephanie were together at Mikey Barube's pool party a few weeks ago."

"They were not!" said Maria. "Knock it off, Jules. Jimmy was there and he said Tommy was with him the whole time."

"Well, that's what I heard," snipped Jules. Lizzy's brush caught in her hair and Jules pulled her head forward. "Ouch!" She slapped Lizzy's brush away. "Jesus, Lizzy, watch it." She bent away and Lizzy sat still, not knowing what to do.

Jules rubbed her head before continuing, "Speaking of Stephanie, did you see what she was *wearing* at the movies last weekend? That shirt and those jeans." She grimaced.

"I know, right?" agreed Sarah.

"They were *boot cut*," added Lizzy, piling on, but when she smiled her new braces caught on the inside of her lips, halting her face in a stiff semi-grin like a toddler's when prompted.

Jules looked up at Mel, who hadn't said a word. "Mel, you're kinda quiet. Do you think that outfit was cute?"

Mel heard herself swallow and hoped the others hadn't. She felt her generic high-waisted denim shorts bunching around her narrow hips and her mind began to spin. Inside her surged the worry that someone would notice her hand-me-down shirt was closer to last year's fashion than this year's. It suddenly felt too tight along her back and she casually hunched her shoulders and angled her arms inward until its sleeves hung lower on her arms.

"No, I didn't see it."

Jules eyed her with suspicion but remained quiet.

"You didn't miss much, Mel," said Sarah.

Lizzy pushed her bracelets up again. "Ya, except that Donna McCarthy was with her." She laughed and poked Jules's back with a finger. "She washed off that makeup you helped her with in the food court the other day."

Maria burst out laughing. "Oh my gosh, that was hysterical. She looked like the lead in *The Rocky Horror Picture Show*."

They all laughed and giggled. Maria had finished with the construction paper and held up a small square chatterbox. In each corner of the surface was a different-colored dot. She slipped her fingers in beneath it and flexed them wide, opening the paper up to show only even numbers in each corner from two to eight. She closed it and flexed her fingers in the opposite direction causing odd numbers from one to seven to appear. She and Sarah grinned at each other, a job well done.

"Okay, Laur, you go first," instructed Maria.

Laurie's eyes widened and she leaned over the end of the bed to see Maria's hands more clearly.

"Um...will Tommy ask me out?" she blurted then giggled and plunged her face into her hands. Her feet kicked up and down, slapping on the pillow.

Maria held the closed chatterbox up in front of her. "Choose a color."

Laur peeked through her laced fingers. "Red."

Maria opened the box beneath the red dot and the even numbers showed. "Okay, pick a number."

"Six."

Sarah reached over and folded open the flap with a six written on it. Maria turned it toward her and read aloud what she and Sarah had written earlier beneath that fold.

"As I see it...YES!" she said with excitement.

"Ahhhh," screeched Sarah, and they all laughed and wiggled around in their spots. Mel rolled onto her back and, as she laughed loudly, her outstretched hand met Laur's and the two held hands in the air and giggled together at the ceiling for what seemed an eternity.

Chapter Seven

MEL COLLECTED HERSELF and was about to turn off the engine when there was a soft rapping on the passenger's side window. The door opened and in slipped the slender, sinewy frame of Annie Elkins. Her spandexed legs slid easily onto the leather passenger seat and she looked Mel squarely in the eyes.

"How ya doing?" she asked with her plain-spoken directness.

Annie was the epitome of all natural, inside and out—no artificial colors, preservatives, or additives. She was one hundred percent organic, non-GMO natural. Born and raised on one of the farms in town, being outdoors and active had been imprinted on her at birth. She raked her dark curly hair with calloused fingers and drew Mel's attention with bright, clear eyes.

"Still processing," Mel replied with great effort, hoping any trace of mascara didn't have Annie looking at a raccoon. The cabin of the Jeep fell quiet and Mel listened to the muted yells of enthusiastic kids and parents pulsing from the soccer fields.

Mel and Annie first met in junior high when Mel befriended an equally shy, nervous homeschooled twig of a girl who joined the school's track and field team without knowing anyone. Mel too knew how it felt to not belong. She knew her mom drank too much and lived in constant fear of anyone from school meeting her. And by junior high Mel had realized her house was not like the houses she saw other kids running to from the bus. So when Annie's mother brought their two dogs to that first practice, Mel—not allowed to have pets of her own—got her fix and a new friend in the process. Then, having not seen Annie since graduating high school, when Mel moved back to town about five years ago the first thing she did was get her dog, Fred. And since Annie was Fred's foster caretaker for the shelter, the two reconnected.

But it was about two years ago when they began to grow much closer. That was when, after eighteen years of marriage, Annie found herself in the midst of a venomous divorce as she watched her once-solid marriage crumble beneath the weight of her husband's serial infidelities. Then, still trying to find her balance, a year later her only child, a teenaged daughter named Billie after Annie's long-deceased father, died of a drug overdose. And Mel had been by her side throughout it all.

Mel shifted in her seat to better face Annie. "Hey…why are you here?" Her voice was soothing, supportive.

"Checking on you," Annie said, as if it was obvious. "Mel, you're my closest friend. Hell, my only friend lately. I'm worried about you."

"No, here," Mel clarified with a gesture to the soccer fields filled with teenaged girls running and screaming and laughing. "The fields. Why are you at the fields?"

Annie's perfect posture gave way and her shoulders slackened. "I know, I know, it's"—she made air quotes—"*not healthy* as my therapist used to say. But this is the only place I remember Billie being genuinely happy," she explained. "Sometimes I come here just to walk around and hear the noises of happy kids."

"I get it."

Annie shook her head as if shooing away a fly. "Enough about me. I still can't get over the news about Sarah. Are you scared?"

Lizzy's words played in Mel's mind.

But someone murdered Laurie and Sarah. What if we're next?

"Absolutely terrified, ya."

"Do you want to come stay with me?" Annie shrugged. "I've got lots of room."

Mel shook her head. "Nah, I've got the new security system. I'll be fine, but thanks. Don't you forget to use your alarm system too, right?"

A loud cheer drew their attention back to the fields. Mel noticed a gathering of parents standing between two of the fields. Portable chairs lined each sideline and beside the parents was a small cluster of younger kids carefully kicking a soccer ball around in a circle. She watched as the number of adults steadily swelled in size. The parents were talking amongst themselves, ignoring the soccer games taking place on either side of them. Word of Sarah's death had spread.

"Are you going to write about it?"

Mel looked back to Annie, head tilted slightly. Mel was the creator of Kendalton's only online newspaper, *The Meetinghouse.*

"Oh, I, ah…" She twisted her mouth to one side. "It's all too raw right now."

"I totally get it," said Annie almost apologetically. She gestured to the crowd of parents. "I just thought, you know, the gossip and rumors and all. Might be good to have some facts out there."

Mel noticed Jim Lincoln walking through the gate to the fields with two people she assumed were the FBI agents Maria had talked about. The man was tall and husky with broad shoulders and the wingspan of a swimmer, and something in his stride said he was in charge. The woman had a more casual gait that told Mel she was younger than he was. She was tall for a woman and slender, and her red hair was fashioned every which way into a punk style. Annie touched Mel's arm and snapped her from her thoughts.

"I better get back to my walk. We still on to walk tomorrow morning?"

"Absolutely." Mel knew that now that Annie was alone she looked forward to their get-togethers more so than before. And given the past few years that Annie had endured, Mel was damn sure she wasn't going to let her down.

Annie popped her door open and stepped out with ease. She paused before closing it, then stuck her head back inside.

"Be careful, okay? Text if you need anything." And she was gone.

Mel looked back to the fields to see the chief and the two

agents headed straight toward Jules. Jim nodded hellos to some as he passed but the agents' determined strides tugged him along. And as they rounded the corner of the field the man looked back toward the parking lot, and for the first time Mel saw his face. She saw the look of intensity, of suspicion. But, worst of all, she saw patience, confidence. Not the forced confidence usually accompanied by bravado and showmanship but the quiet, reserved confidence of someone who has proven to themselves their ability to get things done. And Mel felt a wave of heat swell inside her chest.

Chapter Eight

"MARIA SAID YOU wanted to speak with us," said Jules after Jim introduced Gus and Vanessa. Jules had a smooth, seductive voice and the subtlest trace of a lisp, one diligently beaten down over the years that Gus guessed only added to her confidence. She removed her KREWE sunglasses and Gus noted stress lines tugging at each eye. The warm sun drew color to her high cheekbones.

"This is my husband, Shane."

Shane had a five-o'clock shadow trimmed neatly to sculpt his jawline and his light eyeglass frames offset thick black hair and eyebrows and dark, deep-set eyes. A sharp, mechanical alarm stabbed the air and Shane took his phone from the pocket of his nylon windbreaker. He tapped its screen to stop the beeping and sheepishly raised it.

"Sorry." He turned to Jules. "I've got to head in, hon."

Jules simply nodded as he scurried off with his phone pressed to his ear.

"Shane's the director of the National Oceanographic Institute. They're doing some time-sensitive biological research."

"The one in Newbury?" asked Vanessa.

"Yes, have you been?"

"No, but I've got a friend who's studying marine biology and she's gone. She said it's lit; best in the country."

"It is very impressive," confirmed Jules with an air of satisfaction.

"Do you work outside the home, Mrs. Russell?" said Gus.

"Yes, I volunteer part-time at the high school in the principal's office and head up the Ed Foundation we started a few years ago to supplement the school's operating budget."

Two women walking by excused themselves to the group and one after the other leaned in and hugged Jules. They each whispered their condolences to her before hugging again and, after nodding their appreciation toward Gus, walked on.

Gus was raised in a small town the size of Kendalton and he knew how small towns worked. He watched how the other women carefully addressed Jules, how they spoke to her with complete deference, and how she carried herself because of it. Gus had been with Jules Russell for all of five minutes, yet he already knew her well. He had met dozens of Jules Russells in his life, and they all acted as if they were always center stage, the world around them their supporting cast.

He glanced around and noticed an inordinate number of people paying more attention to their conversation than the games being played on the fields. He gestured toward a remote spot near a wooden fence behind the far soccer goal and the four of them made their way to it. The sun had inched below the tops of the trees, and it had cooled off considerably since they arrived at the fields. Jules folded her arms across her midsection as Vanessa pulled out her cell phone and placed it on the fence post between them. She tapped the recorder app.

"Mrs. Russell, can you think of anyone who would want to harm Laurie or Sarah?"

"No," she said, her voice shaky. "The girls and I spoke this morning and we can't think of anyone who'd want to do something like this."

Gus got side-eyed by Vanessa at the word *girls* but ignored it.

"Can you tell us about your relationship with Sarah Nelson? It's come up that you and she didn't always get along."

Jules looked to the ground as her head slowly rocked side to side. "No, we didn't. And it all sounds so stupid now." Her voice cracked and she took a tissue from her pocket and dabbed at her eye. "We did bicker a lot but we were like *sisters*. I loved her and I know she loved me too."

Vanessa finished writing a note in her notebook and Gus paused when he noticed Jules distracted by the spinning pen in her hand.

"V," he said, grabbing her attention. Realizing what Gus was doing, Vanessa grasped the pen to a halt and Jules flashed her an impatient glance before turning her attention back to Gus.

"How would you describe Sarah's marriage?" he continued.

"She wasn't happy. I'm sure Maria mentioned she'd been unfaithful to Steve for years."

"Anyone you think who might've wanted to hurt her? A bad breakup, maybe?"

"I don't know. I never met any of them."

"Mrs. Russell," interrupted Vanessa, "can you tell us where you were on the mornings of the two assaults?"

"Absolutely. I was running. I run most mornings."

"On the Land Trust trails?"

"No, I usually run on the roads on the outskirts of town. It's quiet out there. The trails aren't good to train on for marathons."

"Did anyone see you this morning or the morning of Ms. Turner's assault?"

Jules pressed her lips tight. "I don't know, maybe. But, like I said, I usually run where it's pretty remote."

Gus made sure to establish eye contact before asking his next question. "What can you tell us about Rebecca Munroe?"

"Maria said you thought Sarah's death was connected somehow to Becca." Jules paused a beat as uncertainty crept into her features. "Uh, I don't know, probably the same thing others will tell you. Rebecca was a sweet girl, kind of geeky." She raised an eyebrow and shrugged her firm shoulders, searching for more to say. "I don't know—we were in very different crowds."

"Can you think of any connection between Rebecca and Laurie or Sarah? Classes together? Maybe in the same club or on the same bus?"

"Not really, no. Rebecca was this mousy, geeky kid. I seem to remember her around the drama club; not *in* plays but more behind the scenes, like helping to build sets and doing lights, stuff like that. But, neither Laur nor Sarah were into that kind of thing. And, Rebecca lived over by the quarry, probably closer to where I grew up, but I never really took the bus so…"

"Did you ever wonder why she committed suicide?"

Jules's eyebrows arched. "I guess like everyone else I just assumed she was gay. Her parents were very religious—her father was the pastor at their church—so the thinking went that she couldn't bring herself to tell them that she was."

"What made you think she was gay?"

Jules's mouth twisted as she searched for the right words. "Rumors, I guess. She really only had one close friend: Maury Ferguson. They were inseparable and I think it was just the way they acted around each other: a little too touchy with each other, if you know what I mean."

Gus thought a moment. "Is there anything else you can think of that might be important?"

"Yes, yes there is," she said, catching Gus by surprise. "Laurie's and Sarah's deaths aren't the first things to happen to our group recently. We've experienced vandalism and some other weird things." She looked to Jim. "You told them about my car, right?"

Jim's gaze snapped to Gus. "I started to…"

"The chief and I talked about it earlier," Gus said, rescuing Jim. "But I'd really like to hear it from you. The smallest of details or subtleties can make a difference."

Jules's head dismissively twitched side to side. "There *are* no subtleties. This past spring our Range Rover got keyed along the entire passenger side and rear end. We had to have it completely repainted."

"But Jules," interrupted Jim, "remember, we were never able to determine if that was targeted at you or just some random vandalism done in the mall parking lot."

Jules eyed Jim with skepticism before looking back to Gus. "And then a few months ago our house was broken into." She glanced to the chief. "Think they knew we lived there, Jim?"

"Was anything taken?" asked Gus.

"A few things. We were away for Fourth of July weekend, and when we got home I noticed some of my jewelry was missing."

"But, again, Jules," interjected Jim, "there was no sign of a break-in, nor was there any evidence that anyone had been in your home."

Jules's eyes widened with disbelief. "Lizzy found her dog *dead* in her backyard. And Sarah's pool got contaminated with this weird algae a few months back. It took most of the summer to get rid of it and she loved that pool. And, Jim, someone put antifreeze in Maria's gas tank last month; seized the engine."

Gus turned to Jim. "Can I take a look at the incident reports on each of these?"

"Sure thing. They're at the station."

They spoke for another few minutes, then concluded the interview when the final whistle blew, ending Jules's daughter's soccer game. Gus gave her his card and asked her to call if she thought of anything else that might be helpful. As soon as they left Jules, she was immediately surrounded by a throng of other women hugging and consoling her.

It was dinnertime and Gus knew people would be on their commutes home or settling in with their families for the night, so he and Vanessa headed to the Kendalton Inn to drop their bags. But before leaving Jim, Gus had him call Lizzy Porter and make plans for him and Vanessa to meet with her after dinner at the spa she managed in Ashby, the town next door. Jim then headed to the police station to look for the cold case file for Rebecca Munroe's suicide in the archives database system.

Chapter Nine

LIZZY PORTER SLIPPED into The Blend, easing its wooden screen door shut to avoid the stares she had felt all day. Its familiar *slap-slap-slap* had provided a comfortable kick-start to her day for the better part of three years. But there was nothing familiar or comfortable about this day. Sarah was dead—another member of the Posse murdered. And the renewed questions about Becca's death had let a familiar coldness in, one she hadn't felt in decades, and it gnawed at her insides. Seeing the others in their usual spot by the fire, she headed straight over.

There was a nervousness in the air, one that mirrored her own, and the smell of fear so palpable it made Lizzy's scalp tighten. She saw dread in the eyes of those who looked up as she made her way past the various tables and chairs. It was just after six o'clock and The Blend was closed, yet only a few scarce seats remained unoccupied. Fidgeting women sat with nervous men, not knowing what to do except gather together and try and make sense of Sarah Nelson's death. In one corner sat a group of entangled teenagers, their eyes darting between each other, each guessing how to act now that their normal fears and insecurities were mixed with murder and frightened adults.

Mayor Babineau sat at one of the larger tables, his tie impeccably straight and his dress shirt pristine, speaking to a group of older patrons. Lizzy overheard some of their discussion on her way by.

"...FBI..."

"...murdered too...?"

Jules was sitting in her usual chair at the end of the small coffee table with two women standing at her side. As Lizzy approached she caught the end of their conversation.

"Don't worry about a thing, Jules, we've got this," one was saying. "The team will have a great awards dinner."

Jules looked to each of them, her eyes red from rubbing, but before she could say anything the other woman leaned close and touched Jules's shoulder.

"Hey, remember, if there's anything we can do for Sarah..."

"Thanks," whispered Jules solemnly, her voice scratchy and raw.

The two of them tipped their heads to the others then Lizzy as they left. Lizzy sat in her usual leather armchair between Maria and Jules. Coaxing the wide leather band of her watch around her wrist, she noticed it was tighter than usual, and her frightened brain smothered all-too-familiar anxieties. She checked the time.

"I'm meeting the FBI at the spa at seven, so only have about a half hour or so." Her voice rose with uncertainty. She felt her heart rate pick up as she looked to Maria.

"Your text said it was urgent?"

Maria was nervously rolling the gold cross hanging from

her neck back and forth between her finger and thumb. She wore a pumpkin-colored shirt buttoned at the collar and pressed khaki slacks. Lizzy caught the faint odor of cigarettes through Maria's spearmint gum.

Jules ran her finger and thumb along the sides of her open mouth and removed a smudge of her signature red MAC lipstick, the classic Ruby Woo. She leaned forward and looked to Maria. "What'd you find out?" she whispered.

"Jim said they found a memorial card from Becca's funeral on Sarah's body."

"Ohhh," groaned Lizzy into her fist. She caught her reflection in a mirror over Mel's shoulder. Her eyes were puffy and her cheeks pulsed from too much blush. She felt the stares of the others and knew they could tell she'd been crying. Maria crossed her legs, one knee tightly over the other, and was about to say something when Jules interrupted.

"Do they have any suspects?"

"Not yet." Maria's voice was hoarse and her chin began to quiver. She bit her lower lip and with her eyes closed was forced to see the image that had been haunting her for decades. A snapshot perfectly framed like an old Polaroid: Becca laughing nervously, the shimmer of campfire lapping her innocent face, the tapestry of a brilliant night's sky her backdrop. She opened her eyes and inhaled deeply.

"What if they reopen Becca's suicide investigation?" interrupted Lizzy. She heard the panic rising in her voice but no longer cared.

"What if they do?" challenged Jules in a whisper. "It's

been twenty-five years. What're they gonna find?" She handed Maria a tissue, then offered them to Mel and Lizzy, whispering, "People are watching." They each took one.

"So, Jules, you were right: It had to be Sarah or Laurie," Lizzy said in a hushed tone. Her words came quickly and her eyes darted around the group. "Mel, Maria, you knew the two of them best. Can you think of anyone they might've told?" Mel and Maria both shook their heads, causing Lizzy to manically continue, "Mel, maybe one of the guys Laurie dated?"

"I doubt it." But even as Mel said the words she pondered the same question in her mind.

"Maria, what about this guy Sarah was screwing around with? You said she had fallen hard for him… Maybe she told him, you know, during pillow talk or something."

Mel leaned over and put a hand on Lizzy's shoulder. "Hey, hey, c'mon. We're gonna figure this out." She leaned in, trying to catch Lizzy's eyes. "It's never as bad as it seems."

Lizzy snapped her head toward Mel. "How would you know? You weren't even there!" Tears began to run down her cheeks. "You didn't see her."

Lizzy stopped abruptly, catching herself, and looked around at nearby tables. Comfortable no one else had heard her, she then looked around at the others but saw only pity staring back. She ran the palms of her hands from her nose to her ears to wipe away the tears. She glanced back at the mirror and a ghoulish mask with panda eyes stared back. Using her tissue she cleaned up as best as she could then cleared her throat in embarrassment. Lizzy had always known they thought of her as lesser somehow; the one with the low self-esteem. And she understood why. They all went to college; she didn't. They all had boys chasing after them their entire lives; she didn't. And now they all had nice, large houses and shiny new cars and took vacations. And she didn't. But she wasn't surprised. Like many raised in an unhappy family, Lizzy never thought her life would bear anything too exciting.

She looked to Maria, with her petite frame and large chest and put-together attitude, then to Jules and her runner's body and model good looks and, finally, to Mel with her dimples, and natural beauty and insanely successful business career. How could she ever compare to these women? She had been dealt a shitty gene pool and had spent her entire life trying to overcome it.

As if reading her thoughts, Jules put a hand on Lizzy's shoulder and began to rub it gently. Lizzy could feel the strength in her friend's touch and watched her arm warily out of the corner of her eye. She felt the space between them close and she stiffened.

"Hey, hey, we're all upset," whispered Jules in her ear. Jules's breathing was slow and rhythmic, and her breath smelled of rum and peppermint. Lizzy felt the slow heartbeat against her shoulder and compared it to the racing of her own. How could Jules be so calm? Jules gave her shoulder a tender squeeze before sitting back in her chair. Realizing she had been holding her breath, Lizzy exhaled.

"It doesn't matter who talked or what they said, for that matter," said Jules, her confidence back. She ran her tongue over her teeth beneath her upper lip. "It's always going to be their word against ours. We just have to stick together, stick to the story we've told forever."

Once outside in the parking lot they all hugged their goodbyes and, as one, vowed to get through this together. The number of people remaining on the street had thinned considerably as dusk took hold. Jules stood by her glistening black SUV, with its tinted windows and sleek curves. She tapped at her phone while Mel and Maria each got in their cars and left. Lizzy anxiously twisted the ignition key of her tired, old Hyundai sedan again and again.

In her peripheral vision Lizzy saw Jules begin to slowly walk toward her. Her wrist ricocheted back and forth but still her car would not start. And as Jules got within feet of Lizzy's side window she stopped and, without saying a word, simply stared down at her weak friend.

After another few twists, Lizzy's car finally sputtered to life. She yanked its shifter into drive and, stepping on the gas, held tightly to the steering wheel as the car lunged onto Main Street. And as Lizzy turned her rickety, old car toward Ashby and her spa and the FBI undoubtedly waiting for her, she couldn't take her eyes off Jules in the rearview mirror staring after her.

And it was at that moment that Lizzy realized she had lived in fear of this woman her entire life. And that may have been bearable when they had each other's backs, when secrets remained secret. But all that was changing now and Lizzy could feel it, like the faint tremble beneath one's feet that foreshadows an oncoming train not yet within sight or earshot.

And after a lifetime of being pushed around by Jules, Lizzy Porter was finally ready to push back.

Chapter Ten

ELEMENTS FITNESS AND Wellness Center was located at the end of a long plaza just off The Green in Ashby's center. The original fitness center, with its treadmills, resistance machines, and assortment of stationary cycling and free weights, was located on one end of the plaza. The wellness center portion of the name came in the form of the adjacent space that held a spa, massage rooms, and a smaller, more intimate-sized room for personalized sessions. But, unlike the fitness center, its windows were a smoky gray for privacy and the entrance was not standard glass and metal, but a light green door with flowered vines teased to grow up and over it. Chalkboards with distressed wood frames held details for yoga, meditation, crystals, and various types of energy-healing classes, all written in Lizzy's elaborate, sweeping penmanship.

Entering, Gus and Vanessa were met with the soothing aroma of incense and the melody of soft music in the air. Lush plants dangled from the ceiling, while larger ones overflowed from colorful planters set on tables and in corners of the room. The entire environment instantly relaxed Gus, making him feel warm and welcomed like a hug from an old friend. A toddler came running from the back room down the hall toward them, arms wide to his sides, making a motor sound and tilting his arms up and down like an airplane. A woman's strained singsong voice followed the little boy into the waiting room.

"Niiicooo."

Nico swooped around Gus's legs as the airplane made a hard turn and its engine was replaced with a giggling call back: "WhaaAaat?"

Lizzy Porter appeared at the opening of the hallway and when she saw Gus and Vanessa stopped short. She greeted them with sad eyes as Nico zoomed around her legs. Her husband, PJ, had called her after she left The Blend to tell her one of his customers had a broken water pipe emergency he had to tend to, so Lizzy had picked up Nico on the way.

The toddler stumbled his airplane into the middle of her thighs and, rolling his head backward, let out an infectious laugh.

Lizzy tilted her head. "He missed his nap so he's a bit amped." Her face was tight, the lines of stress pulling at her eyes and mouth. "You must be the FBI agents Jim called about."

Lizzy pulled a bin of toys from behind the reception counter and dumped them on the floor in front of a large tank built into the wall containing several exotic-looking fish. Nico squatted with the finesse of an old man and started playing with the blocks and toy cars. The adults sat in leather chairs arranged in a semicircle around the tank as if it were a movie screen.

"We just closed so shouldn't be bothered," said Lizzy.

"Thanks for meeting me here. I had to stop by and get my check."

Gus glanced around. "Forgive me, but this is like an oasis in the middle of a strip mall." His finger tapped along to the song on the side of his knee.

Lizzy forced a smile. "Ya, we get that a lot. It's been a labor of love. I started this with Duane—the owner—when I moved back to town about fifteen years ago now." She paused. "Jim said you wanted to talk about Laur and Sarah?"

Gus asked her many of the same questions they had asked Jules and Maria while Vanessa recorded it all with the app on her cell phone. No, Lizzy couldn't think of anyone who would want to do this. Yes, Sarah and Jules were in a constant power struggle and, yes, they argued often. And yes, she knew Sarah was unfaithful to her husband Steve but never talked about it with her. For completeness Vanessa jotted down her alibis so they could be verified.

"We understand that one of your pets unexpectedly died recently."

Lizzy was nodding before Gus finished. "That's right." She swallowed and her jaw tightened. "Last spring our three-year-old shepherd started acting very strangely: lethargic, not eating. Then that night she wasn't able to stand or walk and by morning she was dead. The vet suspected she had been poisoned but the tests to confirm that were so expensive so…"

"If she was, any idea who would do something like that?"

"No. My husband thought it might be hunters; someone pissed off if she scared the deer away with her barking or something. But now, with everything else that's gone on, I'm not so sure."

Lizzy bit the inside of her lower lip. "I know you're just beginning your investigation but, if I can ask, do you have any leads or suspects yet? We're all kinda freaked out."

Gus saw fear mixed with anxiety in her soft eyes. "We are really just beginning, but the obvious common links to both crimes are the walking trails and you and your friends. Both victims were assaulted on them so if you use them be careful."

"The Land Trust trails?" She scowled. "Those trails are a maze. I'd probably get lost if I did."

Gus leaned forward and rested his elbows on his knees, narrowing the space between them. He recalled what Vanessa had told him about Lizzy's past. After graduating high school and watching each of her friends begin college, Lizzy worked as a bank teller at the local bank her father managed for about a year before moving to Vail to be a ski bum. It was there that she got introduced to all sorts of alternative healing practices, such as yoga, meditation, Reiki, and wholistic nutrition, and eventually getting certified, she became an instructor at a healing center. But then, after Lizzy had lived there for a couple years, her mother had been diagnosed with cancer and that's when she moved home to be with her family, eventually getting married and having her first child.

They heard a loud crash and turned to see Nico lying beneath a spilled bucket of toys he had pulled off the coffee table. Lizzy went and got the crying toddler and, with him on her lap sucking his thumb, snuggled him into her chest while she softly rubbed the back of his head.

"Sorry about that."

"Mrs. Porter, what do you remember about Rebecca Munroe?"

"Becca? Not much, I'm afraid. I didn't really know her all that well." Lizzy leaned over and kissed the top of Nico's head but kept her eyes on Gus. "You think she's somehow connected to Laur's and Sarah's deaths. But that's impossible." Her voice rose, startling Nico. She rubbed his head but the young boy continued to squirm. "That was so long ago. How could they possibly be connected?"

"Is there anything you can remember that might connect Laurie or Sarah with Rebecca?"

She bit her lower lip again and shook her head. "No, nothing. We never hung around with her; she wasn't ever at any of the dances. She was just another kid in school." She held Nico closer.

"Jim was telling us how you used to act in the school plays back in high school."

Lizzy rolled her eyes. "That's right. I'm sure I was awful but I loved 'em."

"Maybe you got to know Rebecca a little from those. We understand she helped out behind the scenes building sets, working the lights, that sort of thing."

She thought a moment. "Oh, I don't think so."

"What do you remember about her death?"

An image flickered in Lizzy's mind, like a frame from a home movie projector. A bright, starry sky, frightened screams, arms, legs everywhere. Lizzy frantic, moving, falling, head swimming with confusion.

"I just remember hearing the news the next day from my dad. It was horrible. Everyone was shocked." She gave Nico a lingering kiss on the top of his head again.

"What can you tell us about her family? Were they active in town? Did you see them at the plays or other school events?"

"I think she only had a brother. I remember him a little but he was a few years older." She shrugged. "I don't really remember seeing them at school stuff and we didn't go to church so…"

Gus looked to Vanessa, who pursed her lips and, having no further questions, shook her head. Lizzy tried bouncing Nico on her knee to soothe him but he only squirmed more.

"It's getting late," said Gus, and he stood. "We'll let you get this little guy home." He handed Lizzy his card. "If you think of anything else that might be helpful, please give us a call."

Lizzy said that she would, and Gus and Vanessa left her and Nico to close up the spa. Outside in the parking lot Vanessa checked her phone and found a note from one of the other agents that they'd had interview Steve Nelson, Sarah's widower, and confirmed his alibi of being at work during the time of her attack and that he was unaware of Sarah's affair. She and Gus both leaned against the hood of the truck facing each other. She tipped her head over a shoulder, back toward the spa.

"What d'ya think?"

"Her dog's death?" said Gus, raising an eyebrow.

"Practice run?"

"That's my bet."

Her eyes remained on his. "That was kinda sus at the end there too, right?" She shook her head. "The vibe was off."

"Ya. You see her blanch at the mention of Rebecca Munroe?"

"Couldn't miss it."

"They're all feeding us bullshit. I grew up in a small town—one about this size—and, ya, I didn't hang around with everyone in my class but I sure as shit knew more about them than 'they were kinda geeky.' I knew who they hung out with, who they hated, who hated them. I knew who liked who and who was going out with who. I knew if they were in a band or if they smoked pot or if their father was a drunk." Gus looked back to the warm and welcoming storefront, but he was no longer feeling warmed or welcomed.

"I think it's safe to say these women know more than they're letting on."

Chapter Eleven

GUS AND VANESSA sat in the corner booth of the Kendalton Inn's tavern; Vanessa picking over a huge plate of loaded nachos courtesy of her junk food addiction. Growing up in a household with three siblings and a single working mom provided her with an appreciation for junk food—especially prepackaged, processed foods—from an early age. There were times still, at the age of twenty-seven, that Vanessa longed for Howard Johnson's frozen macaroni and cheese.

The tavern's rustic interior, impressive cluster of beer taps, and haphazard hangings on the walls gave it the feel of an old Irish pub, the kind one would come upon in small, remote villages with stone streets and green pastures with sheep grazing in them. Situated at the end of Main Street, the inn was a converted farmhouse that had been added onto so many times and in so many different ways one could no longer determine its architectural lineage.

"How are these nachos?" asked Gus, looking over Vanessa's second plate.

She looked at him mid-bite. Her piercing green eyes had specks of gold and rust and brown, like a summer meadow succumbing to autumn, and the tips of her cropped hair seemed to sparkle in the inn's light.

"Dude, don't yuck my yum."

It was after eight o'clock and a large group had just left, leaving Gus and Vanessa as the last patrons of the evening. Sitting alone at the bar was the elderly owner, who had checked them in earlier, Darrell Pierce. Darrell had translucent, weathered skin and rough hands from a life of manual labor. His dyed, shiny black hair was smoothed to one side on a head that looked too large for his frail neck to support, and his lips and eyes were surrounded with thin, graying lines as if he were dying from the inside out. He kept rubbing his silver five-o'clock shadow as he stared silently at the television behind the bar and sipped his top-shelf bourbon. A few feet behind him at one of the tables sat the lone remaining waitress—a large, stocky woman with broad shoulders and narrow hips. She kept busy filling salt and pepper shakers while talking at an episode of *The Bachelor* on the television. Gus tapped a finger against his glass to the song playing in the background while outside the window the blackening sky absorbed the final streaks of bubblegum pink left by the sun.

The television screen changed scenes and a red banner appeared across its bottom with the words *Breaking News*. An imposing woman with light eyes and blond hair pulled back tightly on her head looked down over the tavern in a Big Brother sort of way. Her remarks were laced with tantalizing words like *murder* and *scandal* and *serial killer* before the screen split to make room for a young woman bathed in bright light standing at the end of a driveway. She gestured over her shoulder toward a house Gus recognized as the Nelsons' home. He stood and stepped to the bar.

"Can you turn that up, please?"

The bartender did so and Vanessa joined Gus and the inn owner as the banner along the bottom of the screen changed to read *Murder Linked to Decades-Old Suicide?* Gus listened as the woman spoke of Kendalton townspeople being questioned about Rebecca Munroe's suicide twenty-five years ago and the shot cut away from her to an old photograph of a young girl, like one of those pictures on the sides of milk cartons when Gus was a kid. The screen cut back to the reporter and she eloquently spoke of connected crimes and reaching through time before she wrapped up the story with a summary of today's murder and the broadcast went to a commercial.

They sat back down in their booth, the newscaster's words ringing in Gus's mind. He knew word traveled fast in small towns but had hoped they'd be able to keep a wrap on the suicide girl's connection longer. He leaned back in his bench seat and laid his arm along the top. Vanessa took this as her cue.

"Okay, here's what the NVDRS has on the suicide," she said, holding her phone, referring to the National Violent Death Reporting System maintained by the CDC. "Rebecca Gillian Munroe, DoD August twelfth, nineteen ninety-five, sixteen years old at the time. CoD was blunt-force trauma. Says here she jumped to her death into an old abandoned quarry."

He winced. "Parents still alive?"

"Let's see." Her fingers swiped and tapped at her screen a few times. "Her father, Francis, was a pastor at one of the churches in town; her mother, Genevieve, was a stay-at-home mom…her older brother, Derek, was her only sibling…" Her voice trailed off with each statement as she continued to run her thumb over the screen in search of what Gus was asking for. "Looks like the father died from a heart attack a year or so after Rebecca, in ninety-six. And the mother passed away in two thousand fifteen." She slid her glasses up onto her forehead and squinted at the small screen. "The obit has one of those 'in lieu of flowers' things and asked for donations to be made to the National Alzheimer's Foundation."

"How 'bout the brother?"

"Says here his last known address is Santa Monica, California."

"Okay." Gus looked to his glass. "That's not really much to go on."

"I feel ya but, remember, this was nineteen ninety-five. Pre-internet. And we're talking about a high school girl in a small Podunk town. It's not like our databases are gonna be packed with details. We'll get more from the case file in the morning."

Gus raised an eyebrow. "That's if the chief can find a case file that old." He smirked. "Remember, this was nineteen ninety-five…pre-internet."

Vanessa rolled her eyes and continued. "I had the lab hit the funeral card first. There were no fingerprints on it but the age of the stock looks the right age so the card looks legit."

Gus took a drink of his ice water and, seeing Vanessa's smile, followed her eyes to his hand. She had noticed long ago that when Gus held something it never touched his palm; he only used his fingers, the way he held the neck of his upright bass. He gave her a look, then took an ice cube from his glass and moved it around inside his mouth with his tongue.

"When did Rob say he'd have the autopsy report?"

She was getting something out of her front teeth with her tongue. "He thought tomorrow, late morning. The tox screen will take longer." She used the flattened end of her straw between her teeth, then looked at Gus, who was wiping condensation from the side of his glass with a finger.

"You pushed him on the tox screen, right?" he asked without looking up.

"Nah, I told him to take the week off. He's earned some me-time."

Vanessa noticed she too had begun wiping the condensation on her glass and abruptly stopped. They spent so much time together they adopted each other's mannerisms, and she wasn't sure how she felt about it.

"They never did find Nelson's cell phone today, right?"

"That's right."

"Okay, so we have to assume our suspect has both vics' phones. Anyone think to try and trace 'em?"

Vanessa nodded. "I had the techies try this afternoon but nothing."

The waitress brought over another ice water with a lemon wedge and a Diet Coke and slid them onto the table.

"Room charge?" The stocky woman looked from Gus to Vanessa then back again.

"Yes, please," Gus said with a smile that touched his eyes. He looked to the waitress but only got a blank stare in return. She put the check in the center of the table, then pivoted and went back to the shakers and her show. Gus filled it out, giving her a generous tip courtesy of Uncle Sam, while Vanessa took a large gulp of her Diet Coke. When Gus put the pen down she continued.

"I've also got the team going through both of their social media accounts to see if anyone looks interesting."

He shifted in his seat, left to right, then back again as he rolled things around in his head. He looked to the television where two attractive adults pretended to have a private, tender moment on a date in front of blaring lights and undoubtedly a dozen people behind the camera. He looked back to Vanessa, who was tilting her head to the side and lowering another clump of nachos covered with a multi-colored smear of goodness into her mouth.

"You have someone tracking down this George that the Nelson woman was screwing around with?"

Vanessa chewed then swallowed. "Already got a name: George Palin, triage nurse at Middlesex County Hospital. Married, father of three, real stand-up guy." She poked the screen of her phone and it lit up, showing her it was 8:28. "Good ole George gets off his shift at eleven, and when he does he'll pick up a message that we want to speak with him about his relationship with *Mrs.* Sarah Nelson. And he'll no doubt have seen the news by then."

"Bet he'll sleep good tonight."

They each fell quiet as they let everything they had just gone over marinate in their heads. Gus began to sing the bassline of the song playing softly from the speakers in his head as his mind began to chew through something nagging at him, something slithering just below the surface of his thoughts, something elusive he couldn't quite put his finger on.

Chapter Twelve

BLANK PAGE.

Mel had become very successful in the information technology industry at a relatively young age, and much of this success stemmed from her writing. While conceiving and developing businesses around cutting-edge topics such as the advent and potential of social media, the deep web, the next generation internet, big data, and the cloud, Mel had written feverishly on these topics—and more—throughout industry journals, in briefings for chief executives, and for broader business and industry leadership forums.

But no matter how much writing Mel had done in her life, a blank page was still haunted by anxiety's ghost. And it was with this feeling of apprehension, of loss, that she stared at the blank page that would, at some point, contain the words that, woven together, would become the eulogy for one of her closest friends, Sarah. Nora Ephron's words about death being a sniper echoed in her mind.

Mel would always remember the first words Sarah ever said to her. It was the start of seventh grade and Laur—whom Mel sat next to in science class—had invited a painfully shy Mel into their friend group. Mel helped her teacher pick up after class one morning so was late getting to the cafeteria for lunch. And by the time she got her food the table she usually sat at—the Island of Misfit Toys, as she heard some kids call it—was full. But as she stood there alone and exposed in front of the entire seventh grade wondering what to do, the panic swelling inside her, she saw Laur—just plain Laurie back then—waving an arm to her from the "cool kids" table in the far corner. Fear chased relief as Mel shyly headed that way, eyes drawn to the linoleum floor as she went. She found that if she slouched her shoulders just right, the hand-me-down shirts she got from her older yet smaller cousin Mary wouldn't look so short or tight.

As Mel got to the table she could feel the stares. Laurie excitedly scooted over to make room between her and Sarah while the others silently watched. Mel remembered wishing she had a brown bag lunch like the others when she slid her lunch tray onto the table, quickly scooping up the free lunch voucher sticking out from beneath the milk carton. Laurie had started talking about what they were going to do after school when Sarah leaned close to Mel and whispered in her ear.

"Hey, I think I dropped those jeans off at Goodwill last week. They look good on you."

But, despite the rocky start, as the months passed, Sarah would become the first of them aside from Laur to accept Mel into their group. And, as they entered and made their way through high school, she and Mel grew closer, always laughing at that first salvo and Sarah's attempt to be as callous as Jules.

An ember popped in the kitchen fireplace, jarring Mel from her thoughts. Her eyes fell on the fire with its seductive flames and its reflection on her pumpkin-orange wide pine floors. It was a cold, stormy autumn night outside, but her kitchen smelled of warmth and hot chocolate. She was so glad to be home. Like the others, she too had listened to Jules and made a point to be out and seen by others throughout the day. But when they all left The Blend earlier, Mel raced home and hadn't seen or spoken with anyone else since.

She looked to the can of Hormel corned beef hash on the counter next to the jar of pickles and frying pan but had no interest in eating. She'd felt the same when Laur was taken from her and knew she'd eat eventually; it just wouldn't have any taste. Thinking of Laur, memories pulsed in Mel's mind. How the blood hammered in her ears as she high-stepped into the pond, stumbling on unseen obstacles beneath its black surface. Rolling Laur over in the water and swiping at her face, only to expose a void framed by blood-soaked hair. That image would be forever tattooed onto Mel's memories. A gust of wind rattled a window and Fred dashed away, barking again.

"Jesus, Fred!" she yelled, looking to the ceiling. As if her nerves weren't frayed enough, Fred had been pacing around the house and barking at the wind and his reflection in windows all evening. She leaned her head into the doorway. "C'mon, Fred…c'mon. Off! OFF!"

He finally trotted back with growls and grumbles and stood by her side. She rubbed his fleshy neck and his body, warm and pudgy, leaned into her leg as he rested his chin on her thigh.

"You're a pain in my ass, you know that?" she whispered.

The whistling of the wind through the windows grew louder, then softer, with its gusts. Mel took her hand away, and after a few moments Fred lay down at her feet, leaving a damp patch of drool between the paint stains on her jeans.

She had silenced her phone so tapped its screen, confirming she hadn't missed any texts from the Posse. Her eyes settled on the picture of her and Laur that was her home screen wallpaper. They had taken the selfie together last Christmas in front of the tree at Mr. T's house standing arm in arm, making goofy faces for the camera. They each wore red Santa hats and the ugliest holiday sweaters they could find. The soft glow of the holiday lights gave the photo an older, nostalgic look; the feel of a picture found in a dusty attic box. Looking at it, Mel reeled with emotion.

What happened, Laur?

Mel knew all too well how much anxiety Laur had dealt with over the years about Rebecca Munroe's death. And Mel knew why—Laur had told her everything. So, it was no surprise to Mel just how much that had impacted her best friend's life. What began with drinking in high school rapidly escalated until, before she knew it, Laur had flunked out of college and moved back home after just three semesters. Then came the never-ending rotation of starting new jobs and going back to school at night, never sticking with either. She tried counseling but that didn't work. She began going to church again; that too failed. Laur was rudderless, riddled with inner turmoil, and nothing seemed to provide salvation. But then she met Kevin and they married and things seemed to settle down, even out. A new house, a beautiful baby girl in Lisa, a new norm. Laur was happy for over a decade and a half until she just wasn't and they divorced. And once Mel moved back to Kendalton she realized that Laur's demons were back and as strong as ever.

Mel blinked her thoughts away and turned her attention back to her computer and Sarah's Facebook page. She had been scrolling for pictures and posts for the better part of an hour, her thoughts continually yanked down memory lane. She clicked to one of the other dozen or so windows open on her laptop and a mixture of sadness and guilt gripped her so she immediately clicked back. One of these times Sarah's page would no longer be there. Sure, it might be memorialized or have a legacy contact take over for notices and announcements, but eventually, one day, it would just stop being.

Like Sarah.

And Laur.

Mel selected the window with the half page of thoughts and memories she had managed to scribe about Sarah. She wasn't happy with it yet, but as with all her writing she would know when she had it. The fire hissed and popped and Fred moaned as he rolled onto his side. Something Jimmy, the chief, said to her earlier that day had stuck with her.

I know this is probably being overly cautious, but pay attention to anything strange in the comments on your site.

Mel clicked to another window and her online newspaper, *The Meetinghouse*, filled the screen. The lead story, with the headline *Kendalton Education Foundation Sets Fundraising Record*, wove around a picture of Jules at a podium addressing the audience at the recent annual town meeting. The caption beneath the photo read *Kendalton Ed. Foundation President Jules Russell updates town on fundraising efforts.*

Mel continued to look around the site, from post to post, scanning the threads of comments and discussions beneath each. She had been at it—on and off—for much of the night but had yet to find any odd or strange post or any new users that stood out. But she knew Jimmy's words would not leave her and that she would keep looking, and watching.

She picked up where she left off and clicked on an article she wrote about the town meeting and budget. The most recent three posts were from Frank Brown, the owner of Brown Aroun' Town, the local septic service. She scanned his posts but, predictably, found only complaints about the town budget and "excessive spending" by the police department.

Why is it that every time I pass the general store I see a cruiser parked with its motor running? Isn't that a waste of gas that we're paying for?!

One of the older farmers in town replied to Frank's rant, essentially undressing him for all to see, clarifying that the cruisers in town were kept running for the air conditioning, which was needed to keep the lifesaving medicines in them safe and effective, thank you very much, Frank, you ignorant sloth. Mel's face relaxed slightly—as close as she'd come to an actual smile since Laur was murdered—and she noted how good it felt.

A loud noise came from the farmer's porch and Fred sprang into action, barking his way to the window. She turned to see one of her wicker chairs rocking on its side in front of the glass door beside him. She called to Fred but he wouldn't listen, so eventually she got up and joined him. Squinting into the dark glass she strained to see the backyard but couldn't get past the apparition of herself staring back. She flipped the switch beside the door and the spotlight brightened the entire yard. Trees and bushes swayed in the wind and a large evergreen bush tapped against the blistered, smoky glass door of an old, decrepit shed. Mel saw something on all fours with a ringed tail scurry into the woods.

"It was just Randy," said Mel, referring to the raccoon that frequented her yard and bird feeders. She petted Fred's head but the dog kept grumbling, his eyes locked on the woods.

She switched off the spotlight and, taking Fred by the collar, made her way back to her desk. With a finger tucked in his collar, she lowered his head toward the floor beside her seat.

"Down."

It took a minute but Fred finally settled, and as Mel petted his head the chime on her computer sounded, telling her she had a new post to *The Meetinghouse*. It was a private message with a username she didn't recognize.

Awkward7.

She clicked on it only to find no message but, instead,

attached to it was a JPEG file. Mel opened the attachment and up popped a picture of her, from the back. She was wearing the same outfit she had on right then, sitting at her desk, Fred lying at her feet. It was grainy and slightly out of focus and was shot between the sashes of her old, peeling window that looked out onto the farmer's porch. The hairs on the back of her neck tingled. Then the dominoes fell.

The sound of breaking glass shot from the back of the house.

Fred charged toward the sound, barking and growling, teeth bared.

Mel grabbed her phone and ran.

Chapter Thirteen

GUS SAT ON his bed at the inn and propped the pillows against his back once again. The room they had given him was on the small side, but what it lacked in square footage it made up for in comfort. It's imperfect, antique horsehair plaster walls were painted a calming soft green and held various paintings, each with a small placard identifying the local artist and location of the scene painted. Rockport, Woodstock, Monhegan Island, among others, were listed, each painting more impressive than the last. Long silk curtains with a touch of green matching the walls lined each window from ceiling to floor. And framing the space was an elaborate crown molding around its top. He glanced toward the far corner and the round bow case leaning against it then scowled at the oversized instrument case between that and the armoire.

Over the years, Gus had become a snob when it came to his instruments. Like most jazz bassists he learned on a German bass: sturdy, functional, a workhorse of an instrument through and through. But as with cars, the Germans often sacrificed style for functionality. So as he embarked on a professional career, Gus graduated to a beautiful Italian Giuseppe Marconcini bass built in the early 1800s. And she had immediately become the love of his life. But with experience and age comes wisdom and compromise, and Gus soon realized that in order to juggle life both as an FBI agent and working musician he needed to be able to practice while on cases that took him away from his condo in Charlestown, Massachusetts. Hence, the unsightly foldable upright bass plopped in the corner that he rented for times like this. And to make matters worse, it didn't even have European strings; it had American-made ones, which he believed generally sucked.

One of his playlists played softly in the background from his portable JVC speaker. He craned his head upward and stretched his neck and shoulders. Graphic photographs of each victim were spread out in a semicircle before him like a dealer's deck of cards. There were shots of the bodies taken from every angle and close-ups that separated each victim's wounds into discrete slices. Gus stared at them for long, uninterrupted intervals trying to find that detail, that something different that seemed out of place or just off somehow. The photos of Laurie Turner showed that most of the bones in her face had been broken, some crushed, by blunt-force trauma. Gus read words like *temporal bone*, *supraorbital foramen* and *nasal bone*, *contusion* and *hemorrhage*. But then he went back through the pictures of Sarah Nelson and, unlike the Turner woman, there were no signs of physical trauma other than the cut on her neck and shoulder; just the needle mark at the base of her neck and the weird skin discolorations near it. They would have to wait for the toxicology report to find out what she had been injected with.

Gus closed his eyes tightly and rubbed them with his finger and thumb, trying to scrub away the images. His thoughts drifted to the set list for the upcoming tour and his mind began to sing the bassline for one of the harder songs he'd been rehearsing. Blinking away that and the stress of whether he should do the tour—knowing that would mean walking away from the case—he turned back to his computer. On and off for the past hour he had stalked both Laurie Turner and Sarah Nelson across Facebook, X, and Instagram while he mindlessly pressed and released the tension tool he used to strengthen the fingers on his right hand, his plucking hand.

Having exhausted all of the photos on each woman's pages and feeds, Gus shifted to finding photos they were tagged in by others. He typed *photos of Laurie Turner* into the Facebook search field and before he could blink his screen filled with images. There were only a few pages of pictures and as he scrolled through them he realized he had seen them all before.

He then did the same search for Sarah Nelson, but as he began to scroll through hers he quickly realized there were just as many photos he didn't recognize as those he did. The photos he had seen on her page were filled with her friends, her husband, and daughters, scenes of her exercising and being outdoorsy and active. But the photos she was tagged in by others but that were hidden from her own page showed a very different woman. Gus saw photos of her and a group of others in hospital scrubs making silly faces at the camera in an empty operating room, photos of her and others toasting draft beers to the camera at an all-night diner. He then saw pictures of her saluting the camera holding a red plastic cup, smiling in her short shorts and tight, revealing shirt surrounded by many of those same people. There were other photos of her glassy-eyed, her skin shiny with perspiration, as she danced at crowded nightclubs or at dimly lit bars, her arms around the necks of different men in each. And as Gus finished clicking through these new pictures a saltier image of Sarah Nelson began to form in his mind.

He straightened out his stiff legs, whistling along to a few notes of Duke's "Stomp Look and Listen" piano riffs as he did so. His cell phone buzzed on the bed beside him and, glancing at the caller ID, he tapped its green answer button.

"Hey, what's going on?"

"I knew you'd be up," said Jeff Cattagio. Jeff knew everything there was to know about Gus. He knew Gus preferred wine to beer, red to white, and that Gus spent his nights alone despite frequent offers to the contrary. He knew that Gus had only had one true love in his life but it hadn't lasted; not because they were incompatible or not in love, but because Gus had chosen his music and the transient lifestyle that came with it. And Jeff also knew Gus had become the best agent he had and that he would still be going over his newest case at this late hour.

"Thought I'd check in," continued Jeff. "How'd the day go?"

"Just peachy. Yours?"

"Hit me." Jeff knew Gus's sarcasm well.

Gus told him about the funeral card left on Sarah Nelson's body and what they knew so far about Rebecca Munroe's suicide.

"Never a dull moment. The suicide girl—was she friends with the vics?"

"Don't think so, but not sure. We interviewed several of the other women in that group today and it's obvious they're lying about how well they knew her. We're just not sure why."

Gus clicked on a different box and the Facebook memorial page for Rebecca Munroe filled his screen. The photo on the account was a bit grainy, as if someone had taken a photo of a photo to digitize it. It was of a young girl sitting with her shoulder slightly to the side, her posture impeccably straight. Her hair was flat and tight to her head and curled at its ends, a style from a different era. She wore a light brown sweater that clung to her shoulders and chest and matched the clip in her hair. And the traces of acne along her cheekbones and chin added to the insecurity he saw in her eyes. Gus heard Jeff yawn and could picture him repeatedly running his chubby fingers through his thinning hair, a habit Jeff had when he was stressed.

"Listen, Gus, you were right: this case is only getting more and more complicated. I can get another team up there and pull you two out."

The line fell quiet again for a long beat as Gus thought about it. He thought about the tour he'd committed to and of all the great jazz venues they'd be hitting across the south. His eyes were drawn back to the autopsy photos of Laurie

Turner and the horrific injuries she had sustained. Gus was constantly amazed at the pain and suffering one human was willing to inflict on another. His mother's voice echoed in his mind.

Whatever you do, regardless how big or small, do it right.

"Give me another day or two with it."

"You sure?"

"Ya."

"Okay. Need me to feed Roscoe?" asked Jeff, referring to Gus's large Maine Coon cat.

"Nah, I've got a new pet-sitting service."

"You found *another* one that would do it? I'd have thought you burned through 'em all by now. Or at least that word had gotten out." Jeff chuckled.

"Hey, listen, it's not my fault that the last lady was skittish."

"Dude, Roscoe's dangerous."

"He's protective," said Gus, his own words sounding a little too defensive even to him.

"I've known Roscoe since you got him. There's something off there."

There was a pause, the line filling with a low static. Jeff cleared his throat. "What d'ya make of the different MOs?"

"The Nelson woman today got away, got off lucky. That scalpel cut along her neck and shoulder says our guy had more planned, much more. He just didn't get to it. That's what concerns me the most."

"What, that she got away?"

Gus reflected on it for a moment. "Ya, now he's going to

be angry, hungry." He shook his head slowly. "He's not satisfied, not by a long shot. This won't do it for him, so he'll find another one, and soon. And he'll make sure the next kill is perfect. He'll plan it, he'll rehearse it, he'll make sure he has all the time he needs."

Jeff's breathing filled the line as Gus stared at a photo of Laurie Turner.

"But, I don't think that's what drives him. This case isn't about the MO. How he does it is just a means to an end." He slid the photo aside and pulled one of Sarah Nelson toward him. "It's about the women. These two vics were close friends in a small group of friends, in a *very* small town. What were they like? Were they nice, were they mean? What were their habits? Did they have other friends? Who were their enemies? What secrets did they have?" He looked back and forth between the two photos. "Trust me, when it comes to small towns, there are always secrets."

Jeff began to say something when Gus heard another call beep in. He looked at the caller ID and saw it was a local number.

"Hey, I'm getting another call. Hold on." He clicked over to the other line. "Gus Wheeler."

"Agent Wheeler, it's Chief Lincoln." Jim's voice was loud, hurried. Gus could tell he was in a car. He sat up.

"Hey, Chief, what—"

"We just got a call in to 9-1-1." The line crackled then went flat. Gus thought the call was dropped, but then the crackle was back. "...someone breaking into Melainey Idlewilde's house. The woman who found Laurie Turner?"

Gus's eyes flashed to a glossy autopsy photo of Laurie Turner sitting on top of the case folder. Her disfigured, pulpy face with its lifeless, doll-like eyes stared back.

"I remember..."

"Agent, Mel's still in the house!"

Chapter Fourteen

GUS'S TRUCK FILLED the narrow driveway that sliced through the woods to Melainey Idlewilde's house. He saw the flashing lights from Jim Lincoln's cruiser as it pulled to a stop in front of a stout saltbox-style home. To the right of the house leaned a large barn, its front doors cracked open, and in front of it was a modest yard dotted with clumps of shadows.

Gus pulled to a hard stop in front of the barn and saw Jim spring from his cruiser, then hesitate for Gus and Vanessa to join him. Gus got out and rounded the tall hood, the aggressive treads of his hiking boots biting into the uneven gravel as he went. The familiar, metallic taste from adrenaline saturated his mouth and the cool night air carried the distant sound of a barking dog.

"She has a dog?" asked Vanessa as she stopped short, arm still on her opened door. Unlike Gus, Vanessa didn't grow up in some small country town where dogs chased sticks or geese in the local pond. The dogs she knew growing up in Detroit either chased rats or people, both for food.

"That's right," confirmed Jim.

"Awe-some," she deadpanned.

"Don't worry, he's a lapdog."

"The big kind?" Her eyes were fixed on the house.

Gus stepped between them. "Besides the dog, anyone else live here?"

Jim shook his head. "No, just Mel."

Gus slid his hand inside his worn leather jacket and pulled the 9mm Glock from its holster. The house was largely dark, except for a faint glow he saw through a side window. The front and side porch lights were on but otherwise the yard and immediate surroundings remained black. The microphone clipped to Jim's shoulder crackled.

"Caller notified officers on-site."

"Mel's locked in the pantry," said Jim. "She's on with 9-1-1. She knows we're here."

"Which door's closest to the pantry?" asked Gus, his eyes sweeping the area.

"It's sort of in the center of the house but probably closest to this side door, here, and the back door. You try this one; I'll go around back."

"I'll go with you," said Vanessa. She touched the chief's shoulder, crouching slightly to look into his eyes. "We go side by side, flashlights sweeping as we go. Got it?"

"No one enters the house without a verbal from me," added Gus. Not waiting for a reply, he headed toward the door closest to them. He stepped onto a small set of granite steps, smoothed and rounded from years of wear, and immediately noticed two deadbolt mechanisms on the door, one near the top and the other near the bottom. He tried the doorknob but it was locked.

He leaned to his side, careful to expose just one eye in

the window frame, and shined his light through its glass. Coats lined the wall inside by the door and beyond was a short hallway leading to a shadowy kitchen. His radio came to life.

"Gus," scratched Vanessa's voice, "we've got a broken window beside the back door."

"On my way." Gus heard muffled dog barking somewhere deep inside the house. He jogged around back and as he reached Jim and Vanessa immediately saw the broken glass a few feet from the door. It was the only part of the window that swallowed the beam of his flashlight.

Vanessa used her jacket to turn the doorknob. "It's open."

Gus pushed the door ajar with his forearm and waved his flashlight across an empty room. He noticed that, like the side door, this one too had deadbolts high and low. The dog's barking ramped to a frenzy, pulling him to the interior of the house.

"Ms. Idlewilde!" he yelled again and again but felt the house was swallowing his voice each time.

"Mel! Police!" followed Jim.

Vanessa and Jim flanked Gus, each a step behind, as he led them through a large family room, then a dining room, the barking becoming clearer with each step.

"Ms. Idlewilde, FBI," Gus called again, and this time he got more than a bark in return.

"Here!" He heard knocking on a door coming from the next room. He eased around a long table and through a doorway that brought him into the kitchen, the Glock in his outstretched hand leading the way. To his right was a fireplace, its dying flames now just a flicker in the cozy room. The barking had turned frantic and was now mixed with growls. He heard the click of a lock to his left and turned to see a wide door made of thick, rustic wooden planks. It had large cast-iron hinges and a matching sliding lever that remained unhitched.

"Ms. Idlewilde, are you okay?" asked Gus through the door.

"Yes, I'm fine."

"Okay, stay where you are until we check the rest of the house." Gus looked to Vanessa. "You take the upstairs. Chief, you check the basement. I'll finish this level."

After several minutes the three of them were back at the pantry door, the house having been deemed clear of intruders.

"Ms. Idlewilde, it's safe to come out," said Gus. He holstered his gun and the others did the same. He heard a click, then another, and the door creaked open. The first thing Gus saw was a chubby yellow Labrador retriever scamper into the room, its teeth bared as it stood its ground growling at Gus. Out of the corner of his eye Gus saw Vanessa's hand slide atop her firearm as she shifted backward. The room bristled with energy.

"Fred!" Mel emerged into the dim firelight and grabbed the dog's collar, and Gus was immediately struck by her natural, understated beauty. She had skin the color of honey and soulful eyes cradled by high cheekbones. Her hair was pulled back into a single ponytail that hung lazily between her shoulders and, as she knelt down and hugged Fred, Gus noticed large, delicate dimples blossom on her cheeks. She looked from Jim to Gus for answers.

"Mel, you okay?" blurted Jim a little too loudly from over Gus's shoulder.

Eyes wide, she gave a stiff nod. "Ya. Ya, I'm good." She continued to rub Fred's head. "It's okay, boy. It's okay."

Gus held out his fist and Fred slowly stepped forward. After a few sniffs the dog began to wag its tail, convinced Gus was on the right side of the evening's activities. Vanessa walked around the island, keeping her eye on Fred the entire time.

"Can you tell us what happened?" asked Gus, his hand rubbing Fred's head.

Mel told them about Fred being antsy all night, barking at shadows out windows all around the house, and about the noise and knocked-over chair on the farmer's porch. She spoke of the private message she'd gotten with the grainy picture of her taken through the window and how the window at the back of the house broke right after she got the photo.

"Then what happened?"

"The picture freaked me out, but once the glass broke I knew they were coming in. So, I made a run for the pantry."

He glanced back to the pantry door. "Do all your doors have double deadbolts?"

Her jaw clenched. "Ever since Laur's…" She nodded. "Yes. I had a security firm come in and do an assessment of the house. They took one look at the woods all around me, the seven-hundred-foot driveway, and the remote country road with no streetlights and ordered up the works."

"Shocker," said Vanessa a little too loudly from across the island, and Gus shot her a look.

"So, I ordered an alarm system and had every door fitted with locks and deadbolts, high and low." She glanced to the pantry. "That, we made into a sort of panic room. Its locks are keyed differently from the rest of the house and it has its own phone line in an underground conduit straight into the cellar, not like the regular line from the pole."

"Legit," breathed Vanessa.

"Security cameras?" asked Gus.

"Inside and out." Mel took her laptop from the desk in the corner and, pushing a napkin holder and a few small trinkets aside, set it on the end of the island. "The video feeds into a monitor in the pantry and here," she said, referring to the laptop's screen. "But..."

Mel launched a screen that looked as if it were filming in the middle of a snowstorm. She leaned away from the computer slightly as she used the arrow key to flip to different cameras, showing each screen as fuzzy as the last.

"They were all scrambled," she said at last.

"Jamming device." Gus sighed.

Mel took a deep breath and Gus could see her hand trembling beside the keyboard. He noted the ashen color that had spread across her face and her rapid breathing and recognized the look in her dilated eyes. Fear is a chameleon and grips everyone differently but always looks the same in the eyes. He pulled one of the tall wooden stools from beneath the front of the large island.

"Here, sit for a minute." He helped her onto the stool. Her arm was firm, her hand soft and warm.

Mel sat and slid her arm onto the island and, as she did so, her elbow pushed a single key to the side. Its clinking on the thick soapstone rang loud and she picked it up. Gus noticed her confused look.

"What is it?"

"This wasn't here before." Eyes wide, she looked from it to Gus. "This isn't mine." Her voice rose and she dropped it back onto the counter, then stood and instinctively leaned away from it. Gus and Vanessa stole a glance at each other as he got a paper towel and picked it up. The room vibrated with tension as he studied it more closely.

It was an ordinary-looking, gold-colored key that any hardware store in any town would carry. There were probably a thousand just like it at the nearest Home Depot. He walked over to the side door and opened it. Crisp air rushed into the kitchen and the smell of pine and cow shit filled his senses. He slid the key into the outside lock of the doorknob and it fit perfectly, but didn't turn. Which was exactly what he expected. Because Gus had known immediately what this key was for.

He walked with purpose to the pantry door, slid the key into its lock, and turned it with ease.

Chapter Fifteen

"HOW THE HELL'D he get a key to my pantry?" asked Mel to no one, and everyone, her voice slicing the air with fear. Her words were followed by an intense silence that smothered the room. The blood had drained from her face, leaving it a creamy white, and Gus could see deep lines of stress and anxiety forming throughout her forehead. He thought she must make that expression a lot. Gus eyed her with concern and caught the flickering firelight mirrored in her dusky brown eyes. She wore a ratty sweatshirt with holes and worn spots that was frayed at the bottom and hung just over the waistline of washed-out jeans. She stared at the lone key on the counter and licked her lips but they remained dry.

"Ms. Idlewilde—" began Gus cautiously.

"Please, Mel," she interrupted.

"Mel, I'm afraid whoever did this has more than just the key to the pantry."

Mel's gaze remained on the key, her eyes unblinking.

"The back door," added Vanessa, her voice low, unassuming.

"They also have a key to the house," continued Gus, stealing Mel's attention back. "The window beside the back door was broken too far away from the door for someone to be able to reach the deadbolts inside. If that door was locked, the only way in is with a key."

"It was definitely locked," she said with conviction.

Gus saw panic flash in her eyes and took a step closer. Academy training had dedicated countless seminars and courses to teach its recruits that most people felt safer and were more apt to cooperate in closer proximity to others. But Gus could tell Mel wasn't like most people so remained an arm's length away; inside the same orbit, but not the same atmosphere.

"You're sure."

Mel locked eyes with him. "I'm sure. If you had asked me before Laur—it would've been a different answer. But since then I've kept all the windows and doors locked constantly."

Gus began to work through the possibilities and didn't like where he kept ending up. If their suspect had a key it was not only possible but probable that they had been in the house previously. And with a key how would anyone know? So, when was he here and why? He'd have to know when the dog was and was not home. Which meant he was either watching the house or her, or both. He looked back to Mel and tried to sound much less concerned than he was.

"Have you noticed anything missing or out of place in your home recently?"

Mel's eyes widened with understanding. She looked around her kitchen, as if only now seeing it for the first time. "You think he's been in here before tonight."

"Do you leave your dog here when you go out?"

"Sometimes, but he mostly goes where I go." Her eyes darted around the room.

"Do you leave your keys where someone might have access to them?"

"No. I don't leave them in the car, and they're here with me when I'm home."

"Who knows about the deadbolts or the pantry?" asked Vanessa.

"Ah, I don't know." Mel blinked quickly, thinking out loud. "I mean, my friends, I guess. I haven't blogged about it or anything, but I certainly haven't kept it a secret."

"We'll need the name of the security company you used."

Mel hesitated, then stood and walked past the island to the counter. She pulled a business card from a drawer beside the refrigerator and handed it to Vanessa.

"Can we see the photo you received?" said Gus. Mel took a deep breath and exhaled, trying to regain her composure. She stepped back in front of her computer and, after a few swipes of the touchpad, a grainy, slightly dark photo of her from the back, sitting at her desk, filled the screen. She pointed to the cluttered desk in the corner.

"I was sitting there and, given the angle, the photo was taken from that window back there."

"Can anyone post to the site?"

"Once they register, yes." She pointed to the blog icon on the top banner of the page. "The blog is interactive for that very purpose—so people can discuss things."

"How about this *Awkward7*? Do you recognize who that

is?"

"This is their first message and they haven't posted before, so I don't recognize that name or the email associated with it."

Vanessa stepped around the island to Mel's side. "Can I see something for a minute?"

Mel swiveled her stool to the side to let Vanessa have access to the keyboard. Using her middle finger, Vanessa immediately scrolled over the photo and pressed two fingers down on the Mac's touchpad, launching a box of information.

"What's that?" asked Gus.

"Metadata," said Mel and Vanessa in unison, and Gus saw Vanessa slowly grin.

"Well, it was definitely taken earlier tonight," Vanessa confirmed. "We'll have to verify the coordinates but they likely match this location." She turned to Gus. "We'll get this photo and the user details from the post to the techies, see if they can trace it."

"Is there anyone you can think of who would want to harm you or your friends?" Gus opened his arms wide in the cool kitchen and gestured to the pantry, then the key. "Or do this?"

"No. And, believe me, I've been thinking about nothing else for six months." Tiny tears collected on the rims of her eyes. Embarrassed, she quickly grabbed a napkin from the counter and dabbed at them. "I'm sorry. Laur and her parents were the only family I've really ever had."

"Was there anything odd or out of the ordinary about

the morning you found Laurie?"

"No, it started off like a typical day."

"And you saw no one on your way to her? No one walking or running on the trails? Maybe a strange sound in the woods?"

"No, no one." She wiped her nose. "But it was a really crappy, rainy morning. No one was on those trails. She and I wouldn't have been out there if we hadn't missed the prior few days."

"Your statement said you got a distress text from her. Did she have her cell phone when you got to her?"

Breathing heavier now, Mel thought through her motions as she ran from the trail into the pond, censoring a gruesome Laurie out of the picture. Gus watched the pain burn in her eyes and had the strange urge to comfort her, take her heartache away.

"No, I didn't see it. The stateys asked me the same thing. They never found it?"

Gus shook his head. "What can you tell us about her ex-husband?"

"Kevin? Other than he's an ass, not much. He's remarried and lives in Chicago."

"And Laurie's daughter?"

"Lisa. She lives with him now." Mel paused, as if retracing past decisions. "Mr. T—Laur's father—and I wanted her to stay here but"—she raised an eyebrow—"he is her father. And, in hindsight, it might not be such a bad thing. She and her friends had been in and out of trouble a lot the past few years, so maybe a change of scenery will do her good."

"What kind of trouble?"

"Trouble at school; it started a few years ago, when she and her friends got into high school." Mel paused and tried to catch her breath. "Lis hung around with the others' daughters…Jules's, Lizzy's, Sarah's, and Maria's. They've all been friends since they were babies. Parents began to complain to the principal that they were bullying other girls at school but they always denied it. But then, they got in trouble for smoking pot before school, and they accused another young girl in their class for reporting them to a teacher. This other girl denied it but they didn't believe her. So, they all began texting this young girl nonstop day and night and intimidating her at school. And, as if that weren't bad enough, Maria's daughter, Cheryl, posted some pretty nasty messages about the girl online. Then others piled on and made the girl's life a living hell. The principal stepped in but by then it was too late; she had to shut down all of her social media and change her cell phone number."

"Today's version of stoning in the streets," remarked Vanessa.

"Was Laurie overly involved in this somehow? Maybe made an enemy?"

"No more than the others, no."

"Mel, the others told us of other incidents that had happened in the past few months: vandalism, the strange death of Lizzy's dog. Anything odd or strange like that happen to you?"

"No, nothing I can think of." Her eyes flicked back to the key. "Well, that I'm aware of."

"Did either Laurie or Sarah have any friends you maybe didn't know or any enemies? Or how about hobbies? Did either have any particular interests or activities in town at all?"

"No, they were pretty easy to get along with; everyone liked them. Sarah had other friends through work, but Maria would know more about that than me. And, as for stuff in town, both their girls played sports, so they'd go to games and team activities, typical parent things. Sarah was on the board of the Land Trust and was working with a friend of mine, Annie Elkins. But I've known Annie since we were kids. They'd started to create a GPS app for the trails."

Vanessa leaned forward. "Annie Elkins? We don't have her in your group."

"She's not in our group. Annie's more my friend than the others'. She does a lot in town with the animal shelter and the Land Trust and the 4-H club. And, about a year or so ago, her daughter Billie died of a drug overdose, so Annie's become very active in drug prevention."

"Gus"—Jim leaned in—"that's the young high school girl I mentioned this morning."

"It's become a real passion of hers, for obvious reasons," added Mel. "She started the local chapter of the US Foundation for Drug Prevention. They do awareness seminars at the middle and high schools, things at town meetings, fundraisers like the 5K race this weekend, all sorts of stuff to get the word out."

Vanessa made a note for them to interview Annie Elkins before Gus continued.

"One last thing: How well did you know Rebecca Munroe when you were younger?"

Memories of sitting at a long Formica lunch table in the Kendalton Elementary School cafeteria, its benches attached with round silver tubing, crashed Mel's thoughts. An odd group of kids with her, all misfits in their own way, squeezed together out of necessity and solidarity. Mel squashed between Becca and Stanley Bogle—Booger to his classmates—while they ate their hot lunches with heads lowered and shoulders hunched. The bullying from kids at nearby tables rang loud as they shouted the occasional taunt or shot the random spitball from their straws.

She forced her body to relax. "Maria said you'd probably ask. But, sorry, I didn't really know Becca that well."

"Did she ever hang out with Laurie or Sarah? Or maybe was in the same class or something?"

Mel felt her heartbeat skip and her face begin to flush. She was pissed at herself for reacting this way. She knew they'd ask; she'd rehearsed her reaction. She had thought long and hard whether she should tell them about what happened that night: of Laur's anxieties, of how that one night had ruined Laur, crushed her spirit. But then she remembered what Jules had said at The Blend that afternoon. *We just have to stick together, stick to the story we've told forever.* And she thought maybe Jules was right; maybe they just needed to stick together as they always had. It was always going to be their word against anyone else's. And there was Mr. T to think about too. He had already lost Laur. And, now, Lisa too was gone. Mel was all he had left. Could she risk exposing him to the type of scandal the truth would cause or, worse, her going to jail and, hence, leaving him too? It'd only been hours since Sarah's death. Mel needed time to process it all. She cleared her throat.

"She might've been, I'm not sure."

"What about other activities? Can you think of anything they would've done together?"

She thought for a few moments, her head slowly shaking the entire time as she dismissed things in her mind. "I really can't think of anything or how they'd be connected."

It was late and Gus was exhausted. He thanked Mel, gave her one of his cards and asked her to call if she remembered anything else, then stood from his stool.

"Mel, we understand you moved back to town about five years ago," said Vanessa as she put her notepad away and zipped up her jacket.

"That's right."

"You seem to be the only one of your friends who moved away from Kendalton for any real length of time. Just curious: Why'd you come back after all those years?"

Mel paused at some forgotten memory. "I had been traveling internationally nearly nonstop for as long as I could remember, probably a dozen or so years at least. I was living in Australia at the time and was just burned out and really homesick."

"And what do you do for work now?"

Mel shook her head slowly. "Oh, I moved back to Kendalton to slow down a bit. So, I'm on a few boards and stuff but that's all."

Gus noticed Mel glancing around her kitchen with trepidation, like a widow at the end of a funeral reception dreading the solitude that awaits. His eyes were drawn to the dark windows he could see in nearly every direction and knew he and Mel were thinking the same thing: This place was a security nightmare. And, almost instantly, Mel's face had that washed-out coloring again. Gus put his hand on her shoulder and their eyes met.

"Hey," he said confidently, tenderly. "It's going to be all right. Why don't you get some things and come back to the inn with us?" he suggested, feeling a tinge of excitement at the thought. Visions of the inn's empty parking lot popped in his mind. "I'm sure they have room."

"Might wanna take your own car," mumbled Vanessa.

Gus watched as Mel's eyes softened and her face relaxed ever so slightly.

"No way old man Darrell will let you into the inn with Freddy," scoffed Jim. "Just come stay with us, Mel. Maria and the kids would love to have you and Fred at the house."

Gus noted a change in Mel's demeanor, subtle but there, an idea forming. He removed his hand from her shoulder as hers dropped to Fred, who was standing by her side.

"Thanks, guys, but I think I'm good."

Gus leaned in and their eyes met again. "But, Mel, you have to go somewhere safe, right?"

Mel slid her laptop into a ragged old backpack and zipped it up tight. Then, tossing it over a shoulder, she grabbed her car keys from the desk; Fred's tail wagged at the jingling. She took one last look around her kitchen, biting her lower lip as she did so.

"Don't worry," she said with renewed confidence, "I'm going to the safest place I know."

Chapter Sixteen

GUS'S BODY JOLTED awake to the loud, incessant barking of a dog. His vision was blurry, the early-morning sun sandpaper on his eyes. He closed them tight and shook his head, trying to understand what was happening. Had he dreamed of a dog?

Bark, bark-bark, bark.

Frantically, he fumbled his way up onto an elbow and squinted at the clock. It was 7:30 a.m. It had been nearly 2:00 a.m. before they left Mel's house and gotten back to the inn. Gus could handle a lot of things, but sleep deprivation wasn't one of them. He struggled to get his bearings and looked around the room. His brain wrinkled at something different, something off, but before he could wrestle it down the barking was back.

"What the fuck?" He growled and snapped his head toward the nightstand.

Fucken' V.

He grabbed his phone and through straining eyes read *Private Caller*. Gus swiped its screen.

"Hello." His voice was raspy. He swallowed, then tried to quietly clear his dry throat.

"Gus, it's Rob." The pathologist's voice was clear, crisp.

Gus knew he'd been up for hours. Rob was the type of guy who liked to see the sunrise on his morning run.

"Rob, hey. What's up?" Gus's head dropped back onto his pillow. He pressed the phone to his ear and rubbed his forehead and face with his free hand.

"We just finished the autopsy on Sarah Nelson."

Gus sat up. "Already? What'd you find?"

"Well, a few oddities, for sure. And they raise some interesting questions."

Of course they do. Gus's headache was building. He needed coffee, or sleep. What he didn't need were more questions. "Like what?"

"Well, for starters, the autopsy showed Ms. Nelson to have cerebral edema."

The pathologist's words hammered at his ears. "Brain swelling?" He pinched the bridge of his nose again.

"That's correct, but we typically see that where there's head trauma involved or if there's a tumor or some sort of significant infection, such as sepsis. But there was no evidence of any of these present. We also found her to have cardiac dilation. That's when…"

"The size of the heart cavity becomes enlarged or stretched. Ya, I get it."

"Normally, this would be caused from inflammation of the heart muscle. But there was none here." Rob paused. "Do you know if Ms. Nelson was a heavy drinker?"

Gus's thoughts drifted to the pictures of Sarah Nelson he found last night online, the ones she was tagged in by others: nightclubs, bars, parties with red plastic cups, sloshy smiles.

"She might've been."

"That could explain the cardiac dilation. We also found petechial hemorrhaging across her abdomen and chest."

"Isn't that usually associated with strangulation?"

"That's right. They're the distinctive red and purple dots on the skin caused when the small capillaries just beneath it rupture. But with asphyxiation they're found around the eyes and face, not the abdomen. So, their location here is very puzzling. And, recall, the red and blue coloring around the injection site—the ischemia and cyanosis. During the autopsy we also found necrosis in that area and in a few other regions of the upper torso."

"Rob, it sounds like this is all over the place."

"Yes, I'm afraid it is. But these oddities may work in our favor here to identify the toxin she was injected with. Especially when we consider the symptoms the witness who found the deceased described. The Lincoln woman reported a number of traits that are fairly common: poor coordination, speech difficulties, vomiting, overall weakness. Those on their own aren't really indicative of any specific class of toxin. But she also described two symptoms that aren't very common: drooping eyelids and that she seemed to rail in agony when touched."

"Ya, I remember."

"Drooping eyelids is referred to as ptosis and, if due to natural causes, is most commonly found in newborns from a birth defect or in the elderly when the nerves controlling the muscles and tendons of the eyelids begin to degenerate. But Sarah Nelson was neither. And the sensitivity to touch as described is likely paresthesia; again, another uncommon symptom. Its presentation can range from tingling and slight sensitivity to a deep burning sensation that's often described as if your flesh is on fire."

"So, these should help you identify the toxin more quickly then."

"That's correct. The initial tox screen already ruled out all the usual suspects."

"Okay." Gus's mind was spitting and sputtering to make sense of it all. "What was the ultimate cause of death?"

"Sarah Nelson died of cardiac arrest."

"Heart attack," breathed Gus. His thoughts skipped back to the autopsy report he'd reviewed for the first victim: Laurie Turner.

"Rob, did the ME find any of this with the Turner body? Or a needle mark for that matter?"

"Let's see...I've got it here somewhere..." Gus heard pages turning through the phone, then the *click-clack* of a computer keyboard. "Let's see...findings...severe lacerations, craniocerebral trauma, frontal lobe fracture..." There was a pause and the pathologist's voice was replaced with heavy nasal breathing. "No, there are none of these findings with the Turner woman. And I don't see any mention of a needle mark either."

"Did they do a tox screen?"

"Of course, but it was all negative."

Gus heard a muffled voice through the phone before Rob said, "So, that's where we are. We're compiling a list of specific toxins given the symptoms and findings we've discussed and will test for those next."

"Excellent. So…"

"So, this is where you ask me how quickly we can have the final tox results done," said the pathologist, interrupting Gus. "And when I say: Gus, you know toxicology tests take three or four weeks or more, depending on the toxins tested. Then you say: That's too long. To which I say…"

"Okay, okay, I get it."

"Trust me, Gus." The pathologist's voice became serious. "I get it too. We've got our lab guys focused on this. And, heck, it wasn't hard; they like the challenge of something out of the ordinary, so there's a lot of energy around this one."

"Thanks, brother," said Gus with sincerity.

They ended the call and Gus dropped his phone onto the bed. Boz Scaggs's song "Lido Shuffle" began playing in his head. He had never really listened to Boz Scaggs, but for some unknown reason this particular song would pop into his head on a fairly regular basis. Especially in the middle of the night. Three a.m. bathroom runs to "Lido Shuffle" were a thing. He didn't know when it started, but it'd been his brain's go-to song for as long as he could remember.

He stood from the bed and pulled his boxers out of a wedgy. Two bodies in six months, another woman psychologically terrorized, and a string of other escalating activities before that. All friends, all the same age, all grew up together in town. And a decades-old suicide. What had these women done to attract this level of malice?

He turned to head toward the bathroom and his brain stuttered again, but this time his eyes caught up. Lying on the bureau beside the door was a silver thumb drive. He walked over to it and studied it closer but there wasn't anything else to see. It was silver and it was a thumb drive. That was it; no note, no writing on it, nothing.

But he knew it wasn't his.

He got a pair of latex gloves from his bag and, picking it up, turned it over. Still nothing. He thought back to last night, sitting on his bed, going over the case reports on the Turner and Nelson women. He had the files on the bed with him; the bureau top was empty. Then the call from Jeff and the call from the chief, the scramble out of the room, then the late-night return. He would've heard the door opening this morning; hell, he heard the dog barking. He held the thumb drive up at eye level. This was left for him while he was at Idlewilde's house.

Gus knew the protocol: Send it to the FBI's Cybercrimes group in Boston where they would scan it for viruses and malware and discuss it and work their way through a list of protocols as long as his arm before accessing it. But he didn't have that kind of time, nor the patience.

Gus toyed with the idea of firing this data stick up on his laptop. He blinked away the sleep, enjoying the possibility, running it through his mind again and again like beach-warm sand through his fingers. He sat at the small table, opened his computer, and once it booted up, a few taps of his touchpad disabled the Wi-Fi and Bluetooth settings. His computer was now a rock, a deserted island; barren, fruitless, isolated from the FBI's vast intranet and resources and the internet as a whole. If something fried his computer it would be isolated; risk mitigated. He plugged the flash drive into the USB port and a box popped up suggesting the file it contained be opened with the music player app. He double-clicked it, then tapped the sideways triangle to play the file. The audio was scratchy and muffled and there was a lot of background noise: music, voices, laughter. A party.

"Shut up, Sarah," said a distant, slurring voice just slightly louder than a cacophony of faint noises.

"Brilliant, Jules. Have another one," an irritated voice shot back, sizzling above the ambient noise.

"Sarah, she's right," said another voice. "You're being kinda cranky."

"Oh, shocker. Maria defends Jules."

"C'mon, ladies," said yet another woman, her voice sultry yet weak. Her voice was louder, clearer than the others, as if speaking right over the microphone. "Please, not tonight."

"Be careful, Nelson," warned Jules, her voice deliberate, sharper, as if now closer to the mic. "It'd be a shame if Steve found out about your boy toy Georgie. Or…" The line filled with ambient noise, then Gus heard heavy breathing. "…if your precious girls found out about Mommy's little secret. How d'ya think that'd go over at family dinner?"

There was the slightest of pauses and the recording filled with unidentified muffled sounds, like the static that fills an open walkie-talkie line when no one speaks.

"We each have our secrets, Jules," said Sarah finally, her voice measured, confident. "The difference is: Mine won't land me in jail."

The audio became unrecognizable, as if it was suddenly in the middle of a swirling windstorm. Then the recording abruptly ended.

Chapter Seventeen

GUS HAD WOKEN Vanessa with his call to tell her about the data stick left for him in his room, so they were now parked at the police station, waiting for the chief to arrive so they could get the case file for Rebecca Munroe's suicide. Gus stood beside his truck, leaning on its fender with his phone pressed tightly to his ear. He told Jeff about the break-in to Melainey Idlewilde's house, the photo sent to her by her attacker, the key left on her counter and, finally, the data stick left for him in his room at the inn.

"Dude," drawled Jeff, grating Gus's nerves. Jeff was always trying to sound cool, always trying to speak like the musicians he'd met through Gus. "We'll need forensics, the cybercrimes guys… Behavioral sciences will want to get involved." Gus reluctantly agreed. "This case has popped. So, I guess now's the time: You want out? I can have a new team there by lunch."

Gus glanced through the windshield to Vanessa sitting inside the truck, the determined look on her face as she munched away on her breakfast sandwich while staring down at her lap. He thought of Mel and how scared she'd been last night, and he looked around at all the innocent tourists, smiling and laughing as they strolled by shops and took selfies in front of some of the buildings, going about their normal lives completely unaware of the dangers that lurked so close by. The tour suddenly seemed oddly trivial, selfish even.

"Nah, I've got it. I can find a sub for the tour…there'll be others."

Gus ended his call and climbed back into the truck. Vanessa held his laptop, listening to the audio of Jules and Sarah. He waited for it to stop, then told her they'd be on this case to its end. He looked to The Blend next door and at the steady stream of customers going in and out.

"I wish we had some context for that conversation."

He took the laptop from her, flipped it shut, and, after putting on a fresh glove, pulled the data stick out. "There are a lot of things that Jules Russell could've done that are illegal, some far worse than others."

"True, but I think the implication's clear. Regardless of what secret Jules has, it's no coincidence that we get this recording of Sarah Nelson threatening her about it the day after Sarah turns up dead. And, who knows? Sarah could've been the only one who knew about the secret she refers to. Problem solved."

"I'm not sure the woman we talked to yesterday has what it takes to commit murder."

Vanessa raised a cropped eyebrow. "Depends what the secret is."

He slid his computer into his worn leather saddlebag, then dropped the data stick back into the evidence baggie and, sealing it up tight, also put it in the bag.

"Maybe it was for insurance," tossed out Vanessa. Gus waited for her to continue. "Maybe Jules has something on the person who recorded it, whether it was Sarah or someone else there. And they had or have a secret of Jules's and this now proves it in case they're not around to."

"Well, if Sarah was the one to record it she clearly gave it to someone else who's now sent it to us." Gus peeled off the plastic glove he'd been handling the data stick with and dropped it into the pocket of his door. "But, regardless, why give this to us now? Unless they think Jules is going to give up their secret and they want to beat her to the punch."

"Or they fear that, like Sarah, they won't be around to tell anyone about it themselves."

Vanessa squeezed her shoulders into her neck and turned up the heat. Outside was a crisp September morning and, given the thin metal doors of Gus's truck, inside was the same.

"Let's play it for the chief. Maybe he can help us figure out when or where it was recorded. If we know who else was there we might be able to put some pressure on and get some answers before we speak with Jules again."

Vanessa nodded her agreement, then tore back into her breakfast sandwich with vigor. Gus sipped his coffee and watched as groups of people strolled by on Main Street, their breath pluming in front of them as they talked and laughed while peeking in shop windows as they went. He had opted for a large coffee with two espresso shots from The Blend to help nurse his headache. Vanessa took one look at the espresso machine, the glass cases with signs that read *Savories* and *Sweets* and made Gus bring her to the Dunks at the gas station a few miles away.

Without saying a word, Gus tossed his phone onto Vanessa's lap. She tilted her head toward the roof and guffawed with a mouthful of half-eaten egg sandwich. After a few large chews and an exaggerated swallow she turned to him, her fuzzy, cropped hair flicking straight. She had a playful look on her face, her smiling mouth partially open.

She scooped up his phone and went to work. Gus marveled at the ease with which her fingers flew over its screen as she swiped and poked and tapped at it. And while they both were very comfortable with technology, he couldn't help but think of his hippie parents with their ponytails and nomadic existence as noble warriors in the Peace Corps ("The ToughestJobYou'llEverLove!") and their generation. They barely used email and were proud of it. He wondered where—when—was that moment when they stopped learning new things when it came to technology and of all they were missing because of it.

"Here you go." Having changed his ringtone back to the default setting, she slid it onto his thigh. "Back to boring."

Gus put the phone in his jacket pocket. "Found some interesting things on these women last night." Vanessa dropped the last of her sandwich in the bag, crumpled it into a ball, then tossed it over her shoulder into the back of the truck while eyeing Gus with mock disdain as he continued, "Certainly an eclectic bunch. On the one hand, there's Maria who married her high school sweetheart, commuted to Fitchburg State for an accounting degree, and has never lived away. And on the other, there's Mel who went to Bates, moved to Boston right after then lived abroad in Australia for a decade or so."

"You see the shit show that was Mel's home life though?"

"I saw a reference to DSS, but no details."

"Well, I didn't see any mention or reference to any family anywhere on her social media so I dug deeper," she said. "When she was in high school her mother—who, from what it looks like, was a raging alcoholic, in and out of treatment centers—just up and left."

"How old was she when that happened?"

"About sixteen, eleventh grade. And the DSS connection? They stepped in but before Mel got into the system the Turners—Laurie's parents—petitioned and got legal custody of her. So, Mel went to live with them."

Laur and her parents were the only family I've really ever had.

"The father wasn't in the picture?"

"Nope."

Gus thought of the frightened woman he was with last night and his heart sank at the thought of a sixteen-year-old version of her having to go through that.

"You'd never know speaking with her that she had that background." He thought a moment before moving on. "I did see some of the info you told me about Lizzy: living in Vail, the crunchy alternative lifestyle thing. I saw two arrests for marijuana possession but not much else. Doesn't look like she went to college."

"No, seems she kicked around town for a year or so after

high school before moving out west. One interesting thing I found was a missing person's report filed for her when she was seventeen; she'd been gone for several days without a trace. Apparently, she hitchhiked to a U2 concert in Toledo with some guy the family didn't know." Gus silently shook his head as she continued, "She was only in Vail a few years before moving back home, getting married, and having her first kid, a daughter who's a teenager now. She also has the little guy we saw at the spa."

"Jules, on the other hand," began Gus, "seems to have maximized her collegiate experience: two drunk-and-disorderlies at UMass and a citation for streaking on campus."

"I saw that. All while underachieving for a marketing degree and president of her sorority…a walking stereotype. Did you see the death of the pledge to her sorority?"

Gus turned to her. "No."

"The fall of her junior year a freshman student died of alcohol poisoning while rushing Jules's sorority. Jules was in charge of the recruiting process, and some of the other recruits who rushed said she was guilty of some pretty intense hazing."

"Jesus."

"Apparently, Jules had the group of recruits strip down to their underwear and sit around in a circle in the sorority house's unfinished basement and drink warm, cheap wine until everyone threw up on the girl to their right. The one who held out the longest was immediately accepted into the sorority and got a pass on other rush activities. And this was

December. In Massachusetts."

"What happened to her?"

"Nothing, really. There were some pretty damning statements in the case file from other recruits that paint a terrible picture of Jules specifically. But, in the end, an investigation was done but no charges were filed. She seems to have kept her nose clean senior year, then she moved with Shane when he went to UT in Austin for his doctorate."

"Jesus, nice work, V. All I found online were pretty pictures."

"Fear not, my young Padawan, the Force is strong with this one."

He then told her of the pictures he found of Sarah Nelson on other people's feeds, the ones of her at parties and nightclubs and with red plastic cups. She said she'd dig into those further.

Gus checked the time on his phone and looked toward the police station and its empty parking spots. He told Vanessa about his conversation with the pathologist, Rob Pappas, and about the odd findings and the tox tests being done on Sarah Nelson. He then thought about her murder and how it was so dissimilar to that of Laurie Turner.

"The Turner murder," he said, looking out his side window at a group of women going into The Blend. They were each dressed in loud, colorful leggings, baggy shirts, and bright white sneakers; going to or coming from yoga or Pilates or whatever the current fad was, he guessed. The first woman opened the door, began to enter, then backed out quickly, holding the door open. Jules Russell stepped out of

The Blend and tipped her head in a thank-you to the woman, and Gus watched as each woman down the line made a point to say something to Jules as she passed.

Vanessa used her tongue to get something out from between her two front teeth.

"What about it?"

"Well, you said yourself: The MO was very different than that of the Nelson woman. So, what do they have in common, besides being friends?" Gus didn't wait for a reply. "They were both done by someone who each of them let get up close and personal."

"Someone they knew."

"Right, but what if that's not all? Turner was beaten to death, then dumped in that pond. There's no way she sent Idlewilde that text that morning."

"I feel you on that."

"So, assuming our guy sent that text to Idlewilde, why didn't he just wait for someone to find the body? She was floating in a pond right off one of the trails. It wouldn't have taken long."

Vanessa rolled that over in her mind, then turned toward him. Her eyes too were drawn to the entrance of The Blend. Jules had stopped to help a young woman pushing a baby stroller. She picked up a small stuffed animal from the ground, then knelt down and playfully gave it back to a miniature flailing hand.

"Maybe he didn't want to wait."

"Maybe," Gus said softly into his window. His breath fogged a small circle that swelled then disappeared. "Or maybe he didn't want just anyone to find her; he wanted Idlewilde." He turned to her and saw on her face the faraway look of someone working it out in their mind.

"Think about it: Idlewilde and Turner are best friends, like sisters according to Idlewilde. And she's the one who finds Turner dead. And Maria Lincoln and Sarah Nelson are best friends according to Maria. And she finds Sarah, who then dies in her arms."

"So, he's especially sadistic," she concluded. "It's not like we haven't seen that before."

"But that's not all. With Nelson, Rob said that given her condition she couldn't have made it twenty, thirty feet tops before collapsing."

Vanessa's head slowly tilted up then down. "Which means he was close," she said, taking his lead. "And likely still nearby when Maria Lincoln got to her."

"And if he did send that text to Idlewilde he could've been close by there as well."

This time it was Vanessa who prodded. "Which means."

Gus turned back to the window and watched the truck's heavy exhaust evaporate in the driver's side mirror.

"He likes to watch."

Chapter Eighteen

Mel lay still beneath the covers, the wool blanket tucked tightly beneath her chin as she strayed around sleep. She hadn't slept much at all, tossing and turning while images of ski-masked intruders hiding in the shadows of her house invaded her dreams. She rolled onto her side and, pulling an arm from beneath the covers, began rubbing the side of Fred's head. The dog had been glued to her side since they stepped out of her pantry just hours before and had managed to curl up next to her on the narrow twin bed. Annie's words from the day before had echoed in her mind the entire night.

Are you scared?

Mel texted the Posse about the break-in to her house last night and asked if each of them was okay, and much to her surprise at this early hour, the thread immediately blew up. Mel was not the only one not sleeping these days. Maria texted that Jim was suggesting to the FBI that they provide protection for them. Lizzy asked if they should all go to the FBI before someone else gets hurt or worse. Jules reminded them texts weren't good and that they should all be careful and speak later.

Mel dropped her phone on the bed next to her and

looked past the small pine nightstand to the window. The early-morning sky was stained a brilliant pink as the sun crept toward the horizon. She heard the distant yipping of a coyote or fox somewhere in the distance and felt Fred perk up.

Mr. T had answered her call around 2:00 a.m. on the second ring, and by the time she left her house and drove the ten minutes to his, the lights were on—inside and out—and he had already put fresh sheets on her old bed. She had forgotten how good her bed at the Turners' always felt, its sheets tightly tucked around the sides and bottom and its comforter at just the right height beneath the pillow. Mr. T insisted on making the beds in the house, a skill he learned as a young man while in the air force.

Mel's tired morning eyes were drawn to the other twin bed lying beneath the window, and the laughter of late-night talks with Laur came back to her. She lazily looked around the small room with its sloping walls that followed the roofline. There were two matching dressers on the wall beside the door and two desks placed side by side opposite the beds. On the narrow wall between the window and far corner of the room were six petite handprints, each pressed in a different color paint and signed beneath by the members of the Posse. Lizzy's was the only multi-colored one. It was red with swirls of orange and yellow throughout, and her signature beneath was done in a beautiful calligraphy. They had razzed her for bringing her creative talents even to a handprint.

Mel's eyes settled on a stack of books and notebooks on

top of a moving box between the beds and one in particular caught her eye. She reached over and slid it from beneath the stack. It was a three-subject school notebook with a spiral wire binding, and written across its pale, faded cover in Laur's handwriting was *Microbiotics*. Mel's insides warmed at the memory. Laur would title her notebooks that contained personal or secret information something she thought her mother would find boring and leave alone. But just as quickly as it had appeared, the memory was replaced with anxious thoughts: Laur's and Sarah's deaths, the FBI nosing around about Becca, the break-in to her house, the key left on her counter.

Suddenly Mel was engulfed by fear: fear of the intruder, fear of being the next victim, fear of the FBI learning about Becca's death. And as she lay there alone crying, Mel held the soft, ragged notebook firmly to her chest, wishing with all her being that Laur could be there with her.

Chapter Nineteen

UNABLE TO GET back to sleep, Mel texted Annie to see if she could walk earlier than they had planned. Mel knew Annie to be a borderline insomniac, so it was no surprise when she texted Mel right back that she was already up, dressed, and ready to go.

The Kendalton Land Trust was formed nearly thirty years ago with the donation of land by a group of farmers on the outskirts of town. The official story was one of altruism: A group of concerned citizens were seeing each of the towns surrounding Kendalton sell their souls to businesses and developers alike for the almighty tax dollar, and they wanted Kendalton to remain a rural country town for generations to come. But there was another, juicier story that involved the four most prominent families in town colluding to create the Land Trust to evade the tax man on what would be hundreds, if not thousands, of acres. Regardless of which story was closest to the truth, in the thirty years of its existence the Kendalton Land Trust had amassed close to two thousand acres throughout town, most of it connected by trail.

The morning sky was a silky royal blue with white, cotton-like clouds that seemed to float just above their heads. Mel was still exhausted, physically and emotionally, but she looked forward to her walks with Annie, and she knew how much Annie looked forward to them as well, now that she was alone. They walked side by side while Fred and Annie's foster dog, a snorting and rambunctious French bulldog named Reggie, chased each other on and off the path ahead, their noses glued to the ground, hoovering all the smells the woods had to offer.

Once they had settled into their walk, Mel told her about the picture taken of her from the farmer's porch and sent to her by private message from Awkward7, of the break-in to her house and her using the pantry, of the key left for her on her counter, and of the late-night visit by Jim and the FBI. Annie placed a hand on Mel's shoulder, stopping them on the trail.

"Mel, he has a key to your *house*?" she said in astonishment, her eyes wide with anger. She pointed a finger at Mel's face and leaned in closer. "I told you…I said you should be careful," she scolded like a mother.

Mel watched as the expression on her friend's face morphed from anger to a look she had seen before. Her thoughts skipped to the bright red lights of the ambulance pulsing off of Annie's house, Annie feral with fear and panic as she climbed in its back with the EMT attending to her daughter Billie on the stretcher. Mel leaned her head in close to Annie's and they held each other's eyes, as intimate as lovers.

"Hey, hey. I'm not going anywhere. You hear me?"

Mel could see Annie biting the inside of her lower lip and the embarrassment on her face. Annie took a deep breath and pulled her hand away slowly and, with an arched eyebrow, said, "You better not. Or I will hunt you down, this side or the other."

She turned and walked on, and as Mel fell in beside her again Annie said, "I saw that FBI guy at The Blend this morning."

Mel looked to the ground, knowing full well what Annie was getting at. "Easy on the eyes, huh?" she replied.

They both grinned and Mel realized how good it felt. It was a brisk morning and the fresh air and a new day's sun cleansed her psyche. For the first time in the past twenty-four hours her mind wasn't gnawing its way through tragedy and her chest wasn't warm with anxiety. And she knew that wasn't due to fresh air and sunshine alone. Being with Annie always made Mel feel good. Annie was such a positive person that just being around her seemed to lift Mel's spirits. And with all that she had been through, Mel didn't know how she kept going. Mel had no idea what it was like to have a child, so she certainly didn't know what it was like to lose one. But Mel had seen divorce through Laur's eyes, including the dark times that followed. She knew how tough that could be, but to compound it with the loss of a child—your only child—left Mel in awe as to Annie's inner strength.

Annie cleared her throat. "Well, it's good that the FBI's involved now, right?"

"Ya, it is," said Mel with confidence, hiding her inner anxieties.

"I bet they catch this guy in no time." Annie paused. "I mean, I assume they think Sarah's is connected to Laurie's."

"They do. They're also thinking that Rebecca Munroe's

suicide may be connected somehow too."

"What?! Why?"

"Beats me," she said, and a tiny pinch of guilt squeezed her innards. "The FBI asked me and the others all about Becca."

"Holy crap."

"I know, right? Oh, and they also asked about Sarah's hobbies and activities around town, so I told them about the Land Trust and how you two were creating an app for the trails."

Annie's eyes bulged. "You mean how Sarah was creating it and I was watching in awe."

"You underestimate yourself all the time. No one knows these trails like you."

"Says the woman who gets lost walking in her own backyard." Annie smirked. "It's all relative."

"Ya, ya. But the FBI agents said they wanted to speak with you at some point."

"You know, I was thinking about finishing that app. Sarah was teaching me some of the technical stuff, and I still have some of the online tutorials she gave me." Annie glanced down. "I was thinking it'd be something good for me...give me something to do."

"I think that's a great idea."

"Ya, I think people would really use it, and it'd get me out of the house more, for sure."

Mel put her arm around Annie's tight shoulders. "I think that's a great idea," she repeated more slowly, her voice softer this time, as if the idea had settled in comfortably.

Annie turned to Mel and caught her eye. "Seriously, Mel, you okay? He *came into your house*," she said in awe. "The offer stands to come stay with me. There's safety in numbers."

"Fred and I are staying at Mr. T's until I can get the security firm back out. So I think I'm good, but thanks."

"How are the others handling it? They must be basket cases."

Mel thought for a moment, her mind sifting through what she could say.

"Ya, not great. The FBI clearly thinks we're all targets even though they won't say it out loud. Maria seems the strongest but, then again, she has blind faith in Jimmy so... And Lizzy's scared but probably no more than me. She just wears it on her sleeve like everything else."

"And how's Margaret dealing with things?" asked Annie.

Like most women in town, Annie had encountered the tsunami that was Jules Russell and referred to her as Margaret Hamilton, the actress who played the Wicked Witch of the West in the *Wizard of Oz*.

"Well, she's not in control, so let's just say she's thrashing about as you'd imagine."

"There is a god."

Mel had always known that's how it was with Annie: Good people did good things; bad people did bad. There was no gray in Annie's world, only white hats and black hats.

A light breeze chilled the sweat on the back of Mel's neck, giving her goose bumps. Slices of sun rained down on them through the thick canopy and lit the multi-colored autumn leaves around them as if they were on fire. She looked around and realized Annie had led them down a narrow, partially overgrown trail.

"Where are we now?"

Annie pointed to the woods on her left. "We're over on the Ashby side." The dogs took off chasing another sound in the woods up ahead. "Just wait, the view is amazing."

Mel's tired brain wandered. "I was surprised you were at the fields yesterday. You doing okay?"

Annie rocked her head side to side. "Some days are better than others. Sometimes I just find myself rattling around that big house all by myself, not knowing what to do."

"You? What with the Land Trust and the shelter and the foundation stuff? You're the busiest person I know."

"That's different—that's mostly outside the house."

"I get it. Remember, you're talking to one of the biggest introverts and homebodies around. How about James, though? Does he still come around?" she asked, referring to her daughter Billie's longtime boyfriend at the time of her death.

Annie's mouth scrunched. "Not really, not anymore. And, really, he's just a high school kid, so it could be considered kinda sketch anyway."

They fell quiet, each watching the dogs racing through the woods until Annie spoke again, her voice cracking. "It's just hard sometimes to get it out of my head."

"That's normal. You know that, right?"

"I guess."

Mel turned to her. "You lost your only child and it's only

been about a year. It's gonna take time to get through it."

"No, I know that," whispered Annie, and Mel saw the shine in her friend's eyes begin to flicker out. "It just shouldn't've happened." Her jaw tightened as she looked to the ground. "That's all that keeps swirling in my mind. I think about it all the time. We were working through the depression; we had that under control. But it was the drugs." Annie looked back to Mel and through clenched teeth said, "There's a special corner of hell waiting for the person who gave her the drugs."

Mel wrapped her arms around Annie and they hugged tight, as they had done so many times since Billie's death, and Annie cried into her shoulder. "How could I have not seen it?"

Mel hugged and Annie cried for a long time until, finally, the crying stopped and they continued on in a rugged silence. They came upon a beautiful, remote meadow with views to the mountains in the distance, a scene straight from a postcard.

"Tada," croaked Annie, sweeping her arm in a wide semicircle before the view.

"This is amazing," marveled Mel.

"I love it out here."

They soaked in the sun for a while as the dogs chased each other around the meadow. Then, after Mel was sure Fred was tuckered out, they started back toward their cars.

"We should start a new routine and walk together in the mornings," declared Annie. "It'd be good for both of us. We'd get to hang together, get exercise, be outdoors. They say vitamin D is the key to happiness."

Mel's thoughts crash-landed onto memories of her morning walks with Laur, the two of them joking and laughing as they huffed and puffed along the trails, Mel goofing on Laur for robo-dating after her divorce, Laur telling Mel her vajajay would seal up tight if she didn't get some soon.

Mel's hesitation caused Annie to stammer, "Oh, Mel, I'm so stupid. Of course it's too soon. I didn't mean to suggest I could ever replace Laurie or…"

Mel smiled weakly and swooped her head casually to the side. "Ah, don't worry about. It's not a bad idea. Let's think on it for a bit though, okay?"

"Absolutely. Totally."

Mel made sure to smile and make Annie feel better as they approached the parking lot. She watched Fred, his nose glued to the ground, as he zigged and zagged through the underbrush in search of something that had seized his attention, and her thoughts turned to the day ahead. She knew the FBI wasn't going to stop asking questions about Becca's suicide. They were going to poke and prod at every detail until they turned over the right rock. They too had gotten the scent. And she knew she needed to be ready. She wondered what others who only saw Becca from afar would remember about her.

"Hey, what do you remember about Becca? Anything?" asked Mel as casually as she could.

"Nothing, really. I mean, she lived in the next house over from ours, but our farm was over a hundred acres, so that was easily a mile or so down the road. But I didn't really know her at all." Her eyebrows arched upward. "The downside of being homeschooled: The only kids I really ever met were on the track or cross-country teams. Why?"

"Dunno," Mel said, shrugging it off. "I just haven't thought about her in years," she lied, feeling that pinch inside again. "I guess all the questions about her just dredged things up."

They walked out of the woods and made their way to their cars. Mel put Fred in the Jeep and joined Annie at the rear of her SUV, where she was coaxing Reggie to jump onto the open tailgate.

"So, if you're free tonight, we could grab some dinner somewhere." Annie wiggled her head in mock excitement. "Two wild single women out on the town."

"Sounds awesome, but I'll have to take a rain check. I promised Mr. T I'd make him dinner." Mel did her best impersonation of Annie's wiggle. "It's taco night."

Chapter Twenty

"I UNDERSTAND YOU folks stayed at the inn last night," said the mayor, Beady Babineau. He had accompanied the chief to the station to meet Gus and Vanessa. He rubbed the cold out of his hands, and Gus noticed long, uncut fingernails protruding from his arthritic fingers.

"That's right," said Gus as he looked for a chair to sit in.

"We've had four presidents stay there over the years."

Jim spun one of the desk chairs around and turned on his computer and motioned to Gus and Vanessa to pull chairs over from nearby desks.

"It was very nice," said Gus, distracted. He noticed a younger Jim and Maria Lincoln in a family photo on the corner of his desk. Two girls and a younger boy sat in front of their parents, each with a wide, forced smile on their face. Gus saw an unmistakable resemblance of both parents blended into each of the children but, if pressed, wouldn't be able to pinpoint any one specific feature. The daughters looked close enough in age to be interested in similar things, but far enough apart to not have the same friends. Jim looked exactly the same as he did today, while Maria's pixie haircut and lack of makeup gave her a boyish appearance.

Gus took in the photo, with its quaint, wholesome vibe

and wondered if that could've been him. An image of his former love from college, Rachel, shot to the front of his thoughts. He wondered if maybe somewhere in some alternate universe there was a photo just like this one with him and Rachel and a few adorable kids sitting atop some intimidating FBI desk, or maybe even a desk in some college of music somewhere. Beady's voice snapped him back to the real world.

"The inn's usually booked solid through the fall, with all the leaf peepers and such. You're lucky you got a room." The mayor's eyes dropped to Gus's worn hiking boots with their yellow safety laces and beefy treads. He smiled as he met Gus's eyes. "You hike, agent?"

"Hike?" questioned Vanessa with enthusiasm. "He used to be search and rescue."

Beady's face lit up, but before he could speak Gus said, "I used to *help* search and rescue teams." He smiled at Vanessa, then looked back to the mayor. "I was a hiking guide growing up, so when there was a search and rescue and they needed extra bodies I'd help out."

Beady's smile remained and he gestured out the window. "You'll find some of the best hiking in the country in those mountains. People come from all over to experience 'em."

"Oh, they've been on my list," assured Gus before gesturing to Jim and his computer. "Maybe when we get things sorted out here."

Beady was about to say something else but then appeared to pick up on the body language of the room. He lowered his head, then ran the palm of his hand over his blue-and-white paisley tie, smoothing it top to bottom. He looked back to Gus as he buttoned his suit jacket.

"Well, I'll leave you folks to it." He straightened his posture and nodded gracefully. "But, please, if there's anything I can do, don't hesitate." He raised his chin in Jim's direction. "The chief here knows how to get ahold of me at all hours of the day or night."

And with that Beady strode toward the door and left the station. Gus watched out the window as the old man climbed into an old cream-colored Cadillac Eldorado the size of a warship and marveled at its long, sloping front end and hidden headlights. He immediately recognized the car as the same one his uncle had when he was a child.

"Sorry about that," said Jim. "He's quirky but he means well."

"No worries," dismissed Gus.

"Hey, before I forget." The chief took a thin stack of papers from his desk and handed them to Gus. They had row after row of numbers on each page and were held together with a large silver paperclip. "Laurie Turner's cell phone records from the months leading up to her death."

Gus flipped them for a moment, then handed them to Vanessa.

"Thanks, Chief," she said.

Jim's face relaxed. "Oh, no problem. We already got them so I just thought we'd save you the hassle of dealing with Verizon."

Gus took his laptop from his saddlebag and flipped it open on Jim's desk. He took out the baggie with the data stick and held it up for Jim to see.

"This was left in my room last night while we were at Mel's house."

"What's on it?" asked Jim as Gus went about putting a latex glove on and removing the data stick from the baggie. Once his laptop had booted up he plugged it in and played the audio for Jim. Jim leaned in toward the laptop's speaker while Gus played it a second time.

"Any idea what secret Sarah Nelson's referring to?"

"No, no idea."

"Do you recognize any other voices on it?"

"Sure, Sarah points out Maria at that point defending Jules. And the other voice is Lizzy's; she's asking them all to just stop arguing. And I can tell you this was recorded at Sarah's house. If you listen closely you'll hear the gong of the grandfather clock in her foyer in the background."

"Do you remember their argument or when this might've been recorded?"

"I don't, but the women have a sort of rotation going where one of them is having a get-together for the families most every weekend. So, essentially, every month or month and a half or so we'd be at Sarah's house when it came around to her turn."

Gus's thoughts went back to Jules's checkered past that he and Vanessa discussed earlier.

"Jim, what do you know about Jules's time in college?"

"Not much." He shrugged. "I mean, I've heard bits and pieces over the years about her sorority and the parties and stuff. But she went to UMass and she was always a little wild anyway, so nothing all that surprising. Why?"

"She also ran into some legal troubles there." Gus told Jim of Jules's drunk-and-disorderlies, then of the death of the young woman rushing her sorority.

"The drunk-and-disorderlies? No surprise," said Jim with a touch of sadness. "Having a hand in someone's death? That's a whole new level, even for Jules."

Vanessa arched an eyebrow. "This Jules woman doesn't sound like a very nice person."

Gus leaned over and put his elbows on his knees. He held the chief's eyes. "Jim, things are starting to get…complicated. And we're going to be digging deeper into each of these women, and your wife is among them. So, if you need to recuse yourself…"

"Absolutely not," said Jim in a tight, clipped manner. "Gus, you have my word that everything about this investigation remains between us and stays confidential. I take my responsibilities very seriously. But, equally important, I know my wife. And if this investigation leads to one of these women, I know Maria is in no way a part of that."

Gus heard confidence with a dash of hope in the chief's voice and looked to Vanessa, who only stared back. They both knew they needed the chief to navigate the inevitable obstacles they'd encounter in a small, close-knit town like Kendalton. The chief had been put on notice, and if information began to leak, Gus would know where it was coming from.

"Okay. For starters, we need you to pull together all of the odd events over the past year or so; activities like the ones

Jules told us about—her car being keyed, Lizzy's dog likely being poisoned, and the others—as well as others you now think might be strange or odd. It feels to us like these are escalations of our suspect, so we may want to interview some of those people."

"Sure thing. You'll have it tonight."

"Great. Were you able to find the file on the Rebecca Munroe suicide?"

"Yes." Jim swiveled in his chair to face his keyboard and tapped a few keys. "We had a lot of case files digitized a few years back. And I remembered last night"—he launched a program with his mouse—"the Munroe file was one of 'em." He typed something in the search bar. The screen blinked and Jim nodded.

"There it is. The case file and the autopsy report." He turned the color printer on, and after a few moments it began to slowly inch the first page out. He spun his chair around and gestured to his computer screen. "This really rocked the town. But I can't imagine how it could be connected to Sarah's and Laurie's deaths."

Gus looked to the printer as it shuddered out the first page. It whirred, as if taking a deep breath before tackling another. He looked back to Jim.

"What do you remember?"

"Well, I remember it happened on a Saturday night, so most of us heard about it that Sunday at church." He blinked a few times, reliving the feeling. "The trails to the quarry were taped off so a bunch of us gathered at the front gate. I remember watching the ME's van come down its dirt road, then drive away. We all knew Becca was inside."

"What was she like?"

"She was an average kid, seemed as happy as anyone else. She didn't have a large group of friends but everyone seemed to like her."

"How well'd you know her brother?"

"Derek? I knew him a little. Why?"

"Were the two of them close? Maybe he knows why she did it."

"I think they were as close as any brother and sister. But he was much older than Becca. I think he was either just out of college or finishing up when she did it. But either way he hadn't been around for years. After he moved away to college he just never came back here."

Gus looked to the growing stack of pages on the printer tray and his thoughts went back to the Facebook pages of Laurie Turner and Sarah Nelson he'd scoured last night. And, although most of the photos were of them as adults, they both had posted old photos of themselves as kids on various anniversaries throughout the years. Gus was no expert but, liked or not, Rebecca Munroe was nothing like the two victims.

"But she didn't hang around with the Turner or Nelson women or their friends at all?"

Jim shook his head and scowled. "No. I think they liked Becca and all, but that was probably because she wasn't a threat. She didn't compete with them in any way, boys or otherwise. They pretty much left her alone."

"And she didn't leave a note, right?"

"No."

"Jules said everyone thought she was gay. Do you think she was?" interrupted Vanessa.

"No." The printer pushed out the final page of its job. Its fan hummed low in the background. "But it doesn't matter what I or anyone else thought. Becca wasn't gay," Jim said dismissively. He leaned over and took the case report from the tray of the printer, tapped its edges so they were straight, then handed it to Gus. The pages were tight and warm to the touch.

Gus lifted the first page and began to scan the second. "How can you be so sure?"

Jim leaned forward and rested his elbows on his knees. His head dropped and he looked to the floor, as if trying to reconcile conflicting emotions. When he looked back up Gus saw sorrow in his eyes.

"The former chief, Chief Martin, was a crusty old coot," began Jim slowly. "Police matters were not discussed outside these walls. And he ran this office with an iron fist. You did nothing without his permission."

Gus looked to the report, then back to Jim, confused.

"*Nothing*," Jim emphasized. "Especially question his orders. So, when he had this case file marked confidential and sent to storage, that's where it stayed. For twenty-something years." He took a deep breath. "You see, he and his wife were close friends with the Munroes, Becca's parents." He shook his head and his eyes narrowed.

Gus tilted his head to the side. "Jim, I don't follow."

Jim sat up, his back straight in a perfect posture. "I

couldn't sleep last night after Mel's, so I logged in from home and read through that for the first time." He tipped his head toward the file in Gus's hands. "Becca wasn't gay. And if she was, that was the least of her problems."

Gus began to quickly flip through its pages but Jim beat him to the punch.

"Gus, Becca was pregnant."

Chapter Twenty-One

JIM LINCOLN HAD no idea who the father of Rebecca Munroe's unborn baby could be but reminded Gus and Vanessa of all they'd heard about her: a geeky bookworm with horn-rimmed glasses and braces who was somewhat of a loner. It didn't exactly scream sex symbol or promiscuous lifestyle. The loner part created a challenge in finding someone to speak with whom she may have confided in. Becca's parents had died years ago and her father was her de facto pastor, so that took a confessional off the list. A quick internet search found that their family doctor and the school's guidance counselor at the time, each of whom she could conceivably have spoken with, were also dead. And there were no living relatives from the area that Becca might have confided in. Jim was going to call her brother Derek, but he shook Kendalton off his shoes the day he moved away to college and never looked back. So that left just Becca's childhood friend: Maureen Ferguson.

Miss Ferguson worked at the Ashby Town Library, an old building with a slate roof, built in an era when structures needed to survive generations. It had tall antique-glass windows resting on weathered granite sills and a two-story porch with plump white columns. The steps spanned the entire front and matched the sills of the windows, and the library's oversized entrance was pretentious, yet oddly inviting.

The library was situated on The Green, an area about the size of a baseball infield in the center of Ashby surrounded by an elongated rotary that collected roads from all parts of town. Its grassy center had a small path dotted with cast-iron benches, a copper water fountain weathered to an avocado green, and several statues commemorating various town figures prominent during the Revolutionary War. Over the years The Green had found its way into several movies trying to capture the essence of a classic New England setting.

The library wasn't yet open, but Jim had called ahead so the door was unlocked. Gus followed Vanessa and the chief into a cavernous open space. Beams of sunlight pierced windows lining the top of its vaulted ceiling and brightened the otherwise dark interior. The area before them was filled with row after row of long community tables, and circling above on all sides was a balcony filled with shelves of books rising stories to the ceiling. Dark ladders, their tops connected to round wooden rods by shiny golden wheels, leaned against the shelves awaiting a purpose.

The large, sweeping room reminded Gus of the library at Loyola, and he recalled the long nights he spent there doing the research paper for his philosophy minor his final week. It explored the differences in student-teacher relationships through ideas and thoughts passed on from Socrates who taught Plato who taught Aristotle who then taught Alexander the Great. It was his last assignment senior year and held a special place in his memories, if only for that simple fact.

A tidy square booth, complete with green banker's lamp, acted as the buffer between the books and the front door. Jim tapped the small silver bell on its counter with an open palm before quickly grasping it to stop the ringing. A woman's faint voice rang from somewhere deep within.

"Be there in a jiff."

A heavy-set woman came around one of the bookshelves with a small stack of hardcover books in her arms. Her button-down sweater draped broad shoulders and she had wide, sturdy hips. The muscular legs jutting from her beige skirt were supported by wide feet in black flats. Her eyes rounded as she gave a big smile at the sight of Jim.

"Well, hello, Mr. Policeman," she said in a sassy tone.

Jim smiled and Gus realized it was the first time he had seen the chief look happy.

"Hey, Maury," he said in an aw-shucks cadence. He gestured to Gus and Vanessa. "Maury, these are the FBI agents I told you about on the phone. Agents Wheeler and Lambert."

She plunked the stack of books onto her desk, rubbed her hands free of dust, then shook each of theirs. Maury Ferguson had always been a bookworm and, never marrying, had developed a penchant for town news and gossip as well. And, being the adjunct library for the Ashby-Kendalton regional school district, the Ashby library hosted mostly stay-at-home mothers and their children during the day and in the evenings. So Maury's days were happily filled with books and drama, beginning to end. She tilted her head toward the nearest table.

"Let's sit."

"Thank you again for meeting with us. Jim tells us you and Rebecca were best friends."

Maury Ferguson had kind eyes that seemed to soften at Gus's comment.

"Inseparable. She was—and is still—the kindest person I've ever known."

"We're trying to get some more information about her and, maybe, why she did it. What can you tell us about her health or her state of mind around that time? Did she deal with depression or anxieties or anything that might've driven her to take her own life?"

"Heavens no, Becca didn't deal with anything like that. She was always very happy. Heck, she even got voted most cheerful in our ninth-grade class yearbook." Gus caught a side-eyed glance from Vanessa. "She was always goofing around, always playing practical jokes."

"How was her family life? Was it a close family?"

"They were an extremely close family; she had a great upbringing. That was very important to her mom. So if Becca was struggling with anything like that they would've known."

"Looking back, do you remember her acting differently, maybe preoccupied or distant?"

"No, nothing." Gus noted her voice rising slightly and her cadence had quickened. "She was the same old Becca right up until she died."

Gus paused, questioning Maury's response in his mind.

"What about her interests? Did she have any hobbies?"

"Oh, Becca was very creative. She sang in the choir at the church and she would always do the decorations for the Sunday suppers and other events. But most of all Becca was a prolific writer. You name it, she wrote it: poems, short stories, she even helped her father write some of his sermons. And her journal—she was always writing in her journal. She took it everywhere."

Vanessa leaned in. "Do you know if there was anything in there about why she did it?"

Maury's shoulders twitched upward in an apologetic shrug. "We never found it."

"What do you mean, you never found it?" parroted Vanessa. "Did you look for it?"

"Not specifically, no. But I helped her parents pack up her room after, you know, and we noticed it missing. There was a stack of them in her closet; when she'd fill one up she'd start a new one. She said that's what all great writers did: document life as it happened." Maury's face relaxed at the memory. "But the last journal on the stack had a final entry months before her death. We just assumed she had her current journal with her when she…"

"How about her social life? Was anything troubling her?" probed Gus.

"Social life?" Maury's eyes widened and she waved open hands along herself. "You're looking at Becca's social life."

"What was her relationship with Laurie Turner and Sarah Nelson and their friends?"

Maury looked to Jim and smirked. "She dealt with some bullying from them but that was about it." She shrugged.

"Just the usual high school crap."

"So, they never hung around or did things together."

"No, but not from a lack of trying on Becca's part." Picking up on Gus's quizzical look, she continued, "Agent, those girls were the coolest of cool kids. Everyone wanted to be part of that crowd. It was junior high and high school. Becca was no different."

"Maury, I know this may be difficult, but were you aware Becca was pregnant?"

Maury swallowed and looked to her hands. "Yes," she whispered, her voice raspy.

"Why didn't you tell the police or someone at the time, Maury?" asked Jim.

"I was going to but then I guess I just chickened out. I mean, Becca was gone. And I know her parents were searching for answers, but I thought it'd be worse if I told them. I figured they'd find out from the medical people, so why make it worse by letting them know that I knew also."

"Can you tell us more about that time?" continued Gus. "What her mindset was?"

She rubbed an eye, then cleared her throat. "She was terrified. She didn't know what to do." She took a deep breath and exhaled slowly. "And there's no way her parents would've let her get an abortion. We actually found a place that would do it, but they needed parental consent. She was gonna forge the form, but there was also the cost." Her eyes softened. "She had no money. *We* had no money. So there was just no way."

Maury got quiet, her mind clearly dredging up old

memories. Her face grew remorseful, angry.

"Freakin' Becca." Her voice was pleading. She licked her lips and continued, trying to provide some context for it all. "She had always been committed to waiting until she got married; that's just how she was raised. It was spring of sophomore year, end of May, and the seniors were having all kinds of graduation parties. So, we got brave and went to this one big one at Eddie McKay's house."

Her eyes grew distant. "We were *so* mischievous. She told her parents she was sleeping at my house and I told mine I was sleeping at hers. The place was packed. I mean, people everywhere. When we walked up we saw a guy jump off their porch roof into the pool. It was nuts. And we were so excited to be at a cool kids party. Then we got inside and some guy gave us each a beer from the keg so we sipped them in a corner, wincing the whole time."

She took another long, sobering breath.

"The next thing I know we've had several beers and we're both drunk. Becca was always prettier and more outgoing than me so she was talking to people, joking, laughing, having a blast. I just stood quietly by her side and took it all in. But then after a while I began to feel sick so I went outside. I don't remember much after that. The next thing I know, I wake up on one of the poolside lounge chairs with Becca shaking my shoulder. It's early in the morning—just after sunrise I think. There are people sleeping on the other chairs and on the grass beside the hot tub. I feel like death warmed over, but when I look at Becca it's obvious she's been crying."

"Did she tell you why?"

"No, she just wanted to leave, so we did. It took her a week to finally tell me."

"Had she been forced?" guessed Vanessa.

Maury shook her head. "No. Taken advantage of? That's a different question. But raped? No. She said it was late and they started kissing in a dark corner behind the house, then went into the basement. She then remembered helping him take his pants off, then kissing his stomach."

Maury blushed at what she thought of next but didn't say a word. She looked down at her hands again and Gus waited for her to continue.

"Anyway, she did remember having sex with him and wanting to, not being forced to. And that's it. The next thing she remembered was waking up alone on the couch in their basement with just a T-shirt on. Her pants and underwear and bra were on the floor beside her, next to an empty tequila bottle. She said she started crying uncontrollably at what she'd done. That's when she got dressed and came to find me."

"And this was May you said?" asked Vanessa, her pen rotating through her fingers.

"Yes, late May. I remember because graduation was that following week."

Gus bent his head slightly to make eye contact. "Did she ever tell you who the boy was?"

Maury hesitated and the kindness in her eyes had been replaced with the sneer of doubt, suspicion. Gus knew the woman across the table from him had held a secret so long it had become stitched to her DNA. He leaned onto his forearms.

"Maury, we have reason to believe her suicide may be connected to the recent crimes in Kendalton. So, please, if you know who the father was, we have to speak with him, if nothing else than to rule him out of the current investigation."

Maury's chin trembled as she looked to the table and nodded ever so slightly.

"I knew immediately who it was," she said in a whisper. Her voice had a sheepish, guilty tone to it, as if she were still betraying Becca after all these years. She looked straight at the chief. "It was Troy Robinson," she said at last. "They had been seeing each other secretly for months at that point. She was crazy about him and he, her."

"Why secretly?" asked Vanessa. "Because of her parents?"

"Troy?" interrupted Jim in disbelief. "And Becca?"

Maury nodded to Jim before turning back to Vanessa. "Partly because of how strict her parents were. But mostly because Troy had been seeing Jules, and Becca didn't want to get on her bad side."

Gus looked to Jim. "Who's Troy Robinson?"

"Ahhh," mumbled Jim hesitantly as he struggled for something more specific to say. "We hung around in high school. He was sort of the star athlete around here—all-state in everything it seemed. Really popular. He went into the army for a long time; got out a couple of years ago and moved back. He took over his family's hardware store on Main Street. You may have seen it when you drove through the center: Robinson's Hardware and Security."

Chapter Twenty-Two

MEL SAT ACROSS from Mr. T at the small square kitchen table, one leg pulled beneath her. Her sneakers—muddy from her walk earlier with Annie—sat in a heap beside the door. The simple wooden chair with its frayed rush seat felt familiar, felt good. Because it was her chair. It had been her chair for as long as she could remember, and she had some of her best memories in this chair, in this house. The Turners had made their home Mel's home all those years ago, and she always felt a special inner peace being there, being home. And after the events at her house last night, that feeling of home was precisely what she needed.

The wall behind Mr. T was lined with pine cabinets stained a honey brown, and Mel's eyes were drawn to the cupboard nearest the refrigerator. She and Laur always thought the swirls of woodgrain and knots just above the handle looked like an old lady picking her nose with a long, bony finger. On the counter below the cabinets sat a white butter dish with denim-blue designs, its handle partially broken. Mrs. T had loved that it matched the blue-and-white ceramic backsplash beneath the cabinets. Mel thought it odd that in the decades since Mrs. T's death, Mel's memories had come to serve up images of her as being lit from behind like some sort of angelic vision.

Mr. T took a sip of his lukewarm tea, and Mel once again wondered if he had gotten the age spots on his hand looked at. Mel had always been protective of him, but now with Laur gone that feeling was on hyperdrive. She was painfully aware of the empty chair to her left, and to her right. He was all she had and she wasn't going to muck it up. She looked back to him, with his papery skin and silver hair. He was only in his mid-seventies—by no means old by today's standards—but he had aged significantly in Mel's eyes since Laur's death. But, then again, she had glanced in a mirror or two these past few months and the gaunt, pale face looking back had seen better days as well.

Mel watched him nonchalantly slip Fred a piece of egg beneath the corner of the table. She used her fork to push the eggs and grilled toast around her plate. She hadn't been eating much lately but was still surprised to find she had no desire for even a few bites of Mr. T's famous popeyes. Many a weekend morning when she was young was spent eating this same breakfast with the Turners. Mr. T would cut a loaf of crusty Italian bread into thick slices, carve out the centers and cook eggs inside them, all soaked in lots of butter. Laur always had him poke a knife through the egg whites as they sizzled on the grill so that there were no "runnies." And Mel would steal Mr. and Mrs. T's buttery, toasted centers when they pretended they weren't looking. Mr. T rubbed his bloodshot eyes and guilt gripped her.

"Tired?" she asked.

"No more than usual." He ran his hand over his forehead and face. "Tough to get old." They both smiled slightly. He had been saying that since Mel first met him as a middle-schooler.

"You wanna lie down for a bit? Fred and I'll be outta your hair in a little while. We've got to meet the security people at my house in about an hour."

"Maybe later," he answered. He pulled his hand from Fred's head and was about to stand when Mel caught his eye.

"Thanks again for last night. I know it was late."

Without hesitating he reached across the table and gently placed his large hand on hers. His fingers were thin, his palm rough to the touch. He gave her his caring yet serious look—the "Dad look" as Laur used to call it.

"You know it's never a bother, and last night doesn't have to be it. You and Fred are always welcome to stay here as long as you like. Even just until things…" He paused, searching for the right words. "Sort themselves out."

Mel put her hand on his and it warmed her palm. "I know. And thank you." She felt that stinging in her eyes again. His face softened in return, and Mel knew what he was thinking because she was thinking it too. In all the years they had known each other, not once did either one of them say *I love you* to the other. And they weren't about to start now.

Mr. T squeezed her hand lightly and his expression turned serious. "Mel, I worry about you being alone, spending all your time with an old man like me. You deserve to be happy, to have a life of your own, to have someone you can build that life with, feel safe with." Mel squeezed his hand and, as she did so, became unnerved when Gus popped in her mind and by how with just a few words that's precisely how he made her feel last night: safe. She chased the thought away, forcing her attention back to Mr. T.

"I won't be here forever," he finished.

He stood and slid the chair neatly back into place before going to the counter to rinse his dishes in the sink. Mel noticed the old, worn leather wallet she and Laur had gotten him for Father's Day years ago protruding from the back pocket of his neatly pressed khakis. He opened the cabinet beside the refrigerator and Fred scurried from beneath the table to the old man's side. He pulled out a tennis ball and a curved plastic rod used to toss it long distances. Fred's tail and rear end began to feverishly wag and the two of them made their way to the back door.

"I think I'll toss the ball to Fred for a bit. I've got him bringing it back each time now." Mel's face cracked into a tiny smile. Only he could train an otherwise untrainable dog like Fred. Mr. T nodded toward Mel's computer on the table beside her. "Now, you go on. You've been polite long enough, humoring an old man. I know you want to get on that thing."

Mel watched out the window as the only dad she had ever known tossed a bright green tennis ball around with Fred in the backyard, and a swell of memories and emotions washed over her. She tapped the corners of her glassy eyes with her fingertips as she was, once again, smacked with the realization of just how massive the void was in their lives with Laur gone. How was Lis supposed to have a normal adolescence without her mom? How was Mr. T able to get through each day with constant reminders of how his daughter was taken from him? And as Mel's tired brain churned through these and other quandaries, it occurred to her that in addition to assuming Laur's role—as best as she could—in Mr. T's and Lis's lives, she had also assumed her anxieties. And that's when she realized that at her core she was simply lost, floating in an abyss she feared she might not escape.

Pushing those thoughts aside, she picked up her phone and saw she had a new text message in the Posse's group thread so tapped on it. Jules had removed Sarah and Laur from the thread and sent around a short note that simply said *"Rest in peace our loved ones. You will always be in our hearts"*. And it was followed by a broken-heart emoji.

Mel had cried enough these past few months for a lifetime and simply had no more to give. She glanced past the top of her screen to the cozy living room where they would play cards and board games growing up. She thought about what Mr. T had said. Maybe it did make some sense for her and Fred to stay here a while, at least until things got back to normal. She could easily have an alarm system put in, and she hadn't felt as safe as she did right then for a long, long time, despite all the measures she had taken at her house. It was a good idea and she'd think about it.

She opened her browser and her site, *The Meetinghouse,* blossomed before her and immediately the chimes of new posts began to ring. She looked at the aerial photo of the town center she used for her site's backdrop as the number of posts continued to tally. The stout town hall stood firmly on The Commons in the morning sun with the white church next to it, its steeple yearning skyward. The lines of shops strung along Main Street, its sidewalks dotted with locals and tourists alike. She gazed beyond downtown to the Johnsons' farm and could almost smell the fertilizer and churning of soil that filled the springtime air.

Mel turned her attention back to the counter as the number of unread posts settled at ninety-four. Someone had started a new discussion with the subject *No One is Safe*. She clicked on the link and immediately recognized the username from the night before: Awkward7. Her heart sank. They had posted a new comment to *The Meetinghouse*, but unlike the private message to Mel the night before, this one was posted for everyone to see. Mel's heart raced as she read its one sentence.

C'mon, people, wake up. It's time we stopped trying to hide our crazy.

She then clicked play on the video attached to it. She watched in horror as the greenish night vision brought her through the kitchen and up the old staircase to the bedroom door she knew all too well. The door was ajar and Mel recoiled slightly as a gloved hand came into view and slowly pushed it open wider, careful to not make it squeak as it was apt to do. She heard faint breathing getting louder as the video slowly made its way bedside. It then lowered straight over the pillow and the gloved hand reappeared to carefully inch back the thick covers.

Mel's breathing became labored as she watched the gloved hand gracefully flow left to right, waving a large, jagged hunting knife over the sleeping face of Mr. T.

Chapter Twenty-Three

THE FBI'S CYBERCRIMES group had been monitoring *The Meetinghouse* since Mel received the picture of herself last night, so as soon as the post from Awkward7 hit, both Gus's and Vanessa's phones blew up with alerts. Vanessa immediately pulled the site up on her phone, and after watching the video to its end, Jim recognized Mr. T in the final frames. He made a quick call to Mel's cell and confirmed she was there with Mr. T and that they were both safe. He had them stay inside and lock the doors, then they raced to the house and now stood in its small kitchen.

Mel stood beside Gus at the kitchen table, her heart still racing, her mind spinning. This video brought the threat right to Mr. T's doorstep so her protection instinct for him was on hyperdrive. She looked around the cozy kitchen, then into the sitting area and her heart sank. This monster had stripped her of all the happy memories this house held, of the only real home she had ever known. But, worst of all, he'd stripped her of the one place she'd ever truly felt safe.

Vanessa was sitting at the table in front of Mel's computer. *The Meetinghouse* was open and the video filled its screen. The late morning sun cut across the speckled Corian countertops and the house smelled faintly of bacon and grease.

Vanessa pressed play again and leaned closer to the screen.

"All you can really see is the hand and part of the shirt sleeve."

Gus remained quiet, lost in his own thoughts. He watched the video play all the way through again, hoping to see anything that might give them a clue to work with. But there was nothing, just a gloved hand and a dark, long-sleeve shirt in the midst of a grainy greenish video of Mr. T's kitchen, stairway, and bedroom.

"And this night-vision thing makes it tough to see any details," continued Vanessa. The video finished and she leaned back in her seat, absentmindedly twirling her pen back across her hand to rest between her thumb and index finger. "We'll get the techies to go through it frame by frame."

"This couldn't have been filmed last night," said Mel wearily. "Fred would've gone nuts."

Vanessa's chair creaked as she leaned toward the computer and hunched back over the keyboard. "There's no simple way to get a date stamp on videos like there is with photos but let's see…" Her fingers flew over the keys and then, after a few moments, she pulled back. "Nah, nothing. But maybe the tech guys can figure it out."

"Well, I can tell you it wasn't filmed any time recently," said Mr. T.

Gus looked up at the old man who was standing by the window just inside the living room. Fred sat obediently by his side as he slowly pet the dog's head.

"Why do you say that?"

Mr. T joined them in the kitchen and stood just behind Vanessa's chair. Keeping his back straight, he bent at the knees so that he was beside her, then gestured to the computer.

"Can you play it again? And pause it when I say, please." His voice was calm and even and had the patient cadence of a teacher.

Mel leaned in to get a better look at the video, and Gus's senses filled with a fruity, floral musky scent. Their shoulders touched gently, but neither moved as Vanessa played the video again.

After a few moments Mr. T pointed at the screen. "There," he said.

Vanessa clicked pause and they all stared at the frozen green screen.

Seeing nothing different from the last ten times, Mel asked, "What, Mr. T?"

He pointed at a spot on the screen. "It's right there, Mel. Hard to notice, but it's there."

"The wall?" asked Gus.

Mr. T straightened and Gus heard the faint cracking of joints as he did so. The old man pointed toward the half wall separating the kitchen and living rooms.

"That's correct. The half wall," he said patiently.

Gus followed his outstretched arm and looked over the screen of the laptop to the waist-high wall beside the boxy white Kenmore refrigerator. Its top was a small shelf stained a light brown to match the kitchen cabinets, and it had several intricate layers of crown molding framing it. He looked back to the video and saw what Mr. T was getting at. That same wall in the video was a simple, plastered wall with just the shelf on it, no molding.

"The shelf," said Gus.

Mr. T nodded, just once. "The shelf," he echoed. "I trimmed out the living room, including that half wall, last Memorial Day weekend. It's only halfway done in this video."

"That was four months ago," said Gus, disappointment in his voice.

He and Vanessa stole a look at each other, and Gus saw her face blanch and her thin, copper-red eyebrow bent upward. Gus's eyes went back to the half wall with its pristine shelf that demarked the two rooms, and his mind began to spin with information and thoughts: pools contaminated, cars keyed, dogs poisoned, night-vision videos. What next? He knew they needed to get more information on these events but he was beginning to understand what they would find: a very tight, orderly timeframe. Because it was all tied together: countless hours of planning, numerous events and activities, all building up to the main event.

Mel touched Gus's shoulder and he turned to her. Her dark eyes were clear and bright, but the stress lines were back along her forehead.

"He was in here five months ago?" Her eyes pleaded for a different answer.

"It appears so, yes." His voice was steady, confident.

"Well, there's more then," Mel continued, her jaw clenching. "Gus, you asked me last night if I'd noticed anything missing from my home."

"That's right." Mel had his full attention.

"Well, not in my home, but in Laur's. I hadn't thought about it in months. She had this toy from her childhood, one of those pull-string toys where you turn the arrow to point at a farm animal and pull the string to hear what the animal says?"

"The Fisher-Price See 'n Say," blurted Gus. His eyes lit up. "We had one of those growing up too." Visions of his brother Jake holding it up high and away from him while he futilely jumped to get it ricocheted around inside his head.

"Well, Laur's was especially special to her." She flashed Mr. T a knowing look. "She and her mother would play it every day when she was younger and she had great memories of that. I'm sure you're aware of it by now, but not only was Laur an only child, Mrs. T was also a stay-at-home mom. So the two of them were extremely close. When Mrs. T passed about ten years ago Laur kept that toy as a sort of keepsake."

"Okay," said Gus, his voice hesitant.

"Well, I know Laur still had it before she died. We pulled it out of the attic one night at her house after dinner when she was feeling nostalgic. But then when we sold her house we were packing up her things and couldn't find it anywhere. I wanted to keep it to remember her by, sort of a keepsake of a keepsake. But it was gone."

"When was that?"

Mel had wrestled with this same question earlier that morning so didn't miss a beat.

"About four months ago now."

Chapter Twenty-Four

Gus and Vanessa stood in silence in Mr. T's driveway, each lost in their own thoughts as they digested what they had learned during the past few hours. Vanessa was leaning back against the truck's door, Gus beside her, his outstretched hand on its roof. She rolled her head along its window and stared at the large, beefy tire secured to the hood. Invariably, Gus's truck had her thinking of *Out of Africa* and Meryl Streep and lions.

I had a farm in Africa…

Gus could see the top of one of her tattoos just beneath her collar. He had asked her about her tattoos once, years ago, when they first began working together, but she had skillfully avoided the question. He knew of her childhood—growing up in the gang-infested inner Detroit projects—and of her early career years as part of the vice squad at the Detroit Police Department, but her tattoos looked neither gang nor drug-related. They looked artistic, creative even. He followed her gaze to Mr. T's house.

"Penny?" he asked, their verbal shorthand for "penny for your thoughts."

"I'm thinking we've got a guy who's prepped for game day," she said, and Gus was thinking the same thing. He lowered his head and ran his forehead along his shirt sleeve and, as he did so, caught his reflection in the split window. His olive-toned skin spoke to the slice of Native American heritage from his mother's side of the gene pool but the ice-blue eyes cradled in laughter lines looking back were undeniably his dad's. He stood there for a beat and realized that as he got older he took on more and more of his mother's looks.

Vanessa rolled her head toward him. "Did you notice how carefully that video was shot? The camera angles?" She looked up to the sky. "That was fire."

Gus found himself in a constant wobble when it came to deciphering Vanessa's slang in his head. Her formative years in Detroit had imprinted in her the ability to always know the latest slang. But she'd used that phrase before and he thought he knew what it meant.

"Ya…fire."

"Please don't," she said flatly, her eyes fixed on the sky's blue canopy polka-dotted with clouds. "Our guy's definitely got game. Any ex-military guys that know these women come to mind?"

Gus nodded. "That's where I'm at. We start with Troy Robinson."

Vanessa closed her eyes, her face tilted toward the sky to absorb any semblance of sunlight available. Vanessa was not a health nut but she did subscribe to the notion that sunlight and, specifically, vitamin D were critically important to one's health and psyche. She would joke it was the single most important takeaway she'd gotten with her behavioral psychology degree.

"He is connected to the Munroe girl so the funeral card would make sense," she added.

Gus was about to reply when the screen door to the house creaked open and Jim stepped out onto the front porch followed by Mel and Mr. T. Fred squirmed through their legs and scampered straight to Mel's Jeep. He jumped up and put his front paws on the passenger door and looked back to her and Mr. T, tail wagging. Jim led the way down the steps and, rubbing Fred's head as he passed, joined Gus and Vanessa.

"They're heading over to Mel's to meet the security people."

Gus pushed away from the truck. The rumble of thunder off in the distance drew his attention and his eyes settled on the woods beyond the house. There was something nagging at him but he couldn't grab hold of it. His gaze drifted to the modest cape-style home with its white clapboards, black shutters, and thick center chimney, its top stained black from years of smoke. He noticed a lone granite piece laid in amongst the faded bricks. It had the year 1952 chiseled into it.

"What is it?" asked Jim.

Gus's lips were pressed tightly together and his head shook slowly side to side. "How far have you gotten on pulling together those prior escalation incidents we talked about earlier?"

"It's going a little slower than I anticipated. It's amazing how many other trivial incidents we've had in town over the past year or so that I have to sift through."

"Like what?"

"You name it. Bonfires, drinking in the fields or woods at night. People have had their mailboxes smashed with baseball bats, their gas tanks siphoned. I mean, heck, farmers are constantly chasing kids out of their fields at night to keep 'em from going cow-tipping."

"Cow-tipping?" spat Vanessa. She looked to Gus, excitement in her eyes. "That's gold."

Jim smiled at her reaction. "I'm going to head back to the station now to get it done."

Gus glanced from Jim to Mel pushing Fred's wagging rear end into her Jeep. Mr. T was standing beside her holding the door open wide as the dog's back legs scratched at its side for purchase. He slapped the thin metal roof of the truck causing Vanessa to startle and push away from its door.

"All right, we'll follow you there?"

But before they moved, a sleek black Range Rover with smoked windows and large, glossy black wheels turned into Mr. T's driveway and came to an abrupt stop behind Mel's Jeep. Jules Russell hopped out and in one fluid motion swiftly rounded the driver's door and headed straight for Mel.

"Oh shit," said Jim, and he immediately stepped between Gus and Vanessa and headed straight toward the back of Mel's Jeep, the precise geometrical intersection point between Mel and Jules's forward progress. Gus fell in stride beside him.

"What's wrong?"

Without taking his eyes off Jules, Jim said, "I've seen that look before and, trust me, it never ends well when she has it."

Jules quickened her pace and Gus saw the look of confusion on Mel's face as Jim took off in a full sprint and intercepted Jules just a few feet before reaching her.

"You fucken' bitch, Idlewilde!" screeched Jules.

Jim had his arms wrapped around her thin waist and was slowly pulling her away from Mel. Gus instinctively stepped in front of Mel and put his arms straight out behind him until he felt the curve of her hips against his forearms. He felt the warmth of her hands resting on the back of his shoulders and he sensed her leaning around him, watching Jules. Jules clawed and pounded at Jim, trying to break free.

"Jules, what's wrong?" asked Mel, her voice rising with uncertainty.

"Let go of me!" she screamed into the side of Jim's face. She then threw her cell phone at Mel but it hit the back of the Jeep, narrowly missing her. Jules looked over Jim's shoulder at Mel.

"What the fuck were you thinking?" she yelled.

Mel remained behind Gus. "Jules, what are you talking about?"

Gus looked over his shoulder and met Mel's eyes and with the slightest nod told her she was safe. After a few moments Jules calmed down enough for Jim to lessen his hold on her. She carefully gained her footing while Jim stood in front of her as a precaution. She wiped strings of saliva from the corners of her mouth and licked her full, red lips.

"Why, Mel? Why would you *ever* do something like that?" she pleaded.

Mel stepped beside Gus, her hand remaining on his arm. "Jules, do what? I have no idea what you're talking about."

Jules gestured to her phone in the dirt beside Mel's Jeep. "The post you put up on your site," she said hoarsely as she absentmindedly scratched at her forearm.

Mel looked to the phone. "What post? I haven't posted anything."

Mel pulled her own phone from her back pocket, spun it around in her hand and noticed two missed calls from Jules. She had silenced her phone when the FBI arrived to look at the video of Mr. T and hadn't looked at it since. She swiped its screen and Gus leaned over and watched as she tapped her way to *The Meetinghouse* site. She selected the blog from the menu and a stream of posts lined the screen. Gus watched as she tilted her head in confusion at a post entered a little over an hour ago from the user *Idlewilde* that had the title "Whose Child Has She Not Given Alcohol To?" There was a video file attached. She looked up at Jules.

"Jules, I didn't post this. I swear."

"Don't," spat Jules. "You're the only one not in the video but I can hear you talk. Don't try and tell me you didn't record that."

Mel hit the play button. A group of women milling about in a large, dimly lit kitchen filled the screen and Gus immediately recognized Jules leaning against the counter beside the sink. She wore a tight-fitting blouse unbuttoned low on her chest. Her hair was a little tousled and draped over both shoulders. To her right stood a smiling and radiant—and alive—Sarah Nelson. Another woman was leaning opposite them against the island with her back to the camera, but from her short hair and height Gus guessed it was Maria Lincoln. And next to Maria stood Lizzy Porter. Other people walked partially in and out of the frame, some adults, some teenagers. The music and ambient noise of a party filled the background and the window over the sink was black with night. A young girl with long, curly hair rinsed a glass in the sink, smiling to Sarah Nelson next to her, then exited the frame.

"That was Lizzy's daughter, Terry," said Mel quietly for Gus's benefit.

Gus watched as Jules picked up a large liquor bottle from the counter and filled her red plastic cup. A teenaged boy entered the frame and proceeded to walk past and Jules immediately put her arm around his shoulder, stopping him next to her. And as Jules leaned in against him, Gus heard Mel's voice as clear as day on the recording.

"No, no, no Jules no…"

Jules then poured a large splash of the clear alcohol into his cup. The young man's eyes lit up, their faces inches apart.

"Thanks, Miss Jules."

"Our little secret," she said, her words sloshing through the air so softly Gus could hardly hear them above the background noise of the crowd.

The boy then walked out of the frame, and Gus heard Maria ask who that was. Jules was watching him walk away and when she turned back toward Maria she swayed against the counter, bumping into Sarah who propped her back up.

"That's Sean, Milly's new boyfriend," slurred Jules, referring to her daughter Emily. Her words blended together and the pitch of her voice seemed to rise and fall with the sways of her head. She bit her lower lip on one side of her mouth. "Yum, right? I'd…" She waved a hand in the air in a flamboyant gesture, then said something else that Gus couldn't hear and started to laugh, a sloppy wide-mouthed guffaw. Maria had stepped to the side and now faced the camera.

"Oh, gross, Jules," she snapped, flashing Jules a questioning look.

"Lighten up, Lincoln," Jules slurred, a wide grin on her face. She stared intently at Maria for several seconds, as if trying to get her eyes to focus. "C'mon, we all know there's a *wild* woman under that turtleneck." She pointed a finger at Maria then, as she said something else, her head flicked to her side at Sarah and she swayed along the counter, laughing as she went.

"He's just a *boy*," said Maria, disgust in her voice, realizing Jules was serious.

"He's eighteen." Jules giggled then, and after a few moments she gestured toward Maria with her cup, splashing some of her drink onto the floor. She laughed toward the ceiling, then the video ended and the screen went black. Mel looked up from her phone and took a step toward Jules.

"Jules, you can't possibly believe I had anything to…"

"Fuck you, Idlewilde! I knew we could never trust you." Jules was breathing heavy and Gus could see the rage in her eyes as she took a step around Jim before he grabbed her tight.

"Jules, it wasn't me, I swear," pleaded Mel. "I'll take it down right now."

"It's too late. The whole town's already seen it. It's gone around every group chat at Milly's school! Why'd you do it? What could you possibly have gained by having Milly disgusted with me? Or by having Shane threaten to kick me out? Is that what you were going for? You're alone so everyone else should be too?"

Gus felt Mel's hand tighten around his arm, but before she could respond, Jules took a step backward toward her car and then, shaking Jim's hands from her sides, turned and pointed at Mel.

"You're dead to me, Idlewilde," she growled. Her voice was sharp, cutting. "I hope you die in a fuckin' hole."

Chapter Twenty-Five

GUS AND VANESSA waited with Jim at Mr. T's house until Jules had left and they were sure she wasn't coming back, then they followed him back to the police station. The bullpen where they sat was quiet except for the faint hum of the refrigerator in the break room and the low, bassy purr of cars streaming by outside. Jim had run next door to The Blend to get them afternoon coffees, and while they waited Gus sat sprawled out in his chair, staring out the window. He watched groups of people meander by on Main Street, each with long, skinny shadows in tow. He used his foot to rotate his chair back and forth, lost in his own thoughts of whom he should call to sub for him on the tour and whether he'd really use that electric fretless bass he'd been coveting online. Vanessa thumbed away at her phone and, without looking up, was the first to speak.

"My brain's a blender."

"Mine too," echoed Gus. He was about to say something else when the first verse of Gwen Stefani's edgy song "Hollaback Girl" began to stab the air around them. Startled, he looked around as Vanessa began to laugh. Gus pulled his phone from his jacket pocket and answered it and the song stopped just as it began another loop through the lyrics.

"Wheeler," he grumbled, glaring at Vanessa. "Hey, Rob, what's up?" Gus listened for a moment, then put the pathologist on speaker. "Rob, I'm here with V. You're on speaker."

"Like I was saying, Gus, after you and I spoke earlier this morning I got to thinking about the toxin we found in the Nelson woman and the odd list of symptoms associated with it. So, before we ran down a rabbit hole of tests I called a colleague of mine at one of the independent labs to get her take on it. And when I brought her through the symptoms and all the toxins we've already tested for that've come up negative, her first thought was that we're dealing with some sort of venom."

"Venom?" questioned Gus.

"That's right. She practiced for many years in Arizona so dealt with snakebites all the time, and several of the symptoms I mentioned seemed to her to be very similar to those she saw with snakebite victims. And that would make sense of all the negative results we've gotten; you can't really test for venoms. They're identified from the symptoms they cause or from witness or victim accounts."

"So, you're thinking it's some kind of snake venom?"

"I didn't say it *was* snake venom; that's just what she's dealt with in the past. This could be from any number of plants or animals. We're still going to do the next round of tests, but I wanted to pass that on."

They thanked Rob for the update, then ended the call as Jim entered with a tray of coffees. Gus and Vanessa each took one while Jim sat at his desk and swiveled around to face them.

"All everyone's talking about in The Blend is that video of Jules."

"I'm sure," said Gus. He took a long pull of his coffee, and as he did so his eyes caught on a large photograph on the wall above Jim's desk. It was a group shot of a dozen or so people, and by the sweeping views in the background Gus guessed it was taken on the summit of a nearby mountain. He recognized each of the women and Jim among a few others. His eyes settled on an excited Jules and his thoughts skipped back to the scene earlier at Mr. T's house.

"Does Jules always amp up like that?"

"Unfortunately, that was classic Jules. She heats up quick."

"Heats up?" questioned Vanessa. "That woman's straight-up off. Why is anyone still friends with her?"

"I've been asking Maria that for years. I think they all just shrug this stuff off as that's just Jules. Like they've become immune to it or something."

"Could you tell where that video was from?" asked Gus.

"That was at Jules's house a few months ago. We were there. Maria didn't get into details, but I remember her mentioning something about Jules flirting with Milly's boyfriend."

"Does she do that often?"

"Not necessarily that, specifically. But let's just say it's not uncommon for there to be stories about Jules's after parties."

"What about the giving alcohol to minors thing?" sniped

Vanessa.

"Yes, that's a thing. She's always wanted to be"—he did air quotes—"the cool mom. It got so bad a few years back when Milly—her oldest—started high school that several parents filed complaints with us, so I had to speak with her and Shane. As you saw, some habits are hard to break."

Gus thought about Jules drunk in the video and his brain tapped along the various infractions she had in college. "Has she always drunk a lot?"

Jim pondered the question for a moment. "I don't know. I think we were all typical teenagers in a small town: parties in the woods, bonfires, that sort of thing."

"Do you think Idlewilde dropped that video?" asked Vanessa.

The chief shook his head. "I don't know. Mel's no wall-flower. If she had a problem with Jules she'd say it to her face."

The question struck a chord with Gus. As far as he could tell, the only thing posting that video achieved was the public shaming and humiliation of Jules Russell. Other than involving Jules and other women in their group, he was struggling to see how it was connected at all with their investigation. He was about to change the subject when Vanessa spoke.

"Well, the techies are reviewing it as we speak. They should be able to figure out where it was posted from even if it's in someone's account in the cloud."

Gus nodded as if he knew what Vanessa was talking about, but he understood the cloud about as well as he understood quantum physics. Jim tapped a few keys on his keyboard and the printer whirred to life. He then took a couple of pages from its tray and handed each of them one.

"Here's the list of all the odd or unusual incidents we were notified about in the past year."

Gus scanned the list quickly. It was short and worked back from Mel's break-in last night. There was the antifreeze in Maria's gas tank in late August, about a month ago, then the break-in reported by Jules on Fourth of July weekend. Then in late May the odd algae contamination of Sarah's pool and, a few weeks before that, in late April, Lizzy's dog being poisoned. The last one on the list was Jules's Range Rover being keyed in early April.

"This is everything?"

"Everything that wasn't typical or explained."

Gus looked over the list again. "The timeline's interesting, right? Everything on this list has followed Turner's murder. I think we can agree our guy's a planner. But Turner's murder was chaotic, frenzied. It has an element of impulsiveness, recklessness. So, did that kick all of this off for him? And, if so, why? Did Turner do or know something that triggered him?"

"Maybe Laurie was his real target and all of this other stuff is just to hide that fact?" suggested Jim.

Gus's mouth twisted. "Uh, I don't think so. It's not like he's just killed another woman. He's gone over the top planning and executing all of these other things."

Gus's eyes remained on the paper but his mind began to ricochet off the odd and growing tally of leads and events they'd encountered since arriving in Kendalton yesterday morning, until one observation rose above the tempest of his thoughts, like steam from a pot.

"No matter how I think about this—everything that went on in the past months, what's happened in the past few days, all of it—one name keeps popping in my head: Jules Russell."

"I was just thinking the same thing," commented Jim. "How do *you* get there?"

"Oh God, don't ask how that dyslexic brain of his works," warned Vanessa.

"Well, there's the audio recording on the flash drive left in my room of her and Sarah arguing. And the video we just saw of her at that party. Then her showing up at Mr. T's looking to lay into Idlewilde. I don't know…" His eyes scanned the wall behind Vanessa. "Her name keeps sticking in my mind. It's like she's all over this."

"Completely agree," said Jim.

"Are you suggesting she's a suspect or a target?" asked Vanessa.

"The suspect, right?" interjected Jim.

"I don't know what I'm suggesting," clarified Gus.

"She really could be either, right?" offered Vanessa.

"How do you mean?"

"She could be either," she repeated. "She could be a target for a number of reasons. First, to state the obvious, she's in that group of women. And that's two for two so far. And"—she tipped her head toward the paper in his hand—"she's the only one on that list twice."

"The video posted earlier today certainly targeted her for something," pointed out Gus. "If you wanted to trash her reputation you'd be hard pressed to find something more damaging."

"Ya, but why would Idlewilde drop that? Does she hate Jules Russell that much?"

They both looked to Jim, who was shaking his head. "No, it's not really in Mel to hate anyone."

"Then we need to be asking who *does* hate Jules Russell that much," said Gus.

"That's a pretty long list." The chief sighed. "You've seen how brash Jules can be; she's left a lot of people in her wake over the years."

The room fell quiet for a few moments; there was nothing else to add.

"Well, in terms of her being our suspect, I start with her sheet from college," Vanessa jumped in. "The drunk-and-disorderlies are sort of her thing as far as we can tell. But anyone with a brain can see she was responsible for that young woman who rushed her sorority, accident or not. And based on witness accounts, Jules abused that poor girl and all for flirting with her boyfriend. That hits differently."

"Agreed," said Gus.

"Then there's the audio file on that flash drive," added Vanessa. "Sarah clearly had a significant secret she was holding over Jules." She looked to Jim. "Any ideas what that could be?"

He shook his head slowly. "Jesus, with Jules's behavior over the years it could be anything. But nothing that could land her in jail that I know of, sorry."

Gus looked back at the list in his hand. "You know, there are a few more incidents not on this list." They waited for him to continue. "We know that video taken inside Mr. T's house was taken last Memorial Day weekend, so about four months ago. And when Sarah's lover, George, was interviewed by one of our agents he said a couple interesting things. Apparently, Sarah called him early one evening about a month or so after Turner's death. She was freaked out that someone had been in her house. She walked through it with him on the phone but it was empty. There was no sign of a break-in and nothing was taken or seemed touched, but Sarah said it just felt like someone had been in there; she felt an energy or something."

"We never got a call."

"No, she felt stupid calling the police and the house was empty and secure. But George also said that Sarah often had the feeling of being watched from the woods behind her house."

"So, the Mr. T video goes in the Idlewilde column since it was done after Laurie Turner's death," pointed out Vanessa. "And the potential break-in at Sarah Nelson's house adds another incident involving Sarah to the list. So now Jules *isn't* the only one on the list with two incidents—Idlewilde and Nelson each have two as well."

"That's right," lamented Gus. His cheeks puffed out as he loudly exhaled.

Vanessa spun her pen across her hand as her mind wrestled with the swelling list of leads. "Well, and now how about Rebecca Munroe's suicide? How does that fit into all of this?"

Gus leaned forward and, feeling overwhelmed, briskly rubbed his face with his hands. "Maybe the connection's to the baby daddy, this guy Troy. You get anything on him yet?"

"I requested his background info…" Vanessa said as she picked her phone back up and swiped at it a few times, then sat forward.

"Here we go. Troy Frederick Robinson. Enlisted in the army in nineteen ninety-seven, honorable discharge in two thousand nineteen as a sergeant first class. In two thousand and two he became a member of the army's Special Forces."

"Green Beret?" questioned Gus, perking up.

"A number of operations listed here," continued Vanessa. "Afghanistan, Republic of Congo, Syria… Says here that Troy was in the unit's security force assistance and special reconnaissance outfit." Vanessa lowered her phone and looked to Gus. "There's a lot more here but I think we get the gist. Mr. Robinson's got game in the surveillance department."

"Well, and there's the Awkward7 posts to Mel's site," added Gus.

"I'd be surprised with this background if he didn't have the computer chops to post those without being traced… It is Robinson's Hardware and *Security*, after all," she mocked.

"He is connected to things," added Gus. "Dating Jules and secretly dating Rebecca Munroe when she committed suicide and the pregnancy, of course." He looked to Jim.

"How's the relationship between Troy and Jules?"

"They definitely don't like each other. But does he hate her? I don't know."

"Maybe he's our guy and he's feeding us info to set up Jules?" pondered Vanessa.

She spun in her seat to get up, but as she did so something caught her attention. She stopped short, spun partway back, and steadied herself in the wobbly chair. In front of her were three other officers' desks, each organized similarly to Jim's. Each had the same black-and-silver telephone, the same silver computer, and the same widescreen monitor the size of a billboard. But one was different and she immediately realized why.

Vanessa spun back around while simultaneously sliding her chair between the monitor and Gus and he saw the panicked look on her face. Vanessa touched her finger to her lips, then mouthed four alarming words.

That computer's camera's on.

And, just like that, a deadened silence smothered the room.

Chapter Twenty-Six

IT WAS A beautiful Sunday morning in Kendalton. Plump, creamy clouds floated by, the sun playing peekaboo with the large crowd milling about on The Commons. Police manned the crosswalk on Main Street, stopping traffic continually so pedestrians caught in that look-left, look-right ritual could cross and join the festivities. Tables and elaborate booths formed a wide perimeter as vendors and farmers sold everything from homemade breads and bakery items to farm-fresh produce, meats, and cheeses. The gazebo in the center had a large white banner hung across its front with bright purple letters that read *Billie's Run* and beneath that *The US Foundation for Adolescent Drug Prevention's 1st Annual 5K Race for Life.*

Gus wished he could enjoy the festivities around him but was distracted. The FBI's Cybercrimes group went to the Kendalton Police Station last night to evaluate the hack to the station's computer camera but was yet unable to trace its feed. It wasn't lost on Gus that that type of security breach was likely something Troy Robinson could do in his sleep. Gus was already eager to speak with the army vet given his connection to Rebecca Munroe and her unborn baby, but now with this breach at the station, he was able to focus on little else. Robinson's store was closed on Sundays and they still hadn't heard back from Troy.

One of the vendors started their tractor and birds scattered in the air like confetti. Gus noticed the Posse, as they called themselves, standing together beside the gazebo. Jules wore a flattering form-fitting shirt with matching green-and-black runner's tights. Her shiny blond hair, perfect body, and meticulously applied makeup gave Jules the appearance of a celebrity trainer readying for the camera. Next to her stood Maria and Lizzy, each dressed in jeans and thick coats, content to be spectators.

Gus noticed several women sneaking glaring stares at Jules while others subtly gestured her way while talking with others. With one single video Jules Russell had become a pariah. Gus watched as Jules too saw those women out of the corner of her eye.

Realizing Mel wasn't with them, Gus scanned the crowd until finally seeing her near one of the vendors. His eyes lingered on her for a hot moment. She wore a long-sleeve T-shirt that hung past her waist and plain white exercise pants. Gus watched as a young boy with Down's syndrome standing next to Mel caught her attention, then leaned into her and gave her a hug. The boy's father seemed to apologize to Mel, and Gus saw Mel wave him off as she smiled and returned the boy's embrace. Mel spoke with the young boy for several minutes, smiling the entire time, until he and the man playfully waved their goodbyes and wandered away.

Gus followed the young boy until his eyes fell on a group of teenaged girls hovering near the Posse. They were snickering and stealing glances at each other as they fluttered around someone in the middle of their tight circle. Two of the daughters parted enough for Gus to see a young, meek-looking girl with large, bright red circles on her cheeks, far too much red lipstick, and dark raccoon circles around each eye. Gus felt Vanessa take a half step forward as she too saw what the daughters were up to. Then they all separated in unison, laughing and joking, happy with their artwork, as the other young girl naively walked away clown-faced into the crowd.

"Jules has had a rough twenty-four hours," said Jim.

"How so?"

"Apparently, she got suspended from her job at the high school after that video of her giving a minor alcohol made the rounds. And Maria was saying last night that she's also been asked to step down from the sports scholarship committee and she's been banned from all school events until further notice."

"Sounds like she's not living her best life right about now," remarked Vanessa flippantly.

"I'm not sure you understand," said Jim, turning to them both. "To Jules, that's *everything*. Involvement in those activities—especially the scholarship committee—is who she is. She runs those groups and is in the know about everything going on here in town. Her world just blew up."

Gus looked back to Mel as a slender woman tapped her on the shoulder, and when Mel turned to see who it was the two of them hugged. Mel's face lit up and her entire body became energized when she was excited, and Gus imagined the young girl she must have been. He watched as the two women talked and nodded, genuinely enjoying their conversation.

"That's Annie Elkins," said the chief. "You wanted to speak with her, right?"

"Ya."

"We'll never get her once Beady starts talking so let's grab her now, before the race."

Jim stole Annie away from Mel and the four of them now stood beside the vendor booth on the end, which provided as much privacy as they were apt to find. Gus noted her clear, bright eyes, tanned complexion, and earthy vibe. Annie Elkins radiated good health.

After Jim did introductions, Vanessa gestured to the banner atop the gazebo. "Billie's Run. Your daughter, right?"

Annie's face tightened. "That's right."

"Was she a runner like you?"

Her lips bent into a smile. "No, not at all. And, believe me, I'm not a runner." She opened her arms and looked to her outfit. "These are my ex-husband's. He's a crazy runner. We just thought this type of event, outdoors, family-oriented, would fit with our cause."

"We understand she passed a year ago."

"Thirteen months, six days," corrected Annie. She took a deep breath and exhaled and her eyes widened. "Enough about me. Jim said you folks had some questions about Sarah?"

"Yes and thank you for speaking with us," began Gus. "We won't take much of your time."

Annie waved a hand in front of her. "Please, agent, take as much time as you need. Those deaths were just as tragic and senseless as what we're trying to prevent with fundraisers like this."

"We understand you and Sarah were developing a GPS app for the Land Trust trails."

Annie sheepishly glanced at the chief. "I think it's more accurate to say that Sarah was developing it and I was sort of helping out around the edges."

"How do you mean?"

"Agent, I am anything but computer savvy," she said matter-of-factly. "Sarah, though? She really knew her way around a computer. So, she did all the techie stuff. She loaded an app on my phone that would log the route I took on the trails. So, afterward she'd download that data and add it to the map of the trails she was developing."

"Did you see Sarah much outside of the Land Trust?"

"Not really, no."

"And, how about Laurie Turner? Were you and she friends?"

"Nah, not really. I mean, she was Mel's best friend and Mel and I are close friends but that didn't really extend to Laurie. Or the others in that group, for that matter, including Sarah." She looked to Jim. "Jim knows, Maria's in their group. They sort of stick together."

Jim simply nodded his agreement.

"Can you think of anyone who might want to do this to either of them?"

"No, not at all. I can't think of anyone who'd want to do

this to anyone."

"Are you aware of anything else odd happening in town recently, other than these incidents?"

Annie slowly shook her head. "Nothing comes to mind."

"Can you tell us where you were the mornings of each attack?" interrupted Vanessa.

"Sure thing. I was at the animal shelter in Ashby. I volunteer there."

Gus looked to Vanessa, then back to Annie, struggling to think of anything else to ask. Annie wasn't in their group of friends, nor did she seem to have any real connection to either victim other than living in Kendalton and being a member of the Land Trust with Sarah.

"Is there anything else you can think of that might be important?" asked Gus finally.

"No, sorry. Nothing else comes to mind," Annie replied.

"If you think of anything, please let us know." Gus gave her one of his cards and, as he did so, looked around The Commons. "This is quite an event you've put on here."

Annie smiled. "Oh, thank you. But, believe me, there were a lot of people who put in a whole lot more time than I did to pull this off."

"Is this your main fundraiser?" asked Vanessa.

"We only formed this chapter of the foundation about six months ago, so we'll see. Our first fundraiser was a huge success though, so that will be tough to beat." Annie gestured to Jim. "The one that Jules helped organize early this summer at the institute."

"Jules Russell?" interrupted Gus.

"That's right," confirmed Annie. "Her husband, Shane, donated a tour of the oceanographic institute. And they could only accommodate thirty-five people so it became this special, very exclusive event. But the night…the night was truly amazing. They study and do research on marine animals and plants from all over the world—their behaviors, ecosystems, biological research on their venoms, all sorts of neat stuff."

Vanessa shot Gus a look. "Fascinating."

"Then, as if that wasn't enough," continued Annie, "they brought us out on their research vessel and showed us how they find and track specific marine animals they study. It was so cool."

"It really was great," agreed Jim.

"Well, and the night wasn't without a bit of drama too." Annie looked to Jim and then back to Gus with a sheepish smile. "Jules had a bit too much to drink so wasn't up for the boat ride. She stayed back at the institute alone to get a second wind."

Jim, with an eyebrow raised, looked to Gus. "Jules."

"If that's all," interrupted Annie, "I better get over there." She raised her chin toward the gazebo where Mayor Beady was climbing its steps.

They thanked Annie for her time, and as soon as she headed toward the gazebo to join Mayor Beady at the podium, Vanessa turned to Gus.

"Marine animal venom?"

"I know, right."

Seeing the confused look on the chief's face, Gus told

him about their conversation yesterday with the pathologist and the thinking that the toxin they were trying to identify was likely a venom.

"Can you call Jules's husband? We need to have their inventories inspected ASAP."

And as they made their way across the street and back to the police station they heard the crowd on The Commons begin to chant as Annie took the podium.

"Billie...Billie...Billie!"

Chapter Twenty-Seven

JIM CALLED SHANE Russell on his cell from the station and arranged for Gus and Vanessa to meet him at his work. Vanessa spoke with the team in Boston during the drive, leaving Gus to be in his own head. Annie Elkins's passionate remarks at the fundraiser kept replaying in his mind and left Gus realizing once again just how much someone's selfish act could shred its way through a family. Gus's older brother, Jake, had dealt with addiction for much of his adult life, and Gus had put long stretches of his own life on hold to try and help him. Annie's account of losing her daughter Billie to drugs and the hole it had left in her life had Gus thinking once again of Jake, and he questioned, for the millionth time, whether he had made the right choice by simply walking away. He wondered if he should reach out to Jake, see if he had finally slayed his demons. It had been over two years, could have happened. He'd give it some focused brain time when this case was over. He downshifted as he exited the highway, the truck's engine roaring in protest. Vanessa ended her call.

"That was Tony," she said, referring to another agent running logistics from Boston, Tony Blackford. "Nothing yet on the police station's hacked computers."

The National Oceanographic Institute was a nonprofit organization dedicated to ocean research and exploration. Spanning several acres along the coast, it contained eight research departments, over forty different labs, and employed nearly eight hundred scientists, ship's crew, and experts in a myriad of related areas. Shane was waiting for them in the lobby and escorted them through a maze of inner corridors and hallways to his surprisingly large, well-furnished office. The world of government grants was treating him well.

"Thank you for seeing us," said Gus. "I know this is a difficult time for your family."

Shane tossed his security badge onto a small, misshapen pottery dish on the corner of his desk with child's handwriting on its side, then pulled out his chair and sat.

"Not as difficult as it is for Laurie's or Sarah's families, I'm afraid."

Gus leaned forward slightly with interest. "Shane, we've come to understand that Sarah Nelson knew a very important secret about your wife that could potentially have Jules in legal trouble. Do you have any idea what that might be?"

Shane's eyes flicked from his desk back to Gus's. "I don't know of anything specific but, agent, I'm sure Jim has told you of Jules's sordid past." Shane paused and licked his lips. "And, as evidenced by that video I'm sure you've seen, there are things I just don't know."

Gus sidestepped his bitter tone. "How about Laurie or Sarah? Any idea who might want to harm either of them? Maybe someone with a grudge or someone they might've had a conflict with?"

"No, I'm sorry, but I'm the last one you should be asking." Seeing Gus's confusion he elaborated, "Agent, I'm the one outsider in that group. They all grew up together. I married in."

"Understood," said Gus before switching topics. "Shane, we have reason to believe our suspect is using some sort of venom to incapacitate his victims. And according to the Department of Health and Human Services, this is the only research facility in the northeast registered with an inventory of dangerous venoms."

"That's correct. We have, probably, three, four hundred different toxins and venoms in various stages of clinical research here at any given time."

Vanessa pulled her phone from her jacket pocket and tapped on her email. "The pathologist sent us a summary of the symptoms we've gotten from eyewitness accounts and autopsy findings."

"Okay." Shane shifted the monitor on his desk so they each could see it. He clicked on an icon for the inventory database and then opened a large search box. "I can search by key words to see what matches we get to the characteristics of the various toxins and venoms we have in inventory."

Vanessa read the symptoms aloud slowly as Shane typed them into the database search field, watching his fingers intently as he did so.

"Cardiac arrest…" She thought of how Maria described Sarah the morning of her death. "Paralysis, nausea." She then ticked through the symptoms from the autopsy findings.

"Paresthesia, ptosis, dysphagia, ischemia, cyanosis, and necrosis."

After reviewing the field quickly to check spellings, he pressed Enter and leaned back in his seat.

"Agent Lambert, many of these symptoms are fairly common. But it's the combination of the paralyzing attributes, the paresthesia, which is a neurological condition that heightens the pain receptors, and the comorbidity of cyanosis and necrosis that distinguishes this particular agent."

The screen populated with results, and Vanessa and Gus leaned forward to get a closer look. There were eight animals listed and next to each was a picture of a colorful, exotic-looking seashell. A field to the right of each contained the various words he had entered highlighted in yellow to signify which symptom matched each particular animal's venom.

"Precisely what I was thinking: cone snail venom." He thought a moment. "Your suspect is one smart cookie. Cone snail venom is unlike any other known venom."

"How so?" asked Gus, his geek brain snapping to attention.

"Cone snails can actually control their venom composition depending on whether they're hunting or defending themselves. When they're defending themselves, the composition of their venom targets the predator's pain receptors to significantly increase the pain felt, which naturally keeps them away. But when they hunt, the composition of the venom released from this same snail is modified to target paralyzing their prey. And their venom contains up to six or seven hundred different toxins, making it nearly impossible to derive an antidote. It's truly fascinating."

"What do you do here with a venom like this?" wondered Gus.

"All sorts of research into pain management, sedative qualities, that sort of thing. A famous example of a similar agent is tetrodotoxin or TTX, most commonly found in pufferfish. That's been synthesized to be used for pain relief in cancer patients, for migraine management, a whole host of uses. And it has none of the addictive properties of morphine or other opioids."

He printed out the search results, stood, and gestured through a window to the lab next door. "We keep the inventories of these in this lab here."

The laboratory had dozens of individual workstations along long, shiny black tables that reminded Gus of high school chemistry class. Technicians in pristine white lab coats busily worked away at most of them, some performing analyses on computers while others fussed with microscopes and other more advanced equipment.

Shane led them to a set of tall chrome coolers with glass doors that spanned a large portion of the back wall, like the freezer aisle of a supermarket. He scanned the log sheets affixed to each door until he found what he was looking for toward the middle of the coolers. Opening the door, he ran his finger over the fronts of the trays until he found the first one on his list: *Conus striatus.* He eased out the drawer, counted the vials it contained and matched it to the inventory on the sheet of paper. He then did this process for five more trays before pulling out the next one, and his hand stopped short at several open spots with no vials. He looked between the sheet and tray, then pulled the tray out and rested it on the counter beside the cooler.

"What is it?" asked Vanessa, but they each knew the answer.

"*Conus geographus*. There appear to be four vials missing: two harvested from predatory snails and two harvested from defensive snails." He then clarified, "We put the animal in different situations to elicit either a predatory or defensive reaction then harvest the venom."

Shane called one of the lab techs over and asked her to go through the entire cooler's inventory to verify the four vials were not mixed in with other trays. Vanessa's cell phone rang, so she stepped to a quiet corner and answered it.

Gus looked around. "I assume the security at the facility is fairly tight."

"Absolutely," confirmed Shane. "You need a security badge to enter past reception, and only the highest security level is allowed to enter the labs where we store the inventories. And, of course, we have 24/7 security personnel throughout the facility as well as a security system."

"So, if someone wanted to enter here..." began Gus, gesturing around the lab.

Shane pursed his lips and shook his head. "Impossible. Not without approved access." He held up his plastic security badge. "And one of these."

"Can you get me a list of attendees at the fundraising event you hosted this past summer?"

"Sure thing. Security will have it in their sign-in logs."

The other lab tech finished her review and came to the same conclusion that Shane had: Four vials of venom from the *Conus geographus* snail were missing. Vanessa rejoined them as Shane thanked the tech, who went back to her workstation. He then looked to Gus and Vanessa with embarrassment.

"I don't know how this could've happened." He removed the receiver from the wall phone and punched in a few numbers. "Yes, this is Director Russell. We've identified a potential inventory discrepancy. Laboratory P6. Also, could you bring a copy of the visitors list from the charity event this summer? Thank you."

He hung up the receiver, then said, "We'll have this evaluated, and if we can't reconcile the inventory we'll have to file an NOI—Notice of Incident—with HHS immediately."

A few moments later a security guard arrived with a copy of the visitors' log for the night of the fundraiser. Gus asked the young man to organize the security footage for the night of the fundraiser and said that another agent would be by later in the day to review it. But, given how the security footage at Mel's house had been scrambled, Gus wasn't optimistic they'd get anything from it. He and Vanessa then thanked Shane for his time and the guard escorted them to the lobby while members of Shane's team began a complete reconciliation of the inventory in question. Once in the parking lot, Vanessa excitedly held up her phone as they quickly headed toward the truck.

"The team got Turner's cell phone records from the

phone company. They're still combing through the texts and data but the morning of her death she made a 9-1-1 call."

"No shit."

Vanessa nodded, her eyebrows raised. "We've got the recording. Listen."

"Nine-one-one. What's your emergency?" asked a nasally voice.

"I want to report a murder." Laurie Turner's voice was soft, meek. She didn't sound anything like the self-assured, confident-looking woman Gus saw in her Facebook photos.

"When and where was this murder committed?"

"It was committed decades ago, but I'd rather not say where right now."

"Have you spoken with your local law enforcement?"

"I can't. They're compromised. Who else can I speak to?"

"That would be the state police or the FBI. I can put you through to the FBI if you'd like."

"Is there a statute of limitations on murder?"

"No, ma'am, there is not. Were you involved in this crime?"

No answer.

"Ma'am, if I can just get your—"

The audio ended as they got to Gus's truck. "That's when Laurie hung up," said Vanessa.

Gus leaned against the front fender. Vanessa stopped in front of him, holding her phone up.

"A murder…decades ago," she pressed.

"Rebecca Munroe," finished Gus.

"It's gotta be," she stressed. "That's gotta be the secret Sarah Nelson had on Jules. If Laurie Turner also knew about it that could explain her murder as well."

"Ya, totally fits. But Jules Russell on some killing spree to shut them all up?"

"We've seen stranger."

"True." Gus thought a moment, mashing this together with all they knew, connecting sporadic dots. He caught his partner's eye again. "You notice Shane's routine when we got to his office?" Vanessa squinted at him so he continued, "He unlocked his door and, as he walked around his desk, without even looking he dropped his security card onto a small clay cup on its corner that looked like one of his kids made it for him." The corner of his mouth flicked upward. "Didn't even have to look for it. Just tossed it in."

"Like it was a habit," finished Vanessa.

He held up the copy of the visitor list. "I'll bet anything that security badge was just sitting there that night for anyone to grab. We need to see if anyone else who attended that event has motive or the computer and surveillance skills we're seeing."

"Troy Robinson on that list?"

"He is," said Gus with a quick nod and after a beat added, "His background certainly puts him top of the list: the home invasions, the night vision, the surveillance and audio and video recordings. And the Rebecca Munroe tie could easily be the unborn baby…*his* unborn baby."

"So, what? He somehow finds out that these women had something to do with Rebecca's death and decides to pick them off one by one?"

"We've seen stranger," tossed Gus with a raised eyebrow. "And, you heard the chief: He and Jules don't like each other. So, he leaks that video of her to trash her reputation in town, or maybe, to distract us. Diversion: One of the five basic military tactics they teach you in boot camp."

He thought about the extensive covert background Troy Robinson had and all of the missions listed in his file, and he wondered how many other classified missions weren't listed.

"And the reality is: With his training, if Troy Robinson wanted to get that toxin—that night or any other night—no one would ever know."

Chapter Twenty-Eight

IT HAD BEEN a long afternoon for Gus and, with the events at the oceanographic institute, one that quickly bled into the evening. He called Jim Lincoln on the drive back to Kendalton, but the chief had yet to hear back from Troy Robinson. And, while they now had a high degree of confidence of Jules Russell's involvement in Rebecca Munroe's death, Gus wanted to speak with Troy to understand his potential involvement before confronting her. So, he and Vanessa decided to head back to the inn for a late dinner before calling it a day.

As they made their way up the front steps Gus got a call from Jeff looking for an update. So, Gus now stood huddled in a corner of the wraparound porch next to one of the dozen or so brightly painted rocking chairs with his phone pressed to an ear, his leather saddlebag at his feet. A large evergreen had grown through the slatted railing as if giving it a hug and small pin lights strung along the ceiling gave the porch a fairyland feel. Gus could picture older couples dressed in their Sunday best slowly rocking away on warm, lazy summer days with iced teas in hand.

While Gus was on the phone, Vanessa checked in with the tech group and now leaned on the railing beside him, repeatedly pinching her fingers together and apart on her phone screen. Gus ended his call and leaned against the railing next to her. When she didn't look up he leaned closer.

"Whatcha got?"

But before Vanessa could reply, something out of the corner of Gus's eye caught his attention. He turned to see Mel step from the shadows.

"Gus, you have a minute?" Mel asked through the slats in the porch.

"Sure." He gestured to the rocking chairs. "C'mon up and have a seat."

Gus and Vanessa shot each other a knowing look as Mel made her way to the stairs and onto the porch. They knew this case revolved around this group of women, and if one was willing to break from the pack it could blow things wide open. Gus pulled three chairs together in a group and they each sat. Seeing tears pool in Mel's eyes, he leaned forward and rested his elbows on his knees. His face was inches from the side of hers and he waited to make eye contact before speaking.

"Rough couple of days?"

Her glassy brown eyes widened and her cheeks puffed out as she exhaled. "Ohhh." Her voice shuddered. "You have no idea." She dabbed at the corners of her eyes with a shirt sleeve. "I mean, one of my closest friends was murdered the day before yesterday so…"

Mel's voice hitched and she looked to her feet and swallowed. The silence stretched on while she took a few steadying breaths, then continued.

"But in that time, I've been psychologically tormented at my own house with that photo of me taken from my porch, had to race for my panic room when someone—likely the same person who killed Sarah and Laur—broke into my house, only to find out they had keys to my house and that panic room. Then, while staying at Mr. T's—the only home I've ever truly had—the town gets a menacing video of an intruder waving a knife over him while he's sleeping—the only *father* I've ever had. And, if that's not enough, we come to find out that same person had broken into *his* house months before to film it." Her voice rose with a mixture of disbelief and awe. She looked up at Gus, the tears streaming down her cheeks. "What is *happening*?"

He put his hand on her knee. "Mel…"

"That was rhetorical," she said, steeling herself with a shake of her head. Vanessa handed her a napkin from her jacket pocket and Mel wiped her cheeks and blew her nose. She paused a moment before continuing.

"But in that same time, I've also seen Jules, someone I thought was a friend, go batshit crazy and accuse me of all sorts of things. And I've witnessed my other friend, Maria, the reserved and proper one become"—she held Gus's eyes—"calculating."

When she didn't go on, Gus asked, "Mel, why are you here?"

She sat up and took a deep breath. "At first, I couldn't believe it might be one of us, one of my friends," she said, ignoring Gus's question. "Sarah and Laur were our friends, our sisters. And, you… Well, I didn't know you." She looked from Vanessa to Gus. "I foolishly thought being loyal to my friends was the best thing to do. I didn't know who else I could trust."

"But…" prompted Gus.

"But over the last two days I've come to realize"—her head shook slightly—"they're not my friends. They never were. Laur and Sarah were my only friends and they're gone. The others are just…friends by proximity."

Gus knew she'd continue. Witnesses and suspects always did once they got going. He held her gaze and remained quiet and watched as the anger faded, leaving sorrow and regret in its place.

"They were with Becca the night she died," Mel said at last. "All of 'em." She slowly shook her head again. "Becca didn't commit suicide. They were all out at the quarry, smoking pot and drinking. Laur told me that at one point she felt sick so went into the woods to throw up. Then she heard screams and yelling and when she caught up to them down one of the trails she found them all standing around Becca, who was lying on the ground, her head next to a rock and all bloody. They all just started telling Laur how it was an accident, how Becca ran away from them and fell, hitting her head on the rock. Then they all started to freak out and panic. And that's when Jules had the idea to make it look like a suicide. So they carried her way down to the quarry's edge and made it look like she jumped."

"You weren't there?" he clarified.

Mel's face relaxed a little. "No. My mother was a lot of things—a drunk, abusive, absent—but lenient wasn't one of them. Until my mother left I was in the house by 9:00 p.m. every night. No exceptions."

Vanessa leaned forward, mimicking Gus's pose. "So, Laurie told you all this?"

Mel nodded. "The next day. She was so upset, so scared. That night ruined her life." Mel paused and collected herself. "Laur was a very kind person." She bit her bottom lip. "Kind. You don't hear many people described that way these days. But that was Laur. The others went on with their lives, pretending that night never happened. But Laur always struggled with it. Then Annie's daughter, Billie, died of a drug overdose last year and Laur's guilt came flooding back. You see, their daughters were…not very nice to Billie."

"They bullied her," goaded Vanessa, and Gus heard the shards of experience in her voice.

"They did. And Laur was convinced that all of their daughters' bullying, at least in part, contributed to Billie's drug use and eventual death. Jules and Maria and Sarah used to pick on Becca and others in school. And when Becca started hanging around with us we all got a sense of just how horrible it was for her. Laur always remembered that. So, after Billie's death Laur was on them nonstop to have their daughters stop bullying other girls at school. She didn't want anyone else to get hurt."

"Did they? Talk to them, I mean?" asked Gus.

"They said they did, but who knows? But it didn't matter. Billie's death brought back all the traumatic memories for Laur of that night with Becca. She became obsessed; she felt she had to confess. To someone. Jules and Maria were constantly talking her down. They'd challenge her: Who would listen after all these years? What good would it do now? What would it accomplish besides ruining our lives? Laur wanted to do the right thing; she really did. But each time, she'd eventually listen to them and do nothing, but it constantly gnawed at her."

Gus took a few moments to process all he'd just heard as random thoughts and images sizzled in his mind. He remembered a traumatized Maria suspiciously staring at him and Vanessa as they spoke to the statey and pathologist and took in the Sarah Nelson scene, and a nervous Lizzy clearly lying about not knowing Becca while asking if they had any suspects. He thought of speaking with a confident Jules at the soccer fields and of how the other women who approached acted around her, deferred to her, as if she were superior to all of them. Vanessa's words echoed in his mind, what she had read to him from the case file of the young college woman who died rushing Jules's sorority and how witnesses described Jules and her behavior. *Abusive. Tormenting. Psychological torture.* And his thoughts immediately went to the photo sent to Mel of herself at home alone and the key left for her on her counter. And, finally, his thoughts settled on what they heard from Laurie's 9-1-1 call.

I want to report a murder.

This all swirled together as one in Gus's mind, like cream stirred into coffee, and he looked back to an exhausted Mel.

"Did Laurie believe it was all an accident?" asked Gus. "Rebecca's death, I mean."

"She did at first, but as the years went on she questioned it, for sure."

Chapter Twenty-Nine

WHEN MEL WAS finished and they had no more questions for her, they thanked her for coming forward, then watched her walk back to her Jeep and slowly drive away. Gus sat back in his rocking chair and steadied it so that his face was beside Vanessa's.

"Didn't see that coming," he said.

"That killing spree theory of mine is making more sense all the time."

"It is starting to come into focus, I'll give you that. But Mel wasn't there that night. Everything she just told us is third party hearsay; it'd never stand up. We need the evidence or at least a confession from one of the women who *was* there that night."

"But it does confirm these women have been flat-out lying to us about not knowing Becca."

"That it does," agreed Gus. "That it does. And we're going to hit each of them with that, but first we need to know more. There's more going on here, I can feel it. And I want to know what it is before we speak to these women again."

Vanessa rocked back and forth a few times, then pulled her phone from her jacket pocket and swiped it awake. She leaned toward Gus and held it up so they could both see its screen.

"The lab thinks they got a reflection off the window from the picture at Mel's house." Vanessa showed him the original, dark photo, then swiped to a duplicate that had been lightened to clear the blurry spots. The phone the suspect used to take the picture took up most of the frame so that only a small portion of their cheek and the outside corner of an eye could be seen.

"You can't see much." Vanessa twisted it side to side but the decorative porch lighting was more for ambiance than illumination. "It looks like a curly lock of hair above the eyebrow though."

"Maybe," Gus hesitantly replied. "Or it could be a shadow...tough to tell. I need to look at it on a bigger screen."

She tapped her phone off and slid it back into her pocket. "The techies also picked up something from the night-vision video of Mr. T's house in one of the still frames. A reflection in the chrome toaster. They think it could be a logo but they'll need more time to process it."

Vanessa then stood and gestured toward the door. "C'mon, I'm fried. Let's eat."

"Let me just dump my bag in my room before we hit the tavern."

She rolled her eyes, then pivoted and followed Gus as they made their way inside and through the cozy lobby, past the unattended reception desk and the oversized fireplace that Gus swore could fit a VW Bug. Gus cringed at the faint, soulless music oozing from the speakers overhead. It was "The Girl from Ipanema"—a generic, homogeneous melody devoid of percussion instruments, the type of tune you heard in elevators or dentists' offices or, Gus was sure, hell.

Along the way Vanessa updated him on a few other items discussed with the team in Boston. The techies had finished their evaluation of Laurie Turner's and Sarah Nelson's computers and social media accounts, but nothing noteworthy was found. Their analysis of the audio recording of Sarah and Jules arguing that was left for Gus in his room was complete, but they weren't able to clean up the resolution of the background noises enough to make anything useful out of it. But, they noted that whoever had recorded it had removed all of the metadata from the file so there was no way to trace it to even the type of machine it was recorded on, let alone who recorded it.

"They also found that video of Jules drunk on Idlewilde's cloud account." She continued, "It was in some random subfolder along with some pictures from years ago. But Jim was right, the video was filmed back in July: just over two months ago."

"They figure out what that muffled dialogue was?"

"Still working on it. Oh, and Tony looked at the surveillance footage at the oceanographic institute from the night of the fundraiser," she added, referring to the other agent, Tony Blackford. "As we suspected, it was jammed; nothing but snow."

Once at his room, Gus moved the sign that read Do Not Disturb aside, slid his key card in, and slowly pushed open the door. He took a few tentative steps inside, then stopped and scanned the room slowly, taking it all in. The bathroom light was still on and his towel from that morning still hung from its door. The curtains were pulled away from the windows and Gus could see the fat orange moon just above the treetops. His foldable bass stood in the corner where he'd left it and his bow was leaning against the wall beside it, again where he left it. Vanessa stepped beside him.

"Maybe Cato's in the armoire," said Vanessa, referring to the martial arts sidekick tasked by Inspector Clouseau to surprise attack him regularly in the *Pink Panther* movies she knew Gus loved as a kid.

He looked down at her but didn't say a word. After the break-in to his room the night before Gus had spoken with the old innkeeper, Darrell Pierce, and learned that not only did the inn have no security cameras but that the front doors had the same flimsy locks as the rooms. And Gus knew that these days anyone could get a remote cloning or relay device online that would allow them to copy key cards and, hence, open a variety of electronic locks, including those used by hotels. And given how sophisticated their suspect appeared to be with their computer prowess, Gus was betting that getting into the inn and his room would be child's play to them. He shut the door and threw the lock out of habit. He slid his bag onto a small round table in front of the windows as Vanessa looked around at the small room.

"What is this? A room for ants?"

Gus glanced at her with a confused look, and she was once again disappointed at his inability to understand her favorite Will Ferrell movie references.

He took off his coat and slung it over a chair and, as he

did so, noticed something he'd missed when they entered the room and jolted to a halt. Vanessa placed a hand on her firearm.

"What is it?" Her eyes scanned the bed, side tables, and the bureau beside the door.

"The bed."

"O-kay," she said slowly. The bed's pillows were partially piled on one another, its sheet hanging to the floor on one side and the comforter resting askew across it.

"Didn't have time to make it this morning?"

While Vanessa and Gus had never been a couple, they had spent as much time together as most couples they knew. And this included crashing at each other's apartments when the circumstances warranted it. And, as a result, Vanessa knew that one of Gus's many quirks was that he always made his bed, even in hotels, but he made them so poorly no one but he could ever tell.

"I made it," he said, his voice laced with indignation.

"Looks like the work of a small child."

"Beneath the pillows, smartass."

Without taking her hand off her Glock, she craned her head farther to the side, and that's when she saw the corner of a manila envelope jutting out from beneath one of the pillows. They each put on latex gloves from Gus's bag and stepped beside the bed. He carefully held the envelope and pulled back each gold-colored clasp holding its flap down and opened it. He peered inside, then slowly pulled out a yellowed, aged piece of lined paper. One of its corners was missing and three of its sides were jagged and flaky, while the fourth was cut perfectly straight. It was written in elaborate, sweeping cursive penmanship faded to a pastel bluish-gray color. Gus gently placed it on the sheet so they both could read it.

June 26, 1995

Dear Journal,

Today was a great day, a wonderful day. When I got to work at Eddie's Jules was there. She usually doesn't work Mondays but the manager told me she had volunteered to work today. It was a little weird at first because I didn't know what to say but she made it really easy. She was different today. She was super nice and super fun to be around. We even laughed a lot at each other's jokes. But then the best part was when her ride got there, before she left she smiled at me and said—and I quote—"WE SHOULD HANG OUT SOMETIME." Aaaaaaahhhh!!!! Journal, I can't even imagine it: I could be hanging around with the cool kids. Unbelievable!!

Until next time,

—B

The two of them read and reread the short note in silence several times before Gus sat on the bed beside it. She gestured toward the paper with a lift of her chin.

"You think it's legit? It's from Rebe—Becca's—journal?"

Gus had a case a few years ago where the age of the document in question was a key factor in determining the outcome. And as a result, he had learned more than he ever wanted to about the various factors a forensic document examiner evaluated to make their determination: watermarks, composition of paper, office machine defects, identification of the writing instrument, determining the printing technology used and more, much more. But Gus didn't need any of that extensive forensic analysis to tell him the page lying on the bed beside him was from Rebecca Munroe's missing journal. He knew it the second he read it.

We should hang out sometime.

"No doubt," he said as he leaned back on his hands and looked up at his partner's intense, curious eyes. "But the question is: Who has the journal now? Who's pointing us toward Jules Russell?"

"Mel?" questioned Vanessa. "She was clearly here waiting for us tonight. She could've slipped in before we got here."

"Nah, I'm not feelin' that at all."

Vanessa's eyes bulged. "Shocker." When Gus didn't reply, she continued, "Dude, a blind person could see you're attracted to her." Gus opened his mouth to say something but Vanessa held up her hand. "Just sayin', be careful. She's in the thick of this."

When Gus remained silent, Vanessa moved on. "Becca's friend Maury could be lying about not finding the journal, but I don't think so. The obvious answer is Troy. He was dating her around the time of her death. He could easily have it." She paused, looking the page over again. "But, regardless, there's Jules again, front and center," she pointed out.

"Right. And look at the date. That's about a month or so

before Rebecca's death."

Gus carefully turned the piece of paper over and back.

"It looks like you may be right," Vanessa said slowly, watching Gus examine the brittle paper. "If Jules *was* our guy, she wouldn't be leaving us clues leading back to herself."

Gus probed a molar with his tongue. "I wonder where Mr. Robinson was tonight."

His thought hung in the air for a brief moment before the loud ring of Vanessa's phone stole her attention away. She listened intently to her caller for nearly a minute without saying anything other than "hey" when she answered and "thanks" when she hung up. She met Gus's eyes with a widening grin.

"Dinner'll have to wait." She took hold of the strap on Gus's saddlebag and held it out to him. Confused, he stood.

"Why, what's up?"

"They just traced the Awkward7 posts to the Ashby-Kendalton Regional High School."

Chapter Thirty

GUS HAD VANESSA take a picture of the page from the journal with her phone so they could continue to refer to it as needed. Then, before heading to the Ashby-Kendalton Regional High School, he repeated the drill he had done with the data stick left for him: he sealed the journal page inside an evidence bag, documented the date, time, and location at which it was found and put his signature over the sealed opening to the bag. Vanessa would arrange for a secure courier to bring it to the Boston lab so they could evaluate it more closely.

The computer room at the high school was located just past the front office between the library and music room. It was an internal, windowless space about the size of a storage locker. Gus, Vanessa, and the chief crammed just inside its door and watched two cybercrimes techs peck away at a cluster of terminals against one of the walls. It was late and the overhead lights were bright and harsh. Gus rubbed his eyes with the palm of his hand but they remained watery from fatigue. He told Jim of the page from Rebecca Munroe's journal left in his room earlier and of the entry written on it describing Jules befriending her. He considered telling the chief about the visit from Mel and what she told them but decided to hold off for now. Mel's story clearly implicated Jim's wife Maria, so until they learned more, Gus would keep that between him and Vanessa.

"I have to say," began Jim, surprised, "I didn't think Jules had it in her."

Gus tipped his head toward the stack of servers. "But, these posts and the hacking of your station's computers and the whole B-and-E element to this…it all has a sophistication to it. And, besides, Jules wouldn't be leaving us leads like that journal post that steer us back to her. No, seems someone's trying to set her up."

"Or pointing us to her," countered Jim. "Seeing how she was, outside Mr. T's house…not only the rage but the desperation." He shook his head. "Like I said, Jules's reputation in town is *everything* to her. It defines her. And right now, her whole world is falling down around her."

"And people tend to become fairly irrational when their world falls apart," added Vanessa. "I've seen this movie before."

"Let's just say it is Jules," said Jim. "Why now? What's set her off?"

Vanessa looked from Jim to Gus. "The Turner 9-1-1 call." She held back from adding "duh." She then played the audio of that call for the chief and his face blanched.

"Holy shit. Gus, yesterday you asked me if Jules always drank this much. And that got me thinking. It seems to me, in hindsight, she started to stand out with her drinking the beginning of junior year in high school. And that would be just a few months after Becca's death. Now, it could be a coincidence; some of us were getting our licenses, we were out more, teenage hormones, whatever." He raised an eyebrow. "Or it could not."

"Okay, it all started with the Turner woman," began Gus. "She made a 9-1-1 call the morning of her death. It's clear she wanted to talk to someone about an old murder; we're thinking it's Rebecca Munroe. So, let's say Jules did have something to do with that and she gets wind that Turner knows and is going to drop a dime on her, so she confronts her to talk her out of it."

"But she can't," added Vanessa.

"But she can't," Gus echoed. "The two of them argue and, in a fit of rage, Jules snaps and kills Turner."

"She panics so rolls Turner into the pond and gets away before Idlewilde gets there," finished Vanessa.

"That explains the different MOs." Gus grimaced. "Six months ago Jules Russell isn't a murderer, she's just a frightened woman with a hot temper."

"That all holds." Vanessa nodded.

"But, whatever Turner knew so too does Sarah Nelson. It could be the secret Nelson had on Jules, the one she mentions on that audio recording."

"So now, in for a penny in for a pound," added Jim.

"But Jules is smart." Gus continued, "She knows Nelson is a more formidable opponent. This time she plans it out."

"The drug," explained Vanessa.

"The drug," repeated Gus. "That takes away any fight Nelson could've mounted. And the two of them were friends so..."

"Jules is able to get close enough to use the needle," finished Jim.

As this all settled into Gus's thoughts it began to make more and more sense. "It definitely hangs together."

They each fell quiet, letting it marinate. The dedicated air conditioning system hummed in the background as it strained to keep up with the surge of body heat now in the room. Trevor Hamilton, the head of the Boston Cybercrimes unit, said something to his colleague, then stood and stepped over beside Gus. Trevor was a large man with an elaborate goatee and long, bushy sideburns that ran to his jawline like pillars for his bushy mop of hair. He wore sturdy, square black eyeglasses that resembled those used by jewelry makers when working on the finest of details.

"Hey, sorry this trace has taken us this long." Trevor paused, watching something the other tech was doing on one of the computers. "You check out that unreleased Coltrane record yet?"

Gus and Trevor had worked together on several cases over the years and the two of them had clicked over their love of jazz music.

"No, it's on my long list of things to do."

"Why was this one so difficult?" asked Vanessa.

"This guy's no script kiddie. He…" Seeing the confused look on their faces, Trevor held up. "Script kiddie. A novice, a beginner. Anyway, this guy knows what he's doing. His posts hop-scotched through servers all over the map." Trevor gestured to the server stack in the corner of the room. "This is the seventh one."

Gus followed Trevor's gaze to a metal rack with a tinted glass door. Inside were eight or ten computers stacked on shelves from floor to ceiling, their green and red lights blinking angrily.

"With each server, we don't know if it's the one or not, so we can't just follow the IP address and go in there and take it and potentially spook our suspect." Trevor continued, "We have to see what's on the server first and to access it we need to get a warrant which, as you know, takes time. When we get the warrant, we access the server remotely, look at the mail logs and identify the exact dates and times of the traffic, in this case the posts, to see who was logged onto the server during those times. Then as we rule those users out we also look for malware, remote access software, which leads us to another server in the chain. That entire process takes time." Trevor pointed his finger in the air and rotated it like a propeller. "So now repeat it over and over for each server in the string until you find the one."

"That's nutty," commented Vanessa. "So, how are you sure this is the last one?"

"This server points to a specific user." Trevor ran his hand over his goatee. "And, we've not found any malware or remote access software, so as we suspected, this looks like the server the various posts to that site, *The Meetinghouse*, originated from. We're going to take the server back to the lab to validate it."

"How about the sender? Do we know who that is yet?"

"We believe so, yes. We've identified all of the users that were on the system during the times when each post was sent. Our suspect has tried to mask that information by altering the creation and last modified dates on the files but we've been able to cut through all that. So, we then ruled out and removed anyone who wasn't online for all of them. Luckily, the first post sent—the one with the picture of the Idlewilde woman—was sent very late at night, so that helped narrow the list considerably. So, vetting all of that's left us with only one user who was on the system when all the posts were sent: a Jules Russell."

Vanessa looked to Gus and simply smiled.

Trevor gestured toward the tech in front of the computer. "I better get back."

Gus nodded and lightly bumped fists with him. "Thanks, brother."

As Trevor stepped away, the theme from the movie *Jaws* spilled from Gus's phone, alerting him to a new text message. He tilted his head in annoyance at Vanessa, and then, looking at its screen, confusion immediately spread across his face. He tapped the text app and a new thread opened with several phone numbers listed, one on top of the other, and an emoji of a yellow face with its finger in front of its mouth in a "shhh" gesture.

"There're no names, only numbers," said Gus. "Is this spam? None of these numbers are in my contacts."

"What the..." mumbled Jim. He pointed to the screen. "That's Maria's number."

Gus thumbed his way down past the emoji as Jim took his phone out and typed the sender's number into his contacts.

"I don't have the sender's number in my phone," said Jim, the panic rising in his voice.

"Fuck," bit Gus. "Another audio recording." Gus hit play and they each listened intently.

"You can't tell me you're not scared shitless," said a women's voice shakily, as if on the verge of crying.

"That's Lizzy," noted Jim.

"I didn't say I wasn't scared. I'm just saying don't freak out. Keep it together."

Jim tilted his head. "That's...Maria," he said, confused.

"Why shouldn't I be freaked out? Someone's definitely talked about that night," said Lizzy. "But, ya know, maybe it's about time Jules got what's coming to her." A long silence filled the audio before she continued, "Don't lie: You never wondered if *she* was lying? None of us saw what really happened."

"I don't know," said Maria with an edge to her voice. "I just don't know," she repeated quickly, her voice harder. "But you can't really believe Jules is responsible for Laur and Sarah?"

"Unless she's paranoid that one of us'll talk," choked Lizzy.

Then the audio ended. Gus pushed his phone toward Jim.

"Who else got this text?"

Jim tapped numbers into his contacts and read each of the names as he verified them.

"Mel...Lizzy...Laurie...Sarah...Jules."

"And Maria."

"And Maria," confirmed Jim.

Gus gestured toward the computer terminal. "If that really is Jules"—he then held up his phone—"and she got this too, Lizzy and Maria and maybe Mel could be in danger."

"I'll call around, make sure they're all safe," said Jim.

"And make sure you find Jules," insisted Gus, his voice steady with resolve.

Chapter Thirty-One

MEL STARTLED AWAKE.

It took her fuzzy brain a few seconds to remember she was no longer at Mr. T's but back in her own bedroom. She looked to the bedside clock and sighed when she saw it was 3:23, the witching hour. Jim Lincoln had woken her with a call around midnight, checking that she was safe. He directed her to the text she had on her phone from an unknown number and told her that he had already spoken with Maria, Lizzy, and Jules and that they each were safe. He remained on the phone with her while she verified her alarm system was on and house secure. But, given the hour, she knew when she ended the call with Jim she was in for another restless night.

The full moon steeped her bedroom in a warm golden glow as ribbons of light stretched across her floor and nightstand at odd angles. She blinked and rubbed her eyes with stiff fingers but they remained blurry. Moving her leg beneath the covers, she felt Fred's plump body snuggled along the outside of her thigh. She heard him snore and nudged him to stop.

Finding herself anxious all day, Mel had foregone dinner and, soothed by the warmth of her favorite long-sleeve shirt taken from the dryer, decided to go straight to bed. But each time she relaxed enough to drift toward sleep, images and whispers from her subconscious forced her awake.

She thought of Laur and how much she missed having her best friend in her life. She reflected on how Laur's life might've been better had things been different. She missed seeing Lis every day, but took comfort in how well she was doing. She thought of Mr. T and what he said to her and feared she was destined to be alone. Her thoughts then drifted, as they were apt to do during her 3:00 a.m. wake-ups, and settled on Gus and how she felt like a giddy teenager when he was around. She couldn't remember the last time she felt that way, and it both unnerved and excited her.

She rolled onto her side and faced the window. The frigid nighttime air starched the pillow and it stung her cheek. Fred stirred at the sudden absence of warmth but didn't wake. She glanced at the panel for the alarm system on the wall by her headboard and the neon blue letters told her it was still armed and secure. She pulled the thick down comforter up and tucked it beneath her shoulder then, rocking backward, her chin. Taking a deep breath, she lazily closed her eyes.

Forcing all thoughts from her mind, the comfortable nothingness enveloped Mel again. Her breathing slowed, her body stilled, and she flirted once again with sleep. But then she heard the faintest of sounds, stirring an awareness deep within her, and her eyes snapped open. She waited and listened and it took nearly a minute before she heard it again. Recognition was just out of reach, but she could tell it was coming from outside.

Mel carefully rolled the sheet and comforter to the side and slithered out of bed, taking her phone from her nightstand in the process. With her back to the wall, she moved stealthily through the shadows and came to settle beside her open window. She squatted so that the side of her face was pressed against the cold windowsill in its bottom corner and surveyed her backyard and the long meadow beyond sprawling to the wood line. She saw bushes and trees and clumps of shadows, but nothing unfamiliar and nothing that moved. Then from somewhere in the darkness Mel heard the sound again, but this time immediately recognized its familiar melody.

"The cow says mooooooo."

Pooling tears compromised her vision and a swell of heat engulfed her chest as images of a happy Laur pulling the string on her Fisher-Price See 'n Say toy popped in Mel's mind like the flashbulb of an antique camera. The toy's playful sound began to play over and over from somewhere deep within the woods but then became muted by a guttural moan that filled the room, one so foreign Mel questioned its source.

Her knees buckled and she slid down the wall, onto the floor. And as the chills ran up her spine, Mel realized that the toy's once-endearing, playful sound had forever turned her life's happiest memories rancid. Terrified, she swiped with shaking hands at the tears clouding her vision until the numbers on her phone were visible. Then she dialed the only person she knew would make her feel safe.

Gus answered on the first ring.

Chapter Thirty-Two

GUS MADE IT to Mel's house in nine minutes and was met by a frightened, skittish Mel at the door, Fred glued to her hip. She told him about the sound from the toy in the woods and how it had played nonstop, the same cow's moo, over and over until he pulled into her driveway. Gus secured the house, top to bottom, and searched her immediate yard, front and back, yet stopped short of entering the woods. Gus had seen enough since arriving in Kendalton to know two things with near certainty: Their suspect was thorough enough to anticipate Gus entering those woods so was likely long gone, and they clearly knew those woods a whole lot better than Gus ever would.

Gus didn't want to leave until he was sure Mel was comfortable, so the two of them now sat on a small wicker sofa on Mel's three-season porch, Fred sprawled out between them. It was nearly 5:00 a.m. and the sky glowed a brilliant light blue with diffused, predawn light. Mel's porch looked out to an old, dilapidated wooden gate on the edge of a small meadow surrounded by dense woods. They enjoyed the strong coffee she had made for a few moments, then Gus turned to her, pulling a knee up onto the sofa.

"How ya doing? You okay?"

Mel ran fingers through her hair, meeting Gus's look. "What if they're still out there? What if they're watching us right now?"

He saw traces of fear lingering around her eyes, and his mind spun for ways to make it go away. "They've got nothing to gain by sticking around. They did what they came here to do. They're gone." Gus thought a moment, his eyes back on the dense woods. "Do the Land Trust trails run back there?"

"Ya." She gestured with her coffee mug toward the side of the meadow. "One of the trails is about a hundred yards back that way."

Gus remembered what Mel said the other night. "Does that Annie woman have access to the GPS app of the trails she and Sarah Nelson were developing?"

"I think so. She just mentioned yesterday that she's thinking of finishing it."

"Check with her, will ya? I need to get a better sense of where they go."

They drew quiet for a time, each nursing their coffee. The meadow was beginning to glimmer as the sunrise quickly approached.

"It was scary that they were in the woods behind my house, for sure," breathed Mel, turning to Gus. "But, the creepiest part was what they were playing: The cow says moo. Of all the animals on that stupid toy, that was Laur's favorite." She held his eyes, looking for answers.

"Who would know that?"

"Well, me and Mr. T, obviously. And, her daughter,

Lis."

"How about the other women?"

Mel tick-tocked her head. "Maybe…"

"How about Jules?"

Her jaw tightened and Gus saw the desperation in her eyes. "Do you really think Jules or any of them could be responsible for all of this?"

Gus raised an eyebrow. "What you told us earlier was pretty compelling. If it's true and it really happened that way, each of those women has a lot to lose, including Jules."

They each grew quiet and Gus saw the pain lingering on her face. He wanted to make her feel better; he needed to.

"Remember when you said that Laurie wanted to do the right thing but was always dissuaded by the others from saying anything?" he asked. Mel met his eyes. "Well, she did," he continued. He lowered his head and his face relaxed. "She did do the right thing. The morning of her death she called 9-1-1 wanting to report a murder from decades ago. She got flustered and hung up before they could get any details, but she tried." He held Mel's gaze, looking for any sign of relief. "Just thought you should know."

Mel's eyes welled up and her chin began to tremble. But Gus knew these were not tears of sadness. He felt a swelling urge to comfort her, to hold her, but Vanessa's words rang in his head.

Be careful. She's in the thick of this.

He was about to put his hand on her shoulder and tell her he knew what it was like to feel loss when his attention was drawn to snapping sounds up beyond the gate. And when he looked he saw a deer galloping away along the edge of the meadow. He thought of Troy Robinson and his hunting that Jim had talked about, and then, like a flat stone flicked across a smooth pond, his mind skipped to Rebecca Munroe's pregnancy and to the page left for him out of Rebecca's journal suggesting that she and Jules were becoming friends until, finally, landing on Troy's military background.

"How well do you know Troy Robinson?"

"We don't hang around or anything but I've known him since we were kids. Why?"

"What can you tell me about him?"

"He's sort of a loner, but nice. Does a lot of hunting and fishing. I can't tell you how many times I've driven by his house and he's got a deer strung up in front of his garage bleeding out."

"Hunters." Gus shook his head. "I grew up hiking and camping a lot, so at one point I got certified in animal tracking. I'd help tourists and photographers who wanted to find animals in the wild and I'd also track game for hunters; it never ceased to amaze me what they'd do and think was normal." Gus felt some of the tension melt away and liked how good it felt. "This guy Troy and Jules dated back in high school, right?"

"Ya, for a couple of years."

"Do you ever remember him dating anyone else?"

"No." She kept her eyes on the meadow and sky. "You think Troy's involved in all this somehow?"

"Oh, I don't know. We're really looking at this from every angle." He took another long pull on his coffee, then reached out and touched her shoulder. When she turned to him he said, "Hey, we've been provided some information concerning the case from an anonymous person." He paused; their eyes locked. "You know anything about that?"

She shook her head and her eyes relaxed. "Nope."

"Any idea who it could be?"

She held his eyes. "Depends on what it is."

He shrugged it off, then looked back to the gate and meadow and Mel did the same. Gus recalled the young boy from the road race.

"I saw you at the race with that young boy with Down's syndrome."

She smiled. "Ya, it's kinda my thing. I'll be in a store or a restaurant and if there's a person with Down's syndrome anywhere around I'll inevitably get a hug. It's the coolest thing." She looked to her side at Gus and he saw a tenderness in her eyes, a vulnerability he hadn't seen before.

"Vanessa asked me the other night why I moved home from Australia. What I said was true; I was burned out and homesick. But that's not the whole story. Laur had been really struggling. Her mom had died a few years before and she and Kevin had finally decided to get a divorce. Mr. T was needing more care and she was nervous about that and her anxieties around the secret about Becca were back in full force. I could tell she was drinking more; she'd call me late at night her time three, four nights a week and we'd talk for hours." Mel tipped her head to the side and her mouth turned up slightly. "I just knew it was time to come home.

Laur needed support and it was time to take care of Mr. T the way he'd taken care of me when I needed it most."

"I totally get it," whispered Gus in return.

The sky had become so bright it looked as if it were electric, and they both watched as the sun breached the horizon.

"I love sunrises," she said softly, changing the subject. "When I lived in Sydney, it'd come up over the harbor and just wash over the bridge and opera house. It was incredible." Memories flooded her mind. "Laur turned me onto sunrises when we were kids. She and her mom would get up to watch them together, especially at the end."

"The sunrises in New Orleans are pretty amazing too," said Gus, his eyes on the meadow and tree line. "It lights up all the pastel blues and yellows and pinks of the buildings and terraces until they glow."

Mel's gaze was back on the sky. "I'll have to check it out sometime."

The two of them sat on Mel's porch for a long time watching the sun settle into its day, neither feeling the urge to interrupt the comfortable silence.

Chapter Thirty-Three

Stepping into Robinson's Hardware & Security had Gus feeling like Marty McFly as he blinked fifty years into the past. In this era of warehouse-sized, forklift-laden, supersized construction materials stores Robinson's was the exception. The store was about the size of the lobby at the Kendalton Inn and the décor, with its pegboard walls and speckled white linoleum flooring, reminded Gus of advertisements from his local paper when he was a kid.

But while the style of the store was 1970s retro, the inventory was clearly twenty-first century. Sure, there were aisles of paints and cleaners and row after row of nuts and bolts and a plethora of screws. And from the upper halves of the walls lining the store hung rakes and all sorts of small motorized leaf blowers and chainsaws. But the entire back wall was dedicated to some of the most sophisticated security and surveillance electronics available, some of which Gus recognized from the FBI toolkit. Gus's eyes wandered up and scanned the tops of the walls and ceiling, noting the telltale pinholes of surveillance cameras throughout the entire space. He and Vanessa made their way to a small checkout counter area in the middle with several employees milling around it; Gus estimated one for each aisle.

"Can I help you?" asked a young, plain-looking woman. Her baggy T-shirt with the store logo was knotted below her belt as if she was trying to hide her beauty, be one of the guys.

"Yes, is Mr. Robinson here?"

"Troy," hollered the woman. A thin man with long, gangly arms and wavy black hair appeared in the doorway behind her. His tanned skin stretched over skeletal features.

"Can I help you?" he asked as he leaned a shoulder against the doorframe. Troy Robinson was not a tall man—Gus guessed five-ten or so—or an imposing figure. But he moved with an agility that gave off an air of confidence. Troy Robinson wasn't the type of guy you'd want to meet in a dark alley.

Gus held out his badge. "Mr. Robinson, is there a place we can talk in private?"

Troy took a step back and motioned them to join him in the back room. Stepping past the former soldier, Gus noticed a glossy John Deere calendar pinned to the wall above a long set of desks pushed together. Apparently, September's beauty was a shiny green-and-yellow farm tractor the size of a lake house. Troy closed the door and leaned against the end desk, and Gus saw a poster-sized framed photo on the wall behind him. It was of an old barn, which Gus thought he'd seen somewhere in town, with a large American flag hanging on its sagging side. Its paddock was filled with horses of all sizes and colors grazing along vast lush fields. The early-morning dew sparkled on the fence posts like tiny fairy lights, the sky awash with streaks of purple and pink.

"Like it?" asked Troy, his voice clear, precise.

"It's incredible," remarked Gus as he leaned in to take a closer look. "You take it?"

"Yes. It's difficult to capture the sunrise at the exact moment when its light angles like that." Troy looked to Vanessa. "So, I take it this is what Jim's been leaving me messages about."

"We're investigating the recent murders in town," said Gus. "And your name's come up."

Troy instinctively leaned back, his chin angled toward his chest. "My name? How so?"

"How well did you know the victims: Laurie Turner and Sarah Nelson?"

"Well, we all grew up together and hung around as kids. I saw them less these days; really just occasionally at a gathering or town event."

"So, you weren't friends with them."

"Agent, in a town this small you're friends with everyone. But, did we see each other regularly? No."

"How about the other women in their friend group? Are you close with any of them?"

"Not especially, no. Like with Sarah and Laur, I see them around town but that's about it."

"We understand you and Jules Russell don't exactly get along," suggested Gus.

Troy paused, as if contemplating this for the first time. "No, not really. We're not enemies or anything; there's just a lot of history there." His voice was monotone, unemotional. Troy was either nervous or repeating what he'd rehearsed.

"By history, you mean you two dating in high school?"

Troy's eyes narrowed as he eyed Gus warily. "Yes, that, and about forty years of knowing each other. We're just very different people."

"Troy," interrupted Vanessa, "we understand you were in the army for twenty-plus years. A Green Beret, in the unit's security and special reconnaissance outfit."

"Yes, ma'am. Twenty-one years, Green Beret for nearly fifteen of 'em."

Gus looked from the line of computer monitors along the desks behind Troy to the row of server stacks on the adjacent wall similar to the one at the high school. If number of computers meant anything, Troy had multiples of the computing power of the entire Kendalton school system.

"What type of security do you specialize in these days?" asked Gus.

"We sell and install monitoring equipment and software, intrusion detection devices, video surveillance equipment, remote monitoring networks, audio and video communication systems. All the latest technology, really."

Vanessa pulled out her small notepad and flipped it open. "Can you tell us where you were the morning of Ms. Turner's death?"

"I was probably here but I'd have to check, ma'am. That was some time ago."

"How about this past Friday morning, when Sarah Nelson was attacked?"

"Friday was the first day of deer season. I took the day off, went hunting."

"Did anyone go with you?" probed Vanessa.

"No." He opened his palm to the ceiling. "I'm usually here seven to five, Monday through Saturday, so I get my fill of people. That was a day for just me and the woods."

"Did you stop anywhere along the way? Maybe for coffee or gas?"

"No need. The best hunting is the state forest—twenty, twenty-five minutes away."

"We'll need to verify where you were those mornings, so anything would be helpful."

"There was a forest ranger at the gate of the dirt lot. Maybe he'd remember me."

Vanessa jotted this all down in her notebook. "And last night?"

"Last night? I was home. Why?"

"All night?"

"Yes, ma'am."

"Were you with anyone? Can anyone vouch for your whereabouts?"

"I live alone. But I suspect you already knew that." Troy looked from Vanessa to Gus, his brow furrowed, his demeanor now guarded. "Agents, what's this all about?" he asked slowly.

The room fell quiet as Gus considered how best to proceed, leaving the faint whir of computer fans to fill the void.

"Troy, what can you tell us about Rebecca Munroe?"

"Becca? What…?" Confusion tugged his voice higher.

"We understand you two were dating at the time of her death."

Troy paused a moment before replying, "That's right. Who told you—Maury?"

"We also understand that you and Rebecca kept your relationship a secret and that you may have been dating Jules Russell, ah Marshall, at the same time."

"You're correct that Becca and I kept our relationship quiet. Her parents were very strict; she wasn't allowed to date. But as for Jules and me, I broke that off. I'd never do that to Becca." Troy's eyes narrowed. "Why are you asking about Becca? That was so long ago."

"Mr. Robinson, were you aware Rebecca was pregnant at the time of her death?"

Troy tilted his head slightly to the side. Gus watched as his jaw tightened, and he could almost see the tumblers in Troy's mind locking into place.

"No, sir, I wasn't. Was it…?"

Gus spared him the torture of saying the words aloud. "We can't be sure."

Gus let the uneasy silence slip into awkwardness and hang in the air as thick and heavy as a harbor's fog. Troy's body language had shifted and he no longer knew what to do with his hands, eventually clasping them in front of his midsection. Gus searched the man's steeled eyes, trying to get a read on his reaction, but only got a vacant stare in return. Had Troy known about Becca's pregnancy all along? Was this not a surprise? If Becca had told him he would've processed it decades ago, come to terms with his role in the chain of events that led to her death, and put this chapter of his life away in its own little box, sealing it up tight and stowing it somewhere deep in the annals of his mind. Troy's eyes roamed the room before settling on the photo hung on the wall.

"Agent, Becca and I were in love." He cracked a knowing smile. "I know what you're thinking: We were just kids. We were, absolutely. But it hit us both like lightning bolts. Agent, have you found your true soulmate, that one person you just know you're destined to be with?"

Gus's thoughts flashed to his former love, Rachel, and her puffy, red-lined eyes, when he told her he wasn't following her to New York like they had planned but, instead, remaining in New Orleans to pursue his music career. But, then he was in Mr. T's driveway, Mel's hips between his arms, the tender touch of her hands on his shoulders. Surprised, he blinked it away.

"No," he lied, "can't say that I have."

"Then you won't understand. It's something that can't really be put into words."

"Can you think of any other reason Rebecca would've committed suicide?"

"No," said Troy in a trancelike tone. "I've always wondered how I didn't see it coming."

Gus thought of what Mel had told them about that night but knew he couldn't tell Troy that maybe Becca hadn't committed suicide after all, however well that might've eased the man's pain. Gus's thoughts then went to the journal post left in his room.

"What was her relationship with Jules and the other women in that group? Did she hang around with them?

Were they friends, enemies?"

Troy swallowed and exhaled deeply. "No, Becca didn't hang around with any of them. Becca was nothing like them." Troy looked from the floor to Gus. "Agent, why all the questions about Becca?" His tone was low, protective. "What does she have to do with your investigation?"

"We have reason to believe Rebecca's death may be connected to the deaths of Laurie Turner and Sarah Nelson."

"How? Becca committed suicide," snapped Troy, the change in his voice, his cadence, obvious to everyone in the room. "Right?"

"Do you have any information about the recent murders, Mr. Robinson?" Gus pushed on.

"Nothing other than what I've seen on the news."

Gus's eyes were drawn back to the row of monitors and stacks of servers. The small room looked like command central in a war games movie. Everywhere Gus looked small green and red lights snapped at him through tinted glass. Gus waited for Troy's eyes to follow his.

"And you've seen the posts online? The threatening video of Mr. Turner and the one of Jules intoxicated?"

"Of course. Everyone in town's seen 'em."

"And you've had no involvement in either recording or posting those videos?"

Troy's eyes narrowed. "Of course not."

"Mr. Robinson, our suspect has demonstrated very sophisticated computer and surveillance skills." Gus held his eyes, the implication clear. Gus then chose his next words carefully so as to not divulge anything they might need later.

"And we've received sensitive information regarding Jules Russell through various channels… Are you the person sending us that information?"

"No, but if I was, you'd never know it."

"You yourself said that you and Jules don't get along."

"Very true. But, not getting along with someone and incriminating them in a murder investigation are two very different things."

"How would you feel about the FBI's computer forensics team taking a look at your computers and system?"

Troy raised an eyebrow. "Like my civil liberties were getting raped."

"We'd simply like to rule out your involvement, given your unique skill set."

Troy's mouth formed a thin line. "Do you have a warrant?" His tone was flat, all business.

"Do we need one?" Gus tried to smile casually but knew it fell short.

"Agent, I've spent the better part of my life fighting to protect the freedoms and liberties afforded citizens in this country. And the last time I checked the First Amendment was still in effect, so I'd say I've been fairly successful in that endeavor."

Troy then pushed off the desk and stood.

"It would help us enormously," tried Gus again.

Troy gestured toward the door. "If that's all, I really should get back."

Chapter Thirty-Four

"OKAY, GUYS, GET settled and hit your homework."

Maria Lincoln tossed her car keys onto the small hutch beside the front door and, punching in the code to reset the alarm, flipped its lid shut. Her three children shuffled along behind her like penguins as they silently paraded toward the kitchen. She pressed the play button on the home answering machine and listened to a message from one of her vice presidents of the PTA asking her another question about the upcoming fundraiser. She audibly grunted. Being a member of the PTA was hectic enough, but she was quickly regretting running for president. Her ego had clearly gotten the better of her. She spun her flat gold wedding band around her finger, wondering whether to call her back, before deciding it could wait. She had more pressing matters to attend to.

Decorative crystals beside the answering machine refracted the midday light, splashing tiny rainbows onto the floor beside Maria's feet. She was reminded of a poem she had read that suggested these were our loved ones who had passed telling us they were okay. She dismissed the thought with a shake of her head and marched down the hall. She passed the stairs and a variety of photos hanging on the Vshaped wall along the way, following the thumps of backpacks being dropped onto the kitchen table. She dropped the plastic bag of arts and crafts supplies for Patrick's school project they had spent the last hour shopping for onto one of the chairs and looked around.

Her sixteen-year-old daughter, Cheryl, was getting a tall glass of water from the tap. Maria noticed the cuts and bruises dotting her muscular legs and imperceptibly shook her head. Cheryl had not only gotten her dad's athletic genes but had also inherited his tenacity and competitive streak. She simply never gave up and, as a result, was usually the scrappiest on any team she joined. Her love, however, was soccer, but she hadn't been allowed to play in today's game. Instead, Cheryl and her friends—Sarah's daughter Jessica, Lizzy's daughter Terry, and Jules's daughter Milly—had bullied a girl in their class and, being repeat offenders, had been suspended from school for three days. So, Maria, Cheryl, and the others had spent the last school period with the principal.

"You guys hear what I said?" asked Maria, irritated.

Maria's younger daughter, Pam, was sitting at the kitchen table, and Maria watched as she silently put down her phone, opened her computer, and pulled her books from her backpack.

"We heard you, Mom," said Cheryl to the faucet, her voice rich with annoyance. Cheryl was in that stage where she and Maria were constantly at odds, convinced she knew more than her mother on all topics, and Maria found herself giving Cheryl a wide berth these days. She knew eleventh grade was a stressful year for teenagers. Academics got much harder—if they were doing it right, which in Maria's world was her way—and the stress of beginning the college search impinged on everything they did. Maria just wished Cheryl would focus a bit more on her studies and less on her friends and the social activities at school.

Maria stepped beside the teenager. "Watch the tone."

Cheryl glanced sideways and Maria saw the disdain in her daughter's eyes. Maria leaned in.

"Cheryl, what were you all thinking?" The teenager didn't say a word but just glared at her mother. "You guys have to stop… Do you know how lucky you are to only be suspended for a few days? This is your third offense. Heck, if Jules hadn't spoken with the principal last year when you posted that stuff online about that young girl you would've been suspended for two weeks, banned from all sports for the year, and not allowed to any after-school activities. *At all.* That's school policy. So, for you to only get a three-day suspension for this, your third time? You should be thanking your lucky stars. And Ms. Jules. But it has to end."

When Cheryl refused to say anything or even look at Maria, Maria shook her head, turned, and walked away. She looked around the tidy kitchen, then into the adjoining dining room.

"Where's Pat?"

"I think he went down to the playroom to play video games," said Pammy, pushing her glasses back up the bridge of her petite nose as she flipped open her organic chemistry book. She pulled a leg beneath her and began to highlight the page and Maria smiled. Pammy was definitely cut from her cloth, right down to the way she tapped her pen against her cheek when she was concentrating. And even though she was only a freshman she was taking advanced classes and already poking around on college websites.

Maria stepped to the open cellar door and looked down into the dim light below. The thin blue carpet running down the stairs was matted in the center and the railing was worn in spots along the top. A few years ago Jim had framed out a small portion of the then-unfinished basement and, calling in some favors, had electricity put in and walls put up to create a small finished playroom for the kids. Its light brown door at the bottom of the stairs was open a few inches, so she called down to Patrick.

"Pat?" She waited for an answer but, as expected, got none. She could picture her eleven-year-old with his large headphones on, stabbing away with his thumbs at the video game controller as he shot and killed zombies and other creatures on the flat-screen TV.

"Cheryl, can you get your brother up here and make sure he does his homework?"

Maria didn't wait for the verbal acknowledgment she knew wouldn't come. She headed back down the hall toward the stairs, passing the small room off the dining room they had turned into a home office on her way. Her eye caught the large ledger sitting beside her computer, reminding her of the quarterly accounting statements she owed one of the small businesses she did bookkeeping for. Between that and Patrick's school project, Maria knew it was going to be another late night, but first she needed to get into some sweats.

She double-stepped it up the stairs and hurried around the corner toward the master bedroom at the end of the hall. She glanced in Patrick's bedroom on her way by and was surprised to see him on the floor on all fours, his butt facing her as he reached for something beneath his bed. Maria stopped short.

"Pat, I thought you were in the basement." Maria leaned on the doorjamb and watched as he stretched his arm farther. She heard a low, feral moan come from beneath the bed.

"What're you doing?"

"I'm trying to get Einstein out from under the bed," he said into the carpet, referring to their tabby cat. "He's acting weird."

"Well, don't freak him out any more. He'll come out when he's ready."

She continued down the hall to her bedroom and, once inside, leaned against the bed and kicked off her flat-soled shoes. She scurried into the master bath and the cool ceramic tiles tickled her bare feet. As she stood in front of the mirror and ran her fingers through her short hair, somewhere deep within her an alarm sounded and she froze.

It took Maria a few seconds before she realized she could smell the delicate aroma of her favorite perfume in the air. But she and Jim barely went out alone anymore; she hadn't worn that in forever. She slowly stepped over to the vanity and makeup mirror and noticed, unlike each of the other makeup products lined perfectly straight in a row, its tiny glass bottle was slightly askew. Her heart pounded in her chest and she looked around the rest of the bathroom but nothing else seemed out of place. She stepped hesitantly back into the doorway to the bedroom.

The windows were closed and locked and the curtains hung by their sides. Both her dresser and Jim's were neat, their drawers closed, just like she'd left them. The door to the walk-in closet was shut and Jim's uniform hung from its handle, still in its plastic sleeve from the dry cleaners. She scanned the floor from the hallway door, around the foot of the bed, to where she now stood but saw no impressions in the thick carpet that weren't put there by her own movements moments before. The bedside tables were neat and orderly, the alarm clock perched in its usual spot, and the bed was tidily made, its throw pillows carefully placed across the top in their usual sequence. Then her eye was drawn to something she couldn't quite make out. She crouched slightly and then leaned side to side, trying to get the angle of the late afternoon light from the windows to rest on the comforter just right. And that's when she saw it.

On Maria's side of the bed was a slight indentation that began in one of the throw pillows and continued down the length of the bed. And before she knew it, Maria Lincoln was sprinting down the hallway, screaming for her kids to get out of the house.

Chapter Thirty-Five

MARIA'S FRANTIC CALL to Jim resulted in Gus and Vanessa and a flurry of cruisers with flashing lights descending upon the Lincolns' house. The first thing they found was Maria and her three children sitting in their car at the foot of the driveway, motor running, doors locked. A thorough search of the house discovered nothing missing, but Gus had Vanessa get forensics there to dust for prints nonetheless. He, along with nearly everyone in town, had seen the gloved hand push open Mr. T's bedroom door in the video posted by Awkward7, so he wasn't optimistic they'd find any prints, but they had to try. "Nothing ventured" and all that.

He and Vanessa now stood around inside the police station's only interview room, and Gus's mind was spinning. When Jim called around to the women last night after they got the text from the burner phone with the recording of Maria and Lizzy talking of their suspicions about Jules, he arranged for Jules to come to the station to speak with them again. So, when she didn't show, Gus had the chief put out a BOLO on her and her black Range Rover. And he had been pacing ever since. He looked to his phone again; it was 4:35. His afternoon had crawled by like an Italian opera.

"Jesus, it's been three hours. How can we not have found Jules Russell yet? There can't be that many places she would be in this town."

"One would think," replied Vanessa, distracted, as she swung in and out of the conversation. She pressed her ear tighter to the phone as she listened to what the Cybercrimes agent was saying on the call.

They had confirmed alibis for about half of the people at the fundraiser and were aggressively pursuing the others, and Gus knew that'd be done soon. The trace of the Awkward7 posts to Jules's user account at the high school was curious, as was the audio recording with Lizzy and Maria panicking that Jules had started some sort of paranoid survival killing spree. Had he misjudged Jules? Did she have it in her after all or was someone trying to frame her? In Gus's mind, the volume of evidence against Jules was mounting significantly. If someone was trying to frame her they were going to extreme lengths to do so, and he generally subscribed to the keep-it-simple-stupid rule for criminals. The need to confront Jules with all they had learned roiled within him.

Gus reflected on their interview with Troy Robinson. Each of the women had in one way or another been watched or had their homes invaded easily by someone. Gus wanted a warrant for Troy's computers but, after discussing it with Jeff, they agreed they didn't have enough evidence yet for one. But Gus wasn't a big believer in coincidences, so they'd start with nailing down Troy's alibis and see where that led them.

But he wondered who else could have Rebecca's old

journal, and why did they provide Gus with that page connecting her and Jules? Troy was the most likely candidate. Had he learned of Jules's secret, figured out it had to do with Rebecca's death, and set out on a revenge spree that he was setting Jules up for? If it wasn't him, then who was it? Could one of the other women in the Posse have gotten ahold of it somehow and, knowing Jules's secret, was now using it to direct them to her? Or what about Rebecca's best friend—Maury? Vanessa was right: She might have the easiest time getting possession of the journal. Could Maury have the journal and be involved? Regardless of who had it, they needed to find out who was pointing them to Jules, why the murders, and why now after all these years. Gus's head was swimming with questions when Vanessa ended her call.

"They traced the number that text was sent from; it's a burner all right. But they were able to clean up the audio from that video of Jules drunk at the party," she said, her voice crackling with excitement. She spun her phone around in her open palm. "What she said to Maria was, and I quote, 'Jesus, Lincoln, stop trying to hide your crazy.'"

Gus's brain wrinkled. "Why does that sound familiar?"

"Because it's the same phrase from that Awkward7 post with the night-vision video of Mr. T sleeping: 'C'mon, people, wake up. It's time we *stopped trying to hide our crazy*.'"

Gus felt another puzzle piece slide into place. "Nice."

"It gets better. The fuzzy logo in the reflection off the chrome toaster in that Mr. T video? It's for an ultramarathon group, North American Adventures. They're in Tewksbury, like forty minutes from here."

"What the hell's an ultramarathon?"

Vanessa laughed. "I asked the same thing. They said it's a marathon on steroids. They're either done by time or distance. The distance ones are usually either fifty or a hundred miles."

Gus's face contorted. "People *run* that?"

"Ya, and all at once. Apparently, they're all the rage. Anyway, you can't buy their apparel. The only way you can get it is to compete in *and finish* one of their events."

"That can't be a long list."

"I feel ya. Also, the lab finished with the old journal page. They dated it to be of about the same age as Rebecca's journal would be; seems legit. They also pulled two fingerprints off it. One was a match to the fingerprints taken from Rebecca Munroe during her autopsy."

Gus nodded; he had known immediately the page was from Rebecca Munroe's journal. "They match the other print?"

"Nada."

"Push 'em on that. That could be our best lead yet."

"Already did." Vanessa gestured toward the door. "C'mon, we need to hit that ultramarathon place. We should be able to get there and back and still speak with Jules today."

"Hang tight," said Gus. "Mel texted. She's on her way here with that Annie woman to go over the GPS app they were making of the trails."

Vanessa tilted her head. "Mel texted, huh?"

"Drop it, V."

Her eyebrow quirked up. "You might want to check yourself on that. You and I both know when it comes to you and dating it's been a minute."

Chapter Thirty-Six

BY THE TIME Annie and Mel got to the station Jim had returned from his home to join them. He cleared off his desk to make room for the maps and plot plans of the Land Trust Annie Elkins brought with her. Having been purchased in numerous transactions over decades, piecing together individual parcels that showed all of the Land Trust land was like assembling an elaborate puzzle with key pieces missing. Jim took a large area map of Kendalton off the wall in the interview room and laid it on one side of his desk, beside the collection of individual, letter-sized documents from Annie. The two of them were assessing each of the smaller pages and then fitting them onto the larger map along common edges and taping them in place. The result resembled something out of a Rorschach test. Satisfied they captured all of the land with trails, they stood and backed away, allowing the others to get a look.

"This covers almost all of Kendalton," remarked Gus as he leaned closer. The late-afternoon light created spots of sun on the glossy maps.

"Nineteen hundred and forty-three acres to be exact," said Annie. She wore a tight, form-fitting Under Armour workout shirt that highlighted firm, muscular shoulders and flat abs. "It's easier to see it first spread out like this to get a sense of the scope and scale of it."

"Nutty," breathed Vanessa.

"So, Mel, where's your house?" asked Gus.

Mel leaned over and turned the map slightly, then pointed. "Here."

Gus considered that for a moment as he took in the entire collage of plot plans, partial maps, and drawings. But he found that no matter how hard he tried he couldn't get his bearings.

"Okay, so where are the entrances?"

"Well, there are three official entrances." Annie reached down, her forearm tight and corded. She stabbed a weathered finger on the map. "Here, here, and…here."

"But there are dozens of other ways to enter the trails," added Jim.

"Oh, for sure," agreed Annie. "When I'd be walking them to map 'em out I'd constantly see people just stepping from their backyards onto a trail or right off the street in some areas."

"Yikes," said Gus, taken aback. "I mean, I get it, small town and people have been using these woods forever. But it's not like there are houses in the middle of it." He gestured to the map.

Annie looked up at him. "I think you're thinking about these woods as one consolidated area," she suggested. "It's not Central Park, it's woven in and around houses all throughout town. There are spots where you can see a house on either side of you that you could throw a rock to. And other parts where you'd swear you were in the middle of the wilderness."

Annie looked back to the map, her eyes roving over it before she pointed to another spot. "Over in this area it threads right along a few streets, right by houses…" She tapped spots along a line. "Right along here, for instance, is where the town garage is… This is the mayor's house… Jules's house is right around here…and this stretch goes right along Pleasant Street."

She looked to one of the computers. "Jim, can you get me on this so I can go online?"

Jim leaned over and typed in his password as Annie pulled out the chair and sat. Annie pulled a well-worn piece of paper from her pocket and unfolded it.

"Sarah wrote me out instructions so I could get to the current version of the site on my laptop. It's still a work in progress. It's not public yet."

She held down the Windows key, then awkwardly pressed the letter *R* and a small dialogue box popped up. She looked back to the paper, then in the program prompt space typed *cmd* and pressed enter. The screen blinked and then turned a solid yellow. There were three lines of text on the screen, the last one with a simple C:\>. Annie had gone to the system's root directory.

Looking back and forth from the paper to the keyboard she typed in a string of letters and characters and, once verifying she'd typed it correctly, hesitantly pressed the Enter button. A colorful picture of the Kendalton Town Hall filled the screen, the old maple and oak trees surrounding it in full bloom. Across the top of the website were several menu options.

"This is the site"—she referred to the paper again—"for the current version and the app Sarah and I were making of the trails." She turned and, with a smile, said over her shoulder, "You folks are the first to see it." Then she turned back. "It's not done yet, but it has most of the trails in it."

She clicked a menu option and the page filled with a map of Kendalton in color. In its center was the downtown area with its buildings, shops, and The Commons. Surrounding this were houses, farms, and other structures throughout town, and the streets had their names written down their centers. Checking the paper again, Annie clicked another option and the screen dissolved into a white depiction of the same map, but the houses and other structures not contained in the Land Trust were removed, simplifying the map considerably. Streets remained and a thick line highlighted the perimeter of the Land Trust and thin black lines ran throughout, depicting its trails.

"There it is." She put the paper on the desk beside the keyboard as the others leaned in.

"Whoa, legit," remarked Vanessa.

"Soooo…" Annie pointed to the screen. "Here are the entrances. And here's Mel's house. But I know of other places people enter here, here, here…" She pointed to over a dozen other spots.

Gus leaned closer until he was beside Annie and the crisp smell of fresh air filled his senses. She pointed to the upper right corner of the area. It was completely devoid of lines, a blank white space like those maps of upper Maine or northern Canada along its ice shelf.

"This area hasn't yet been mapped out, but there are lots of trails there."

The hippocampus area of Gus's brain sizzled as long-dormant memories of his tracking days flooded his mind. He immediately began to view the map differently, more like an animal. Or a hunter. He saw the lines demarking the trails as highways, allowing the coverage of long distances quickly. He knew these highways connected to runs, small, lesser-traveled offshoots that led to feeding areas, as well as sleeping areas known as beds. He knew he needed to get out there, see and smell and feel these places for himself. He was kicking himself for not doing it sooner. There was a time when a younger Gus could track anything, anywhere, and he knew he needed to haul those skills out of storage and dust them off.

"This is fantastic, exactly what I needed."

"Oh, I'm so glad," said Annie, catching Mel's eye. "Sarah was a whiz."

"Can you print this out?" asked Gus as he stood straight.

Annie also stood. "Agent, let me see your phone."

Gus unlocked his phone, then handed it to her. Annie turned the paper over and, after reading it for a moment, launched the phone's browser. Referring to the URL string on Jim's machine, she carefully tapped it out on the phone. Gus saw a white progress line appear on his screen and work its way to its end. Then, after following a few more commands from the paper, Annie held the phone up to show him a white app with the boxy black letters *LTT*.

"Congratulations, Agent, you're now our beta test guinea pig. You should be able to navigate the trails pretty well now with this."

Annie loaded the app on Jim's phone as Gus moved the map around on his with the tip of his finger. "This is great. Thank you."

Annie's eyes shined with pride as she slid the paper into her pocket. "Absolutely. And please, Agent, let me know if I can be of any other help."

Gus played with the app on his phone while Jim pointed out where Sarah Nelson's house was, where Laurie Turner's body was found, and where Mel's house was. Then, seeing all he could from a phone screen, Gus swiped the app closed and looked to Jim.

"What d'ya say? Wanna hit the trails?"

Jim paused. "Normally I'd jump at the chance but"—his eyes flicked toward the bullpen—"I really should get home. The kids are pretty freaked out."

Gus tipped his head, then looked to Vanessa. Her face contorted and she leaned away. "Don't look at me."

"I'd show you, Agent," offered Annie, "but I've got a foundation meeting. I could take you tomorrow."

Mel raised an eyebrow. "Looks like you're stuck with me."

"Oh, Mel, I couldn't..."

She held up a hand to stop him. "Will I be safe?"

"As safe as you'll ever be," said Jim matter-of-factly.

"I don't know the trails as well as others but I'm up for

trying."

And as Gus and Mel headed out of the station, he glanced back at Vanessa only to see her hunch her shoulders and hold two thumbs up in return.

Chapter Thirty-Seven

GUS WAS EAGER to see and experience the Land Trust trails for himself, to be surrounded by nature and the serenity that it offered. But he was also excited to spend more time with Mel, yet equally uncomfortable with that realization. Gus hadn't felt this way in so long it made him uneasy. Mel was incredibly attractive, but a lot of women were beautiful. Mel was different. It was as if she didn't know she was beautiful, as if her beauty came later in life so she'd experienced life through the eyes of someone less attractive, someone who learned being a good person was more important.

Mel rubbed her lower back as they crossed the dirt parking area toward the opening to the trails. "That's some ride you've got there." She glanced back at the Land Rover sticking too far out of its parking spot. "You bring her home from the war?"

Gus laughed. "It was my grandmother's. She used it on her farm, and when I'd go there as a kid she'd let me drive it around in the fields."

"So, she was the cool grandma."

"Oh, I idolized her."

They made their way into the trails and followed the

black-and-white app toward Mel's house for about twenty minutes. Gus felt good hiking again, being back in nature, the feeling of uneven terrain beneath his feet. The thick woods were steeped with relaxing sounds and above them the darkening, sapphire-blue sky. This feeling was everything to Gus: to be immersed in fresh air, to see nothing but nature, not a single manmade object. This was Gus's comfort food.

"You get any sleep after I left this morning?"

"Nah, once I'm up, I'm up."

Gus fell into the cadence of his boots clomping along the path and, catching a glimpse of the late afternoon sun through the trees, thought of Mel's comment about sunrises in Sydney.

"How'd you like living in Australia? I've never been."

"Australia was awesome and the people are so great. None of that pretentiousness you see here. You'd regularly see CEOs socializing with blue-collar workers. Really down to earth. If I hadn't been missing Laur and Mr. T so much I'd probably still be there."

They walked on in silence for another minute or so, each taking in their surroundings, before Mel changed the subject. "Jim says you're a crazy good jazz musician. Apparently, your partner's been bragging about you."

"Well, the musician part, yes," said Gus, distracted. "Crazy good? Don't believe everything you hear."

"He said you've played with some pros and have been on tour and stuff."

The wide trail they were on snaked around stumps and rocks before dropping off over a slight incline. Gus noticed a small clearing beneath a cluster of spruce trees, their soft, droopy branches creating a natural dwelling, like nature's little hut. When he was a kid those were the areas he and his brother Jake would make into forts. He could feel the soft needles beneath him and the pitch that stuck to his fingers and Toughskins as they sat and planned their next mission.

"Played," said Gus, finally. Mel looked at him, a question in her brilliant, dark brown eyes. "I've played with them in the past." He faced forward as they continued walking. "Being a jazz player isn't like being a rock star. You're basically an independent contractor. So, yes, I've played with some really talented people, but it's not like we have a band. There's no guarantee I'll play with them again. There are a lot of bassists they can call for their next gig or next tour." He smiled and raised an eyebrow. "Don't get me wrong, I love it. It's just that it's not as glamourous as it sounds."

"Sounds pretty glamourous to me. He said you just got off a tour with the Preservation Hall Jazz Band. I'd never heard of them so looked 'em up." Eyes wide. "That's pretty cool."

"It really wasn't a big deal. The trumpet player and I went to Loyola together. He asked me to go on tour with them." Gus chuckled at the memories. "It was a lot of driving and fast food."

"I haven't listened to jazz in years. When Laur and I were in high school Mr. T would have it on in the background so it sort of just created this vibe in the house." Mel's eyes were bright, happy, as fond memories flooded her thoughts.

Gus glanced at her knowingly. "Jazz has a way of doing

that. You should check it out again. There are some really great artists these days."

Mel met his eyes. "I will. Maybe I'll even take in a show. I hear there's some great talent out of New Orleans these days on the cusp of breaking through."

They stepped over an exposed root and onto a large rock on the side of the trail. Gus wiped his brow, and the lower front section of his shirt was dark with sweat.

"How do you find the time to be an FBI agent *and* a professional jazz player?"

Gus thought of Jeff Cattagio and how he sold Gus on joining the FBI all those years ago.

"The FBI and I have…an arrangement." He grinned wryly. "It's sort of a work release type of program." He looked from the trail ahead to the app on his phone and noticed the tiny red *x* in the top corner of his screen. "Chief was right; there's no cell service out here."

They had hiked nearly two miles by the estimate in Gus's head and the trails followed the lines on the app perfectly. He heard the rustling of birds overhead and looked down the winding trail snaking away from them until it was eventually swallowed by the forest. Out of his peripheral vision he saw Mel take a pull on her water bottle before pointing to the woods to their side.

"My house should be through there somewhere."

"Let's check it out." Gus used his foot to move the branch of a large weeping tree aside, exposing a small, almost unrecognizable path leading away from their trail. He immediately recognized the shimmering silver light flashing on some of the trees and thought of his mother. She called this special glitter of early morning or late afternoon light off of water “sparkle water.”

He led them down the narrow path and seemingly out of nowhere the woods thinned, and through branches to their right Gus saw a small swamp. Its surface was covered in spots with dusty yellow pollen and patches of lily pads floated throughout. Near one side was a cluster of cat-o’-nine-tails, their brown corndog-like tips bending over. As if imprinted in Gus from childhood, he immediately searched the water’s smooth surface for the familiar bumps of frog and turtle heads. Something caught his attention and he trudged off the path, then knelt in some tall switchgrass.

“What is it?” asked Mel, stepping closer.

“A lay.” Gus looked around. “Makes perfect sense. The water’s right there and they can make a quick escape if they need to through the meadow.”

“A lay?”

“Sorry. Animals create beds, places they return to each night and sleep. But they also create what is called a lay—places they rest less frequently during the day. They’re usually found near feeding grounds or watering holes. This is definitely one.”

“Interesting, but how’d you see it? It just looks like grass to me.”

“I noticed some shine on the switchgrass. Its faint, but it’s there. It starts there on the edge of the path where we were standing and goes in this way.”

“Shine?”

"Ya, shine's the type of track left behind when grass or vegetation is flattened. There's no real print per se, but you can see a sort of path worn through, in this case, the tall grass. The sun reflects off the flattened surface to brighten it as compared to the untouched vegetation. You need the right light but when you see it, it really stands out."

He stood, leaned next to Mel, and pointed. She followed his outstretched finger. "See that tamped-down grass and the bent-over twigs along the edge of the meadow over there? That's a run. That's how animals get from the water and their lays back into the woods."

"Ah, okay," she replied hesitantly.

Sensing Mel's uncertainty, Gus faced her with his hands in front of him as if he were showing her how wide something was. "Think of these woods as a city, with trails being the well-worn paths animals use to cover long distances, like a highway. Runs connect these highways to eating areas, watering holes, things like that. They have much less traffic on them and are used less frequently, sort of like a side road. Every animal in here has a bed for nighttime and many have lays for resting during the day. It's all connected."

Mel looked at Gus with bewilderment in her eyes and a raised eyebrow. "A city, huh?"

He smiled. "Exciting stuff."

Gus took in their surroundings once more. The app didn't have the small path they took to get here, let alone any of this. From this spot he could make out slivers of the back of Mel's house. He recognized the back door and, beside it, the shiny new replacement window. Gus now fully appreciated their current vantage point. On three sides of them was nothing but dense forest. You didn't just stumble into this spot, you had to weave your way through the labyrinth of trails they'd just trekked. Something manmade and red flapped in the breeze at eye level through the trees, catching his attention.

"What's that?" he muttered, causing Mel to turn and look also. They made their way through a cluster of trees and over a large log until they came to a pine grove. Bright green ferns dotted the tiny space and, dangling from a pointy, sharp branch was a clear evidence bag, the kind Gus had used a thousand times. It had large, bright red lettering across it and sealed inside was a single sheet of letter-sized paper. He looked down at the mossy clearing they were standing in and saw a series of footprints in front of them that obviously weren't his or Mel's.

"Don't come any closer. We've got footprints here," he said over his shoulder. "We need to get this area taped off and get the CSI guys out here."

Gus then turned and looked over his shoulder and realized that from where he was standing he had a clear, unobstructed view to the back of Mel's house. And, as he began to think of all the ways someone could use this vantage point to stalk and terrorize Mel, the pine tree beside him exploded into pieces, and shards of wood sprayed the side of his head and face.

And as Gus instinctively turned and tackled Mel to the ground, another bullet seared across the side of his head.

Chapter Thirty-Eight

GUS SAT ON the large fallen tree he and Mel had hunkered behind when the shooting started, their necks firmly pressed against its wet, rotted bark, their feet outstretched into the dirt like soldiers in a foxhole. Mel had immediately texted 9-1-1 before tending to Gus's wounds as best she could, so the scene was now crawling with officers and the FBI's CSI team. Mel was looked at by the EMTs and, having given a statement, was now back at her house, likely watching the activities from the comfort of her living room. Other than a large hit of adrenaline and a twinge of PTSD she'd gotten from having to text 9-1-1 again from these woods so soon after Laur's murder she came away unscathed.

Gus, however, had an EMT attending to his bleeding ear and the pulpy line of exposed scalp along the side of his head. He winced as the young woman finished putting drops of liquid stitches along his scalp and began to apply antiseptic ointment to the side of his face.

"How ya doin', Rambo?" asked Vanessa as she leaned in to take a closer look at the side of his head. She had been on her way back to Kendalton from getting the participants list from the ultramarathon company so made it to the scene just after the EMTs.

He winced again. "I'm good. Just pissed."

Gus had been shot once before, a hunting accident as a kid, and the vivid memory of every second, every sensation was still with him. He was leading his brother Jake across a stream when Jake slipped on a rock and fell. His rifle hit the rocks in the creek bed and fired, sending a bullet into Gus's abdomen just below his lowest rib. The bullet ricocheted off several ribs before exiting below his arm on the opposite side. And, although it caused significant internal damage, Gus remembered feeling no pain at all. Instead, he felt enormous pressure, as if he were being crushed, his vision became blurry, and all he heard were metallic-like sounds. Only later, during rehab, did he come to understand that the bullet entered his body with such force that the tissue surrounding its path died and the shockwave cracked several of his ribs, as well as giving him a concussion.

But this was nothing like that prior gunshot wound. Where that was all-encompassing, crushing pressure, this was searing pain, surgical in its precision.

"Me too," quipped Vanessa. "I leave you for an hour and you go and get yourself shot." She noticed the evidence baggie he held in one hand. "Prizes?"

Gus held it up between them. Written across its front was *FBI Man* in bright red sharpie. Inside was a letter-sized piece of copy paper with elaborate cursive handwriting on it. There were smudged lines across it from a copier and its edges were darker than the middle.

Dear Journal,

Tonight the girls invited me to a party and it was great. James was there and was being kind of a jerk (I think we're done) so I went upstairs and it was just me and Jules. She was pretty drunk so we talked forever about a ton of things—boys, clothes, makeup tricks. She thinks I'd look good with long hair. Then she asked me if I've ever gotten high. When I said no, she pulled out a joint and asked if I'd like to try it with her. I'm sure she could tell I was nervous but like she said: everything's okay in moderation. It was weird at first but she said it gets better the more you do it. She said it's great to do before school—makes the day fly by. She's so cool!!

Until next time,

—B

"No date, but it's definitely from Rebecca's journal," observed Vanessa.

"Agreed," said Gus. "But why's this one a copy?"

"Dunno. In case the bag leaked?"

Gus scanned it again. "I'm betting we know who 'the girls' are that invited her to a party."

"Ya, but who's James? I thought Rebecca didn't have any boyfriends before Troy."

Gus didn't answer; he didn't have to. Neither of them knew anyone in town, especially anyone in town twenty-five years ago. Jim had arrived and was with a few officers as they watched the CSI team work the roped-off area, so Gus waved him over and showed him the baggie.

"Any idea who this James is?"

"James…? There was a Jim Harrington in school but he was an upperclassman. There's no way they were a thing. There was Jimmy Pennington in our class, but no one ever called him James." Jim thought for another few moments. "I'll think on it but I don't know."

"Anyone ever call *you* James?" asked Vanessa.

Jim's eyebrows arched up and he seemed taken aback. He smirked and slowly shook his head. "No one but my priest and only at my confirmation." Jim looked from Vanessa to Gus and then back. "I've always been Jim. Ask anyone."

The EMT dabbed at Gus's scalp and he bit down at the pain before looking to Vanessa. "You get that runner's list?"

"Yep. There's over a thousand names on it but no Jules Russell or her maiden name, Jules Marshall. I sent it to Boston for the names to be run through the system, see if we get any hits."

Gus's head was throbbing so the EMT offered him Percocet, which he refused before taking three Tylenol and slipping his leather jacket back on.

"We were obviously set up." He tipped his chin up toward the tree and the red flag hanging in the spot where the baggie was found. "That might as well have been a target."

"Question is: Who knew you were coming out here?" Vanessa asked.

"Just the five of us at the station, right?"

"So you, me, Jim and Mel and her friend Annie. Mel or Annie?" she offered with skepticism. "That sounds janky."

"I radioed the other officers where you were going," said

Jim hesitantly. "In case anything happened." Seeing Gus's reaction he continued, "Sorry, Gus. I knew I'd be out of pocket for a while."

Gus thought of Troy Robinson and of all the high-tech equipment he had at his disposal, and Gus knew something as basic as a police scanner had to be in his arsenal. Gus's eyes swung back to a clearing far off in the distance on the top of a small hill that he had sent the CSI team to. A large rock formation protruded from a cluster of scraggly bushes like a nose from a bearded face. It had deposits of mica throughout that sparkled and shimmered in the low-hanging sun. Gus had replayed the events in his mind as best he could, trying to capture key seconds in neat, still frames. And, in doing so, recalled that he heard the whine of the bullet pass his head just a second or so before he heard the gunshot so knew it had been fired from a pretty good distance. Looking at this clearing, Gus guessed it was about four or five hundred yards away, the type of distance it'd take a bullet to beat the sound of gunfire. It was on higher ground, which gave it a view of the entire area and, more importantly, had a clear line of sight to the spot where he stood.

Gus took a deep breath before looking to Jim. "How're Maria and the kids doing?"

"Pretty shaken up. I spoke with our security company and confirmed that our alarm system was accessed remotely and turned off for an hour and eleven minutes at 2:32 this afternoon."

Over Jim's shoulder Gus noticed two CSI team members

making their way toward them, returning from the hilltop. One of them handed Gus a small, sealed evidence baggie with two long bullet casings inside. Gus held the baggie up to the fading sun to get a better look.

"That a six millimeter?" asked Jim.

"Nah, it's too big," said Gus, distracted. "You got a lot of deer hunters around here?"

"Sure, guys've been hunting these woods for generations. Why?"

Gus twirled one of the casings slowly around in front of their eyes. "This is a two fifty-seven Bob. Popular in the forties and fifties until Remington made the six-millimeter round in the mid-fifties. We saw these a lot growing up with the older guys." The scar on Gus's lower side throbbed with reminiscence. "My brother inherited my grandfather's old rifle and used these."

The last time Gus had seen a two fifty-seven Bob was in the jar beside his hospital bed when he awoke from surgery all those years ago, a present from Jake. In Gus's experience, it was the bullet of choice of the prior generation. The same guys who still liked the old bolt-action rifles for hunting. But their suspect didn't seem to have any traits of an older man; just the opposite. They were a whiz with computers, handy with cameras and video equipment, and adept and agile enough to make it into people's homes without them knowing. Those weren't typically the traits of the older generation, especially one that prospered in a time of typewriters and rotary phones.

"Jules Russell doesn't hunt, does she?" asked Gus skeptically.

Jim scowled. "Jules?" He shook his head with confidence. "No way."

Gus pondered the casings for another moment. "Troy Robinson's father a hunter?"

"Yes, sir, president of the sportsmen's club."

"We need to find Troy, now. Find out where he was this afternoon."

Jim's radio squawked. "Chief, Anderson here. We're at the opening of the Russells' driveway and we've got eyes on Jules. Please advise."

Jim grabbed the mic from his shoulder as he and Gus exchanged a look. "John, approach with caution, then take her into custody and meet us at the station."

"Roger that."

Gus stood for the first time in nearly an hour and steadied himself. He looked up at the pink smear across the early-evening sky, then to the west past Mel's house. He gazed for a moment into the dense forest and thought of tree forts and playing cowboys and Indians in the woods as a kid and of the crackling sounds of rifles echoing off distant mountain ranges.

Chapter Thirty-Nine

"MRS. RUSSELL, A few things have come up during our investigation we'd like to clarify."

Gus sat across from Jules at the small table in the station's interview room. Jim to his right, Vanessa to his left, her pen spinning quickly back and forth across her hand. The two of them had clustered close to him, as if trying to define distinct sides to the round table. It was dark outside and a fine mist playfully flickered around the decorative lampposts along Main Street, creating tiny, fuzzy halos. The faint rhythmic hum of cars passing by competed with the throbbing in Gus's head. The wound on his ear pulsed sorely but the pain of the seared line along his scalp burned.

"This better be important, after the way I was dragged in here."

Jules's face had touches of that rosy flush from being in the brisk New England air, and Gus noted her hair had that blanched smell of snow. She scratched her elbow through her runner's jacket and Gus picked up a change in her demeanor. The confident woman with the swagger at the soccer fields was gone and in her place sat an uncertain, anxious woman. He pulled the laptop from his leather bag and played the audio recording left in his room two days before.

The clanking and bustling sounds of a party filled the air. They heard Jules telling Sarah to shut up, Sarah retorting, then Jules threatening Sarah with the possibility of her husband and kids learning of her affair with George. Then Sarah's measured voice spilled from the speakers.

"We each have our secrets, Jules. The difference is: Mine won't land me in jail."

Gus tapped the stop button. "It seems Sarah thought you had a fairly important secret you wouldn't want divulged. Could you tell us what that is?"

Jules twisted her mouth dismissively. "That?" she scoffed. "God, Sarah was extremely judgmental of everyone's life but her own, hypocritical one. I'm sure you've heard from at least someone that I've got a tendency, from time to time, to get caught up in the festivities and have one too many drinks." She shrugged. "Anyway, Jim here—and his predecessor—have helped me out of a few…difficult driving situations. Sarah thought it was only a matter of time before I killed someone, if I hadn't already."

"So, let me get this straight," began Gus slowly, skeptically. "The secret Sarah's referring to is that you could, someday, kill someone while driving drunk?"

"No, that I already *have* but that it was a hit-and-run somewhere." She raised an eyebrow. "Did I mention that Sarah was also a conspiracy theorist?"

Gus stole a glance at Vanessa and got a skeptical look in return.

"It seems to us that the tone of Sarah's voice suggests something more specific."

"I don't know what to say. It's not."

"What about the recording we all got on that text?" interrupted Vanessa. She tapped Gus's phone and Lizzy Porter's terrified voice rose up from its tiny speaker, pleading with Maria Lincoln.

"Don't lie: You never wondered if *she* was lying? None of us saw what really happened."

"I don't know," lamented Maria. "I just don't know. But you can't really believe Jules is responsible for Laur and Sarah?"

"Unless she's paranoid that one of us'll talk."

Vanessa's head tilted. "That sounds like they're frightened of something very specific."

"Damn if I know," said Jules, glancing at the table in a way that suggested she did. "Lizzy's always been a drama queen. The things she spins up in her head sometimes are baffling."

Gus's mind flashed to the memorial card of Rebecca Munroe left beneath Sarah Nelson's armband, the card that initially tied their entire investigation to the decades-old suicide. He slid a copy of the page from Rebecca Munroe's journal into the middle of the table for Jules to see.

She leaned over it. "What's this?"

"That's a page from Rebecca Munroe's journal. It's an entry she made six weeks before her death, which clearly states you and she were becoming friends, or at least your invitation to do so."

Jules studied the page for several moments before sliding it back. "I have no idea what Becca was referring to there.

Did we both work at Eddie's Ice Cream? Yes. But so too did a lot of other kids; that place was a revolving door for high school kids. And was I nice to her? Sure, but no nicer than I was to others who worked there. But, did I ever suggest we become friends?" Her mouth twisted again and she shook her head slowly. "No," she said, pity in her voice. "My guess is that's some wishful thinking on Becca's part."

Gus leaned back onto the table. "Mrs. Russell, we now know that Rebecca and Troy Robinson were in a relationship around the time you two were a couple."

"Troy and Becca? Are you sure?"

"Hundred percent," replied Vanessa.

"Are you saying you never knew of them being together?" asked Gus.

Jules jutted her lower lip out and shook her head. "No, never."

Gus leaned an elbow on the table, glancing at Jim in the process. He didn't want Jim to find out his wife, Maria, was implicated in these events this way but found he had no choice. Jules was tougher at getting a confession from than he'd anticipated.

"Mrs. Russell, we know you and some of your friends—Laurie, Sarah, Maria and Lizzy—were with Becca the night she died." Gus felt Jim turn toward him but ignored it and continued. "And we know that Becca's death was not a suicide. What we don't know is: Was it an accident or murder? This is your chance to get in front of this."

Jules held his gaze. "Agent, I don't know what you're talking about. Becca and we were in very different crowds."

She leaned toward him. "We did not hang around together."

Exasperated, Vanessa then played Laurie Turner's call to 9-1-1 the morning of her murder.

"I want to report a murder."

"When and where was this murder committed?" a stranger's voice asked.

"It was committed decades ago but I'd rather not say where right now."

Gus had Vanessa stop the audio. "So, I'm sure you can see, Mrs. Russell, how we've come to believe that you had something to do with Rebecca Munroe's death. Sarah's suggestion of a significant secret you have, Maria and Lizzy fearful of you and speculating about your involvement in Sarah's and Laurie's deaths, Laurie's 9-1-1 call about a murder decades ago and the fact that you and the others were with Becca the night she died."

Eyes squinted, Jules considered this for a moment. "I can see how someone could infer meaning into random suppositions and disparate half statements. But your conclusion is wrong."

"We know you and the others were with Becca the night she died," hollered Vanessa, exasperated. "Jules, this is it. The end of the road."

Jules turned to her. "I don't know who told you that, but I'd question their motives if I were you. And, if it's true, where's your proof?"

Frustrated, Gus sat back. He knew what Jules was suggesting, and she wasn't wrong: They had nothing concrete against her. He decided to take a different tack.

"Mrs. Russell, where were you this afternoon?"

"Like I told John at my house, I was on a run," answered Jules, her confidence returning. "I've got a race in four weeks and today was my long day so I went twenty miles."

"Where did you run?"

She looked to Jim, like a foreigner to a translator. "I went down High Street to Depot, then onto Oak, then I took Hollis and looped around on the other side of the conservation area and came back onto High Street on the upper end, then straight home. It's twenty point one miles."

Jim gave Gus a slight nod, as if approving of her route.

"Did anyone see you running? Anyone outside or any passing cars you recognized?"

"Agent, that's all farmland out there. There's probably seven people who live in that twenty-thousand-acre area. And no one drives out there. That's why I run that route; it's remote and quiet."

Again, Jim tipped his head in agreement.

Vanessa leaned onto the table. "Have you ever run in an ultramarathon?"

"Not yet, why?"

"Our technical team has traced the posts to *The Meetinghouse* site from this Awkward7—our suspect—to your email account at the high school," said Gus, shifting topics.

"Okay," Jules replied, indifferent.

"You don't seem surprised by that."

"I wouldn't say I'm surprised or not surprised. I mean, my account has clearly been hacked. But I can't imagine the high school's security is anywhere near top notch."

"So you don't know how those posts got sent from your account."

Jules recoiled and her eyes widened. "Of course not. Agent, I am the farthest thing from a computer whiz. I barely know how to turn the damn thing on."

"So, you didn't post those messages to *The Meetinghouse*."

"No." Her voice was firm, emphatic.

"You attended a fundraiser at your husband's work this past summer—is that correct?"

"I organized it," she corrected with disdain, and Gus heard the old Jules in her tone.

"And we understand you weren't able to participate in the cruise later in the evening."

She paused. "That's correct."

"We met with your husband yesterday. It appears a very lethal toxin is missing from the institute's inventory and we believe it was used in the murder of Sarah Nelson. Did you remove that toxin from the institute's inventory?"

Jules tilted her head and, as if for the first time truly considering the implications being made, sat back. "Wait, you *actually* think I had something to do with Laurie's and Sarah's murders."

Vanessa noticed Jules was somewhat distracted by her spinning pen so spun it faster. "We've not been able to verify your alibis for either morning."

"This is insane." She turned to Jim. "They can't be serious." She leaned in, making sure she held his eyes. "Jim, it's me...Jules."

For the first time Gus saw fear in Jules Russell. "Mrs. Russell," he interrupted, stealing her attention back. "Do you own a rifle?"

Jules's head snapped toward him and she scoffed, "No."

"So, you don't go hunting," followed up Vanessa in a natural one-two cadence.

"I don't even know how to *use* a gun."

Gus gestured to his wounds and the bandage on his ear. "So, you weren't in the Land Trust trails this afternoon and you didn't fire at me and Ms. Idlewilde."

"Jesus, no!" She looked to Jim, opened her mouth to say something, then, hesitating, turned back to Gus and with a furrowed brow asked, "You were out on the trails with Mel?"

"Mrs. Russell," volleyed Gus, trying to maintain a rhythm, "were you in the woods outside Ms. Idlewilde's house late last night?"

Jules's eyes stayed on Gus, as if staring him down. Then she smiled. "That explains where you got that crazy tale of us being with Becca the night she died." She squinted. "What's Mel now? Your little helper?" She paused a moment, then added, "It's convenient her little fairy tale doesn't have her there with us."

"Please, answer the question."

"No, I was not outside Mel's house last night. Why would I be?" Gus remained silent. He watched Jules try to regain her composure and noticed one of her hands begin to tremble. She shook her head in disbelief. "You can't possibly think I had anything to do with the murders of two of my closest friends." Her voice cracked. "I mean, why would I *ever* do something like that?"

Gus no longer felt compelled to answer and the room remained quiet. Jules took several deep breaths, her eyes trained on the three of them, surveying them. And as the moments passed, Gus could see her confidence slowly reemerge. It was in her posture, her eyes, the way her shoulders straightened. She met Gus's eyes and held fast, asking if that's all they had. Gus knew they were close; he could feel it. The evidence was rapidly stacking up against her, but that last piece was still elusive, like trying to grasp smoke. And, he knew he couldn't prove Jules or the others were with Becca the night she died or that Jules had a role in any of this, not yet. And there was also Troy Robinson to consider. Was he involved and, if so, how? Was he framing Jules? Had he too figured out that she was somehow involved in Rebecca's death and was seeking vengeance?

"Mrs. Russell, if you had nothing to do with Laurie Turner's or Sarah Nelson's deaths can you think of anyone who would want us to believe you did?"

Jules leaned on the table. "Agent, I'm sure you've heard: There are a lot of people that, let's just say, may be envious of me for what I have or who I am. Now, we all know, some people want to tear successful people down to lift themselves up." She bit down on her lip. "It could be any number of people but, last I checked, you're the investigator." She slid the sleeve of her Gore-Tex jacket up her forearm, exposing a black plastic fitness watch.

"I should really be getting home. Is there anything else?"

"No, nothing else for now." Gus exhaled. "But we'll likely want to speak with you again."

Jules stood, sliding the chair back with her thighs but said nothing.

Vanessa stood also. "Once we talk with Lizzy and Maria again, that is."

And as Gus stood he thought he saw Jules flinch at the mention of the other women. But before he could be sure, she was stepping from the interview room, heading toward the large glass door and the freedom that awaited her beyond.

Chapter Forty

Maria Lincoln was scurrying around the stovetop, trying to get some semblance of a dinner on the table before it got too late. As much as Maria didn't want to admit it to herself, Lizzy wasn't the only one struggling to keep it together. Her mind whirred with the day's events, spewing all sorts of gruesome thoughts around in her head. When she learned that Mel and the FBI agent had gotten shot at in the woods she nearly collapsed in a heap. How far could they let this go?

She numbly stirred the wooden spoon around in the pan, longing for things to go back to normal, back to the way they were, when the most stressful thing in her life was her kids' sports tryouts. But she knew that was impossible now. Too much had happened. The disappointment on Jim's face when she told him of the night Becca died was seared into her brain and it crushed her.

Maria and Jim weren't like the others; she didn't bitch about him to the girls and he didn't complain about her to the guys. They were best friends; they didn't keep secrets from each other. At least that's what Jim had thought, until recently. Now, he knew Maria had kept a secret from him since the beginning, since the time when the bedrock of their life together was formed. A secret so horrible she knew he would never look at her the same. And the worst part was the secret he thought she had kept was nothing compared to the real one she still held.

Her hand fell to her thigh and she felt the near-empty soft pack of cigarettes in her pocket. She desperately needed a cigarette, needed a few minutes to just be alone and think things through. Lost in her anxieties, she dumped the crushed tomatoes for the spaghetti sauce into the pot a little too quickly and they washed over the side like a storm surge breaching a dike.

"Ah, shoot!" She grabbed a rag and began to wipe off the burner as the sauce popped and singed, sending a sour burnt smell into the air.

"You okay?" asked Officer Rich Burrows, looking up from the dining room table.

"Ya, Rich, I'm good. Just spilled the sauce a bit."

Rich stood and went to the counter that separated the two rooms like a border wall. He pulled out a stool and plopped on its padded brown seat, its joints creaking in protest.

"Maria, relax. I'm right here with you and Colin's outside in the cruiser. And, remember, Jim already changed the security code." He shook his head. "No one's getting in this house again."

"I know, I know." Her eyes flicked to Patrick, who was watching her closely, hanging on every word. She forced a smile as her brain clicked through the day's events like a slideshow: her oldest daughter, Cheryl, and her friends getting suspended for bullying again, her home being invaded and the message that was intended to send her, and Mel and the agent getting shot at.

"I'm fine," she lied. "It's just been a hectic day, that's all." She casually stirred spices into the sauce. "And I've got some books to close tonight." She gestured toward her home office.

Her phone vibrated on the counter beside the stove and, when she saw it was Jules, her mouth went dry. She waved the phone casually in the air.

"Speaking of work." She turned to go. "I'll take this in my office. Be right back."

Maria walked briskly into the small room off the hallway and closed the door behind her. Pressed firmly against the opposite wall, just out of reach of the door, sat a light wooden desk. Neatly organized atop it was a chocolate-brown leather desk pad, a thick, well-worn laptop, and an old white printing calculator, its keys worn pale from years of use.

"Hey," she said softly. A scratchy, windswept noise filled her ear. "Where've you been?"

"I've been at the station for the past hour and a half. Being interviewed by the FBI and your dickwad husband," bitched Jules.

Maria took a breath to suppress her fear. The line crackled, and as she waited she wondered what Jules was thinking, what she knew versus just suspected. She breathed in and out deliberately, like a swimmer before a race. She did not want to be in Jules's sights anymore, she thought, than Jules wanted to be in hers. But that recording of her and Lizzy was disastrous and she knew it. Jules was too smart, too cunning, to ignore what they all heard: Lizzy and Maria always had their suspicions about her, and now with the FBI nosing around they were cracking under the pressure.

"I've been trying to reach you all afternoon, though. Where were you?" pressed Maria, changing the subject.

"I was on my long run. When I got back there was a cruiser waiting for me in my driveway. They just brought me home now."

Maria looked at the clock on her desk and it read 7:55 p.m. The line filled with the loud swishing of wind. Maria waited for it to die down.

"Jim said the FBI has Becca's journal," she said, trying not to panic.

"I know, or at least a page from it," replied Jules.

"They said it suggested you and Becca were going to start hanging around."

"I blew it off as wishful thinking on Becca's part. But that's not the worst part. Mel's told them about us being with Becca that night, and they know about fucken' Turner calling 9-1-1 the morning she died."

A burning wave swelled in Maria's chest. Images of Becca lying on the dirt trail, her hair soaked with blood, popped in Maria's mind and her heart began to race. Her thoughts then turned to the night of Laurie's death, when she and Jim huddled together like criminals in the dark of their garage, scrolling through the call log on Laurie's cell phone, seeing her final call was a two-minute conversation with 9-1-1. Her watching the sunrise, alone, having stayed up all night praying for forgiveness.

"Oh dear Lord."

"Listen, I called bullshit on what Mel told them. I said it was convenient that in her story Mel wasn't even there that night. And they have no proof and it's been twenty-five years so they're not going to find any."

"But what about Laur's 9-1-1 call?"

"They played the recording of it… She called to report a murder from decades ago."

Maria slumped back against the desk, knocking the mug filled with pens over in the process. Officially, Laurie Turner's cell phone was missing and Jim was never able to request details of that conversation without raising red flags, so they never knew what Laurie had said in those two minutes. Until now. The fire in Maria's chest was spreading and she could feel the slimy film of sweat in her palm against the phone.

"Oh, God, help us," she breathed. "Jules, that's two things. They have to know."

"Well, hold on a second. First, about that night: As long as you, me, and Lizzy stick to our story we'll be fine. Remember, it's our word against theirs. The 'their' now just happens to be Mel. And, as for Laur's 9-1-1 call, it was vague, very vague."

"But, what else could she be referring to?"

"I don't know. But neither does the FBI nor anyone else for that matter, right?" Jules paused, the implication hanging in the air. "And Laur's not around to explain herself so…"

Maria bridled her breathing, steadied her voice. "Okay…okay. What else did they say?"

Jules told her about the posts from Awkward7 being traced to her email account at the high school and of the recording of her and Sarah arguing about a past secret and that the FBI had determined that secret to be about Becca's death.

"They know!" quivered Maria. "They definitely know, Jules."

"They're grasping," replied Jules with confidence. "But, anyway, we've got a bigger problem. Someone's feeding them information. Information only a few of us know about." Maria felt the accusation through the phone but remained silent. "And if it's not you or me it has to be Lizzy or Mel."

"Ya," said Maria, overcoming her concerns at the whiff of a scapegoat.

"Mel posted that video of me. And, she seems all too keen to help out the FBI; not only did she tell them about the night with Becca, she walked that agent guy through the trails today. But, if she's done all that, why wouldn't she just give them this other info—the recording of me and Sarah, the page from Becca's journal, all the other stuff—instead of sending it anonymously? No, this feels more like something Lizzy'd do; not confront me directly but, instead, go behind my back."

"I can find out," said Maria, trying to stay in Jules's good graces.

"Nah, don't worry about it. I've got this."

"*We've* got this," corrected Maria. "We're in this together," she said, reassuringly.

"Never doubted it," quipped Jules. "Where are you anyway…? Home?"

Maria heard the rustling of leaves through the phone and the faint snap of a tree branch. The hair went up on the back of her neck and her breathing hitched. "Ya," she said softly. She separated the white metal blinds on her window and looked out into the black night. She scanned the shadows and woods, imagining movements where there were none. "Why? Where are you?"

"Thanks to everything going on I'm now the newest resident of the Ashby Sheraton."

"You okay?"

Maria could hear Jules exhale deeply. "I'll figure it out. But, anyway, you should watch it. It's not safe to talk in our houses. That tape of me and Sarah was recorded in her house."

Maria hunched her shoulders and, with wide eyes, looked around her tiny office. "Oh my gosh, you're right." Concern gripped her. "What if all our houses are bugged?" she whispered.

"Exactly. How 'bout I come by and get you and we go for a drink?"

Goose bumps erupted up Maria's spine. She and Jules had a very symbiotic relationship when it came to this situation. They both had husbands, kids, lives they cherished dearly; they each had as much to lose as the other. But, more importantly, it was both of them who had continually swayed the others throughout the years to hold the line, to honor the vow they each made that night. Maria knew that the day may come when their interests diverged, when only the smarter one would prevail. She feared that day was here.

"I'd love to, but I've got dinner on and a ton of work to do." Maria's mind was spinning, trying to think of how she could plausibly not see Jules. "Hey, something else happened. Someone was in our house this afternoon while we weren't home."

The line crackled and hissed for a brief moment before Jules asked, "How'd you know?"

Gotcha. Maria told Jules about Einstein their cat acting weirdly when they got home, of the depression on her bed, and of the smell of perfume in her master bathroom.

"Jesus." Jules sighed. "It seems like whoever's doing all this can get to any of us, anywhere, anytime." Her voice was emotionless, an automated greeting telling you to speak after the tone.

Maria's brain whirred. "Good thing the FBI's here with us."

A beat.

"Good thing. A rain check on the drink then." Jules paused and the light sound of wind filled the line before she said, "You know, from the sounds of that tape things are really beginning to unravel. If one didn't know better, they'd think there was trouble afoot."

Maria separated the blinds with her fingers again and her eyes scanned the darkness outside once more. "Ah, don't worry about Lizzy. I'll handle it," she said into the cold window.

"Lizzy…right. Ya know, I'm not really feelin' that's working anymore. Why don't you put your efforts into plying info from Jim so we know what the FBI knows." Jules's steely voice sliced through the scratchy storm of the line. "I'll handle Lizzy."

The line then went dead.

Maria pressed her forehead against the frigid window as her mind replayed every word and nuance from their conversation. Still wondering if she had held her own, she straightened and stepped from her office, and as she walked down the short hall toward the kitchen she felt Jules's breath on the back of her neck the entire way.

Chapter Forty-One

THE CYBERCRIMES GROUP asked Vanessa and Gus to make a trip into Boston to see something else they identified from the Mr. T video on a large, wall-mounted screen with high resolution. Using the known dimensions of Mr. T's sitting room, kitchen, and the half-wall separating the two, and an enlargement of the image of the suspect from the chrome toaster, they were able to triangulate the height of their suspect to be between five foot seven and five foot ten. And, using this same footage, they calculated their suspect's average foot speed at one point four-one meters per second. Knowing the average foot speed of adult males and females at varying ages, they were then able to determine their suspect was either an adult male between thirty-five and forty-nine years of age or an adult female between thirty-nine and forty-nine years of age.

This combination of height and age allowed them to rule out an additional eight people from the attendee list of the fundraiser at the oceanographic institute. So that, combined with the tally of other attendees who had confirmed alibis for the mornings of Laurie's and Sarah's deaths, resulted in their suspect pool shrinking to Jules Russell, Troy Robinson, and three other guests from that event they were still chasing down.

As Gus and Vanessa were wrapping up with the techs, Jeff Cattagio leaned into the doorway of the lab and asked them to join him in one of the conference rooms. They followed Jeff back to a private room beside his oversized corner office where there were two men already sitting around its glossy wooden table. One was facing the doorway, the other the windows, and as they entered, the man facing them looked up.

"Hey, Gus. Vanessa."

"Hey, TJ," they replied in unison. Thomas Jefferson, or TJ to anyone that knew him, was a short, rotund man as wide as he was tall. He had been an agent for nearly two decades, beginning his career in Kansas City—Missouri, not Kansas, as TJ would often clarify as if the Missouri office was somehow larger and more prestigious than its sister satellite office in Kansas. He transferred to Boston about eight years ago after a human trafficking case he initiated led to nearly fifty arrests and gained national attention.

The other man at the table, with his back to the door, dwarfed TJ in both height and width, as well as overall physical stature, and when he stood and turned Gus immediately recognized the state trooper from Sarah Nelson's crime scene.

"Trooper Morrow," said Gus with a tip of his head.

Mike Morrow shook Gus's hand, then turned his attention to Vanessa and, with a smile that curled his neatly trimmed mustache upward and softened his entire chiseled face, he shook hers.

"Agent Lambert. Nice to see you again, ma'am."

They each took a seat at the table. In its center was a black laptop open and facing the trooper. Jeff looked to Mike. "Mike, you wanna go through what you just showed me?"

The trooper leaned forward and rested his meaty forearms on the table. "We've been working a string of robberies that started in Connecticut and have moved through Mass. Petty stuff, really, but someone got shot at one of the scenes so it hit our radar. It's the same suspect and same MO across about a dozen hits." Mike ran his finger over the touchpad on the laptop and its screen came to life. "So, we were reviewing security camera footage from one of the places hit this past winter again to see if we missed anything back then and came across this."

He tapped the touchpad a few times, then spun his laptop sideways so everyone could see. A black-and-white video of a small parking lot full of cars filled the screen. In its upper right corner was a sign for Alice's Diner.

"This is a diner in Ashby on March fourth," he said.

"That's the day of Laurie Turner's death," pointed out Vanessa.

"That's right. Now, this camera's mounted just above the entrance."

They watched as two women stepped out of the diner and began walking toward a few cars parked beneath the signpost. One of the women was noticeably taller than the other and had shoulder-length dark hair and a three-quarter-length heavy coat on. The shorter woman wore a thin, waist-length coat that hung just over the top of khakis. The taller woman pulled what appeared to be keys from her coat pocket, then stopped and turned to the other woman.

"That's Laurie Turner," said Gus, recognizing her from her case file. Then the shorter woman turned also and Gus recognized her immediately. "That's—"

"Maria Lincoln, yes," finished Mike. "I recognized her from the Nelson scene."

Maria and Laurie spoke for a minute or so and by the body language it appeared they were arguing. Then when Laurie turned to leave Maria grabbed her arm, stopping Laurie in her tracks. Laurie's head snapped around to Maria as she tried to tug her arm free. They could see Laurie yelling until finally she broke free and quickly shuffle-walked to her car, leaving Maria standing alone in the middle of the parking lot. Laurie frantically unlocked her car, got in, and quickly shut the door. Mike tapped the touchpad and the video paused.

"That was straight-up sus, right?" said Vanessa.

"You said it." Mike raised an eyebrow. "But it gets better." He tapped away. "This is the security camera overlooking the back lot, less than twenty seconds later."

They watched as a small, distant Maria Lincoln hurriedly walked from the side of the building, wove her way through several rows of cars until finally getting into the passenger seat of a car backed into a spot at the far end of the lot. The driver had their visor down and the car was too far away for Gus to make out who it was, only that they too wore a jacket. Maria and this other person talked for a few moments before this conversation too appeared to become heated. Hands were waved and fingers pointed and finally the driver slapped their hands onto the steering wheel and, keeping them there, leaned forward and rested their forehead between them.

"Do we know who that is?" asked Gus, leaning closer and squinting at the screen.

"Hold on…one…second." The trooper's finger hovered over the touchpad. After a few more seconds the driver raised their head, but before they leaned back against the seat he tapped the pause button. Then with a few swipes of his finger the camera zoomed in on the windshield and Gus immediately recognized the short haircut and small ears of Jim Lincoln behind the steering wheel. Working this case was like grasping at mist.

"That hits differently," said Vanessa.

Gus tipped his chin toward the computer. "What's the time stamp on this?"

The trooper's eyes widened. "That's the best"—he shrugged—"or worst part. This was at 8:14 a.m., and if I remember correctly, Turner's time of death was around nine thirty."

"Nine forty-six," corrected Gus.

Gus's mind ground through Chief Lincoln's involvement in the investigation. He thought of how Jim was convinced neither the break-in at Jules's house or her car getting keyed a few months back were committed by anyone other than Jules. And of how he'd been so enthusiastic lately that Jules was the suspect, even leading them to believe she ran almost exclusively on the Land Trust trails when Gus keyed in on them, only to be corrected by Jules herself.

"Have you looked into these two?" asked Jeff.

Gus looked to Vanessa. "They were each other's alibi for the Turner murder, right?"

Vanessa confirmed silently. Gus stared at the paused video, but his mind was picturing the image of the frozen figure caught in the reflection of Mr. T's toaster, clad entirely in black. Their suspect was about the same height as Jim but too thin to be him. But could it be Maria? His thoughts walked back over the various leads and clues, like fingers atop an open filing cabinet. His eyes flicked around the table, to the laptop, then to Vanessa.

"Jim's been pretty enthusiastic about Jules Russell being our suspect lately but he hasn't really fed us anything directly, right?"

"It doesn't matter," argued Jeff. He gestured toward the computer. "He withheld that he and his wife were with the victim an hour and a half before her murder. How do you know either one or both of them aren't our suspect? And, even if they're not, this video's enough for at least a search warrant, if not an arrest warrant for obstruction. He's a police chief, for Chrissakes."

Vanessa turned to Gus and he saw concern in her eyes. She immediately grabbed Gus's rucksack and began to rummage through it.

"What're you looking for?"

"He..." She pulled out a few sheets of paper stapled together. She looked at Gus. "Remember when we met with him that morning at the station about Rebecca Munroe's suicide?" She held the papers up. "He handed me hard copies of Laurie Turner's cell phone records."

"That's right." Gus looked to Mike. "He said he'd gotten them already when you guys first looked at the Turner case."

"But we always get them straight from the phone company for chain-of-custody reasons," continued Vanessa. She scanned the first page, then the others, before looking back up. She arched a thin red eyebrow. "The 9-1-1 call Turner made the morning of her murder isn't on his list."

"Boom," said the trooper.

Jeff slapped the table. "I'll get the arrest warrant going. We'll have it in an hour."

Gus looked to his phone and saw it was past eleven o'clock. "Okay," he said. "Get the warrant but we take 'em first thing in the morning. I want the team bright-eyed and fresh for the search, not rushing so they can get back home to bed."

Jeff left the room and a moment later they all heard him speaking tersely into his phone. Gus began a mental list of things that needed to be redone and looked to Vanessa. "What else did Jim give us? He didn't have control of either scene; Nelson's was ours."

"It was the state's crime lab team for Turner's," added Mike. "But, he *was* first on the scene. He had the area roped off and he and his guys were waiting for us when we got there."

"So we have to assume the Turner scene was compromised." Gus looked to Vanessa. "We need to go back through everything: photos, evidence gathered, witness statements. But, other than that, we've had lead on all of the other evidence since then, right? The tox screens, autopsies, the computer hacking, everything."

"That's right," confirmed Vanessa.

"He didn't lead the interviews with the women; we did."

"That's right."

"And he wasn't with Jules's husband, Shane, when the missing toxin was discovered, we were."

"That's right."

Gus nodded slowly, his confidence in the integrity of the investigation rising. "And he wasn't with us when we interviewed Troy Robinson," he continued, on a roll now.

"Or, with us when you got shot at in the woods," dropped Vanessa.

Gus's hand went to the bandage on his right ear. "Ya, there's that."

Chapter Forty-Two

"MAMA?"

He toddled into the bedroom—all two and a half years of him—clad in blue, fuzzy feetie jammies. He looked like a character out of *Peter Pan*.

The room was dark. The windows allowed the dim outside light to cast the eerie shadows of predawn onto the dressers and walls. The bed was messy, empty. He made his way quickly toward the small master bath, with the *pat-pat-pat* of feet that don't yet have years of wear and confidence beneath them. The bathroom was windowless and much darker than the bedroom.

"Mama?"

She was not there.

He wobbled back into the bedroom and his small heart quickened in his little chest. His sleepy eyes felt wet; he rubbed them with chubby hands. Mama was always here when he got up. He knew not to wake her if it was too early. If he did he'd have to go back into his own room until it was an okay time to go downstairs. That happened a lot.

"Mama?" he called again, his voice rising.

He wiped snots from his nose onto the sleeve of his jammies. Maybe she was downstairs having her Mama-time. She liked to close her eyes and do her special breathing. It helped her empty out her head. She'd told him just that. She said that when he learned to sit still like a big boy he could sit with her while she did her special breathing, but not right now because she could sit still for really, really long.

The room was getting a little lighter, he thought. Maybe they could have some dippy eggs. He loved to dip his toast in the sunny, yellow part of his eggs. And maybe Mama could make bacon. His tummy grumbled.

He climbed up onto the bed and snuggled beneath the thick, heavy down comforter. The soft sheets were still warm and the pillow smelled of Mama's hair. Soon his eyes were heavy and he struggled to keep them open.

Downstairs, in the porous grays and blacks of early morning, Lizzy Porter lay facedown, paralyzed on her living room floor. A lithe, wiry body sat atop her dressed completely in black. The room was brightening, with shards of sunrise coming in through the bay window. The intruder leaned over and whispered in Lizzy's ear.

"You said you'd say something but we both know you never did." Lizzy smelled the rancid stench of polluted breath. "I hope you rot in hell, Porter, for what you stood by and watched happen."

Lizzy felt hot breath on her temple followed by a soft, lingering kiss on the side of her mouth. Then the intruder stood and a high-pitched, singsong voice filled the air.

"Niiicooo."

Lizzy heard the familiar *pat-pat-pat* of tiny feet and, as the blackness took her, she heard one final sound that told her she was already in hell.

"WhaaAaat?"

Chapter Forty-Three

GUS AND VANESSA and a van of FBI agents rolled up to the Lincolns' house at 8:00 a.m. sharp. While en route, Vanessa received confirmation from Boston that everyone on the attendee list for the fundraiser at the National Oceanographic Institute had confirmed alibis except Troy Robinson and Jules Russell. Gus hadn't slept at all last night so was running on a combination of adrenaline and caffeine. His lack of sleep wasn't due to not getting back to Kendalton until nearly 2:00 a.m. Or because he was in a hotel and it wasn't his own bed. Between his music career and the FBI, Gus had seen more than his fair share of late nights and early mornings and certainly had slept in more than his share of hotels and motels. Gus hadn't slept for one reason and one reason alone: He was pissed. He was pissed at himself for involving Jim Lincoln in the investigation as much as he had, pissed that they now had to use precious time to retrace old ground on the investigation, but most of all pissed that he had been played. And played well.

Gus was very clear in his instructions to the team: There would be no dialogue or discussion with either Maria or Jim. They would be shown the warrant, read their Miranda rights, then handcuffed and taken into custody. One, two, three. He wanted the couple to stew on things, let the severity of the situation marinate in their minds for a while before speaking with them. And that would be done at the FBI's offices, on his turf not theirs.

Gus had been aiming for shock and awe and had nailed it. As soon as Maria opened the front door he saw the confusion on her face. And, after having been officially served the warrant, when the team of FBI agents spilled into the foyer and streamed past her, fanning out into the house, that confusion turned to panic. And, as if it couldn't get better, hearing the commotion, Jim came rushing down the stairs and, seeing the beginnings of a search, began pleading with Gus to know what was going on. Step one: complete.

Then, standing in their foyer, Gus read Maria and Jim their Miranda rights, pausing not once at Jim's repeated pleas to understand what was happening. Gus would later grimace at his behavior, but ego took over and he found himself purposely looking down at the much shorter Chief Lincoln as he did so. Vanessa, standing beside him, played the part of the stoic, silent partner and held up the search and arrest warrant so they could read it. Step two: complete.

And, lastly, Maria and Jim Lincoln were each handcuffed, but not before their sleepy-eyed teenaged daughter Cheryl, who'd been suspended from school, came stumbling down the stairs asking what was happening. Gus had Cheryl brought to the kitchen to sit with an agent and Jim and Maria led to separate FBI sedans where they now sat, undoubtedly watching as agents spewed from their house with box after box of their belongings to the awaiting black windowless FBI van. Step three: complete.

Tony Blackford came rushing down the stairs with a cell phone in his large gloved hand. He had short sandy-blond hair, fine features, and a lean frame. "Gus, Chief Lincoln's phone. We bypassed the security code so you could take a look."

Gus snapped on latex gloves, then flipped through the recent calls and texts, but he found nothing of immediate interest. He handed it back to the agent to be logged into evidence.

"Thanks, Tony. Have we got the wife's phone?"

"It's being worked on now. We should have access in a few minutes."

Gus nodded his thanks and Tony headed back up the stairs. He and Vanessa were standing by a window in the Lincolns' dining room and watched Maria and Jim try to communicate to each other as they sat in the back seats of their respective cars, hands cuffed behind their backs. A Kendalton Police cruiser pulled into the driveway and Gus watched as Officer Burrows began walking to the house, pausing momentarily at Jim's calls from the back seat of the car before continuing on to the front door. Gus met him in the foyer.

"Thanks for coming, Rich." Gus had called the station after securing the Lincoln home and Rich was the one on duty.

Rich stepped inside the door and his eyes narrowed. "Jee-some."

"Give Vanessa here your cell phone number in case we

need to reach you."

Rich told Vanessa his number, then said distractedly, "I'll need to call the mayor. Let him know what's going on." But before he could do so the mic affixed to his shoulder squawked.

"All officers, code 146 at 58 Oak Street. Injured party on the premises. EMTs en route."

Rich looked to Gus in a panic. "That's the Porters'." Rich took the mic from his shoulder. "Angie, it's Rich. What's going on at the Porters'?"

"Terry Porter just called 9-1-1. Someone broke into their house just before sunrise. She's been unable to call until just now."

"Is there anyone else at home or injured?" asked Vanessa, stepping forward slightly.

Rich repeated the question to dispatch.

"Unknown. Terry's in her room, unable to move. Colin's on his way," Angie said, referring to another officer.

Rich told Angie he'd meet Colin there, then signed off. Gus and Vanessa stole a quick glance at each other, and Gus knew they were thinking the same thing.

"Rich, we need to find both Jules Russell and Troy Robinson immediately and verify where they were at sunrise this morning."

Before Officer Burrows could reply they were interrupted by Tony bounding down the stairs again, visibly excited this time. He held out a cell phone for Gus to take.

"Gus, Maria Lincoln's cell phone. Check out the recent calls."

Gus looked to the screen, and at the top were several unanswered call attempts from Maria to Lizzy Porter from earlier that morning. Below those was an incoming call from last night at 7:49 p.m. from Jules that lasted seventeen minutes. Below that was a nine-minute call to Mel and, below those, at least ten unanswered calls to Lizzy from last night.

"Looks like someone's been trying to get their stories straight," remarked Tony.

Gus didn't reply but, instead, turned and walked briskly out the door, down the front steps, and to the FBI sedan with Maria Lincoln in its back seat. Vanessa was right on his heels as he opened the door and, kneeling beside a frantic Maria, held her cell phone in front of her face.

"We know you spoke with Jules last night. What did you two talk about?"

"Uh, she just told me about you interviewing her at the station. That's all."

"Then why'd you try to call Lizzy all night?" Gus growled. When Maria didn't reply he yelled, "Lizzy Porter's family was attacked this morning. Talk to us, Maria."

There was a slight pause before Maria hoarsely whispered, "She said she'd take care of it..." And Gus watched as panic gripped her.

"Who, Maria? Jules? What was Jules going to take care of?" When Maria didn't reply Gus hollered at her, "Maria, what's going on? We know about the night of Rebecca Munroe's death. Is Jules trying to cover that up? Is that what's going on?"

Maria began to cry, so, frustrated, Gus tried one last attempt to get her to talk. "Okay, you stay quiet, stay loyal to her. See how that ends for you. We'll know soon enough. We've got agents on the way to Jules's house now too. So, Maria, time to get in front of this."

She remained silent, so Gus stood and was about to shut the car door when Maria yelled for him to stop. He leaned back over and with his long arm slung over the car's roof looked down at her. She was breathing heavily and Gus saw the stress and anxiety taking its toll as she tried to make life-altering decisions on the fly.

"Last chance, Maria," he pressed, beginning to stand.

"You won't find her at home," she blurted. "Shane kicked her out last night."

"Where is she...? Maria, where is Jules?"

She looked up at Gus through tear-soaked eyes and cried, "I've done nothing. I never knew for sure it was her." Gus said nothing, waiting for her answer. "She's staying at the Sheraton in Ashby."

Gus slammed the door shut as Maria began to plead with him. He turned to the group of agents that had gathered behind him, and through the muffled screams from Maria the tumblers in his mind began to click into place. He met Vanessa's eyes.

"Get a warrant for the Russells' house. We've got enough now." He pointed to Tony and the Cybercrimes agent. "You two, continue the search of the premises. No one else is to enter without my permission." He then pointed to two other agents. "You two bring the Lincolns to our offices for processing. And they're not to be anywhere within earshot of each other at any time."

He saw Rich Burrows at the back of the group. "Get to the Porters and secure the scene."

Gus then looked back to Vanessa at his side, staring up at him with anticipation.

"We're going to get Jules Russell."

Chapter Forty-Four

JULES RUSSELL SAT in her black Range Rover with its tinted windows and big, flashy wheels and looked around the crowded supermarket parking lot. Thick, foamy fog hung over the pavement, held in place by the falling mist. She watched with envy as moms scurried about their morning routines before turning her attention back to her small leather bag on the passenger seat. Somewhere deep in the recesses of her mind had always been the notion, as insignificant as a pebble in a cosmic storm, that this day may come, that the truth would catch up to her. She never really gave it much credence, let alone spent any conscious time thinking about it. But it was there; she always knew it was there.

She scratched at the inside of her elbow through her shirt, then grabbed her purse from beside her. She rummaged around in it for a few moments, sure she had a tube of her prescription cream in there but couldn't find it. She tossed her purse aside and pulled the leather bag onto her lap. She had packed her birth certificate, passport, social security card, her health insurance cards, and her medical and immunization records, thanks to some advice from prepper websites. She remembered how adventurous she felt researching go bags and how to stay off the grid and what to do to create a new identity. It had all felt so exciting and adventurous at the time, but not anymore. She knew she wasn't Jason Bourne, that she was just some rich housewife from a small tourist trap of a town in northern Massachusetts. But Jules Russell had always accomplished what she set her mind to and this was no different. She had this, she kept telling herself, she had this. One step at a time.

She still held out hope that this would all blow over, and it might still. She knew she could talk Shane off the ledge, that he would take her back. Hell, he knew what everyone did: That he was punching well above his weight class to have landed her. And she could explain it to her kids, maybe pull a mea culpa with the drinking. She could even enter a program, do it up big. Surely Shane and the kids would rally around her for that.

And as for the FBI, all was not lost on that front, not by a long shot. They had spilled their goods to her last night and all they had was circumstantial at best. They knew it and she knew it. As long as she and the others stuck to their story they'd all be fine. She'd be fine. If all went according to plan she'd be back in her own bed within a week, maybe less.

She reached in the bag and took out an old, worn letter-sized envelope. Inside was a yellowed slip of paper with the personal information of her college roommate, Meghan Tanner, written on it. She once thought of herself as crazy for keeping it, but not today. On it was Meg's mother's maiden name, the names of her childhood schools, the name of her first pet, and her social security number. Jules had originally gotten this information from Meg one drunken night back in college, then secretly got a credit card in her roommate's name that she quickly maxed out and then threw away without Meg ever knowing it was her. But that was when they lived together and it was easy to intercept the mail and when Meg and Jules looked similar enough for Jules to use Meg's license she stole as identification. The faded license had expired decades ago, and Jules certainly had no intentions of skulking around Meg's neighborhood to steal her mail. So, as she fingered the soft, timeworn paper she couldn't think of a way to use the information the old-fashioned way, but she would keep it. Maybe she could find a way to use it online.

She took a long pull of her Irish coffee—the coffee part courtesy of Dunks, the Irish part courtesy of the nips in her glove box—and it warmed her insides. Her hand rummaged deeper into the bag, past a few pieces of essential clothing and a few unopened tubes of prescription cream she noted for later until she felt the tight stacks of cash at the bottom. The nominal amount of money she had always kept in the bag had been added to significantly in recent weeks with a series of small but regular withdrawals from various accounts so as not to draw unwanted attention from either the banks or Shane. When Jules saw just how unhinged Lizzy was when they met at The Blend the night of Sarah's death she knew it was only a matter of time before the weak bitch cracked. Lizzy never did have the constitution of the rest of them. So that's when Jules freshened up her go bag and stocked up on cash.

Hope for the best, prepare for the worst.

Jules zipped up the bag and slid it back onto the passenger seat. She looked in the mirror and cringed at the roadkill looking back. She raked her hands through tousled hair and ran a finger beneath each eye. She then pinched her cheeks until they were rosy and took out her signature Ruby Woo red lipstick. Applying it to both lips she rubbed them together and instantly felt better. She stared at her reflection and reassured herself that all would be fine.

The Posse had held it together this long and she was hopeful that would continue. But only time would tell. Jules had always made the difficult decisions no one else was capable of, taken the necessary steps no one else could take to ensure their safety, their freedom. But was that enough? This time others would have to step up. But were they able to? Would life soon return to normal or would it never be the same again? She would soon know the answers to these and many other questions.

She leaned back in her seat and trained her eyes once again on the entrance of the Ashby Sheraton across the street. She had to wait only a few more minutes before the old, light green safari-looking truck the FBI agent drove pulled into its small semicircle driveway and parked in front of its entrance. Jules watched as the two agents who'd interviewed her again yesterday at the station hopped out and jogged into the hotel.

Jules then knew she had all the answers she would ever need.

Chapter Forty-Five

GUS DECIDED TO interview Maria Lincoln first, see what she had to say before speaking with Jim. Being in law enforcement, Jim would be tougher to pressure into cooperating. He knew his rights and would know when they were being trampled on. Maria was a different story. Gus had seen the fear in her eyes as they entered her house to search it, and he had seen that fear increase when he told her of Lizzy's attack. He could use that.

Vanessa heard from the team at Lizzy's house on the drive back to Boston. Lizzy, her daughter Terry, and little Nico were all at the hospital and stable. Lizzy and Terry had been sedated, while Nico was with his father, PJ. They confiscated her phone and computers, then, while processing the scene, agents found what appeared to be Rebecca Munroe's missing journal hidden deep in a closet. And, upon further inspection, agents also found a hidden video surveillance device in that same room. They then expanded their search and found similar devices in each room throughout the house. They were still waiting on the search warrant for Jules Russell's home but expected that within the hour, and Vanessa had also requested search warrants for the other women's homes as well. So, the FBI team remained in

Kendalton, on hot standby.

Gus and Vanessa joined Maria in one of the interrogation rooms, where the chief's wife sat alone with no shoelaces, belts, or jewelry. Gus had them handcuff her to the table and had leg shackles put on. He wanted to create the direst possible situation in her mind.

Gus got right to the point. They played the security video of Maria and Laurie in the parking lot of the diner the morning of her death and of Maria and Jim arguing in the car in the back lot. Then they played the recording of the 9-1-1 call Laurie made just after leaving Maria that morning.

"Have you spoken with your local law enforcement?"

"I can't. They're compromised."

Vanessa then read a few of the dozens of texts between Laurie and Maria in the days leading up to her death, texts in which Maria repeatedly warned Laurie about telling anyone and threatened her. And after they were all done Maria began to cry. Gus had seen this reaction hundreds of times: a hard-fought battle with a seemingly impenetrable wall of defense brought down with the smallest crack.

"Maria, we know you've been lying to us from the start." Her eyes were bloodshot and puffy, her skin a blotchy white with lines of stress pulling at the corners. "But now we know you've dragged Jim into it. And, do you know what happens to police officers in jail?"

"No," said Maria in a half moan as she swiped at the tears on her cheeks.

"We show this video to a jury and let them hear Laurie's 9-1-1 call and we bring in Laurie's daughter to testify how her life's been ruined since her mother was taken from her, murdered. Then we show them some of the autopsy pics of Laurie and then, finally, we lay out the whole timeline that puts you fighting with her hours before her death." Gus shook his head. "It won't be hard. I'm thinking...twenty to life for both of you." After another outburst from Maria, Gus cleared his throat, and once he was sure he had her complete attention he finished. "Or, you can tell us everything and, depending on what we hear, we may be able to make things go a whole lot better for you. And for Jim." Maria was nodding rapidly even before Gus finished. "Okay, so let's start with Rebecca Munroe. We know you were all with her the night she died and that she didn't commit suicide."

Maria nodded solemnly. "That's right."

Gus caught the look of satisfaction on Vanessa's face as he said, "Okay, so how does she fit into all of this?"

"I don't know exactly."

Having been raised Catholic, Maria Lincoln had been traipsing her misdeeds out for others to judge her entire life. So, she simply took a deep breath and got to it.

"Jules invited Becca to hang with us out by the quarry that night. It was late and we were drinking. Everything was fine, then Jules pulled out a joint. Becca didn't want to, but Jules really piled on the peer pressure, so she finally gave in. And that's when everything went wrong. There was something in the joint besides just pot, and some of us started seeing things. Becca really freaked out. She started moaning and she just kept repeating that she wanted to go home over and over. Then, out of nowhere, she started screaming and before we knew it she was running off down the trail toward the road. We all froze, not knowing what to do. But not Jules. She ran after Becca. Then a few minutes later we heard Jules yell for help. When we got there Becca was lying on the ground. Her head was against a large rock and her hair was soaked in blood. Jules said she was trying to catch up to her when she saw Becca trip and fall and hit her head on the rock. Sarah felt for a pulse but there wasn't any. She was already gone."

Gus pursed his lips. "So you threw her body in the quarry to make it look like a suicide."

A nod of shame. "That's right. We were all freaking out. Some of the girls wanted to call the police, tell them everything, that it was all an accident. But Jules just kept saying that they'd never believe us. We were underage drinking, doing drugs, that this would ruin all of our lives forever. We'd go to jail. No more college, marriage, kids. Our lives would be over. Then Laur said she was going to get help and turned to leave." Maria's voice cracked. "And that's when I grabbed her arm and stopped her. I agreed with Jules; I told them we had to make it look like a suicide. That it was the only way… *I* was the one who convinced the others that was the best thing to do. Not Jules. And Jules has never let me forget it."

Wet, guilty tears rolled down Maria's cheeks and she rubbed them away with shaking, red fingers. Her cheeks puffed out and she let out a long exhalation before looking back to Gus.

"So, that's what we did. And we all swore to keep that

night a secret and never speak of it again."

"So, only Jules was really with Rebecca when she died. That's Sarah's secret?"

Maria nodded once. "Has to be."

"Do you believe it was an accident?" asked Vanessa.

"I did at first. Jules was as scared as the rest of us. But then a few years later, when everyone else was living away at college, Lizzy and I went out one night and had a little too much to drink. And that's when she told me a story that made me question it. A few months before that night, a few of us were at a graduation party at Eddie McKay's house—he was a senior. It was late and we were about to leave when Lizzy couldn't find her sweater, so she went out on the back porch to see if she left it on one of the chairs. And in a dark corner of the house behind a bush, Lizzy saw Jules's *very* recent ex-boyfriend, Troy Robinson—who she'd been trying to get back—kissing with Becca."

"Did Lizzy tell Jules what she saw?" asked Vanessa.

Maria's eyebrows arched up. "She did, the next day. But only Jules. None of us knew anything about it. But, looking back, it was only a week or so later that Jules started befriending Becca and then only another month or so until that night."

"And the night of Becca's death is the night you and Lizzy were talking about on that recording we got." Maria nodded, so Gus continued, "Okay, so let's fast-forward to Laurie. What were you two arguing about that morning outside the diner?"

"Laurie was convinced she needed to confess to someone

about that night." Maria thought a moment as distant screams and arguments permeated her thoughts. And when she spoke again her voice was quiet, remorseful. "She was just in this constant crisis of conscience. That morning was me trying to talk her down again."

"How was Jim involved?"

"I told him about that night with Becca. Well, most of it."

"Most of it?" parroted Gus.

"I told him we were drinking, smoking pot, and that Becca started acting weird." She looked down at her hands. "Then that Becca left without us noticing and that we heard a loud scream, then a splash. And that we panicked and fled, only to find out the next day that she committed suicide."

"How'd he react?"

Maria bit down on her lip. "Not good. We were working through it, and for a while I thought we'd be okay. But then Laur's death spun everything out of control. Jim was first on the scene and all he could think about were the calls and texts between me and Laur, some of which were from earlier that morning. So, he panicked and took her cell phone. And he's resented me for it ever since."

The room fell quiet and Gus waited for Maria to wipe away tears with her shirt sleeve.

"Maria, did you or Jim have anything to do with the deaths of Laurie or Sarah?"

"No. I loved them like they were my sisters."

"Do you know who did this, who murdered them?"

Maria exhaled deeply and her eyes latched onto Gus's.

"It has to be Jules. I'm convinced now that Becca's death was no accident. Jules knew of her and Troy—that's why she befriended her, drew her in. She has the most to lose if that ever gets out." Then with a knowing tone she added, "It was Jules in my house yesterday. There's no doubt. It was a message to me to fall in line or else. And last night when she called she sounded…scared, desperate even."

"How could she think she'd get away with all of this?" asked Vanessa.

Maria cracked a forlorn grin. "Agent, I've known Jules my entire life. She's always gotten what she wanted, whether through manipulation or from her good looks. She's a classic narcissist. And the fact that she practically runs this town behind the scenes, what with all the groups she controls, has given her a god complex. There's nothing she can't control in town if she wants to."

"Why is this woman still your friend?" asked Vanessa, exasperated.

Maria looked Vanessa hard in the eye. "Would *you* want to be on her bad side? Especially given what she had on all of us?"

"We checked the Ashby Sheraton," interrupted Gus. "She wasn't registered there. Do you know where else she might be?"

Maria tightened her lips. "No, sorry."

Gus thought of Rebecca Munroe's journal at Lizzy's house. "We believe Lizzy's been feeding us information, pointing us to Jules."

"I can see that. She was fed up with Jules's bullying, with

Jules in general. And once Laur died Lizzy became manic that it was Jules, that Jules had lied to all of us about Becca's death."

"But if it was Lizzy, why would she text all of us that audio of you and her talking about Jules?" Vanessa challenged. "It made her look straight-up horrible."

"But it plays right into her hand. Lizzy's always played the victim; that's her thing. And, remember, it wasn't from her phone so she can deny it was her."

"It appears that she had Rebecca's journal. Can you think of how she might've gotten it?"

"I dunno." She shrugged.

"I assume Jim told you of Rebecca's pregnancy?" asked Gus. Maria nodded but didn't look up. "There was a reference in one of her entries to a James and it suggested they had been a couple. We were under the impression that Rebecca didn't have a boyfriend before Troy Robinson."

Maria considered Gus's question for a moment before meeting his eyes. "I dunno," she breathed, and Gus saw the exhaustion on her face as she added, "But, then again, what's one more secret?"

Chapter Forty-Six

GUS AND VANESSA sat in Gus's office on the fourth floor of the FBI's building while Jim Lincoln was being moved from his holding cell to an interview room, and Maria vice versa. Gus's gaze moved from a small framed black-and-white polaroid of him as a young boy sitting with his grandmother on her front porch to a framed cover of the album *The Greatest Jazz Concert in the World* that hung on the wall above his desk. Gus found himself staring at a laughing Oscar Peterson as the flurry of Charlie Parker's bebop lines danced in the air. Lost in his thoughts, he ran his fingers along the calluses on his plucking hand.

The information they got from Maria clarified a lot, and she had certainly painted a damning picture of Jules. He glanced to Vanessa sitting beside him. The smoky sunlight highlighted yellow specks in her brilliant green eyes, making them look almost catlike.

"You think everything she said in there was legit?"

"I do," said Gus. "I think Maria Lincoln knows she's down a hole at this point."

"Then what's wrong?" She flashed a knowing look. "I know you too well. You think something's janky."

Gus looked past her to a framed painting of Preservation

Hall hanging on the wall beside the door, its brilliant blues and greens and reds popping off the canvas. He thought of that first weekend living in New Orleans, walking its streets, soaking up its vibe, excitement fusing with confidence that he would figure out the unknown that lay ahead, and wished he had that same feeling now. His brain wrestled again with what had been nagging at him since getting to Kendalton.

"I can get my brain around Jules for the murders. The evidence is piling up, for sure. And Lizzy Porter feeding us info to settle a score after all these years sits right. But that funeral card on Sarah Nelson's body just doesn't fit."

"You heard Maria: Jules has always had a god complex, and she held the fact that Maria was the one to convince the others to make it look like a suicide over Maria's head all these years. Maybe Jules thought she could frame her for it all." Vanessa eyed him. "You're thinking Troy Robinson."

"I don't know what I'm thinking." He counted points off on his fingers. "He does have the skills to do all of this, the Rebecca Munroe connection…" He raised an eyebrow. "He doesn't like Jules at all." He tilted his head so she could see the wound along his scalp. "And, he's a shooter. But, problem is: We've got nothing on him except lack of alibis."

Vanessa's cell phone buzzed and, recognizing the caller ID, she answered the FaceTime video call. "Hey, Tony, what's up?"

Tony was standing in what looked like an unfinished cellar. His tall, lanky frame had him lowering his head and hunching his shoulders like someone running to a waiting helicopter. Gus saw exposed rafters overhead in the background with copper pipes running through them, and behind Tony was a fieldstone foundation with cobwebs lining the top where it supported the wall. The agent struggled to keep the camera steady as he angled it to include a tall chrome refrigerator with a smoked-glass door.

"We're in the Russells' basement." His voice was choppy and the video froze intermittently. His other gloved hand entered the frame. "This is their wine fridge." He opened the door and the light immediately popped on to reveal row after row of wine bottle tops angled downward. He tilted the video down to show an open spot near the bottom. "We looked behind each of the bottles top to bottom."

Tony knelt down and for a moment the image on Vanessa's screen showed the dusty cement floor before angling back to the bottom two rows of the wine fridge. He then narrated what he was doing.

"And when we pulled out the bottle in this spot we found this." His gloved hand reached deep inside the empty bottle slot and Gus watched as he removed a glass vial with yellow, syrupy liquid in it. He rotated it in his hand so the label faced the camera and read its contents out loud.

"*Conus geographus.* Predatory venom. National Oceanographic Institute Lot number NOI-MX-940284. There are three of these vials in here."

"Boom," declared Vanessa, and Gus felt a surge of adrenaline. He squinted at the screen.

"But, hey guys, the institute's inventory log shows *four* vials were taken."

"She's gotta have the other one with her," concluded

Vanessa.

"Tony, log those into evidence but keep 'em there," directed Gus. "We're on our way."

Vanessa ended the call, then excitedly spun her phone in her hand. Gus stood, and as she followed, her phone rang again. Seeing it was another agent in Kendalton, she hit the speaker button.

"Hey, Katie, I'm with Gus. You're on speaker."

"We just got done going through all the security footage at Robinson's store. We've got Troy Robinson on tape in the store the morning of Turner's murder then, again, the afternoon when Gus was shot at in the woods. We'll have the techies take a look to be sure the footage wasn't altered but it looks legit to me."

Vanessa ended the call and broke for the door first, once again reading her partner's mind.

"I'll get an APB out on Jules immediately."

Chapter Forty-Seven

JULES ENDED HER call with Shane and dropped her phone onto the bed beside her. She sat forward and, planting her stocking feet firmly on the crispy carpeting at the foot of the bed, vigorously rubbed her face. It took her a minute to get her bearings after what she just experienced. She thought it a simple task to make amends with Shane, but she'd been wrong. He was not the least bit sympathetic, nor was he in any way open to discussing her coming home. Shane hadn't finally answered her call after dozens of attempts to calmly and compassionately discuss reconciliation. He had answered the call angry and hostile, his voice rising as he scolded her about her many indiscretions over the years she never realized he knew about. And he became angrier still as he told her about the FBI visiting his work and embarrassing him in front of his coworkers.

But it was when Shane spoke of the girls hysterically crying in their rooms that his voice became filled with vitriol. He spoke of the endless hurtful comments each had been the target of on social media and of the explicit gossiping they'd seen about Jules and her illicit behavior.

When her off-color promises of sex failed to bring Shane around Jules became contrite, resorting to commitments of getting counseling. And when those too failed she vowed to attending Alcoholics Anonymous and promised that, with Shane's and the girls' support, she would be successful and they as a family would get through this. To all of this, Shane repeatedly said no. But it was his emphatic dismissal of them ever being a family again that shredded her, cut her to the core. Shane ended the call by telling her not to contact him or the girls again.

She angrily grabbed her phone again and checked her texts, but there was still nothing. As part of her go bag she had purchased a burner phone so she couldn't be traced. But before turning her phone off for good, she had reached out to dozens of other mothers in town, ones whom she shared committee seats with and with whom she had organized sports activities for years. But none had replied. Jules had seen the news reports of the break-in at Lizzy's and heard the conjecture from "unnamed sources" that she was a person of interest, and she had watched as this evolved throughout the day to becoming an all-points bulletin out for her apprehension. She knew there would be no reply texts and no make-up calls with Shane or the girls, but she had to check one last time. But it seemed that Shane had spoken for everyone: Jules was on her own.

She tossed her phone onto the bed beside the package containing the burner and bit her lower lip in frustration. She looked around the tired motel room with its scuffed-up doors, faded wallpaper, and dusty veneered furniture and the severity of her situation crashed down upon her. She cupped her face again in her hands, and her thoughts went back to that night all those years before at the quarry with Becca, the night all of this nightmare was set in motion. Images of her feeling her way along the dark trail dusted her thoughts, branches slapping her body and face as she chased Becca. The clomping of footfalls and the sounds of her heavy breathing filled her ears. She could feel the sensation of grasping Becca's hair from behind in her fingers as she caught up with her, and the pain of the two of them tumbling down together on the hard earth. Anger surged inside her, as it had that night, and Jules was shaken from her memories at the pain of Becca's fingernails digging into her scalp.

She slowly stood and went to the vanity in the narrow space separating the bedroom from the tiny, dingy bathroom. She grabbed hold of the edge of the vanity and lowered her head. She took several deep, cleansing breaths before looking up at herself in the mirror. Her eyes were bloodshot from lack of sleep and she could see the stress lines throughout her forehead and face, the result of violent mood swings from heavy anxiety to uncontrollable rage. The inside of her forearm and elbows itched so she took her prescription cream and applied it vigorously.

Jules had chosen this motel to get some distance between her and Kendalton but was now questioning that decision. If she continued to run it would only confirm her guilt. She could go back and fight, clear her name and hunker down until things blew over, then re-establish her reputation in town. She had heard the FBI's case against her and it was thin. If it was just her she had to worry about, she knew she'd be fine. But there was also Mel and Maria and Lizzy to consider. Mel had folded like a shitty hand of cards and, after seeing the FBI show up at the Ashby Sheraton, Jules knew where Maria stood. And she'd lost Lizzy weeks ago. But Maria and Lizzy were there that night—they had as much to lose as she did, so there was a chance they only told the FBI just enough, but not everything.

But Mel had gone all in. What would she say when reasoned with, when *her* options were laid out for her? Jules thought of the Benjamin Franklin quote her mother would often recite with sarcasm while Jules was navigating the hormone-laden, gossip-rich waters of high school.

Three may keep a secret, if two of them are dead.

She knew this advice rang true now more than ever. She looked back to herself in the mirror and, as she did so, felt her world closing in. Her family had left her, cast her adrift. Two of her closest friends were dead and the others had shunned her like a pariah, too afraid to be near her. She'd even lost that crappy, demeaning job at the high school. And, now, she was here: sleeping in a fleabag motel she paid for with cash, alone, trying to figure out where to go and what to do.

And it was at that moment that Jules realized there was only one thing left to do: She had to save it all. There was no other choice; her very existence depended on it. She began to pack her toiletries bag when she heard the chime of her phone on the bed telling her she had a new text. Hoping it was one of her friends reaching out to help, or maybe even one of her daughters, she raced to it only to find it was from an unknown number. She read its four simple words and froze.

FBI on way. Run.

Chapter Forty-Eight

MEL DUCKED INTO the entryway of her house and shook off the freezing rain as water seeped into her scalp like the bile permeating her gut. With hunched shoulders, she hugged herself and shivered, cold to the bone. The black clouds that hung over Kendalton for much of the day had finally burst, as if Mother Nature knew the town was in need of a cleansing and was all too happy to oblige. The inside of her house, with its small windows and low ceilings, was bathed in varying shades of gray, like scenes from a black-and-white movie.

Fred scampered past her down the narrow hallway, and moments later she heard his violent shaking from the kitchen. Having made sure Mr. T had something for dinner, she had left him to his latest woodworking project and headed home for some much-needed quiet time. So much had happened since this morning and Mel needed to process it all.

Her day began with a call from Annie alerting her to reports of police at Lizzy's house. After racing to Lizzy's and seeing the cruisers and FBI for herself, she repeatedly called Lizzy's husband PJ only to get his voicemail with each attempt. She then tried Maria and, unable to reach her, tried

Jim on his cell but got voicemails all around. She finally coerced one of the officers at Lizzy's house to have Rich Burrows come speak to her, and that's when Mel confirmed the break-in at Lizzy's and learned of Maria and Jim being taken into custody by the FBI. With no one else to call, Mel had stood alone at the crime scene tape feeling lost and helpless until Annie arrived, frantic at Mel's lack of response to her increasingly anxious texts. So for hours, the two of them stood and watched in awe as the FBI and medical teams buzzed in and around Lizzy's house. Annie hugged Mel the entire time, willing her to be okay.

Mel locked her front door, threw the two deadbolts and reset the alarm. She then peeled her waterlogged coat off like a wetsuit, kicked her old ratty Blundstones onto the mat in the corner, and headed for the kitchen. The sound of the howling wind and pelting rain was replaced with creaks and groans from her old house. Guided by familiar shadows, she dumped a scoop of dry food into Fred's bowl, got a can of Diet Coke from the fridge, and stood zombielike at the island.

Mel too had seen the reports of the FBI's search for the missing Jules. She hadn't spoken with Jules since that morning in Mr. T's driveway when the video of Jules drunk dropped on *The Meetinghouse*, so she had no idea what was going through her friend's mind. But Mel was sure Jules was beginning to unravel as she flailed about trying to save her reputation. Then Maria called Mel in a panic last night after she and Jules spoke. Maria told Mel of Shane forcing Jules to move out of their house and of Jules being interviewed a second time by the FBI and of their growing interest in her as a suspect. She told Mel of the FBI tracing the posts from Awkward7 to Jules's email account at the high school and how Jules had no alibi for the mornings of Laurie's and Sarah's deaths. She described the recording the FBI received of Jules and Sarah arguing about some dark secret Sarah knew of Jules, and they talked about the recording they all received in the text, of Maria and Lizzy sharing their suspicions of Jules as well. And, finally, Maria told Mel of the intruder in her home earlier that day and how she was convinced it too was Jules.

As when speaking to Gus the day before, Mel couldn't believe Jules could actually murder anyone, let alone their closest friends. She had always known Jules to be a narcissist and pathological liar, but murderer? But then doubt began to creep in. Both Laur and Sarah were murdered by someone who was able to get close to them and Jules was absolutely capable of that. And what were the chances someone else went through all the trouble to have the Awkward7 posts traced to her email account? If they were that good, they'd have made the emails completely untraceable. Then Mel thought of that night with Laur's favorite toy playing for her to hear from the woods. Everyone in the Posse knew how important that toy was to Laur, and that was precisely the type of sick thing Jules would do. And there was the lack of alibis: What were the chances that no one saw her either morning? And, what if Jules was the intruder in Maria's house? Why was she there? What was she after?

Mel's thoughts drifted to Becca's death all those years

ago and of Laur's growing suspicions about Jules's hand in it. And Mel had seen firsthand how the guilt of that night ate away at Laur each and every day since. And she understood why; Mel too harbored a deep-seated guilt from that night and she wasn't even there. And over the years, she had sensed a similar pain held close by Maria and Lizzy and Sarah emanating from that night as well. But not Jules; never Jules. In the twenty-five years since that night Mel had not once gotten even the faintest sense of remorse or guilt from Jules about that night. To Jules, it seemed, that night simply never happened.

These thoughts had swirled around in Mel's mind all day, bleeding like dye into the grief she had been carrying for months. And Maria's words had only reinforced Mel's growing beliefs. Mel stared blankly at the spot on the island where the lone key had been left nights before. This kitchen—the one she had designed herself—was once a haven for her, but that intrusion to both her home and her psyche created a chasm in Mel's emotions, one she knew would take significant time and energy to traverse. Mel was an introvert by nature and, as such, generally enjoyed being alone. But as she sipped her soda in the quiet, still house, she realized that she was not just alone anymore, but lonely. Sure, she had Mr. T and she loved him dearly, but she also knew he wouldn't be with her forever.

With the exception of a few fleeting relationships, Mel had been single her entire adult life. She never seemed to need anyone; she always had Laur to lean on in times like this. Maybe Mr. T was right. Maybe she needed a partner, someone she could build a life with. She had found herself thinking a lot about Gus lately and how she felt when she was with him. He was clearly a good-looking guy, but what Mel found most attractive was his personality, his strong sense of self. Gus knew who he was and that was a good person. Mel once thought of herself as a good person also, but that had changed. Would a good person lie about someone's death? Mel feared now that Gus knew the truth, he wouldn't think of her as a good person either.

As she thought through everything that had happened—not just during these past months but during the past several decades—Mel realized that she too had been living with guilt about the night Becca died. She had, until now, unknowingly harbored it deep inside, living around it all these years. And she knew, deep down, that had to end.

With new purpose, she pulled a can of Hormel corned beef hash from the cupboard and a jar of pickles from the fridge and set them down on the counter next to a frying pan. As she reached for the can opener her cell phone buzzed beside her with a text from Annie.

"Hey, got ambitious, got a pot roast to make for dinner, veggies, mashed potatoes, gravy. Will have wine. Wanna come over?"

Mel leaned against her new dark blue Lacanche range, its sturdy metal knobs boring into her lower back. She shuddered inside her damp clothes and thought of Annie puttering around a cozy kitchen, steam rising from pots on the stove, the room aglow and warm as she sang along to songs in the background. It was a scene Mel often dreamed of, both as a child and an adult, yet never experienced, and she now wondered if she ever would. Her fingers tapped away.

"Thanks but just got home—gonna hang in and decompress from today. Talk tomorrow."

She put the phone back onto the counter, then noticed Fred playfully trot past the island with his tail wagging as he headed toward the family room at the back of the house. And a moment later Jules stepped from the darkness to the opposite end of the island. She was dressed in black running attire with a hood draped over her head, hiding most of her face. Using the palm of her gloved hand she slid the hood back and held up her other hand. Mel's breathing hitched.

"I know what they're saying, Mel. But it's not true. You have to believe me." Her eyes were wide, pleading. "I could never hurt Laur or Sarah or Lizzy…or anyone for that matter."

"I know that, Jules," said Mel wearily.

"Then why are you helping the FBI, Mel? Why did you tell the FBI about that night and bring that agent out on the trails?"

Mel froze. She willed herself to respond, to keep Jules preoccupied, but couldn't think of anything to say.

"Why, Mel?" asked Jules again, this time her voice was hard, cutting.

Mel's mind began to spin and, as it did, she watched Jules begin to slowly creep along the side of the island toward her. Mel rehearsed the next eight seconds in her head: spin, five steps to the pantry, throw her right elbow back and up at a lunging Jules, swing around the door using her body weight to close it, throw the middle deadbolt.

"Jules, stop," commanded Mel. But as she and Jules looked at each other, Mel stared into her friend's vacant, doll-like eyes and had no doubt that Jules would never stop.

And that's when Mel spun.

Chapter Forty-Nine

GUS AND VANESSA were on their way to Jules's house to meet with the search team so Gus could see her house and belongings for himself when they got a frantic call from Rich Burrows telling them that Jules had invaded Mel's house and Mel was, once again, locked in her pantry. They were just entering Kendalton so diverted to Mel's and met Rich in her driveway. Having cleared the house, as before, they were now all standing and sitting around Mel's island. As they had done before. Mel brought them through what happened from when she got home to her scamper into the pantry.

"What did she look like? What was her demeanor?" asked Gus.

"She looked…rabid," said Mel, her eyes still slightly dilated from the adrenaline. There was a quiver in her voice that spoke of deeper emotions than just fear. "That's the best way I can describe it. She had this sort of crazed look to her. I've never seen her look like that. She's always the confident, composed one."

Gus pulled out the stool next to her and sat. "What did she say, exactly?"

"She said she didn't do any of it and asked me to believe

her. Her voice was so soft, so fragile but her eyes, her eyes were just…dead."

Gus looked around the kitchen and to the keypad for the alarm system beside the side door.

"How do you think she got into your house?"

"No idea." She held Gus's gaze. "Do you really believe she could've done all of this?"

Gus paused momentarily and thought how best to answer that. He had been in situations like this before, when victims or families of victims were confronted with the truth that evil isn't always distant, in some unknown, faraway place, but rather residing right next door.

"The evidence has become overwhelming."

And with that one sentence the emotions of Laur's death, of Sarah's death, of all the chaos and tragedy that had afflicted her friends and their town came crashing back onto Mel. Pooling tears breached her eyes and streamed down her cheeks.

"Did you know that a month or so before that night Rebecca was seen at some graduation party kissing Troy Robinson? They had been seeing each other secretly."

Mel cocked her head to the side. "Troy and Becca? No. Laur never told me that."

"We don't think she knew. Lizzy saw them and only told Jules about it."

Vanessa tapped at her phone and brought up a picture of the first page from Becca's journal Gus had received in his room at the inn, the one in which Becca wrote about Jules suggesting they hang out. She held it out while Mel read it.

Vanessa then swiped at the screen and the picture changed to the later entry from Becca's journal they found in the woods, the one in which Jules gave Becca her first experience with marijuana at a party. Vanessa gestured to her phone's screen.

"Mel, do you know who this James is? We were under the impression Rebecca hadn't had any boyfriends except for Troy."

Mel pursed her lips. "No. There was Jimmy—the chief—and another Jim in school but no one that went by James."

Gus leaned in. "Mel, we believe Lizzy's the one who's been providing us information about that night with Rebecca and Jules. Can you think of any reason why she'd want to do that?"

"I'm not sure. But Lizzy was always being pushed around by Jules, ever since we were kids. But, lately, we all noticed a change in her. She started talking back to Jules, she stopped hovering around Jules like a little lapdog and even began to ignore some of the things Jules would tell her to do. So, I don't know, but it seemed to me like Lizzy had just had enough."

"Straight up," commented Vanessa.

"We received an audio recording of Sarah and Jules arguing over some secret that Sarah held over Jules. We now believe it was about Becca's death. We found the original recording of that on Lizzy's phone."

"And the original video file of Jules drunk at that party, the one posted from your account to *The Meetinghouse*?" added Vanessa. "The tech guys initially found that in some random folder in your cloud account but they also just found it on Lizzy's phone. And her browser history was filled with searches of how to hack someone's cell phone, computer, how to remotely enable video and audio on other people's devices and a lot more."

"And those pages from Becca's journal we showed you?" interrupted Gus. "We found Becca's entire journal at Lizzy's house. So, now you see why we believe Jules did all of this. She lied about knowing Rebecca at all, but Rebecca's diary and Maria both tell us otherwise. It seems to us that all of this started decades ago with that kiss Lizzy saw between Rebecca and Troy. When Lizzy told Jules about it I'm sure she had no idea of the cascading events she was putting into motion. We can only guess that Jules befriended Rebecca with ill intentions, whether from jealousy or curiosity or whatever. Maybe it was just to understand what she had that Jules didn't or maybe it was more sinister, we may never know. But then that night at the quarry happens. And, from what we now know, only Jules was with Rebecca at the end, so only she really knows what happened. Maybe Rebecca really did slip and fall. Maybe she was pushed, or worse. But, regardless, Rebecca winds up dead and Jules knows that if the police investigate she'll be the one under suspicion for Rebecca's death. So she convinces the others that they're as much in it as she is, so they all agree to dump Rebecca's body into the quarry and make it look like a suicide."

"But, if all that's true, why were the police back then so convinced Becca committed suicide? Surely there must've been some evidence or at least some doubt about it. Becca was always such a happy, positive person. It just doesn't make sense."

With all that had happened, Gus saw no harm in telling Mel the truth that had been withheld from her for all of these years.

"The autopsy report discovered that Rebecca was pregnant. And we've gone over her case file; her injuries were consistent with a fall from that height. Suicide was a reasonable conclusion."

Vanessa's phone rang and, turning away, she answered, then listened intently to the caller.

"Mel, did Jules say anything about where she was going?" continued Gus. "Or can you think of anywhere she might go?"

"No, sorry."

Vanessa turned back toward them and with a hand over the screen of her phone said to Gus, "This is Tony. They're finished at Jules's house. They confiscated all the computers and other devices but Jules's cell phone wasn't there. But..." Her eyes flashed to Mel, then back.

He nodded. "We're good."

"Hidden in the back of their basement they found an old rifle that looks like it's been fired recently and a box of two fifty-seven Bob shells."

Gus's hand went to the stitches along the side of his head. "I thought Jules had never used a gun."

"That's crap," said Rich Burrows with a scowl.

Gus spun on his stool to look at the officer who had been there the entire time, as quiet as a mime. "What's that?"

"That's crap," repeated Rich matter-of-factly. "Jules may not hunt but she certainly knows her way around a gun. Our dads were friends. They taught us both together how to shoot a rifle when we were kids."

Chapter Fifty

Gus asked Officer Burrows to stay with Mel while she packed some things to stay at Mr. T's for a few days. Not knowing how Jules entered her house, Mel needed to get the security company back out before she would stay there any longer. At Gus's urging, Vanessa confirmed they'd still heard nothing regarding the APB put out on Jules that morning. They had tracked her cell phone to a remote seedy motel a few towns away that afternoon, but by the time they got there she was gone and her phone shut off. The FBI had issued a picture of Jules to all state and local police across New England and Jeff Cattagio held a press conference earlier that afternoon asking for the public's help in finding her. Vanessa was monitoring events online and had told Gus that social media was on fire with the story. By her tone, he took that as good thing.

After speaking with Maria Lincoln earlier in the day, Gus's thinking shifted hard to Jules likely being their suspect and that Lizzy was the one leading them to her. Then, when they confirmed Troy Robinson's alibis he knew that was their answer. So, then, like Montresor's final brick in "The Cask of Amontillado," Jules sealed Gus's convictions they were right when she broke into Mel's house. They would get her—he knew it. Jules was no Whitey Bulger. It was just a matter of time now.

But feeling confident she'd be apprehended and actually apprehending her were two very different things. And Gus was getting more antsy with each passing minute that she was not in custody. So, with nothing new on that front, he decided to stop by the hospital to see if Lizzy Porter had awoken. And, if not, maybe he could speak with her daughter, Terry. Maybe the teenager saw or heard something during the break-in earlier that morning that would shed light on what happened. Mel walked him and Vanessa to the front door while Rich Burrows made himself comfortable on a stool at the island in the kitchen.

The rain had not let up, so Gus zipped up his leather bomber jacket and flipped its collar up, readying for a sprint to his truck. He hoped the rear sliding window hadn't vibrated open again on the ride over. Mel thanked them for coming and, with a touch to his arm, asked Gus how much longer they planned to be in town.

"We've got a few things to chase down, but once Jules is in custody we'll be heading back to Boston."

Mel tipped her head in understanding, then Vanessa's and Gus's phones chimed in quick succession with alerts. Jules had been spotted about forty-five minutes away in Burlington leaving a small gas station convenience store. A state trooper had called it in and was approaching to detain her. Vanessa used a secure app on her phone to listen in to the radio chatter and put it on speaker so Gus could hear also.

"Suspect fleeing the premises on foot," said a winded man's voice. "Officer in pursuit."

"Car fifty-two three minutes out," said another male voice.

Mel leaned closer to Gus to hear what was happening and out of the corner of his eye he watched a hand go to her mouth in concern.

"Roger, car fifty-two," came the steady voice of a female dispatcher.

The phone fell silent and Gus felt a mixture of excitement and tension rising within him. He thought about heading to the scene, being there to speak with Jules when she was apprehended. But he knew by the time he got there she'd most likely already be on her way to Boston in the back of some trooper's car. The hurried voice of the officer on site spilled from the phone.

"Suspect entering a vehicle at the corner of Bedford Street and Route Sixty-Two. Black SUV, plate number Juliet-Echo-Whiskey-Echo-Lima-Sierra."

"Roger that," responded the dispatcher. "All units, officers on site. Suspect may be armed. Approach with caution."

Gus sighed. "It's over. They've got her."

"Officer down," yelled the officer. "I repeat: officer down. Suspect on the move at high speed, heading toward south side exit."

"Roger that," confirmed the dispatcher. "Additional backup en route, eight minutes out."

"What is she doing?" whispered Mel in disbelief.

"All units, all units, ten-fifty at the corner of Route Sixty-

Two and Bedford Street," strained the officer at the scene. "Suspect's vehicle involved in a multiple-car collision."

Gus needed to speak with Jules before she was in a hospital, potentially sedated, lawyer by her side. He pulled his keys from his pocket.

"V, let's hit it."

The dispatcher's voice clipped Vanessa's reply. "All units, critical trauma at the scene. Jaws of Life requested; ambulance en route. Twelve minutes out."

"Fuck!" spat Gus before seeing the disbelief on Mel's face morph into fear. He put his hand on her shoulder, prompting her to look up at him. His face softened; he shook his head slowly.

"Hey, hey, don't worry. The troopers at the scene are pros, and it's common to have the Jaws of Life brought in in accident situations. They don't want to risk further injury by pulling the injured out of the car."

But, no sooner had Gus gotten those comforting words out to Mel than the dispatcher was back with another, more somber update.

"All units, be advised car fire reported at the scene. Repeat, car fire involving suspect's car in progress. Be aware of perimeter established."

Gus's emotions flooded with dread. If Jules had suffered a critical trauma they wouldn't be able to speak with her at the scene, but he also knew if they couldn't get her out of that burning car no one would be speaking with her at all. He felt Mel lean into him.

"All units, all units, fire rescue has control of the scene," alerted the dispatcher. "Repeat: fire rescue has the scene. Multiple fatalities reported."

Gus clenched his jaw in frustration. He looked to Vanessa. "I want to speak to the trooper in charge of the scene, now."

Without saying a word, Vanessa spun her phone in her palm, pivoted on a heel, and headed back toward the kitchen. And, as she left, Gus felt Mel's shoulders begin to shudder into his side. He moved his hand along the top of her back and, pulling her into him, held her close.

Chapter Fifty-One

MEL MINDLESSLY TOSSED some clothes into a bag, loaded Fred in the Jeep, and followed Officer Burrows out of her driveway, leaving Gus and Vanessa sitting in his truck, each on their phone. Mel's mood swung from fury to sorrow and back as she rode an emotional pendulum decades in the making. How had all of this happened, how had it gone this far? While packing the bag in her bedroom, Mel had put on the television to see what they were saying about Jules on the news. So now, as she numbly drove to Mr. T's house, she couldn't get the image out of her mind—the firefighters dousing Jules's charred Range Rover with steady streams of water, steam wafting into the air.

Mel dropped Fred and her bag off at Mr. T's before heading straight to the hospital to look in on Lizzy and her daughter, Terry. They had been admitted to the Middlesex County Hospital for observation early that morning, so she was hoping they'd be allowed visitors by now. After speaking with a helpful older gentleman at the information desk in the lobby, Mel found herself stepping out of the elevator onto the fifth floor. She checked the room numbers beside each door, quietly making her way to room 512. She peeked through the viewing window and saw Lizzy in the bed closest to the window. She was lying still, eyes closed, and had an oxygen mask affixed to her face and several cords running from her arm to a large monitor.

In the bed beside her was Terry. Terry's eyes were closed but there was no oxygen mask on her, and Mel thought she saw her arm move. Mel was about to find a nurse to see if she could go in their room when a very tired-looking Maria stepped from the small bathroom in the corner and sat in a seat beside Lizzy's bed.

Mel pushed hesitantly into the room and met Maria's eyes. The two of them held a stare for several long, anguishing moments before Maria stepped forward and hugged Mel.

"I'm so sorry for everything," she whispered into Mel's ear.

Mel hugged her back, long and hard, just as she had done that morning in Maria's living room after Sarah's death. And after a minute, Mel released and swiped at the tears on her cheeks with an open palm. She looked into Maria's shame-filled eyes.

"What're you doing here?" she asked. Her voice was hoarse. "I thought you and Jim…" Her thought dropped off.

Maria nodded, choking back tears. "We were. We were released on bail." Maria told Mel about her and Jim's confessions to the FBI, how they got a lawyer and how he thought that they would be able to strike a plea arrangement that kept the both of them out of jail.

"Maria, that's amazing."

"I know. We're so thankful for a second chance after all that's happened." She pulled the gold cross out from beneath her collar and kissed it.

"Where's Jim now?"

"He's at home with the kids. We sat down with them earlier and told them everything...well, almost everything." She eyed Mel. "There are some things I couldn't bear for my kids to know."

Terry stirred, catching Mel's attention. "Has anyone spoken with PJ?"

"Ya, I called him from home. He's pretty confused, still trying to understand everything that's happened."

"Did you...?"

Maria's eyebrows scrunched together. "Oh, heavens, no. Once he told me that they expect Lizzy to make a full recovery I thought it best she tell him what she wants. But, when we spoke he and Nico were at home, and I just couldn't bear the thought of Lizzy and Terry here, alone."

Maria followed Mel's eyes to the Bible in front of her chair on Lizzy's bed.

"I thought I'd need some help for this one," said Maria, answering Mel's unasked question.

They both chuckled through drying tears. Mel met Maria's eyes again. "You've heard about Jules."

Maria replied with two quick nods of her head as her bottom lip quivered. "Jim wanted to call the doctor to get me some Valium I was so upset."

"I was with Gus...the FBI agents when they got the alert that she'd been spotted. It was hell listening to it live."

The two of them spoke for a long time about Jules and Becca and things that were said and done decades ago, trying to make sense of the senseless. They then lamented all that had happened since: the lies, the secrets, the deceit, the disgusting behavior of all of them. They questioned everything, they got mad, they got sad. And when all that was done they talked about Mr. T and Jim and the kids. They talked about PJ and Nico, Terry and Lizzy and how they'd each be there for them. And for each other. But neither of them spoke of the future, of what was to come. Maybe it was intentional, maybe not. Maybe in their own way, they each realized they knew nothing of what was to come. And maybe, just maybe, for the first time in decades, they were each comfortable with that.

Mel hugged Maria again and, as she did so, glanced toward the door and saw Gus standing in the hallway looking back at her. They held each other's eyes, and for a fleeting second Mel wondered if Gus had come to think less of her, disappointed in the secret she had held from him and many, many others.

And just when she had convinced herself that was the case, Gus's faced relaxed into a smile that touched his brilliant, ice-blue eyes.

Chapter Fifty-Two

GUS WANTED TO go to Mel, be with her, but he knew he couldn't. Mel went back to speaking with Maria and his eyes were drawn to an unconscious Lizzy as Sarah Nelson's former lover, the nurse George Palin, entered the room. He nodded hello to Mel and Maria, then checked Lizzy's chart and IV bag hanging from a tall chrome pole beside her bed. He then went about reading Terry's chart, lingering. It was times like this that Gus questioned his choice to join the FBI. Musicians didn't have to deal with murders and toxins and pathologists, and they sure as hell didn't have to tell a sixteen-year-old girl her mother had been sedated to help save her life.

Gus felt Vanessa step beside him followed by another person. He turned to see Tony Blackford.

"How was the Porter scene, Ton?" asked Vanessa, rubbing her strained eyes with a finger and thumb.

"Looked like the place had been tossed. We found the toddler locked in his room playing with some toys and, other than messing his pants, he seemed okay. But the mother and daughter were wrecks. We had the CSI guys go over each of them head to toe and bag their clothes before the EMTs took 'em away." He raised a thick, fuzzy eyebrow. "Nothing of note from the daughter, but the assailant was all over the mother so we got a few good things from her."

Gus looked from a still Lizzy Porter to Tony. "Like what?"

"They pulled a long blond hair from the mother's collar. They're running DNA tests on it now." He pulled a few large color photos from a manila envelope. "And we found this."

The first photo was a headshot of Lizzy Porter from the scene. Her face was bloated and an odd shade of white that reminded Gus of a frog's belly. The bright crime scene lights highlighted every imperfection. Tony immediately slid that photo beneath the next one. "This is the one I wanted you to see."

The second picture was a close-up of the side of Lizzy's face with her mouth in the center. Her lips were a deep, shiny red that juxtaposed her pasty face.

"Lizzy Porter doesn't wear makeup." Vanessa then turned to Gus. "That's the same shade of red lipstick that Jules wears. I'd know it anywhere."

"There's more," Tony said, pointing to the corner of Lizzy's mouth. "If you look closely you'll see traces of lipstick across the corner of her mouth there."

Gus could just barely make out a faint oval of the same red lipstick stretching at an angle over the corner of Lizzy's lips.

"A kiss?" questioned Gus.

"You got it," confirmed Tony.

"They can get DNA from that, right?" asked Vanessa

excitedly.

"Yes, they can, provided there's some saliva. But they said they'd be surprised if there wasn't at least a trace. It's in the lab as we speak."

"Boom," breathed Vanessa, her eyes still on the photo. "That's not circumstantial," she added for Gus's benefit.

As Tony slipped the photos back into the folder he added, "They found the same injection spots on both the mother and daughter as they found on the Nelson woman."

Gus gestured to Terry, who was stirring awake in the next room. "We should speak with her while we can."

Tony nodded. "Sure thing. But, before you do, we got the ballistics back on that rifle found in the Russells' basement too. It's a match to the shell casing they got from that ridge in the woods." He jutted his chin toward the wound on the side of Gus's head. "The shooter."

"Fingerprints?"

Tony shook his head. "Wiped clean or they wore gloves, or both. But, also, the agents checking security footage near the Ashby Sheraton spotted the Russell woman in her Range Rover in the parking lot across the street. The footage shows her being there for just over three hours, and as soon as you two arrived at the Sheraton she left." Gus's jaw tightened in frustration. Tony continued, "The forensics folks also confirmed that the moldings of the footprints found by that tree in the woods where you got shot at are size eight—the same size as the Russell woman. They didn't confiscate any sneakers with a matching tread pattern from her house, but a few agents are there now taking a second look. And, the page from the Munroe girl's journal left in that envelope on the tree? They got no fingerprints or any trace from it. But, saving the best for last, the handwriting *does not* appear to be the same as the other page you got."

Gus's forehead wrinkled. "What?"

"They're having another handwriting specialist look at it. It's close, but our guy says it doesn't seem to be a match but, rather, a very good copy."

"What the hell does that mean?" bitched Gus.

Vanessa tilted her head toward him. "It means that somebody who knows more about handwriting than you or me is getting a second opinion."

Gus noticed Terry open her eyes so looked back to Tony. He tipped his head. "Nice work. Thanks, brother."

"You got it. I'll get back to you when we get the labs back on the lipstick."

Tony left and Gus and Vanessa went into Lizzy and Terry's room. Before speaking with Terry, they asked Mel and Maria and George the nurse to wait in the hall so they had the room to themselves. A young female doctor had followed them into the room and was now leaning over and speaking quietly with Terry. After stating her objection to Terry being interviewed, she finally agreed but limited it to just a few minutes, then left the room. Gus pulled two chairs over beside the bed, so he and Vanessa sat.

"Terry, we're so sorry you had to go through that ordeal," began Gus, and he noticed he was speaking in the same soothing, hushed tone the doctor had been using. "We wanted to ask you a few questions if that's okay. Did you get a look at your assailant at all?"

"I did," she said immediately, her voice raw and angry, and he could see her look to her mother, by the window. Gus was startled at the sharpness of her tone, the wired look in her eyes. He was more accustomed to picking fragments of clues from victim statements. Vanessa held a cup of water and guided its straw between the young girl's chapped lips and she eagerly drank. She cleared her throat. "I did catch a glimpse when I was rolled out of bed: tight black running clothes, black gloves, tight black ski mask. But it was Jules Russell. Fucking Jules Russell attacked us."

"If you didn't see their face, how do you know it was her?" asked Gus.

Terry shakily raised her head off the pillow and spoke through gritted teeth.

"I smelled her," she growled and Gus recoiled. "Jules has some sort of skin condition—eczema or psoriasis or something. She uses this special medicated cream that has a very unique smell to it; she has for years. I'd recognize it anywhere."

Terry's head dropped back onto the pillow and she closed her eyes. The young doctor, who had been watching through the window from the hall, stepped back into the room. Gus thanked Terry, then they left the room.

Out in the hallway, they awkwardly stood with Mel and Maria for a moment, watching the doctor tend to her patient. Gus knew he had gotten what he came for. The evidence against Jules continued to stack up. A commotion coming from the nurses' station down the hall caught their attention, and they each looked to see Annie Elkins rushing toward them.

"Mel!" said Annie a little too loudly as she hurried to her friend and gave her a hug. "*The Meetinghouse* chat room is going *crazy* and someone said they saw police rush up your driveway so I freaked. You okay?"

"Ya, ya, I am now, thanks."

Annie took a deep breath and tried to collect herself. She looked around at the others. "I'm so sorry for interrupting, but when you didn't return my texts I went to your house and I saw the FBI crawling all over the place… I didn't know what to do."

Mel put a hand on her friend's shoulder and Annie's eyes bulged in embarrassment. "When you weren't home I went to Mr. T's and he told me you came here so…" She chuckled at herself and Mel pulled her into a half hug.

"You okay?" she asked, smiling.

Annie laughed and nodded. She then looked to Maria and reached out and touched her arm. "How are you doing? You okay?"

Maria glanced to Gus, then back to Annie. "In process but, God willing, we'll be fine."

Annie gestured to the window beside the door. "How're they? Are they going to be okay?"

"Yes, looks that way," said Maria. "The doctor said they should make a full recovery."

"Oh, thank God," said Annie, rubbing her forehead.

"They just need to rest now," interrupted a deep voice, and Gus turned to see the nurse, George, step around the corner. He looked to the women and tipped his head. "I'm so sorry for your losses."

He entered Lizzy's room and closed the door behind him.

Chapter Fifty-Three

MEL WAS STILL reeling from her encounter with a feral Jules and from the tragedy of Jules's death and found herself pacing nonstop around Mr. T's living room, filled with anxious energy. Mr. T had tried everything to help Mel settle, from offering to talk about it to getting her a glass of whiskey to leaving her alone so she could process it all in her own way. But nothing seemed to work. Finally, at his wit's end, Mr. T suggested to Mel that she go see one of her friends, go be with someone who could talk about everything that had happened in a way Mr. T couldn't. It took some convincing, but Mel reluctantly agreed before realizing that with Laur, Sarah, and Jules all gone there was actually no one left in the Posse to be with. Lizzy was in the hospital with her daughter Terry, and Maria was home trying to save her family and her marriage. Then Mel thought of Annie and wondered why she hadn't thought of her first; she always felt better after being with Annie. A quick text exchange and Mel was soon off to Annie's for a glass of wine and a much-needed home-cooked meal.

Mel was met at the door by Annie's latest foster dog, Norman, a gentle twelve-year-old golden retriever with soft fur and an even softer tongue. Van Morrison sang softly in the background, and as she stepped into the warm, inviting kitchen she caught sight of the steaming stovetop pots. Mel thought of dinners at the Turners', Laur and she laughing with Mr. and Mrs. T as they ate at the small square kitchen table, and it warmed her.

Annie was in her element as she worked her way around the kitchen with ease. Mel folded her coat over one of the stools at the island as Annie poured her a glass of red wine from a decanter in the shape of a duck. She put Mel to work cutting vegetables at the thick block of wood on the island and gestured toward the small muted television affixed to the bottom of her cabinets. On its screen was a newscaster in front of the vacant intersection where earlier Mel had seen Jules's burnt SUV being attend to by firemen.

"Did you see any of the videos of Jules's chase or her car on fire?"

"I caught one of the breaking news stories," said Mel with a tone of regret.

"It went up just like that." Annie snapped her fingers. "They said she was probably unconscious but even if she wasn't there was just no time to get her out."

Mel closed her eyes. "That's horrible."

"True, but given all the things that woman did…" Annie let the thought hang in the air as Mel fidgeted with the carrot she was cutting. Annie checked the pot roast before sliding it back into the oven. Mel gestured toward one of the pots and Annie nodded, so Mel dropped the sliced carrots into its boiling water.

"Well, and especially how her actions will affect each of

those young girls for the rest of their lives," continued Annie, wiping her hands on the front of her apron. "You said it yourself when Laurie died: at sixteen years old, Lisa will need therapy for years to work through the trauma of losing her mother."

Mel nodded.

"And as you and I've talked about many times—especially before Billie passed—those girls had real issues even before losing their mothers."

"Ya, but bullying's one thing, losing your mother's a different level."

"For some," replied Annie sourly. "It's just incredible, though. How much one woman can impact so many lives. I mean, the murders are horrible enough. But, if you think about it, it doesn't stop there. Lisa uprooted her life and moved to Chicago after Laurie's death, and I heard the Nelsons' house is coming up for sale; Steve and the girls just can't get over Sarah being found in their yard. And PJ and Lizzy and the kids—will they ever really feel safe in their own home again? And Maria and Jim's kids? Their home was also violated, and now their parents might be going to jail? And, of course, there's Jules's own kids: I can't imagine them ever coming back to town. Jules is like our own modern-day Lizzie Borden."

Annie took another drink of wine and tried to comfort Mel by rubbing her shoulder. The home phone rang and she read the caller ID. "Ah, shit, it's the foundation. I have to grab this, sorry."

Mel watched as Annie rushed up the stairs to take the

call. She stirred the carrots then, sipping her wine, wandered into the living room when something bright caught her attention through the partially open door to Annie's small den. Hearing Annie's muffled voice from upstairs, Mel pushed the door further ajar and leaned inside the dark room.

Against the wall beside the door was a computer and large desktop monitor, its wide screen split into multiple smaller screens with names in solid white boxes in their lower left corners: *Mel*, *Lizzy*, *Maria*, *Sarah*, *Jules*, *Police Station*. Each screen was filled with a snowy video feed except for the box labeled *Jules*. Confused, Mel held the doorjamb and leaned closer and watched as FBI agents walked in and out of its frame. She jolted and as she did so a partially open drawer of the desk caught her attention. Inside was a thick stack of paper with dark copy lines bleeding from its edges like black tears. Mel pulled it out and stiffened at what she read: *My Wonderful Life, Becca Munroe.*

Mel's heart raced as she scanned the entries, her eyes following the flowing cursive handwriting and, as she did so, she recognized a bunny-eared one as the entry from Becca's journal that Vanessa showed Mel on her phone, the one in which Jules gave her marijuana and the one in which the unidentifiable James was mentioned. Mel's eyes drifted to the corner of the desk and a framed picture of Annie's daughter, Billie, and her boyfriend at the time of her death: James.

Mel's brain hiccupped as she looked back to the post and her eyes went to the bottom of the entry. Like all the others, it was signed simply *B*.

What the…?

And that's when Mel felt the needle prick at the base of her neck and heard Annie's soft, sad voice whisper in her ear.

"And I'd hoped we'd get past all this together."

Chapter Fifty-Four

IT HAD BEEN several hours since the story broke of the FBI's manhunt for Jules and her resulting death, and the video of her fiery crash was in constant rotation on news channels and being spewed online. And with Jules now confirmed dead, Gus and Vanessa set about tying up loose ends before heading back to Boston to get a jump on the paperwork.

They started with the only other potential suspect they had identified: Troy Robinson. While Troy had provided video footage from inside his store to prove he was there during the times of Laurie Turner's death, as well as when Gus was shot at in the woods, Gus couldn't get past his counterintelligence background. So, ever the perfectionist, Gus had directed agents to review all available independent security footage near or around Robinson's hardware store for the periods of time in question and, following up on that, confirmed they were able to validate Troy's alibis.

It took only an hour or so for the agents at Mel's house to find the same surveillance equipment in her home as they had found at Lizzy's. Gus then had agents dispatched to both Sarah's and Maria's houses but knew they'd find the same equipment in their homes also. Laurie's house was a question mark; Gus felt comfortable that her murder was not planned like Sarah's, but more one of opportunity. He would have her house searched also, if for no other reason than to test his hypothesis. And, as for Jules's house, the agents who had gone back to look for other pairs of Jules's sneakers had just made it back to Boston when Gus had them turn around and head back to now look for surveillance equipment. Once Jules's death hit the news, Shane had taken his daughters to his parents' house in Connecticut to ride out the media storm, so they knew the house was now empty.

Vanessa had heard from the attorney general's office that both Maria and Jim Lincoln had been released on bail, which they already knew. Jim would be charged with obstruction of justice for removing Laurie Turner's cell phone from her murder scene and later destroying it and for altering that phone's voice and data records before providing those records to both the state police and FBI. Gus knew how this would play out: Jim would be placed on long-term, unpaid leave from the Kendalton Police Department pending resolution of the case.

"Do you really think Jim will go to prison?" asked Rich from Jim's former desk chair. Gus was sitting on the corner of an adjacent desk with Vanessa standing by his side. He noticed Rich's attempt at a five-o'clock shadow had been cleanly shaven off and his hair was trimmed shorter and neater, and his uniform had a crispness to it.

"I can't say for certain." Gus shook his head. "But I don't think so."

"And Lizzy's obstruction charges? You think they'll

stick?"

"Don't know." Gus contemplated this. "But by feeding us information directing us toward Jules instead of coming straight to us, she did impede the investigation."

"Maybe she admits to it once she wakes up, but she denied it was her before."

Gus scoffed, "I don't buy it. We found Rebecca's journal at her house and the video of Jules on her hard drive, and her search history goes back months searching for hacking others' devices, ways to break security alarm codes, and a whole host of other things."

"But you also found surveillance equipment in her house."

"That's right," jumped in Vanessa. "Surveillance equipment feeding footage back to her own computer. They think it's some sort of do-it-yourself security system. They're still trying to determine if she was getting video feeds from the others' houses."

Rich rocked his head side to side at this new piece of information. Vanessa's eyes were drawn to the television mounted on the wall as video of Jules's fiery car wreck began to play again. She jutted her chin toward the television.

"What d'ya think the vibe'll be like here in town once this makes the rounds?"

Rich's ballooned cheeks resembled those of a pufferfish. "At first: shock and awe. Some would've liked to see Jules hang for all she did, but I think most people will just want to put all of this behind us." Rich caught Gus's eye. "Do you think there'll be any charges coming from Becca's death now that we know the truth?"

"No," Gus said flatly. "Even though there's no statute of limitations on murder, we still don't know if it was that or an accident or even if Jules was complicit in any way."

"No obstruction charges?"

"I doubt it. The only ones who could face charges are Lizzy and Maria, and both have enough legal troubles before them now as it is. I'm not sure the AG will pile it on."

"What about Mel?"

Gus pursed his lips dismissively. "She wasn't even there. What Laurie told her would be considered third-person hearsay." He mulled it over for another moment. "Nah, it was over twenty-five years ago… Rebecca's parents aren't with us anymore and there's only her brother left. I'm not sure anyone wants to open old wounds at this point."

They talked for a few more minutes, then Rich offered to run and get takeout, but Gus said they'd have to take a rain check. He was eager to get back to Boston so they could get their paperwork done and put Kendalton and this case behind them.

Chapter Fifty-Five

MEL'S SORE, DRY eyes followed the end of an eyedropper as it lowered over one then the other and her vision became blurry.

"You should be able to blink and probably talk in a minute or so."

Mel's vision slowly cleared, and she realized Annie was leaning directly over her, their faces inches apart. Mel was sitting back at the island in front of the cutting board she'd been using earlier. She watched Annie rake fingers over an ear to keep her curly black hair out of her eyes.

"It took a bit of practice after what happened with Sarah to figure out the right dosage of this stuff, but I think I've finally got it." Annie's eyes widened. "That Sarah; she was in *far* better shape than I thought. I expected her to drop like a fly. But no; she takes off and almost makes it to her house. If Maria would've just looked back into the woods she'd have looked right at me."

Mel could begin to move her eyes and looked from side to side until they stopped on a black handgun on the island next to Annie. Beside it was a small vial of cloudy yellow fluid and a disposable syringe filled with the same liquid. She wanted to cry out but her mouth refused to listen to her brain. Annie's eyes followed Mel's, and she picked up the gun and slid it into the back of her pants like a pro.

"Don't be scared, Mel. I don't want you to be frightened. I wanted the *others* to be frightened." She raised an eyebrow. "And, believe me, they were."

Mel's thoughts went to the monitor with video feeds from each woman's house, Becca's journal, the needle. She felt her heart beating erratically and her mouth was dry. She slowly closed her eyes and opened them again.

"Good, oh good. It's coming back."

Annie's face was back over hers with a look of curiosity as Mel's mouth moved awkwardly but no sound came out.

"Why?" ventured Annie, still staring at Mel's lips. She began to nod slowly. "I guess you deserve to know, after all we've been through together." Annie's eyes brightened and her eyebrows arched upward. "And, Mel, regardless of what happens, please know that I couldn't have made it through Billie's death without you. You're a true friend. I'll never forget that."

Annie took a deep breath and exhaled, her lips tightly pressed together.

"So much has gone on… I guess I'll just start way back at the beginning. You know Billie had been getting bullied for years by those bitches' daughters, and you of all people know of the struggles with drugs and anxiety and counseling we went through with her. Well, it seems even with all that, I never truly appreciated the extent of it. But then one day late last winter I was having a really bad day; I just couldn't seem to get her off my mind. So, I took a walk out back in the woods—where she used to go—to think and clear my head. And about a mile in I find this old shed or hut built in a little copse of trees. So, I check it out. On the dirt floor is a ragged, old pink backpack, all grimy and grungy, holes in it. And hanging on a nail up under this thick shelf was a black-and-white Billie Eilish backpack; my Billie's backpack. And inside, sealed in a large Ziploc baggie, is Becca's journal."

Mel's eyes bulged and she opened her mouth and coughed.

"I know, right? I was surprised too. So, I start going through it. There are entries in there about Becca seeing Troy Robinson *for months*—who knew?—and of her getting pregnant and how every option she looked at to get rid of the baby fell through. She wrote of all the secrets she kept—her dating Troy from her parents, her pregnancy from Troy, her budding friendship with Jules from Maury—and how it was soiling her soul. It was heartbreaking. But, it was the part about Jules talking with her and being friends that got me." Annie paused and her cadence slowed. "Becca actually thought she was getting into the cool group; she was too innocent to see what was happening. But it was so obvious: Jules knew she and Troy had been together and was spinning her little web around Becca to find out more. Then I find the last entry from Becca was the night before she died. She wrote about how Jules asked her to come out with the girls and how much she was looking forward to it." Annie's face hardened. "And that's when I knew; I knew Jules killed her, I just knew it."

Mel's shoulder twitched involuntarily and Annie abruptly stopped talking. She eyed Mel suspiciously for a moment, then raised an eyebrow.

"Looks like we better move this little party along. So, anyway, then I flip to the next page only to find that Billie had begun adding to Becca's journal. My Billie. I could tell her handwriting anywhere. I knew she used to go for long walks in those woods, but she never told me anything about a shed or Becca's journal or any of it. And then I realize: That shed is about halfway between our house and Becca's old house. And if you walk straight back into the woods from there, what do you come to?" Annie was nodding. "That's right: the quarry. So, my guess is that Becca used to go to that shed too and on the night of her death she left her little, girly pink backpack there not knowing she'd never be back to get it."

Mel's eyes were puddles from the drops, so when she blinked tears rolled onto her cheeks. Annie took a napkin from the counter and dabbed them away.

"I know, heartbreaking, isn't it? But, it gets worse. I start to read Billie's entries and they're *horrific*. They talk about all the abuse she took from those little whores. They'd invite her to parties, pretending to be her friends, then ignore her at school and spread rumors about her."

Annie choked up and her eyes began to bleed tears. "She. Never. Understood. Why." She angrily swiped at her cheeks. "She wondered if it was her. Did she do something to make them hate her? Was there something wrong with her? She wondered why she didn't have any friends."

Mel felt tingling in her arms and chest, and she could

move her toes inside her boots. She stole a glance at the kitchen clock, frustrated at how slowly the minutes scraped by. Annie collected herself and turned back to Mel.

"I watched you the other night," she said, gesturing toward the door to her den and the monitor beyond. "With the FBI. After Jules came to see you. That second page from Becca's journal the redhead showed you on her phone? That was from Billie. One of the parties the girls invited her to was at Jules's house. Jules knew the kids were drinking in the basement, but she not only did nothing about it, she actually gave my daughter drugs! My daughter! The young girl who struggled with depression… Jules introduces her to drugs and alcohol?"

Mel watched as her one-time friend heaved and shuddered at the remembrance of her only child's death. And when she spoke again she did so in a sorrowful tone.

"I've not been completely truthful, Mel," Annie stammered. "There's something that I've not told you." She rubbed her bloodshot eyes with the palms of her hands. "The last entry in that journal by Billie was a goodbye." Tears ran down familiar, salty tracks. "Those little bitches tormented my Billie so much that she thought she had no other choice but to take her own life." Annie bit back more tears. "But, then the more I read of the journal, the more I understood. And that's when I knew: everything…" Annie was nodding faster with each word. "*Everything* Billie went through and *everything* Becca went through…*all of it* was because of Jules."

Annie's head twitched and her eyes blinked quickly, as if

someone had played with her on/off switch. Her eyes were manic. Then as quickly as it had come, it was gone.

"I knew she had to be stopped." She shrugged. "Karma's a bitch," she finished matter-of-factly, her voice light again, as if making small talk. Mel ripped herself away from the wreckage in her head just in time to give Annie an insignificant nod.

"I knew you'd understand," Annie said with relief. "Something had to be done. I couldn't think about anything else, day or night."

Annie took Mel's hand in hers and began to speak faster. "Then about a week later I bump into Laurie on the trails and I tell her Jules is evil and she needs to be stopped." She raised an eyebrow. "And I'm sure I looked like a raving lunatic; I hadn't showered or slept in a week. And Laurie hugs me and tries to get me to go with her. She tells me everything will be all right, that she'll help me make everything all right."

Annie was squeezing Mel's hand so hard now it felt like it might crack. Her face was red, her voice rising with each word.

"But I *don't* want to go with her! I keep telling her that Jules is evil, that all of their daughters are evil and they all need to be stopped! But she won't listen. She keeps telling me everything will be all right, she'll help me make everything all right...and I start to yell at her because I *know* everything will be all right because I'm gonna fucken' *make* it all right but she won't listen so I scream louder and she tries to hug me again and I push her and she gets scared and she tries to run away but I can't let her go so I grab her and push her to the ground and she's screaming and crying and I *can't* let anyone hear her so I grab a rock and I hit her and hit her and HIT HER!"

Chapter Fifty-Six

GUS'S EYES GLANCED to the *Entering Kendalton* sign in his rearview mirror as he headed out of town toward Route 3 and, eventually, back to Boston. Part of him was more than happy to leave the town behind, to wrap this ugly case up. He had gotten a call to perform at a Leroy Jones tribute concert just six weeks away and could use every waking minute to prepare. He'd be damned if he missed this one. But a larger part of him was sorry he wouldn't be seeing Mel again. Maybe he'd give her a call once the dust settled a bit.

Before leaving Kendalton, he wanted to speak with Chief Burrows once more, so after packing up their belongings at the inn, Vanessa hitched a ride back to Boston with one of the other agents. And now, thirty minutes closer to their offices, was on the phone with him. Picking up on his janky vibe, Vanessa said, "Penny."

"Nothing," Gus replied, distracted. His voice was clipped.

She exhaled in a huff through the phone. "Stop playing hard to get; it doesn't suit you."

"We never found that fourth vial of venom."

"Dude, give it up. Jules's car was an ash pile. That's dust

by now."

"You're convinced she had it with her?"

"She got kicked out of her house, then went on the run. Where else would it be?"

Gus knew she was probably right but still wanted to see that vial, touch it, hold it in his hands so he could check it off his list. He thought of the unidentified sneaker prints they took moldings of in the woods. The team was back searching Jules's house a third time, looking for any hidden surveillance equipment, so maybe they'd find the sneakers those prints belonged to also hidden somewhere. But he didn't dare raise that with Vanessa. She'd tell him what he already knew: that Jules either disposed of those sneakers or they too were reduced to ash in her car. Gus pinched his phone between his cheek and shoulder and shifted into fourth gear, steering his truck onto the three-lane highway, heading south.

"What d'ya make of that last text Jules got on her phone?" Gus asked.

The team in Boston had gotten the phone records for Jules's cell phone and called Vanessa earlier while she and Gus were packing up their bags at the inn. There were only a few incoming texts during her final twenty-four hours and none were notable except for the very last one. It was from an unknown number and simply read: *FBI on way. Run.* They triangulated her location using the cell tower data and determined she'd gotten it while at the crappy motel she was hiding out in. But when they tried to trace the number it was sent from they were unable to. It was clearly from a burner phone.

"No idea," answered Vanessa. "Could it have been her husband?"

"Shane Russell doesn't strike me as the type of guy to run out and get a burner. And, besides, he'd just kicked her out of the house. Why warn her? And, even if he would, how would he have known if we were on the way to her motel?"

"Someone in the Kendalton Police?"

"Could be, but why? We had a BOLO then an APB out on her. Everyone possible knew we were looking for her." Gus's mind was amping up so he continued, "And there's the Rebecca Munroe funeral card being left on Sarah Nelson."

"Jesus, Gus, you're like a dog with a bone. Like we said: Jules was a narcissist, she—" But before Vanessa could finish, another call came in to Gus's phone, and recognizing it as an FBI number he let her go and answered it. It was Tony calling from Boston.

"Hey, Ton, what's up?"

"The team at the Russells' house just called. They found surveillance equipment there, too, just like the others' houses."

"Did the feed lead to Lizzy Porter's house?"

"They're trying to trace it now."

"Okay, good."

"But, Gus, we've got some weird stuff going on here. You're far closer to this case than I am. Maybe you can make some sense of it."

Gus gripped the smooth, thin steering wheel tighter.

"Like what?"

"The DNA taken from the blond hair found on the Porter woman was a perfect match to the DNA taken from Jules Russell's remains."

"Excellent."

"It is, but here's where it starts to get really weird. We finally got a hit from that ultramarathon participant list Vanessa sent us. And the only person on it with any link to Kendalton is some guy living in Charlotte. But we just verified he's been in Charlotte this entire time."

"That is weird."

"There's more: We got a match to the DNA found in the kiss on the Porter woman's mouth, but it wasn't to Jules Russell." Gus clenched his jaw as Tony continued, "It was a familial match to the DNA taken from some dead girl a year ago. But get this: She was the daughter of this guy in Charlotte. We're chasing d—"

"What's this guy's name?" interrupted Gus.

"Daniel Elkins. Why?"

Gus's mind spun too fast, like a bicycle's pedal off its chain, and all sound deadened, as if he were in a movie that had been muted. He was back at the hospital earlier this evening, watching Mel getting a hug from a concerned and trusted friend.

Chapter Fifty-Seven

MEL COULD HEAR the water in the pot on the stove boiling over and blinked her eyes, forcing tears down her cheeks. Her thoughts went to cradling Laur that last time in the pond, but she pushed them back into the darkness. The evil that had killed her best friend, her sister, was standing before her. She wanted to lash out, smash Annie's face like Annie had smashed Laur's, but she still couldn't move her arms. She wiggled the fingers on her other hand, the one Annie couldn't see. The tingling was gone in her arms and chest and was fading in her legs.

"Laur did…nt…know how e…vil Julesis," she purposely stammered.

Annie looked back to Mel. "I knew you'd understand. You were never like those women." She paused. "But that was when I *knew* what I needed to do. Billie was gone. Dan—that dirtbag—left me and moved to Charlotte." She opened her palms to the ceiling. "I was all alone, just like Billie was. But *I* could fight back. Jules had to pay for Billie's death, but how? Murder was too good for her. The most important thing to that narcissistic bitch was her reputation, her fucken' social standing. She'd eat her young to protect that. So, that's when my plan crystallized: Each of the women who stood by and let their daughters drive my Billie to her death must pay. I wasn't sure how at first, but they would. But Jules? Jules had to have her social status here in town ripped from her, her reputation ruined, and she needed to spend the rest of her life in jail. But I couldn't trust the Keystone Kops around here to do it. Christ, the chief's married to Jules's best friend. So I had to get the FBI involved, which meant someone else had to die; the feds are always called in for serial killer cases. So, unfortunately, Sarah was the best candidate since it was pretty well known she and Jules hated each other."

Annie's face relaxed, her eyes widened, and she hunched her shoulders. "So, then, I got to it. Turns out it's super easy to hack computers and phones to get access to calls and emails and texts and to gain control of the video and audio recording apps. And it's just as simple to break into homes and plant surveillance equipment. And, wow, the dirt I got on each of those women was amazing."

"Jules is…evil," said Mel.

Annie eyed Mel suspiciously before smiling and nodding. "Don't we know it. And she's also surprisingly easy to frame for murder. Remember that night we had the charity event at Shane's work, when she had too much to drink and I looked in on her?" Annie said devilishly, "I took her keychain with her house key on it. I knew she'd just replace all the keys before she'd ever tell Shane she'd lost 'em while drunk. And while I was there I used Shane's security card to get the vials of toxin from the lab next door as he droned on and on in the other room about the boring research they do there." She paused. "I'd done my research ahead of time and knew what toxins they had at the institute. And, what better way to kill Sarah and frame Jules than to use a poison from Shane's work?

"Then, you gave me the best gift of all: You invited me to the station to walk those agents through the Land Trust trails app." Annie flicked Mel's shoulder and Mel felt it, solid and firm. The fog in Mel's mind was lifting and she was able to think more clearly. Maybe she could actually get out of this, do what neither Laur nor Sarah could do: survive. And just the thought of that had Mel's emotions traverse the wide gulf from terror to determination. She eyed the knife on the cutting board. She just needed to keep Annie talking a little longer.

"You see how I stumbled through getting on the computer and loading the app on Jim's and that agent's phones?" continued Annie. "It was actually hard pretending I knew nothing about computers." She laughed. "So, then, with that app on the agent's phone, I tracked you and him in the trails, took a few shots at him, then simply went back to Jules's house and planted the rifle and shells in her basement along with a few vials of that venom. And, while I was there, I took some hair from her brush, which I left with Lizzy, and a tube of that awful medicated cream she uses, which I wore when I visited Lizzy and her bitchy daughter, Terry. And boom: Jules is the mad person killing her friends and terrorizing the town.

"But framing Jules wasn't enough," Annie continued, energized from telling someone all she'd done. "She needed to be crushed, have the most important thing in her life taken from her: her reputation. With some, I just planted the seeds of doubt—I reminded you while we were walking the trails of how Jules so willingly embarrassed me in public and how awful she treats people. And that day on The Commons I told the agents how Jules got drunk at the fundraiser and stayed behind, alone. And in the police station, I pointed out how Jules's house sat right on the trails. Those little things go a long way in weaving thoughts together, creating a narrative. But I knew I needed more. So, I dropped that video of Jules drunk, hitting on Emily's boyfriend, for everyone to see. Heck, I had video equipment in all of your houses for months, twenty-four seven; I had so much compromising footage of Jules it was actually hard choosing what to use. Most people saw Jules for the horrible person she was, but nobody would ever say anything. But, now they had no choice. So, voila, she's kicked off all her treasured committees, Shane kicks her out of the house, she's banned from school activities and fired from her job at the high school. Oh, and the hack to her email at the high school to make her out to be Awkward7? That was shockingly easy. They really should do something about that."

"Awkward7?" croaked Mel, her voice rising.

Annie tilted her head. "My little joke. I don't know if you remember, but years ago Jules invited me to join you all at her house for cocktails. And, don't get me wrong, I was excited, had a great time. But then afterward, I saw these posts on her Facebook page saying that the party was fun but would've been better if *the awkward seventh one* wasn't there.

Me, the awkward seventh person at her house." Annie shrugged. "Seemed fitting."

"And Lizzy?" Mel asked hoarsely.

Annie shook her head. "Lizzy really needed to stand up for herself, get a backbone. She'd been Jules's bitch for as long as I can remember. It was easy to set her up as the one feeding the FBI info. A few minutes with her computer and she had all this browser history about how to hack computers and phones, what surveillance equipment is best, everything. And, so, I left Becca's journal there, sort of as icing on the cake, and boom: Lizzy had grown a pair."

Mel pretended to have trouble swallowing. "But Jules died," she pointed out.

"I know, who'd a thunk? I followed her to that shitty motel and waited for the FBI to come get her so I could watch. But they never did. So I got a burner phone and texted her that the FBI was on their way to flush her out. But I thought she'd run; I had no idea she'd show up at your house. That was...serendipitous. And then when she did run, I thought for sure she'd cower at the first sight of the FBI, but not Jules. I gotta hand it to her, she went all Thelma and Louise on 'em."

Mel's heart rate had gotten back to normal, as had her arms and legs. Her eyes rolled over the island and the vial of venom with the syringe lying next to it. She knew Annie was almost done; knew she had to think fast. So, as she did earlier when Jules was in her house, Mel rehearsed the next ten seconds in her head: kick Annie's stool away hard, spin away and jump off toward the living room, round the sofa to the hallway and front door, grab doorknob with left hand, throw right elbow up and back, slip through door and run for Jeep.

"So, now you know it all." Annie let out a deep exhalation.

"Why…me? I won't…say…anything." Mel faltered.

Annie's face turned sad. "Oh, Mel, I wish there were another way, I truly do." She then leaned forward and slowly picked up the needle, and when she looked back, Mel saw the evil in her friend's eyes. "But we both know you'll never really be able to forgive me for Laurie."

Mel was about to surprise Annie as she had Jules. But Annie was smarter than Jules. And quicker. Before Mel knew it, Annie was off her stool and had spun Mel around and now held the needle pressed firmly to Mel's neck. Mel was trapped and she felt the now-familiar tingling spreading throughout her neck and chest. She squirmed, trying to break free, but Annie's body was pressed tightly against her legs. Feeling her arms begin to tingle, Mel swatted at the island behind her and, finally grabbing the knife from the cutting board, swung it wildly at Annie. Annie released her grip and staggered backward, and as Mel's limbs grew heavy she noted the warm, wet feeling of blood on her hand.

Mel collapsed onto the floor like a sack of potatoes, suddenly unable to move at all. The sound of her own labored breathing filled her ears as she stared along the kitchen floor to the bottom of the oven. She noted a small spray of blood on the lower cabinets and the sound of stools being pushed aside behind her.

"You. Fucken'. Stabbed me!" raged Annie.

Mel's breathing then became erratic and tunnel vision began to close in, like black water circling a drain. Her thoughts slowed as Annie moaned and grunted behind her and lumbered from the room.

Chapter Fifty-Eight

Gus ended his call with Tony and hunted down Vanessa, who was still in the other agent's car, as he sped back toward Kendalton. He filled her in on his and Tony's conversation that led them to realize Annie Elkins was their killer. Vanessa immediately got into the FBI's databases and brought up Annie's background to brief Gus while he drove.

"Born Anne Marie Taylor, married Daniel Elkins in oh-five, divorced in twenty-twenty. One child, a daughter Belinda or Billie who, as we know, died of a drug overdose a little over a year ago. Annie grew up in Kendalton, graduated high school with the other women but, says here, didn't attend the public schools; was homeschooled." She spoke quicker, her voice becoming clipped. "Michigan State grad, degree in horticulture—shit!—a minor in computer science." There was a brief pause, then she added, "Ah, shit, she was ROTC." The line fell quiet and Gus could picture the determined scowl on his partner's face as she scanned the info for relevant details. "Fuck! Gus, she was a member of the marksmanship team; a club sport at the school. We just didn't do a ba—"

"She had alibis, though, right?" he interrupted.

"She said she was volunteering at the animal shelter the mornings of both murders. One of the other agents confirmed it... Says here the director of the shelter verified she was there both mornings and that she usually worked 7:00 a.m. to about noon, but he couldn't be sure of the exact times those specific days since they don't use time sheets for volunteers." Gus hung on a minute longer as she scanned the remainder of the file, but that was all she found relevant for now. They ended the call with her telling him she was twenty minutes out.

Gus was the first to arrive at Annie's house, and his mouth went dry at the sight of Mel's Jeep in the driveway. Dusk had succumbed to nighttime and, with no outside lights on, the entire area was composed of black hues. He could see a light on deep inside the house, but otherwise it too was dark. He turned his sputtering engine off but kept the headlights on, trained directly at the front door. He then flicked on his large, round roof lights and the front of Annie's house lit up as if it were midday. If Annie and Mel were inside they had heard his truck lumber its way up the gravel driveway, so there was no element of surprise to go for.

The front door was unlocked, so Gus drew his Glock and, easing the thick wooden door open, peered inside. Straight ahead, down a dim, narrow hallway, was the kitchen. Pendant lights hanging over a long island cast the room in a soft, inviting glow. He saw steam pluming from a pot on the stove and could smell something in the oven. To his left was the doorway to a small sitting room. The only light in the room was spilling in from another doorway to the kitchen on the far side. To his right—behind the open front door—was a door he assumed to be a coat closet. Clearing the space behind the front door first, he quickly cleared the sitting room. Then slowly closing the front door, opened the other door and raked his Glock amongst hanging coats, but it too was empty.

Gus carefully made his way toward the kitchen, his gun held confidently before him. His senses were tingling. He could feel energy somewhere close by, but the house was still—too still. The only sounds were the sizzling of water that glurped from the boiling pot onto the stovetop and the soft rhythm of distant music. He then heard movement from a room partway down the hall on the right. It had an open doorway, so he eased his six-foot-four frame against the wall beside it and peered in. It was the dining room, and from behind its table emerged an old golden retriever, tail wagging hesitantly.

Gus began to back out of the doorway, and that's when he saw a shadow in his peripheral vision move past the front door. Muscle memory took over and he began to turn that way, but this time the sound of the gunshot hit his ears at the same time the bullet entered, then exited his side. Blood exploded onto the wall behind him as the force rocked him back into the other side of the doorway. His surroundings turned a blinding silver, then images around him gradually reappeared like a developing Polaroid. He fired back twice and thought he might have caught Annie's arm, but before he could confirm it she had made it through the sitting room and was firing at him from the kitchen doorway behind him.

Gus's side burned with pain as he spun back around the other way and fired back. He watched as Annie's body jolted sideways and she fell from view. The momentum of his gunfire rotated his body and he toppled into the dining room and onto the end of the table. Adrenaline kicked in and his heart raced. He blinked repeatedly to clear his vision and felt his side. It was warm and wet. He heard sluggish footsteps but couldn't determine which way they were headed.

Gus froze and listened intently, trying to get a sense for where Annie was, but heard nothing. The side of his shirt and jacket were now soaked with blood and he could feel the warmth on his right side spreading to his hip. He knew time was not on his side. He tried to stand but got light-headed and fell to his knees.

Mel!

He needed to get back up, needed to find Mel. He leaned against the doorjamb and scanned the hallway, then into the kitchen. He saw blood on the floor beside a stool and, next to that, the bottoms of legs protruding from behind the island. He recognized Mel's Australian Blundstone boots, her thick socks spilling from their tops. Using the wall for leverage, Gus slid to a stand. He rested the back of his head against the wall and closed his eyes, willing for the strength to move.

And that's when the side of the doorway beside his head exploded into the room and the concussive energy from a shotgun at close range rattled Gus's eardrums to a deafening silence.

Chapter Fifty-Nine

MEL WAS FLOATING, her mind soupy with thoughts, when she heard the angry creaking of a door jonesin' for a hit of WD-40. She willed her eyes to open wider but her narrow gaze remained on a slice of the floorboard beside her face. Distant footfalls added percussion to Neil Young's "Harvest Moon" playing somewhere far off in the distance. She heard the moan of a nearby floorboard. Was it Annie? Was she back to finish what she started?

Mel heard a loud noise from the hallway, the scuffle of people scurrying, gunshots. There was a loud boom, a body hitting the floor, a voice. A man's voice. Her mind was jogged. *Gus!* He groaned, then another loud boom, this one like an explosion.

The soft padding of feet across the floor grew louder until Norman the old golden retriever was standing over her. He licked her face and Mel marveled at just how odd it was not to feel his slobbering tongue. Her every sense was strange, detached somehow, as if she were underwater.

Norman stopped licking and looked up toward the hallway. He began to wag his tail, then startled at the loud bang of a stool being knocked over. Another fell and landed by Mel. Someone collapsed onto the floor behind her and a hand slapped her side, then slid down her back to the floor. Dreamy, Mel wondered if any of this was real. Then it all became distant, as if the experience was not her own but someone else's.

A door slamming against a wall.

The vibration of heavy footfalls making her face rattle against the floor.

Vanessa crouching over her in slow motion, her hand going to Mel's neck. The agent's red face was tight with panic, her mouth moving in slow motion without sound. Her head sloshed to the side and the veins on her neck bulged like nightcrawlers as she yelled something over and over.

The world turning black.

Chapter Sixty

IT WAS JUST before midnight on a clear, southern November night. Preservation Hall was buzzing with excitement as the crowd lingered longer than usual to get photographs with Leroy Jones and to remain in the famous musician's orbit as long as possible. Having forgotten how cold November can get in the Big Easy, Gus had neglected to bring gloves and worried that his cold hands had him playing a little sloppy toward the end of the set. He watched the crowd swell toward the stage and could hear the music and noise from Bourbon Street through the window beside him. He made a note to avoid Bourbon and to use the smaller side streets to get back to his hotel. And given the part of town he was in, Gus was thankful he was six-four and had the training to use it.

He picked up his bass and winced at the twinge in his side. The bullet he took from Annie Elkins a few weeks ago had gone cleanly through, missing any vital organs or arteries, but the bruised ribs, severe concussion, and twenty stitches he had gotten as a result left him still on the mend and with two more scars for his growing collection.

Gus carefully lifted his bass and made his way past the drum set, between the rickety wooden chairs, and off the stage with no one stopping him for a photograph, an autograph, or so much as a word. He then ducked into the hallway and, working his way through the throngs of people waiting, made it to the back of the hall before stepping through the curtain and into the alley. It felt no colder outside than inside, and he remembered how poorly insulated the hall was.

He pulled the case for his rented bass from the closet beside the doorway and laid it on the ground. Noticing a small smudge of dust on his suit pants where they rubbed against the historic stage, he brushed it off then knelt down and went about packing up the bass. Lost in his thoughts, replaying his two mistakes from the show over and over, he had set the bass carefully into the velvet-lined case and stored his hand rags beside it before a soft, familiar voice spoke to him from behind.

"Trying to make a quick getaway?"

Gus looked up and over his shoulder to see Mel standing in front of the curtain and his heartbeat quickened. Her hair was lush and styled and shined in the faint overhead light. She wore a thin, form-fitting sweater, dark blue jeans, and new Blundstone boots. He smiled and stood.

"No one ever wants to talk to the bassist," he jokingly lamented. He couldn't remember seeing Mel in anything other than ripped jeans, sweats, or exercise clothes. He tipped his head toward her. "You look different."

She gave him a soft, casual smile. "Thanks."

"New boots?"

She smiled wider, tilted her head, and squinted a playful

look at him.

"You're a long way from home," he continued.

Mel stepped closer until he could feel the heat of her body.

"Someone once told me that I should listen to more jazz." She shrugged and his eyes were drawn to her dimples, her beautiful brown bedroom eyes looking up at him. "So, I figured, where better to get great jazz than New Orleans?" She took his hand in hers and put her other hand over his shoulder. "Besides, I didn't have a chance to thank you for...well, you know, saving my life."

Gus then did something he had dreamed of for months: He put his arms around Mel's waist and, placing his hands on the small of her back, drew her into him. She draped her hands gently around his neck and the two of them kissed slowly, passionately, for a long, long time, until their smiles caused them to stop. They hugged tight and whispered into each other's ears how much they missed each other and how they never wanted to feel like that again. Then they sat, arm in arm, on the steps and laughed and talked and laughed some more until eventually the noise from the crowds had gone and the city grew quiet and the soft glow of the morning sun warmed its sky.

Epilogue

Four Months Later

SPRING WAS IN full bloom in Kendalton, and the town was once again preparing for the 4-H Fair & Livestock Show on The Commons. A lot had happened during the past year, and it would take the town many more to move on from the deaths of three of its women, but most agreed continuing old traditions was a step in the right direction.

There were no charges filed against the remaining women for the night of Becca's death. The only potential witness to what actually happened, Jules Russell, was dead, and the Massachusetts attorney general didn't see the merits of dredging up a twenty-five-year-old cold case with no real evidence, only to ruin more lives.

Lizzy Porter, her husband PJ, and their children, Terry and little Nico, had moved in with PJ's parents while they looked for a new house. Terry was unable to sleep in their home without having night terrors, so they put it on the market for sale, but there was yet to be any interest. Sarah Nelson's widower, Steve, sold their home surprisingly quickly to someone relocating from California; a person who, apparently, had never heard of Google. Steve and his two daughters, Jessica and Abby, now lived in Ashby so the girls could continue to attend the same regional high school.

Although Jules Russell had been proven innocent of committing any of the murders she was framed for by Annie Elkins, the smear campaign Annie had waged against her exposed Jules's many transgressions for all to see. So, as a result, her husband Shane and his two daughters, Milly and Hannah, never returned to Kendalton from Connecticut. Shane left his position at the National Oceanographic Institute and was now a professor at one of the local colleges. He tried to sell their home but after repeated incidents of vandalism found it impossible so simply walked away from the house and Kendalton as a whole. The house remained in foreclosure.

Jim Lincoln had been charged with obstruction of justice for removing Laurie Turner's cell phone from her murder scene and altering her phone records. Given his exemplary service record, he was sentenced to just three years of probation but was prohibited from ever working in law enforcement again. Jim accepted the position of gym teacher at the high school and was the new junior varsity football coach. He was also the first to congratulate Rich Burrows on being appointed as the permanent chief of police for Kendalton.

Melainey Idlewilde added an in-law apartment to her home so that Mr. T could stay with her and Fred whenever he wanted. Mr. T "supervised" the construction, and Mel was thankful he had something to do besides clean and reorganize her basement and barn. Gus split his time between Mel's house and his condo in Charlestown, and he and Mr. T had bonded over fishing and their shared love for Mel. Mr. T approved of Gus and somehow Mel knew Laur would too. Mel adopted Norman, the elderly golden retriever Annie Elkins had been fostering, so now Fred and Mr. T had a new playmate. Mel turned one of her spare bedrooms into a room for Laur's daughter, Lisa, and the teenager had already visited twice. For the first time since living at the Turners' all those years ago, Mel felt she was home.

The teenaged daughters of the Posse remained friends, albeit some now from afar. Mel relayed the course of events in Billie Elkins's life as told to her that fateful night at Annie's. It initially had an impact on their behavior but, as with many things in teenagers' lives, time passed and so too did any guilt they felt and good behavior they adopted.

Annie Elkins had fallen off the grid that day she attacked Mel then Gus at her home, never to be seen or heard from again. They found her blood at the scene so confirmed Mel had cut her with the knife and Gus likely nicked her with a shot, but apparently her wounds were not so bad as to prohibit her from running away through the woods. The FBI's search for Annie remained active, but the only trace they found of her outside her home was a blurry black-and-white video of a woman that could have been her at a bus station in Indiana a month after her disappearance.

Twelve hundred and twenty-three miles to the south of Kendalton, Massachusetts, spring was also well along in Dadeville, Alabama. The scorching sun had just popped above the horizon but it was already nearly seventy degrees, with enough humidity in the air to choke a fish. It was prime strawberry-picking season in southern Alabama, and Sherburne Plantation's harvest manager, Walt Patel, had already been awake for hours getting ready for the first harvest of the season. A group of anonymous seasonal workers milled around outside the main gate wearing wide, flappy hats made of straw and nylon, waiting to begin their long, arduous day in the heat. Walt approached the gate with a clipboard and a cart of handled baskets and the workers naturally slipped into a straight line to receive their equipment for the day.

As each worker stepped up Walt jotted the handwritten name from the sticker on their chest onto his clipboard and noted the number on the side of the basket he handed them as they passed. Having worked with migrant workers for the better part of three decades, the faces all blurred together and looked the same to Walt. There were both men and women, some older than others, but each with the same weathered sheen to their face and hardened look in their eyes.

But on this bright, sunny first day of picking season there was a new face in the group. A tall, slender woman stepped up to Walt, her eyes fixed on the ground before them. Her lean forearms were dark from seasons in the sun, and he could see from her calloused and scraped hands she was accustomed to manual labor. Walt jotted her simple name on his clipboard and handed her a basket. And as the woman passed she raked a long, curly lock of black hair behind her ear and Walt noticed her bright red lipstick. He wouldn't in a million years recognize it for the MAC lipstick, the classic Ruby Woo shade that it was, just that he had never seen it around these parts.

The End

Acknowledgment

As many authors will attest, it takes a team of talented, dedicated people to get a book from the twinkling of an idea to resting on a shelf (physically or electronically). But in my case, I may have needed an even more talented—and certainly more dedicated—team than is typical. To each and every one of you I owe a mountain of gratitude.

First off, I'd like to thank my wife Lisa for, well, everything. Lis, without you the intricate dynamics between this toxic group of women never hit right, Gus isn't Gus, and this book never gets done. You taught me how to write and find my own voice and for all of that—and so much more—I'm eternally thankful.

I'd also like to thank the many other family members and friends that each helped in their own way along this path. To our daughter Mac, thanks for reading this book as many times as I have and yet always finding nuances and inconsistencies my brain skipped past. To our son Sam, thanks for always having the best, creepiest ideas for the villain. I'm so thankful for all your suggestions (your brain is as frightening as it is impressive). And to our youngest, Gabe, thanks not only for your encouragement but also for your superior sense of humor (which I sometimes clung to) along the way. To our niece, Meighan Blanco, thanks for all your superb medical insights and knowledge. The toxin used in this book is very complex and very real, and your expertise made that aspect of the book eerily accurate. And to our dear friend, Jim Newton, for sharing his in-depth knowledge of photography and the photographic process, both old and new. Though the characteristic of *this* villain being a photographer ended up on the cutting room floor, I have a feeling all that knowledge will come in handy in the future.

I'd also like to send a heartfelt thanks into the universe for allowing me the opportunity to work with Dick Marek, however briefly. Dick was an icon in the publishing industry but, more importantly, a kind and gentle man. Why he chose to work with me as my editor, I'll never know. One of the first things Dick said to me was 'It's a re-write, but I can tell you can write.' I only hope he realized the impact those words had on someone in need of them at that particular point in time. I'd like to thank Susan Dalsimer who picked up the baton from Dick, after he passed, and used it to beat the manuscript into something meaningful. Susan, I think back to the first version I provided you and can only cringe at the torture I put you through. Thank you for your patience, guidance and most of all your kindness. And to fellow (I've waited years to be able to say that) author Chris Mooney: thank you for all the help and advice throughout this entire process. You were so right: it's a marathon, not a sprint. But, wow, what a race, what an experience.

Thank you to Eric Jacksch (of Tenebris) and Jack Schafer for the eye-opening and invaluable advice on all technology and cybersecurity aspects of this story. Without your help and expertise, the cyberstalking and surveillance elements in this book would not be nearly as accurate and true, and for that I am grateful.

And an enormous thanks to my wonderful agent, Kathy Green. Kathy, you plucked my submission from the pile and set all of this in motion, guiding me through this murky and sometimes frustrating process with expertise, wisdom and integrity. This industry needs more Kathy Greens and I will be forever thankful I have the original.

And lastly, a very sincere thanks to all the folks at Tule Publishing for taking a chance on this debut author. To Jane Porter for parachuting in over a holiday weekend to let my agent know Tule was interested, and developing a compelling offer. And to all that I've worked with at Tule since joining—Mia, Jaiden, Julie, Meghan, Kelly, Helena, Michael—for making my experience unbelievably enjoyable along the way. And a very special thank you to my editor at Tule, Sinclair Sawhney, for seeing something in Gus and this story and for championing it within Tule to make all of this happen. Your persistence and praise and guidance through the publishing process has been incredible and I thank you for everything.

About the Author

R. John Dingle was born and raised in New England. In fact, despite extensive travel, a move to Australia represents his only bragging right for actually residing outside the six-state area. John and his wife currently call a small island in Mid-Coast Maine 'home', both living, writing and boating from their restored 200-year old house (which they continually assure their three adult children is not haunted). The psychological thriller, Karma Never Sleeps, is John's first novel.

Thank you for reading

Karma Never Sleeps

If you enjoyed this book, you can find more from all our great authors at TulePublishing.com, or from your favorite online retailer.

TULE
PUBLISHING

www.ingramcontent.com/pod-product-compliance
Ingram Content Group UK Ltd.
Pitfield, Milton Keynes, MK11 3LW, UK
UKHW040127080425
457202UK00002B/153

9 781965 640685